paradise

Also available by Katie Price

Fiction
Other books in the Angel trilogy:
Angel
Angel Uncovered

Other Fiction
Crystal
Sapphire

Non-Fiction
Being Jordan
Jordan: A Whole New World
Jordan: Pushed to the Limit
Standing Out

Katie Price

x

paradise

Century · London

Published by Century 2010

2 4 6 8 10 9 7 5 3 1

First published in Great Britain in 2010 by
Century
Random House, 20 Vauxhall Bridge Road,
London SW1V 2SA

www.rbooks.co.uk

Addresses for companies within The Random House Group Limited can be
found at: www.randomhouse.co.uk

The Random House Group Limited Reg. No. 954009

A CIP catalogue record for this book
is available from the British Library

HB ISBN 9781846054846
TPB ISBN 9781846054853

The Random House Group Limited supports The Forest Stewardship
Council (FSC), the leading international forest certification organisation.
All our titles that are printed on Greenpeace approved FSC certified paper
carry the FSC logo. Our paper procurement policy can be found at:
www.rbooks.co.uk/environment

Mixed Sources
Product group from well-managed
forests and other controlled sources
www.fsc.org Cert no. TT-COC-2139
© 1996 Forest Stewardship Council

Typeset by SX Composing DTP, Rayleigh, Essex
Printed and bound in Great Britain by
CPI Mackays, Chatham, ME5 8TD

Chapter 1

Early morning, Santa Monica. Angel Summer was still half asleep. In the distance she could hear the waves of the Pacific Ocean breaking against the shore, the new wake up call in her life. She stretched out her arm expecting to find Ethan next to her, but his side of the bed was empty. He must have already left for training. She would just go back to sleep for five more minutes . . .

But then Ethan's LA drawl cut across her thoughts: 'Happy anniversary, sleepy head.'

Angel opened her eyes and looked straight into the bluer-than-blue eyes of Ethan Turner, star baseball player of the Los Angeles Dodgers and her lover for the last six months. She was puzzled by his declaration, though. Was she missing something? She wasn't aware of any anniversary.

She sat up, pulling the duvet round her. Long white-blonde hair, tousled from sleep, cascaded down her golden-brown back. And that's when she saw that all around the bed were arranged beautiful bouquets of flowers: ice-white roses, delicate pale pink peonies, and dramatic crimson Oriental lilies. The bedroom now resembled a florist's!

'What's all this for?' she asked in surprise.

'It's the anniversary of me first seeing you in Chateau

Marmont.' Ethan smiled the sexy, lazy smile that even now, six months into their relationship, still made her heart flip. 'God, Angel, I sure as hell won't forget that moment. You were easily the most beautiful woman I'd ever seen.'

Angel rolled her eyes at the outrageous flattery. 'And let's face it, Ethan, you've had a few in your time.' She often joked about being one in a long line of his conquests, but actually it was a source of deep insecurity for her. Models, actresses, a top tennis player – she'd checked Ethan's exes out on the net and they were all gorgeous.

The smile went from Ethan's face and the blue eyes turned serious. 'Angel, I swear you're the only one for me.' He slid his strong arms round her and pulled her towards him. 'My beautiful Angel. How is it you can look so good in the morning? You look like Marilyn Monroe in those photos . . . where she's only wearing a sheet and the camera loves her.'

He lightly caressed her bare back, sending shivers down her spine. It was so tempting just to lie back and surrender to his touch but Angel exclaimed, 'I must check on Honey,' and was all set to jump out of bed to see if her two-and-a-half-year-old daughter was awake.

'No need,' Ethan told her, 'Lucy has taken her out. It's just you and me, a rare luxury these days.'

Angel bristled slightly at the suggestion that her daughter was somehow an inconvenience to Ethan. He was not Honey's father: Cal Bailey, the former Chelsea footballer, was. She and Cal had separated just over six months ago. Ethan caught the look.

'Hey, I didn't mean it like that. I love Honey, you know I do. It's just good to have the time with you.' He leant in to kiss her, and even though Angel was not entirely pacified she gave in to the kiss. Ethan slowly pushed her back on the bed and took away the duvet.

'And now I want you to lie back and enjoy every second, knowing that there will be no interruptions. Just you, me and a whole lot of pleasure.'

It sounded like a good plan to Angel . . .

The sex was better than ever, Angel reflected afterwards as she lay in a bath scented with Chanel's Coco bath gel. In fact, life with Ethan was good. She felt connected to him, safe with him, and if it wasn't the all-consuming passion she'd had with her soon-to-be-ex-husband Cal then that was okay, wasn't it? She had always believed that you don't get that kind of passion twice in a lifetime. Cal had been her soul-mate. She couldn't in all honesty say that Ethan filled that role, but she loved him. Whenever she had any doubts about being with him she tried to push them to the back of her mind and focus on the positives. She loved living in LA, had plenty of modelling work there, after being signed up as a Victoria's Secret model, along with her own lingerie range back home, and most importantly her daughter Honey seemed happy.

And even if there were dark days when Angel missed Cal and longed for him, she never forgot that he was the one who had shattered their marriage; he was the one who had been unfaithful. He was the one who had broken her heart. Sometimes she felt the legacy of that pain still within her; the fact that she always had her barriers up. She could never let herself get that hurt again. Much as she loved Ethan, she was aware that she was keeping something of herself back.

'What do you want for breakfast?' he asked, wandering into the bathroom. He'd showered in the black-marble-tiled wet room across the hall – one of the six bathrooms in his vast beach house. He just had a white towel round his waist, accentuating his sun-kissed brown skin. As well as being stunningly handsome and resembling the actor Josh Holloway in looks, with his dark-blond hair and blue eyes, Ethan had the most gorgeous body: rock-hard abs, broad shoulders, long lean legs and the tightest bum. The sight of his half-naked body made Angel want to pull in him the bath for a repeat performance.

It seemed that Ethan had the same thought as he dipped his hand into the water and caressed her between her legs, driving her wild with his slow, knowing touch. Angel gasped with pleasure then took great delight in whipping off the towel and releasing his already-stiff cock. You've just got to love a man who's good to go again, she thought, pulling him into the bath with her. The water sloshed over the side as Ethan thrust into her, but neither of them cared. Two mind-blowing orgasms and it wasn't even 8 a.m. . . .

Breakfast was served outside by Ethan's stylish infinity pool, with its cobalt blue mosaic tiles and a breathtaking view of the glittering Pacific Ocean stretching beyond it. Jose, Ethan's Mexican butler, bustled around pouring out glasses of freshly prepared mango and pineapple smoothies, along with black coffee for Ethan and PG Tips for Angel. Ethan tucked into a plate of scrambled eggs and smoked salmon while Angel had toast and Marmite.

She had never in a million years imagined that she would one day have staff doing practically everything for her. Life with Cal had been luxurious but they had kept it fairly low-key and just had a cleaner, nanny, occasional driver and security. But Ethan had a whole team of people looking after him, headed by Jose and Maria his wife, who was the cook, along with an army of cleaners and gardeners and several chauffeurs – so many that Angel had given up trying to learn all their names.

'I love you, babe, but I don't know how the hell you can eat that stuff,' Ethan said fondly as he watched her take a hearty bite of her toast. Sex had given her a very healthy appetite. It was one of many culture clashes between the couple – he didn't get why she would only drink cups of PG Tips, had to watch *X Factor* (*American Idol* just wouldn't do), and never missed a Chelsea match.

Angel was a life-long supporter of the club. Football was in her blood. Her dad Frank was a football coach for one of the youth teams in Brighton, and her brother Tony was the sports physio for West Ham. And, of course, she had been married to Cal, a Chelsea and England player. She had always loved the game with a passion. Had never simply been a WAG who cared more about her designer outfits and the state of her nails than how England performed in the World Cup. Ethan had tried watching football, or soccer as he called it, but just couldn't get into it.

Of course the cultural differences went both ways. Angel didn't get how so many of the Americans she met in stores always put on the 'have a nice day' act, and she definitely didn't get baseball. She dutifully went to all the big games, cheered Ethan on, put on a great act of being engrossed, but she found it Dullsville after footie. To her, it would always remind her of rounders, a game she associated purely with school and had always thought a bit girlie. But she kept that thought well and truly to herself, knowing Ethan would not appreciate that description of the sport which had made him a multi-millionaire and one of the most widely recognised sportsmen in the States.

'So when you've finished eating that vile stuff,' Ethan told her, 'we're taking a drive into the Hills to buy you an anniversary present. I've got my eye on something in Tiffany's but I want you to check it out first.'

5

'You don't have to buy me anything!' Angel exclaimed. She had never been the kind of woman who wanted men to lavish expensive gifts on her. She had always been fiercely independent when it came to money, and always liked to pay her own way.

'But you never let me buy you anything. I'm over-ruling you this time,' Ethan told her. 'Come on, I know you love Tiffany's.'

That did weaken her resolve somewhat. She adored the store, and always felt like a little girl waking up on Christmas morning surrounded by gorgeous presents whenever she went in. Angel polished off her toast and padded back inside to get ready.

She loved Ethan's ultra-modern beach house, so light and airy, with its glass walls and rooms where you could change the colour of the lights according to your mood, though she did miss her old house just outside Brighton, an elegant Georgian mansion with views of vivid green fields, stately horse chestnut trees and her two horses in their paddock. Inside, the house had been cosy and full of colour. Now, alas, it was rented out to strangers. Ethan's was in more minimalist taste, so there was lots of white and taupe, white marble floors, white-upholstered furniture and white rugs.

He was usually one of the most laid-back people she knew, but when it came to his house he was slightly anally retentive about things being put away and having 'clean lines' everywhere. Well, apparently, that's what his interior designer had told him to do. Angel was forever leaving magazines lying around only to come back into the room and find they'd been cleared away, along with any stray perfume bottles and bags of make-up. She'd had to come to a deal with Ethan that her dressing room, Honey's bedroom and playroom, were not subject to the same high standards. Those rooms were a riot of colour and clutter, much more

6

suited to Angel's personality than the achingly stylish Italian leather sofas, the state-of-the-art light fittings and sleek modern sculptures on display in the others.

She opened the door of her vast closet and wondered what to wear for a trip to Rodeo Drive, which was probably the most prestigious and famous shopping street in the world. Since moving here she'd adopted the laid-back LA dress code and now had an impressive collection of Havaiana flip-flops in every colour, tiny denim shorts, white vests, and long gold necklaces, bangles and ankle chains. She loved that casual look and it suited her, the denim shorts showing off her long slim brown legs and sexy bum, the white vests showing off her impressive curves and enviably flat stomach. But every now and then it was good to dress up and she decided to do just that, going for an off-the-shoulder white dress with a fitted bodice and tight skirt, and a pair of sky-high, hot pink Louboutin heels which had been designed for Barbie's fiftieth birthday – life in the old girl yet, if the sexy ankle-strap shoes were anything to go by!

Angel coiled her hair up into a bun. She would have liked to spend more time on it but already Ethan was calling for her, impatiently. That was something he had in common with Cal: he was always telling her to hurry up. She hastily put on tinted moisturiser, lashings of mascara and a slick of sheer pink lip gloss. She always went for natural make-up in the day, and in truth hardly needed any, so stunning was her beauty. She had flawless skin, just a few freckles on her nose, which only added to her charm, beautiful, intensely green eyes, and full sensuous lips. She grabbed her black Dior sunnies, with the Swarovski crystals at the sides – sometimes it was fun to flash the bling – and was good to go.

As she clattered down the grand marble staircase

which curved elegantly down to the hall, Ethan stood gazing up at her, as if he couldn't quite believe his luck that she was with him.

'Wow, you look beautiful!'

'But do I look like a proper lady?' Angel teased back, putting on her best cockney accent.

'Proper,' Ethan replied, attempting to match her cockney. Not good. Mind you, her attempts at a Californian accent always had him in stitches.

'Best stick to what you know, babe,' she told him as she reached the bottom of the stairs.

'This is what I wanted to buy you.' Ethan pointed out an exquisite green tourmaline pendant. The dazzling gemstone was encircled by diamonds and hanging from a platinum and diamond chain. 'Can we look at this?' he asked the elegant saleswoman, who was dressed in a cream silk blouse and black skirt.

'Of course, Mr Turner,' she replied, promptly unlocking the glass display cabinet. What Mr Turner asked for, Mr Turner got. Ethan was a huge star.

'What do you think, Angel?' Ethan asked as the saleswoman reverently fastened the necklace round Angel's neck. It looked stunning against her golden brown skin, the brilliant green of the stone making her eyes appear even greener.

'It's beautiful,' she said, looking at herself in the mirror. 'But it's a little too grand for me. I want something I could wear every day and you can't exactly see me wearing this with my shorts and Havaianas can you?'

The saleswoman suppressed a smile.

'But I want to buy you something really special, babe.' Ethan came up behind Angel and put his arms round her waist, dropping a kiss on her bare shoulder.

'What about something like this?' the saleswoman

asked, holding up a long necklace with at least fifty small diamonds set in platinum. 'This is something you could wear dressed up or down. It's a piece that will always work hard for you,' she said in typical saleswoman speak that made Angel want to smile. She unfastened the pendant and carefully put on the diamond necklace. It was perfectly lovely, the diamonds sparkling where they caught the light.

'This is more like it!' Angel exclaimed. Then she stopped. 'But it must be so expensive. Really, Ethan, you don't need to get me anything.'

Sometimes she had the uneasy feeling that Ethan was trying to buy her love, that he suspected she might still have feelings for Cal and wanted to do all he could to make her forget her ex-husband.

'I'm buying it and that's final.' Ethan said, adding to the assistant, 'Can she leave it on and I'll pay now?' As they stood by the counter waiting for his credit card to go through, he murmured, 'You know, sometime I'd like to buy you something else from here.'

He paused and gave her a searching look, and Angel knew exactly what he meant without him needing to say the words.

An engagement ring. Oh, God, not this again. As soon as she had moved in with him, Ethan had wanted her to divorce Cal and marry him. But Angel didn't want to divorce Cal for adultery or unreasonable behaviour; she wanted their marriage to end quietly after two years of separation, couldn't bear the thought of getting lawyers in and inevitably having the press pick over every single detail of their lives. And because Cal had been unfaithful, Angel really didn't know if she ever wanted to get married again. She would rather be happy and live for the moment. She was through with making big statements and promises of life-long commitment.

But Ethan longed to marry her; it was almost an obsession with him and he didn't understand her reservations. Angel didn't want the day to be ruined by them taking about the marriage question again so she silenced any further questions by kissing him.

'I'm terribly sorry, Mr Turner, but there seems to be a problem with your card,' the saleswoman said discreetly. 'D'you perhaps have another one?'

'What do you mean, a problem?' Ethan asked. 'I don't think I'm anywhere up to my limit. There must be some mistake.' He seemed agitated and fumbled in his wallet, pulling out another card, 'Try this one.'

But that too was declined. 'Let's just leave it,' Angel suggested. 'Or, if you want, I can put it on my card.' Oops, that had not been the right thing to say at all. Ethan's male pride was not going to stand for that.

He clenched his jaw. 'Of course you can't pay for your own gift. I've got another card I can use.' And he handed the saleswoman yet another credit card. Thank God this one was accepted, but the whole payment fiasco had taken some of the shine off the moment.

Ethan, especially, seemed downbeat when they exited the store. A teenage boy approached him for an autograph and picture. Usually Ethan was only too happy to oblige, but on this occasion he moodily signed the Dodgers' programme and couldn't even manage a smile for the camera.

'I don't know what the fuck's going on,' he muttered once they had settled into the chauffeur-driven Chrysler waiting for them. 'I'll have to speak to Benny, get him to sort out my cards.'

Benny Sullivan was Ethan's PR manager and agent and handled all his press, public engagements, sports sponsorship and advertising deals. He had managed Ethan for nearly ten years. While Angel liked pretty well all of Ethan's friends, she had loathed Benny on sight. He was one of those men with the habit of stripping women naked with his eyes. Angel couldn't believe how blatantly he leered at her whenever they met. It was almost as if he thought it was his right to treat her like that as she was a glamour model. Worse still, it was something Ethan seemed completely oblivious to, and Angel had had to endure Benny's roving eye on many a night out.

She also couldn't help thinking that Ethan relied on his manager a little too much. Why couldn't Ethan phone the credit-card companies himself, for instance? Angel had always kept things on a strictly professional basis with her own agent and wouldn't have dreamt of allowing her to organise things like personal finances. But Ethan liked being looked after, and didn't like bothering with the everyday trivia. He was forever saying to Angel, 'Why sweat the small stuff, when someone else can do it for you?' She didn't like to reply that maybe, if you actually did things yourself rather than delegating everything, you stayed more grounded.

While Ethan spoke to Benny, Angel stared out of the tinted-glass window. LA certainly was Plastic Surgery Central, which made people-watching here all the more entertaining. She was transfixed by a petite blonde in a tiny turquoise sundress and matching heels, who was dressed like a twenty-something but on closer inspection was more like late-fifties, her skin stretched and Botoxed to the limit, eyes almost disappearing into the sides of her head and lips with the swollen, bloated look of way too much collagen. On what planet was that supposed to be a good look? Angel would never criticise anyone for having surgery – she couldn't as she'd had a boob job herself when she'd started out as a glamour model – but some people really seemed to have crossed the line and lost all idea of what actually looked good.

Angel loved it in LA but at times was desperately

homesick for Brighton and her family and friends there. She wondered what they were up to right now. She checked her watch, 2 p.m. LA time, 10 p.m. UK time. Everyone she knew would be winding down for the day. Jez, one of her closest friends and also her hairdresser, would probably be out on the town with his husband Rufus. Knowing Rufus, he'd be eager to get home by now, as he had to get up at half six to go to the gym to start work as a personal trainer.

Gemma, her best friend going all the way back to primary school, who was married to Angel's brother, would either be snuggled up with Tony or out in Brighton with her mates. Tony, had to commute to London every day and often had to work late so he might not be home yet. Gemma worked in her mum's beauty salon in the heart of Brighton's Lanes and liked to go out when Tony was late so she didn't have to sit in the house by herself.

Any minute now, in her parent's house, Angel's mum would turn to her dad, who'd be sitting on the sofa beside her watching telly, and say, 'Right love, that's me done. I'm off to bed.' Her dad would give her a kiss and promise to join her soon. And as for Cal, who would he be with? Angel wondered. No, she wouldn't think of him...She sighed, missing them all. At least in a month's time she would get to see them as she was going back to the UK for Christmas.

Ethan ended his call to Benny. 'So . . . now for your second surprise.'

'Oh, no, Ethan, you don't have to buy me anything else!' Angel exclaimed.

'Nope, this one is priceless and I can't wait to see your face.' Ethan's phone rang again. It was one of his team mates. Angel, who had been lost in her thoughts of home, suddenly realised that they were being driven in the opposite direction from Ethan's house in Santa

Monica, and that if she wasn't mistaken they were on the freeway heading towards LAX – Los Angeles International Airport. Some fifteen minutes later, as they swung into the pick-up area of the vast airport, her suspicions were confirmed.

'So can you guess who we're meeting?' Ethan asked her, his blue eyes alight with mischief as he walked with her to International Arrivals.

'No idea,' Angel replied, scanning the board to give her a clue, but then her attention was drawn to the people streaming through Arrivals – and to one couple in particular: a man in a white trilby and white linen suit, with possibly a little too much fake tan, and a petite woman with jet black hair, dressed in a very fashion fast-forward black dress with studded shoulder pads and insanely high heels.

'Oh my God!' Angel squealed in delight, waving her arms wildly, not caring that she was attracting curious looks from the people around her. It was Jez and Gemma! Angel pushed her way through the crowds and threw her arms round first Gemma and then Jez. 'I can't believe you're here!' she exclaimed, practically jumping up and down in her excitement at seeing her friends.

'Just two words,' Jez said when he could finally get a word in edgeways. 'First class. Ethan paid for us to fly first class! I have never flown in such style before! I had my own bed, my own steward – cute arse, shame about the face. I did think about whether it would count as infidelity if we had a fumble in the loos, but I resisted as I'm a married man. Instead I had as much champagne as I could drink! *And* I got to keep the pyjamas. Gemma was asleep for most of the flight but I was wide awake, loving every single precious minute. It was fabulous!' Still the same old materialistic, wildly camp Jez.

Angel rolled her eyes at him. 'So the highlight is the flight . . . not seeing me?'

Jez eye-rolled back. 'Of course it's seeing you, Babelicious. Looking beautiful as ever.'

'And you're as shallow as ever,' Angel shot back. 'But thank God some things never change. I'd think the world was about to end if you were any different.'

At this they were joined by Ethan, who had hung back watching the friends' reunion. The next few minutes were spent with Jez, Gemma and Angel thanking him profusely for the surprise. 'I figured Angel could do with seeing you guys,' he said, 'I know how homesick she gets sometimes.' Angel thought she had hidden that and was touched that he had realised.

'Thanks so much, Ethan,' she said quietly, kissing him lightly on the lips. 'That was the sweetest thing, the best present ever.'

'I'd do anything to make you happy,' he told her. Angel wanted to say the same, but if anything meant divorcing Cal then she just didn't think she could do it.

Back at the house Jose and Maria had laid on a poolside BBQ with mini-burgers, seared prawns and delicious salads. Honey was back from her day out and thrilled to be with her mummy again. At two and a half, she was a perfect poppet with long dark brown curly hair, big brown eyes, and the beautiful olive skin of her father. She was also feisty and cheeky, and could throw tantrums for Britain. She snuggled on Angel's lap, playing with the diamond necklace, while the friends caught up. Ethan had to go to some business meeting.

Jez and Gemma had visited Angel in Santa Monica once before but were still dazzled by the sheer luxury and size of the house. 'It is so beautiful here,' Gemma said, elegantly sipping her mojito.

She had changed into a stylish purple maxi dress. Gemma was a fashionista through and through, nailing all the new trends. She was constantly on Angel's case trying to make her more fashion aware, sending her links to dresses on Net-A-Porter that she thought were 'must haves'. Every now and then Angel would take her advice, but left to her own devices was always happiest in jeans or tracksuits.

'It's like a dream,' Jez agreed from where he sat surveying the glittering Pacific Ocean and exquisitely kept gardens, the lush green lawn with its perfectly mown grass. 'Are you sure I couldn't move in and be your permanent hairdresser slash slave?' He was only half joking. 'So long as you had space for Rufus.'

'Why isn't he here?' Angel asked; she was sure Ethan would have paid for his ticket as well.

Jez sighed, 'He couldn't get the time off. The gym's not doing very well and Rufus is having to put in extra hours. I hardly see him at the moment. I keep saying I should book some personal training sessions with him. At least that way I'd get to see more of him.' He looked sad for a few seconds before quipping, 'But, hey, absence makes the heart grow fonder and the cock grow harder.'

Angel gestured at Honey, who was fortunately too engrossed in eating strawberries to listen. 'So what's your news, Gem?' Angel asked. Eight months ago Gemma had suffered a miscarriage, and Angel knew it had taken her friend a long time to get over her sadness at losing the baby.

'Work's fine and Tony's good. But my real news is that we're going to try for a baby again. I feel I can put what happened behind me.'

'Oh, Gem, that's so good to hear. I really hope it works out for you.'

And Angel truly meant it. The months following the

miscarriage had been so tough for Gemma. It had also been a time when the two women had grown apart as Gemma had questioned whether Angel had made the right decision when she left Cal for Ethan. What made it all the harder was that Cal was Tony's best friend, so naturally Gemma had divided loyalties.

'So what about you?' she asked.

'Everything is great. I love it out here, though of course I miss all you guys. And it's going really well with Ethan. He's perfect for me, Gem. I'm really happy.' Angel was aware she was gushing – she just wanted Gemma to believe her, and her friend still had a slightly sceptical look on her face. 'You'll never guess what he did this morning . . .'

Angel proceeded to tell them how Ethan had filled the bedroom with flowers and about the trip to Tiffany's. But as soon as she mentioned it, she remembered the incident with his credit cards. He was supposed to be a multi-millionaire, so wasn't it odd that his cards had been declined?

'I thought that looked rather gorge,' Jez said, looking enviously at the necklace.

'It's beautiful,' Gemma agreed, though without Jez's enthusiasm. She still hadn't fully warmed to Ethan. When Angel started seeing him, Gemma had read up about him on the net and much of the press coverage had been about his many short-lived relationships. Before Angel he had been a real player, and Angel knew that her friend believed a leopard didn't change his spots. It was a source of sadness to Angel, who really wanted her friend to accept Ethan. Plus Gemma, like so many of Angel's friends and even her family, had seemed to think that she should be able to forgive Cal for his infidelity and take him back. It was what so many other footballers' wives had done, wasn't it? Forgive and forget, and accept that the odd bit of cheating was part of the territory if you married a footballer. But Angel couldn't do that and knew that she was right not to, whatever anyone else thought. She knew that if she did that, deep down she would always be waiting for Cal to be unfaithful again. Besides, looking at other footballers whose wives had taken them back, it seemed that only a very few never strayed again.

'I saw Cal the other week. We all went out for an Indian meal in Hove. His football academies are going really well and he's got presenting work on *Match of the Day* and 5 Live.' Gemma also seemed to think it was okay to bring up Angel's ex in conversation, acting as if it was the most normal thing in the world, when the truth was just the mention of Cal's name shook Angel up and put her on edge.

'That's good,' she said cautiously. A serious knee injury had made it impossible for Cal ever to play football again. 'I never really know how he is when I see him.'

For the last six months Cal had flown over at regular intervals to see Honey, and Angel had been back to the UK as well. Seeing Cal was always an unsettling experience; there were just too many unresolved issues between them. For the first month after she'd left him, Cal had told her he still loved her and begged her to take him back; Angel refused even to consider it. Then, once he realised she was not going to change her mind, Cal shut down. He was polite to her but gave no hint as to what he was feeling. In some ways this was just as unsettling as his declarations of love – her relationship with Cal had always been so passionate and intense it was hard to imagine that they could ever be just friends.

Angel didn't want to ask the next question but couldn't stop herself. 'So is he seeing anyone?' As far as she knew Cal hadn't seen anyone since she'd left him.

'Is who seeing anyone?' Ethan was back from his meeting. Talk about bad timing! He couldn't bear hearing Cal's name mentioned. Whenever Cal picked up or dropped off Honey at the house, Ethan made sure he wasn't around. It was as if he didn't want Angel to have a past before him, which was pretty ironic given his own colourful love life.

She winced inwardly and tried to say as casually as possible, 'Oh, just Cal.'

Ethan curled his lip and his blue eyes lost some of their warmth, but he didn't react other than to say, 'So is he?'

Gemma clearly guessed that this was a sore point between the couple so said breezily, 'I don't think so . . . he's focussing on work right now. So how's it going with you, Ethan? Jez and I are dying to see a baseball game when we're out here.'

Angel shot a grateful look at her friend and also felt secretly relieved that Cal wasn't seeing anyone. It shouldn't matter to her what he was doing, but it did. She didn't want to think about what that meant.

Ethan duly filled Gemma and Jez in on how the season was going so far – not that either of them had a clue what he was talking about.

'Do you know A-Rod?' Jez suddenly asked excitedly. 'I was wondering if you did, because then you might be able to introduce us . . . and then I might get to meet Madonna! I mean, I don't know if they're still friends, but maybe . . .' Jez *adored* Madonna; had worshipped her since her 'Like A Virgin' days.

'Our paths have crossed a fair few times on the pitch,' Ethan replied, 'and I've met Madonna as well.'

Jez looked as if he might take off into orbit. 'What is she like?' he asked in awed tones.

Ethan shrugged. He was used to mixing with A-listers

18

– hell, he was an A-lister himself – but he humoured Jez. 'Charming, tiny, lovely skin.'

'Charming, tiny, lovely skin,' Jez echoed back, as if he had discovered the meaning of the universe. 'And what was she wearing?'

Another shrug from Ethan. 'Some kinda black dress, I think, the first time. And the second time, a red dress . . . I really can't remember.'

But that was not sufficient for Jez who proceeded to bombard him with questions. Could he guess the designer of the dress? What about the shoes? And what was her hair like? And her lipstick? And so on and so on, until Angel had to rescue Ethan by putting her hand over Jez's mouth and exclaiming, 'What are you like, Jez!'

They stayed chatting by the pool until the sun set. It was as if it was putting on a spectacular show just for them as the sky turned from blue to deep pink to vibrant orange. Angel felt incredibly happy to have her friends with her. She had made a few out here but none were as close to her as Jez and Gemma and she never felt she could quite let her guard down with them, whereas Jez and Gemma knew her through and through and she never had to pretend with them.

Jez and Gemma were jetlagged after their flight and crashed out pretty much at the same time as Angel got Honey ready for bed, both exclaiming about their luxurious guest rooms with en suite bathrooms filled with gorgeous Moulton Brown bath products.

Angel gave Honey her bath and then read to her until she fell asleep. 'Night-night,' she whispered, kissing her daughter on her soft baby cheek. 'Mummy loves you and so does Daddy and so does Ethan.' It was what she said to Honey every night.

She paused for a few minutes in the doorway, looking back at her daughter curled up so snug under her

Tinkerbell duvet cover, then found her gaze drawn to the photograph of Cal with Honey on his knee which stood on the beside table. It was the only photograph of Cal in the house and Angel knew that Ethan didn't like having it there, even though he hadn't said as much. Cal was smiling in the picture, making him look even more handsome. He was half-Italian, with olive skin and jet black hair which he always wore short. His deep brown eyes could appear distant at times, and at others full of passion. The small scar just below his right eyebrow, a souvenir from a collision on the football pitch, only made him sexier. Oh, Cal, where are you now? Angel wondered. She was sure she had made the right decision leaving him but that didn't mean that it didn't still hurt sometimes.

She tried to shrug off the feeling and wandered downstairs to the living room, intending to thank Ethan for the wonderful surprise he'd arranged, but he was on the phone, pacing the room, sounding furious.

'Well, I don't fucking know what to do about it. You're my fucking agent, *you* sort it out. Jesus Christ, Benny, that's what I pay you to do.' He paused when he caught sight of Angel standing barefoot in the doorway. 'Look, Benny, I gotta go, let's speak in the morning.' He clicked his phone off. 'Hey, sorry about that, just some business with Benny.'

'It sounded serious, is everything okay?'

'Everything's cool, baby.' Ethan didn't seem to want to discuss it. 'Now why don't we go outside in the hot tub and have a glass of champagne? It's still our anniversary. And I reckon it's time for the third surprise.'

'Oh, no, you haven't bought me something else!' Angel exclaimed.

'Nope, this one is free.' Ethan murmured, putting his arm round her. 'Let's see if a thirty-year-old man who is very much in love and in lust with a twenty-seven-year-old beauty can have sex three times in one day.'

'Hah, I doubt it!' Angel teased, but when Ethan kissed her and she pressed her body against his, she thought he was probably on to something.

Chapter 2

'So what shall we do today?' Jez asked after he'd finally
emerged from his bedroom the following morning, his
highlighted blond hair carefully teased into spikes.
Ethan had already left for training and Gemma and
Angel were sitting by the pool, while Honey, ever the
water baby, splashed in the water.

'Your favourite thing Jez – retail! We can get a car to
Rodeo Drive, have lunch at The Ivy, and in the evening
Ethan is going to take us to Hyde – that really cool club.'

Angel was expecting Jez to be thrilled by the prospect
of shopping and clubbing; instead he looked torn. 'I
promised Rufus I wouldn't buy any clothes – like I said
last night, things are a bit tight at the moment. He's got
me on a budget and I had to cut up my credit cards.' Jez
said the word 'budget' as if it was the dirtiest, nastiest
thing in the world.

'You don't have to spend any money . . . I want to
give you this.' And Angel handed an envelope bulging
with cash to each of her friends. She beamed, waiting
for their reaction.

'But there's a thousand dollars here!' Gemma
exclaimed as she opened the envelope and flipped
through the notes, 'That is way too much.'

'Too too much,' Jez agreed. 'We can't take your
money, Angel.'

'I want you to have it,' she urged them. 'Buy your-selves something gorgeous.' She wasn't trying to be flash – she genuinely wanted to treat her friends. Money meant nothing if you couldn't share it with the people you loved.

Jez and Gemma hesitated some more before finally giving in when Angel told them to think of it as an early Christmas present. And then they were ready to hit the stores. Lucy, the nanny, took Honey off to a toddlers' art club and so it was just the three friends in the back of the chauffeur-driven Chrysler, laughing and gossiping.

They went into Prada and Jez bought a shirt for himself and one for Rufus. They browsed in Armani, Gucci and Valentino. In Dior Gemma bought herself some stylish black-framed sunglasses, taking nearly forty minutes to make her selection which almost drove Angel and Jez crazy, and Angel ended up buying two bikinis that she didn't need, just for something to do. But that was Gemma: always wanting to make sure she spent the money well, and that she'd bought an 'investment piece', as she called it. Then it was off to The Ivy for lunch and celeb-spotting.

One of the things Angel loved about LA was that she didn't get noticed much, or if she did people were so used to seeing stars they weren't fazed. It wasn't like the UK where the paps followed her every move. The press attention had been intense when she'd first moved over because her leaving Cal had been such a big story, but lately it had become more relaxed and she much preferred it that way. She was not the kind of celebrity who needed to see a story about herself in the paper to feel important, that her life had meaning.

Jez was in his element at the upmarket restaurant as they sat at a table on the patio with the white picket fence that he had seen in many a celeb mag. 'That picket fence is so iconic! It's like the Hollywood sign,' he exclaimed, then added, 'Paris Hilton, two o'clock,' out of the corner of his mouth. 'Christina Aguilera, three o'clock.' He was so excited he could barely eat the lobster ravioli he'd ordered. It was sweet seeing her friend so thrilled.

Gemma, of course, was more cool and restrained, but even she looked excited when she thought she spotted Zac Efron. 'He's so cute!' she enthused. 'Do you think it would count as being unfaithful if I offered him a no-strings-attached shag?' she said cheekily. 'Tony wouldn't mind, would he?'

'Well, there's just the small matter of his girlfriend,' Angel replied dryly, not even sure if the young good-looking guy was Zac.

'But maybe Zac would like the chance to go out with an older woman,' Gemma insisted. 'I could be the sexy Cougar. I reckon I could show him a few moves.'

'Gemma, I never saw you as a star fucker,' Angel told her.

'You're right,' Gemma conceded. 'Anyway I could never starve myself to be a size zero. Never mind that Kate Moss bollocks mantra "Nothing tastes as good as skinny feels", shall we have pudding? I fancy the Key Lime Pie. I can always hit your in-house gym this afternoon before we go out clubbing.'

Pleasantly full from lunch and slightly tipsy from champagne, the three friends linked arms and headed out of the restaurant towards their ride – they planned to go on to the Beverly Centre, an upmarket mall packed with high-end designer boutiques, for yet more retail.

Suddenly a young woman with glossy blonde hair tied back in a pony tail, wearing a smart navy suit and clutching a microphone, stepped out in front of the trio, forcing them to stop. She thrust the microphone out. Just behind her a camera was being pointed directly at Angel. 'Miss Summer, do you have any comment to make about the claim of Ella Richards that Ethan Turner is the father of her little girl?'

Angel stared blankly at the journalist; she had absolutely no idea what she was talking about.

'Did you know about Ethan Turner's relationship with Ella Richards?' the journalist persisted, a fake smile on her blandly pretty face.

'No comment.' Jez took over, marching Angel away from the journalist and into the car as quickly as he could. 'Can you take us straight home?' he asked Raul, the chauffeur. No one felt in the mood for shopping now.

'What the hell do you think she was on about?' Gemma asked, looking at her friend with concern as the car pulled quickly away, denying the journalist any further shots.

Angel shook her head and said despairingly, 'I've no idea. Oh my God! D'you think he's been cheating on me?' She was gripped with a sickening and all-too-familiar feeling of insecurity and doubt. Cal had cheated on her . . . maybe Ethan had as well. She had never believed in a million years that Cal would cheat on her, but he had. It wasn't such a big leap to imagine that Ethan had done the same. Maybe that's why he had gone to all the trouble over their anniversary, the presents and the plane tickets; it was an attempt to butter her up before the truth about his affair came out. She suddenly had a pounding headache and was trembling.

'Don't jump to conclusions,' Jez said wisely, putting his arm round her. 'You know what the press are like, babe.'

Angel knew only too well. Her success as a glamour

model, combined with her great beauty and the fact that she had had relationships first with a boy-band singer and then with a footballer, meant that the tabloids had always been obsessed with her. This had reached fever pitch with the revelation that Cal had been unfaithful during their marriage. He'd had a three-month affair with a beautiful Italian woman who was married to a player for AC Milan during his time playing for the club over a year ago. Back then he and Angel hadn't been getting on – she was crippled by post-natal depression but hadn't revealed that to Cal, who'd had no idea why his wife was being so cold towards him. As soon as news of his affair broke, the press camped outside their house all day and all night and pursued the couple everywhere. The constant intrusion, combined with her pain over the affair, had been unbearable. Angel knew she couldn't go through it again with Ethan. She reached for her phone, then changed her mind. After all, what would she say?

She ran straight into the house and found Ethan in the living room, deep in conversation with Benny. The two men looked serious. Was that a flash of guilt in Ethan's eyes? Before she had a chance to say anything, Benny got in first. 'Angel, could your friends amuse themselves for a while? We need to talk.'

She hated Benny issuing orders like that, but nonetheless turned to her friends. 'D'you want to grab a drink and I'll see you in a bit?'

'Will you be okay?' Gemma asked anxiously.

Angel nodded and sat down on one of the sofas, as far away as possible from Benny. Even at that distance he made her feel uncomfortable. She was aware of his eyes raking over her body, vile man that he was. She folded her arms as if to shield herself from his leer. Benny was sitting on the opposite sofa, next to Ethan.

Talk about Beauty and the Beast. Benny was easily as tall as Ethan but that's where the similarities ended because Benny was definitely not one of the beautiful people. He had blonde, highlighted hair and a perma-tan that veered between orange and deep chestnut brown. He was obsessed with looking young and had regular Botox along with the odd nip and tuck, Angel was convinced. He was always blinged up to the max, too, but in spite of all the working out he did, his face was still pudgy, and he had small cold grey eyes and rather fleshy lips.

She shook back her hair and tilted her chin, making herself appear far stronger than she felt inside. She had been here before and survived, she would survive this too.

'So what do you want to talk to me about? Ella Richards claiming Ethan's the father of her child?'

That took the wind out of their sails. Ethan was the first to speak. 'Angel, I swear I've not been unfaithful to you.'

'And of course you'd tell me if you had.' She couldn't stop herself sounding sarcastic. 'Men are always honest, aren't they?'

'Ethan would never lie to you,' Benny put in. 'He loves you Angel, you know that. The guy wants to marry you, for Chrissake. How's that for commitment?'

Ethan was not doing himself any favours in Angel's eyes by having Benny do the talking. A fact which seemed to register with him as he got up and came and sat next to her.

'I did have a one night stand with Ella Richards, but it was way before I met you. I'm not proud of my past, but it is what it is.' His blue eyes looked pleadingly at her.

'Yeah, right. Where have I heard that one before?'

'Ella Richards is just a whore looking for an easy

27

buck,' Benny piped up again. 'She told Ethan she was on the Pill . . . bitch got pregnant deliberately. But we're not going to pay up. No fucking way! She can dream on.'

Angel bristled on hearing Benny's foul-mouthed description of Ella. She could now add 'sexist' to 'vile'. She ignored him and turned to Ethan. 'If she's your child then you do have some responsibility to her.'

Ethan sighed and run a hand over his short dark-blond hair. 'Actually she *is* my child, we've done the DNA test.'

Angel was stunned by this admission. And he hadn't thought to tell her before? This was a big deal, how could he not see that she would want to know about it? Angel started to wonder if there were other secrets he had been keeping from her. 'So how old is your daughter?' she managed to ask. 'And does she have a name?'

'She's called Megan and she's one,' Ethan said quietly.

Angel sat there feeling numb with shock for a few seconds before asking, 'So why has Ella waited until now to go public?'

Ethan looked over to Benny as if getting his approval to carry on. 'Benny was trying to see if we could come to an arrangement over money. Ella has just decided that the offer wasn't big enough and has gone public.'

'Bitch wants ten million dollars,' Benny said. 'We really want to avoid a court case. The adverse publicity could affect Ethan's sponsorship deals.'

Of course, that's why Benny was so wound up! It was all about the money.

Ethan looked intently at Angel. 'Babe, please don't judge me harshly. I'm not proud of this and I wanted you kept out of it . . . I know you've been through hell with the press and I wanted to protect you. That's why

28

I haven't told you before. It has nothing to do with our relationship.'

'Ethan has only ever been thinking of you, Angel.' Benny again. 'He's been ripped apart with guilt and worry, don't be hard on him.'

Angel *really* wished he'd piss off now. Just then Ethan's phone rang. He looked at the number and groaned.

'It's my coach; he must have seen the story on the news. I'd better take this.' He stood up and stepped through the open French windows and on to the decking beyond. Angel had no desire to stay in the same room as Benny and was all set to join her friends.

But Benny had other ideas. 'I'm sure we can fix this, Angel. It will blow over soon – these things always do.' His description of Ethan's daughter as one of 'these things' only made Angel loathe him even more.

She didn't say anything. Benny carried on, 'So, are you still being managed by Carrie Rose?'

Angel nodded, not wanting to engage with him further. She was still reeling from Ethan's news and didn't want to talk about business, but that was Benny all over, the world's most insensitive man.

'You know, you could really do with an agent out here to raise your Stateside profile. Carrie can't do that in London. I could take you on. I know all the people you should know. It would be good for you and Ethan. I was speaking to Larry the other night and mentioned you. I reckon I could get you a centrefold spread.'

Several years ago Angel had appeared in *LA Dreams*, owned by the legendary magazine magnate and multi-millionaire Larry T. Chance, but since then she'd had Honey and had vowed not to pose topless any more, which ruled out *LA Dreams*.

'I'm perfectly happy with Carrie, thanks, Benny,' Angel said, more calmly than she felt.

'Don't be too hasty, Angel. I definitely think it's something you should consider – not just for your sake but for Ethan's. Two are always better than one, don't you think? And you two make a very attractive package to advertisers and sponsors.' He licked his lips as if relishing the prospect of all that extra money.

Angel looked at him scornfully. He was the last person she would want managing her. The conversation was over. She got up and was about to leave the room to find her friends when Benny called after her, 'And maybe while you're thinking about what we've talked about, you should let me give you the number of a surgeon – those tits of yours could probably do with an upgrade sometime soon, couldn't they?'

The man was fucking outrageous! She wanted to tell him as much and where he could go. Instead she said coldly, 'I'm sure Ethan wouldn't appreciate you speaking to me like this, so shall we just forget your last comment?'

Benny shrugged. 'Whatever. But I'm right, Angel.'

Thankfully Ethan returned at that moment and Benny was prevented from making any further obnoxious comments. Ethan looked completely shattered. 'Benny, I need to speak to Angel now.'

Benny remained sitting.

'On her own.'

Benny did not like being asked to leave, but eventually he stood up. He had reached the door when he stopped and said, 'Oh, and by the way, we need to set up an interview and shoot with *OK* for you guys to put on a united front, so Angel can say how much in love she is with you, and how the fact that you have a child with another woman doesn't change anything . . . blah blah blah. You know the kind of thing.' He raised his arm in farewell and left.

Ethan came and sat next to Angel. He tentatively

reached for her hand which she was reluctant to give him. 'I'm so sorry, Angel, I never wanted you to get caught up in all of this.' He certainly seemed sorry, just as Cal had done when news of his affair had broken.

Angel could sense that Ethan wanted her to say that she still loved him, that she believed him, but something stopped her. She'd become much harder since the end of her marriage. 'I'm sure you are sorry, it's not great for your profile, is it? No wonder Benny wants us to do that interview.' She knew she sounded cold.

'You don't have to do the interview if you don't want to. This isn't about us . . . it's about me.'

Angel sighed, 'And if I don't do it, it will just add fuel to the press stories that we're not getting on, and they'll keep on at us.'

'I'm not putting pressure on you to do anything,' Ethan repeated, 'I just want you to know that I love you.'

But Angel couldn't say it back. She had hoped that her new relationship would be a fresh start for her, but only six months in it was already getting tarnished.

Ethan's bombshell news wrecked the rest of her friends' visit. Whenever Angel tried to go out with Jez and Gemma, they were aggressively pursued by paps who had taken to camping outside the house. In the end they gave up trying to go out and spent the time chilling by the pool, which both Jez and Gemma claimed not to mind about but Angel did. She wanted to show her friends a good time. Ethan was either training or tied up in meetings with Benny and his lawyers, and when he was around he was preoccupied and distant. Every time Angel brought up the subject of his daughter, he said he didn't want to talk about it, which made her feel even more shut out.

He gave her frustratingly few details about what had

31

happened with Ella Richards. Just repeated it had been a one night stand and he had thought no more about it until he got a call from Ella, informing him that she was six months pregnant and the baby was his. Ethan had refused to believe her until the baby was born and DNA tests were carried out.

'But how do you feel about being a father?' Angel asked him, not able to understand how detached he was from his daughter's life.

'It doesn't feel as if she is my daughter,' was his answer. Ethan, usually so laid-back and open about his emotions, was showing a different side and Angel wasn't sure she liked it. And however hard she pushed him, he wouldn't give her any more than that.

On Jez and Gemma's penultimate day Angel was really hoping to take them to Santa Monica Pier for a fun day out, but Benny insisted she do the shoot with Ethan, telling her, 'You've got to pull out all the stops here, Angel. I want everyone to be looking at you, so all thoughts of Ella Richards go out of their tiny brains. We'll start with you in evening dress and go on to the bikini shots.' His cold grey eyes lingered on her as he added, 'Make sure you flash some of that gorgeous flesh.'

Angel resisted flicking him the finger and went upstairs to her dressing room with her friends. Jez had offered to do her hair and Gemma her make-up. Angel now felt even worse. Her friends were supposed to be on holiday but were having to work. She sat in front of her dressing-table mirror as Jez arranged her hair into a chic updo for the first sequence of shots.

'I'm so sorry that we didn't get to go out much – next time you come we'll do some really good things, I promise.' It was about her tenth apology.

'Angel – you don't have to apologise – we've had a great time. We wanted to see you and it doesn't matter about going to exclusive clubs,' Gemma replied, kicking Jez when it looked like he wasn't going to back her up. 'And in a few weeks it'll be Christmas. We can go clubbing in Brighton.'

'Oceania's not exactly the same as Skybar, is it?' Angel said ruefully, naming a club on Brighton seafront, next to the Odeon, which could hardly compare to the über-glamorous Skybar at the top of the five-star Mondrian Hotel, with its breathtaking views of LA.

'True, but would we be able to go for a kebab afterwards here? Got to have a kebab after clubbing,' Gemma put in diplomatically, while Jez pulled an expression of exaggerated disgust. In the past, after they'd gone out clubbing, he had always waited in the car while the girls grabbed their fast-food fix – and then afterwards made a big deal about spraying the car with his Hugo Boss aftershave.

At that there was a hammering on the door. 'Can you guys hurry up in there. The photographer's here and we need to get started.' It was Benny. God, he was unbearable!

'We'll just be fifteen more minutes,' Angel shouted back, even though Jez was almost finished. Let Benny wait. She would take her time.

Ethan was by the pool when Angel finally made her appearance. He was wearing a black tuxedo, the black tie unfastened. He looked stunning, something Angel registered in spite of being angry with him. 'You look beautiful,' he told her, kissing her lightly to avoid smudging her lipstick. Angel was in her red Valentino evening dress, which clung to every curve of her body. She'd gone for old school glamour with her hair in an elegant French pleat, red lipstick, and black eyeliner sweeping across her eyelids.

'The scarlet woman . . . I like it!' Benny cut across

them, ruining the moment. 'So, Ethan, stand behind Angel with your arm round her waist. Angel, look back at Ethan. I want to see the love in your eyes.'

Angel just hated being directed like this, but she wanted to get the shoot over and done with as quickly as possible so she zipped it. But she had to giggle when she noticed Gemma and Jez pretending to be sick at Benny's cheesy over-the-top direction.

'I wanna see that love!' Benny shouted out.

'Sorry,' Ethan murmured in Angel's ear. 'It'll be over soon, I promise, and we can go back to how we were.'

Angel wasn't so sure.

'Show me the love!' Benny shrieked.

'I'll show him something in a minute,' she muttered. 'But it won't be love.'

But Angel was nothing if not a pro and so she plastered a smile on her face and got through the shoot. That night Ethan took her and her friends out to Spago, one of Angel's favourite restaurants in Beverly Hills, which she knew Jez had been dying to go to. Thankfully minus Benny.

'I know what you must think of me,' he said to Jez and Gemma, after they had ordered and the waiter was safely out earshot. 'But I love this girl and I would never do anything to hurt her, believe me.' It was said in all sincerity and didn't sound in any way corny or fake, but Angel knew that Gemma would find it hard to believe. The whole Ella Richards affair would just confirm her suspicions that he was a player.

'So when were you going to tell Angel about your daughter?' Gemma asked, giving Ethan a sweet smile to compensate for the direct question.

'I was about to when the press broke the story,' he replied, trying to stay cool though Angel could see that he was rattled. He wasn't used to being put on the spot. He had clearly thought that his declaration of love would smooth things over between Angel's friends and himself.

Gemma looked at him with her deep blue, almost violet eyes. 'Yeah, Angel's had a lot of that in her life. I really hope, for her sake, there won't be any more surprises, it's been hard on her.' Gemma was not a woman to be won over by an expensive restaurant and emotional speeches.

'There won't be, I promise, only nice ones,' Ethan replied. He turned to Angel. 'She's a tough one, but I like the way she sticks up for you. Can I take it the interrogation's over now and we can order champagne?'

He gave Gemma his best you-can-trust-me smile and she seemed to decide to play nice and stop the questions. The rest of the meal passed happily enough, but Angel was still aware of Gemma weighing up everything Ethan said. And later, back at the house, while Ethan and Jez played on Ethan's Xbox, the two women chatted in Gemma's room.

'You will be careful, won't you, and not rush into anything with Ethan?' Gemma asked, sitting cross-legged on her bed in a pair of pearl-grey silk pyjamas. Gemma had to be stylish even when she slept.

'What do you mean?'

'Don't marry him yet, or have another baby,' Gemma said bluntly. 'I just think you need more time to get over Cal.' She was definitely in the speaking-her-mind zone. Angel was used to it and wasn't offended.

'I don't think I ever want to get married again,' she replied. She knew she wanted another baby, very much in fact, but Ethan's bombshell revelation about Megan had made her cautious about admitting this, especially to Gemma. 'And I suppose I would like another baby, but not for a while. And I don't know why you're dragging Cal into it . . . I am over him.' But even as she said it, she wondered if she ever would be.

*

Later, in bed, Angel and Ethan lay talking. 'I hope this stuff with Ella didn't ruin your friends' visit?' he said.

She turned towards him and saw how anxious he looked. She didn't have the heart to admit that it had cast a shadow over their stay . . . how could it not have? 'It was great to see them, and thanks for inviting them over.' She put her hand on his broad chest as if to reassure him. 'But if they come again, no more surprises.'

Ethan gave a wry smile. 'That's if they *want* to come again. I like them both very much, by the way, even though I'm not exactly sure Gemma returns the compliment.' He frowned. 'Promise me you won't let what's happened come between us? It really does belong to my past. And there are no more surprises.' He put his arm round her. 'I love you so much, Angel. No other woman has made me feel the way you do.'

'I love you too, Ethan.'

But in her head Angel thought, let's just see how it goes. She knew that the shock revelation about his daughter had made her take a step back from him.

Chapter 3

Angel and Honey flew back to the UK the day before Christmas Eve. The original plan had been that Ethan would come as well, but his grandmother, Loretta, was recovering from breast cancer and Ethan had decided to spend the holidays with her. While Angel was sorry about Loretta, with whom she got on extremely well, she was relieved to be spared the ordeal of Ethan meeting Cal, which would otherwise have happened on Christmas Day. She wasn't quite ready to play happy exes/families with the two men; wasn't sure if she would ever be ready for that particular scenario.

Over the last few weeks things hadn't been that great between Angel and Ethan. He was paranoid about her seeing Cal without him being around, convinced that her husband would try to win her back – an obsession which ground Angel down. However many times she tried to reassure him that it was over between her and Cal, she sensed that Ethan wasn't entirely convinced. And on top of dealing with that, she also had her own concerns about spending time with Cal. She knew she wasn't immune to him. She had spent much of the flight back worrying about what it was going to be like seeing him again. And Honey's frequent and excited 'See Daddy?' questions only added to the tension. It had been nearly a month since Angel had last seen Cal, and then he had barely said a word to her as he'd picked up Honey from the house and dropped her off again, seeming to want to get away from Angel as quickly as possible.

As soon as she and Honey walked through Arrivals they were surrounded by paps, clicking away frenziedly. Bloody hell! It was nearly Christmas, didn't they ever let up? Angel instantly picked up her daughter to shield her from the cameras and tried to push her luggage trolley with one hand, no easy feat, especially as the paps had no intention of getting out of her way. She was on the point of losing it with them when a huge mountain of a man pushed his way through. It was Ray, a security guy she had employed in the past.

'Come on, Angel, let's get you out of here. Your mum and dad are waiting in the car.' He took over the trolley, forcing the paps to move out of the way.

'Thanks, Ray,' Angel said gratefully. 'Did Dad call you?'

'No, it was Cal. He thought it would be a good idea.'

Just the mention of his name caused an unexpected rush of butterflies inside Angel. She was about to ask if Cal was in the car when a ripple of excitement went through the paps. They'd seen Cal approaching.

'I thought I told him to stay in the car!' Ray said in disbelief. 'They're going to go mental now.'

'Daddy!' Honey shouted, catching sight of Cal, and stretching out her arms. And there he was, scooping Honey away from Angel and hugging his daughter. Angel would usually keep her expression as neutral as possible when the paps were around, but she was smiling with delight at seeing her daughter and Cal reunited. They both looked so happy. And she couldn't help being struck by how very handsome Cal looked. Oh, God! Maybe Ethan was right to be wound up about her seeing her husband again.

Cal was so taken up with Honey that for a moment he seemed oblivious to the cameras and to Angel. But then he looked over at her. 'I couldn't wait in the car . . . I had to see her.' His brown eyes were full of warmth and happiness at seeing his daughter.

Angel felt a sudden pang of longing for the time when Cal had been as happy upon seeing her as well. If she was like this after a few minutes in his company, what would she be like at the end of two weeks? This visit was getting off to a very bad start.

But if Cal had any internal conflict over seeing Angel again, he kept it well hidden on the journey back to Brighton. All his attention was taken up with Honey; he barely said a word to Angel. They both sat at the back of Frank's Peugeot Estate, with Honey strapped in her car seat between them, while Frank and her mum, Michelle, updated Angel on what was happening with various friends and relatives and on the state of Frank's beloved youth team.

Every now and then Angel found herself sneaking a glance at Cal. He was as gorgeous as ever but looked tired, with dark circles etched under his eyes. He didn't seem to return her interest. He never once looked directly at her. She might just as well not have been there at all. She shouldn't have cared what he thought of her, but she did. Very much. Angel had been feeling exhausted, but seeing Cal again was like a shot of adrenaline. She felt totally wired.

Back at her parents' small terraced house, Cal seemed in no hurry to leave. Though Honey was tired out from the long flight, she too was energised by her father's presence, climbing all over him, insisting that he read her favourite Peppa Pig story.

'He's missed Honey so much,' Michelle told Angel when she went into the kitchen to make a cup of tea. 'That's why he looks so exhausted. He's been driving himself into the ground so as not to have any free time.' Michelle paused from loading the dishwasher, and pushed her ash-blonde hair behind her ear as she looked over at her daughter. Angel had a feeling she wouldn't like what was coming next.

'He's missed you as well, Angel. He would never say it, but I know he has. Do you think you'll be staying in LA much longer? We'd all love you to come home.'

Angel noticed that her mum had so far avoided talking about Ethan – both she and Frank had been shocked by the recent revelation, Frank especially. He'd had a few choice things to say about Ethan not seeing the little girl. Even before that they were convinced that Angel was rushing into things by moving in with him.

Trust her mum to make her feel bad! Happy Christmas guilt trip! 'LA's my home now, Mum. I'm with Ethan. And it's all very well for you to say that Cal misses me, but he's only got himself to blame for that. I wasn't the one who cheated, if you remember?' She was so agitated she spilt tea all over the kitchen table.

At that moment Cal walked into the room. He must have heard Angel's comment, but he didn't let on. 'I was just going to warm some milk up for Honey,' he said calmly. 'She seems to be getting tired, Angel, so maybe I should give her a bath?'

'Sure,' Angel said, as she wiped up the tea, 'I'll get her things ready for you.' Two could play the polite game. Somehow she would rather Cal was angry with her than act the polite stranger. It made her want to shake him up, ask him how he really felt about her. As well as being the most devastatingly handsome man and passionate lover, he was also the most infuriating person she had ever known. No one could wind her up like Cal.

She grabbed her mug of tea and stomped upstairs to her old room, where her mum had set up a camp bed for Honey next to Angel's bed. In place of the posters of pop stars Angel used to have on her wall, her mum had put up an array of family photographs – Angel and Cal's wedding day, Angel pregnant with Honey, Cal with his arm round her. It was like a shrine to her old life with not a single picture of her and Ethan, even though she had sent her mum plenty of them. Angel wasn't at all happy to be sharing a room with so many images from her past.

She was just looking at a photograph of her and Cal fooling around in the sea on Playa d'en Bossa beach in Ibiza, before their daughter was born, when he walked into the bedroom carrying Honey. The room suddenly seemed tiny and Angel felt flustered. She redirected her gaze and busied herself getting Honey's PJs out of the huge suitcase, which was crammed with clothes and bags of presents.

'Still the world's worst packer,' Cal said dryly, seeing the jumble of clothes that Angel had indeed flung into the case at the last minute.

'Yep,' she replied.

'So how's it going with . . .' Cal hesitated. He hated saying Ethan's name just about as much as Ethan hated saying his, by the look of it.

'With Ethan? It's good, thanks,' Angel said, trying to act casual. But it was distinctly unsettling having a conversation in her old bedroom, with Cal, by her bed. Her bed, where she had spent so many nights fantasising about him when she was a teenager and he had seemed so out of reach.

'So you're okay about him having a daughter? Must have been a bit of a shock, I imagine.'

Damn! Trust Cal to bring that up. Because Angel was so well known in the UK, the British press had picked up the story about Ethan and his daughter, and it had been front-page news here as well. Angel shrugged. 'There's no problem – it all happened way before I met him. And I trust him, if that's what you mean. Well, as much as I trust any man now.' She couldn't stop herself from sounding bitter.

Cal sighed, 'Yeah, I heard you talking to your mum, Angel. Thanks for the reminder . . . like I need it. I just hope you haven't rushed into a relationship with Ethan because of what happened with us. Whatever you think about me, I'd hate you to get hurt again.'

Now those brown eyes were less cold as he looked at her across the bed. How the hell was she supposed to respond to that?

'Daddy! I want my bath!' Honey piped up. Saved by her daughter. Leaving Cal and Honey to it, Angel went back downstairs. Cal left for his seafront penthouse a while after that and Angel herself went to bed, too wiped out by jetlag to carry on.

Christmas Eve was a whirlwind of last-minute shopping, with her mum panicking that she hadn't got enough food even though the entire fridge and freezer were crammed to overflowing. In the afternoon Cal had arranged tickets for the whole family to go and see *Cinderella* at the Theatre Royal, a lovely old-fashioned theatre in the heart of Brighton. Honey was far more interested in the light-up, flashing wand he'd bought than in the drama unfolding before her. She insisted on sitting first on Cal's knee then climbing on to Angel's.

Again Angel felt unsettled by being so close to Cal; close enough to get a hit of his Dior aftershave, a scent which he had worn for as long as she had known him; close enough that their legs accidentally touched as Honey scrambled between both parents. The couple had barely said anything to each other but addressed all their comments to Honey.

Gemma was sitting the other side of Angel and must have known how strange this outing would feel to Angel as she kept asking her if she was okay.

'Not really,' Angel finally whispered during one of the big singing numbers. 'I can't get my head round being with Cal, and Mum has even asked him to stay the night so he can be with Honey first thing on Christmas morning.'

Michelle had dropped that particular bombshell while she and Angel were doing a last-minute dash round Sainsburys earlier, and wouldn't take any notice of Angel's protests that she would find it awkward. Angel didn't exactly want to have a stand-up row with her in front of the deli counter.

'Honestly, Gem, I sometimes think my parents worry more about Cal than they do about me!'

Gemma shook her head. 'They just know how much he's missed Honey.'

God! Now she was even getting guilt tripped by her best friend! Angel didn't answer but instead looked at the stage where an extremely camp Prince Charming was fitting the satin slipper on Cinders' foot. Once upon a time, Angel thought bitterly, she believed she had found her happy-ever-after with Cal. Now she knew there was no such thing. 'It won't last,' she said to Gemma, 'I reckon he's got his eye on Buttons.'

'You never used to be this cynical,' Gemma teased.

'I wonder why I am now?' Angel shot back sarcastically.

Back at her parents', Cal insisted on making supper for everyone. He was a fantastic cook who liked nothing better than cooking for a house full of people. Angel felt a sudden pang for Ethan, who was as bad at cooking as she was. She went upstairs with Gemma to do some last-minute wrapping and to text Ethan.

'So is Ethan okay with you spending so much time with Cal?' Gemma asked, sitting in her familiar position for gossiping, cross-legged on the bed, as Angel struggled to find the end of the Sellotape to wrap up the brown and gold monogrammed Louis Vuitton handbag she had bought for her mum.

'Why shouldn't he be? It's not like I had any say in the matter, is it?' Angel knew she sounded defensive but she found talking about Cal really difficult, even with her best friend. And Ethan had sounded far from pleased that morning when she had revealed that Cal was staying the night at her parents' house. In fact, he had been shocked and kept asking why Cal couldn't stay at his own place. Angel could only pray that he didn't see the photographs of Cal meeting her and Honey at the airport, which were bound to appear in the press soon.

Gemma held out her hand for the Sellotape and managed to find the end in no time. That action summed her up: ultra-efficient, always knowing exactly what she wanted.

'Ummm,' was Gemma's reply. 'And has Ethan met his daughter yet?'

Angel glared at her friend; Gemma always went to the heart of the matter. 'Not yet, it's probably going to happen in the next few months. To be honest, Gem, we haven't talked about it that much.'

In fact, Angel had wanted to talk about it because to her it was a really big thing, especially now she had a child and knew how intense the bond between parent and child could be, but every time she had brought the subject up Ethan had avoided it, wanted to block it out. She didn't know if it was because he didn't want to upset her or because he couldn't handle the thought of being a father.

To stop Gemma asking any more difficult questions, Angel resorted to asking her what she thought of the bag for her mum. Instantly Gemma channelled her inner fashionista. 'Well, a Louis Vuitton is a classic. You could have gone for a Mulberry Bayswater, I suppose, but I'm not sure if that's quite your mum.' And from there Gemma went on to describe the Chloe bag that she had her eye on for Christmas, in forensic detail. Angel just hoped that Tony had been paying attention and saving up – hell had no fury like a fashionista who did not get her dream Chloe bag on Christmas morning.

Cal had made lasagne and garlic bread for supper. Once again, as they all sat round the kitchen table, Angel had a flashback to the past. She had sat here so many times with Cal: as a teenager when she was desperately, hopelessly in love with him, and as a couple when they'd finally got together. She found herself sitting opposite him now which made the experience even more unsettling as she was so intensely aware of him and his every move. But, as before, Cal looked every where but at Angel, focussing all his attention on his daughter and making sure she ate her pasta.

'Not like your glamorous LA life, I imagine?' Angel's brother teased her. 'You don't have to lift a finger to do anything there, do you? Gem says you've got your own team of chefs and everything.'

He sounded as if he did not think this was a good thing. Angel had always had a fiery relationship with Tony. They were as different in personality as in looks – Tony dark-haired and dark-eyed, with a cute, boyish face, compared to the blonde, green-eyed striking beauty of his sister. Tony was calm, level-headed, always thought he was right, whereas Angel was impulsive, passionate, often riven by self-doubt and insecurity. The differences were not surprising as she had been adopted as a baby whereas Tony was Frank and Michelle's son, and was a lot like his dad.

'One cook,' Angel corrected him.

'And a butler. And a team of chauffeurs, cleaners and gardeners,' Gemma put in. 'Angel is living the celeb life to the max. You just need a nutritionist, a stylist, and someone to put your toothpaste on your brush and you'll have made it, girlfriend!'

'But luckily I've got all you lot to keep me grounded,' Angel replied dryly as Tony handed her the supper plates.

'So how's your boyfriend spending Christmas?' he asked. He had only met Ethan once and it had been a slightly strained meeting, with Tony being decidedly offhand. While Tony had been stunned by Cal's infidelity, he still believed that Angel should get back with him and they should work through it. Somehow Angel couldn't imagine him being so understanding were Gemma ever to be unfaithful to *him*.

'My boyfriend, *Ethan,* is spending Christmas with his grandmother, Loretta – she's just getting over cancer as I think I told you,' Angel replied, feeling a little put on the spot.

'So he's not seeing his daughter?' Tony continued.

Angel shook her head, and muttered, 'He's not met her yet.'

Frank tutted. 'That's a shame. He should face up to his responsibilities. The child needs a father.'

Perfect! This was all she needed: an in-depth analysis of her boyfriend's failings in front of her nearly ex-husband. She was aware of Cal finally looking at her, no doubt trying to work out what she thought of Ethan's behaviour.

'It's complicated, Dad, but I'm sure he'll see her soon.' Angel hoped she sounded calmer than she felt. 'Not everything is black-and-white, you know.'

Frank looked as if he was about to say something else, but thankfully Michelle gave him a warning look and he kept quiet. Just in case he was tempted to come out with anything, Angel stood up with the plates and took them over to the sink. By the time she returned to the table, thankfully the conversation had moved on.

After supper Tony and Gemma headed to her parents', who lived round the corner. Frank and Michelle watched *EastEnders* while Cal gave Honey her bath and Angel carried on wrapping presents. All the time she was aware of Cal just across the hall from her as he made Honey squeal with laughter and she squirted him with water from her rubber duck. Father and daughter hadn't shared many bathtimes in the last six months. Angel felt another surge of guilt as she realised this. Cal brought Honey into the bedroom, wrapped up in a huge pink towel, and Honey thought it even more hilarious when she turned her rubber duck on Angel.

'You cheeky monkey!' she exclaimed, wiping water from her face while Honey giggled. 'She's never going to settle now.' Angel turned to Cal.

'I'm sorry, I couldn't help it, she's just so great when she laughs,' he replied, kissing the top of Honey's head. Another pang of guilt. 'But I'll stay with her until she goes to sleep if you want to go downstairs.'

Two hours later and Angel had sat through the Christmas specials of *Gavin and Stacey* and *You've Been Framed*, listened to her dad give another blow by blow account of how his youth team was doing and what he thought of Chelsea's performance while her mum continued to fret that she hadn't bought enough vegetables . . . and Cal still hadn't come downstairs.

'Honey never usually takes this long to go to sleep,' Angel told her mum, 'I'd better check she's okay.'

Upstairs all became clear. Cal and Honey lay fast asleep, side by side on Angel's bed, Honey snuggled into her father. Angel stood there for a few minutes, watching father and daughter sleeping. They looked so beautiful together, it was a truly heart-wrenching sight. Then she tiptoed in, grabbed her PJs and tiptoed out again, gently closing the door behind her. She would have to sleep on the sofa bed in the living room.

Her parents went to bed themselves soon after that, entrusting Angel with the task of putting out a glass of wine and a mince pie for Santa plus a carrot for Ruldoph.

'I'll leave you to drink that and take a couple of bites,' her dad told her. 'It always used to be my job but you can have it.' He patted his beer belly, which definitely seemed to have got bigger lately. 'Your mum's putting me on a diet come New Year. She keeps telling me I'm letting myself go, and if I don't watch it she'll find herself a toy boy.'

Angel doubted that very much, but her dad did need to lose weight.

She took a shower, then arranged all her Christmas presents for Honey under the tree, drank the glass of wine, took a bite out of the mince pie and followed it with the carrot . . . *so* not a good combination. She was just setting up the sofa bed when Cal appeared in the doorway.

'Sorry. One minute I was telling Honey a story, the next thing I was out for the count. I was knackered.'

He yawned, stretching his arms and causing his tee-shirt to ride up so it revealed an expanse of olive skin and perfectly flat abs, a thin dark line of hair running down from his navel. The sight sent a shiver of lust running through Angel, in spite of all her best intentions.

'You can stay there, if you want,' she replied.

Cal shook his head. 'I'd better not in case Honey wakes up and wants you.' He looked over at the fireplace, noting the half-drunk glass of wine and half-eaten mince pie. 'So you've done your Santa duty?'

Angel nodded. 'Actually I was going to have a Bailey's, d'you want one?' She suddenly wasn't feeling in the least bit tired, didn't want to go up to bed, wanted to be with Cal. A small voice inside her tried in vain to tell her that this was not a good idea. She didn't listen.

'I'll have a brandy,' he said.

The two of them sat sipping their drinks: Cal sitting on the edge of the sofa bed, Angel sitting on the rug by the fire. 'It's so good to see Honey. I can't believe how much she's grown in the last month. Every time I see her she's changed again and learnt more new words,' Cal said wistfully.

Angel was now feeling thoroughly guilt tripped. She hung her head. 'I'm sorry you don't get to see as much of her as you'd like. I'll try and bring her back to the UK more next year. This year has been difficult.'

'I know,' he said softly. 'And I'm not blaming you.' Angel looked up at him and his brown eyes were warm. 'I'm thinking of renting a place in Santa Monica just along the coast from you, so that I can spend more time with Honey. Seeing her once a month is just not enough. I feel like I'm really missing out.'

Angel could only imagine how much Ethan would hate the idea of having Cal as a neighbour, but she replied, 'I'd like it if you saw more of Honey.'

For a moment they were both silent, then Cal said, 'You didn't answer my question last night, when I asked if you'd rushed into things with Ethan?' It was a question Angel really didn't feel he had the right to ask.

'I don't think so,' she replied, determined to play it cool.

Cal shook his head, and looked sceptical. 'I don't want to upset you, Angel, but it's got rebound written all over it, can't you see that? And, come on, what do you really know about the guy? The news about his daughter must have been a shock.'

He sounded so patronising and judgemental . . . and what right did he have to judge Ethan? Angel saw red. 'It is *not* a rebound thing! And I didn't rush into it. I weighed things up very carefully, wondering if I should stay with someone who had cheated on me and might well do it again for all I knew, or whether I could have a new life with a man who loves me.' She wasn't going to sit back and let Cal rip her to shreds. He certainly knew how to kill a moment! She got up and headed for the door but he was too quick for her. He caught her arm. 'Please don't go.'

'Why not? So you can carry on having a go at me!' Angel glared at him, her green eyes flashing with anger.

Cal didn't answer but instead pulled her towards him. 'I'm sorry, Angel. I just want to know that you're okay. Sorry.'

His voice was soft and low and aroused feelings in her that she thought she had let go of a long time ago. She wanted to tell him to leave her alone, that she was with Ethan, but her body said something different. Just the feeling of having Cal so close, his hands on her shoulders, was setting off a chain reaction of lust and longing within her. And so when Cal ducked down and lightly kissed her lips, she didn't resist him. Instead she found herself kissing him back, and the kiss became deeper, more intense, a passionate, sexy, searching kiss

50

that sent shock waves of desire through Angel's body and made her long to feel Cal's touch.

As if in answer he slid his hands under her tee-shirt and lightly caressed her breasts, circled her nipples in the way which had always turned her on so much in the past. Angel pressed her body closer to his, slipped her hands under his tee-shirt, felt the smooth skin of his back. His body felt so familiar to her, so good. God knows where it would have ended up, because Angel was feeling reckless enough for anything, but suddenly she came to her senses and realised what she was doing.

She pulled away. 'I can't do this,' she said abruptly.

Cal looked taken aback. 'What's going on?'

'I'm with Ethan now.' Once more she made for the door.

'I don't believe you,' Cal called after her. Angel kept on walking.

She barely slept that night, alternately scorched by guilt about Ethan then replaying the kiss, to feel again that rush of desire. Why had she done that? It was playing with fire.

But however conflicted Angel felt, she forced herself to put on an act that she was blissfully happy the following day, not wanting her daughter to pick up any bad vibes. And it was so sweet, seeing Honey opening her presents. Angel and Cal seemed to have bought up most of Toys R Us between them, but with typical perverse toddler behaviour the present Honey liked best of all was a ginger-and-white toy cat which meowed when you pressed its tummy. She was not nearly as impressed by the mini laptop, the Snow White dressing-up costume, the collection of Barbies, the Barbie castle, the Barbie riding school . . . though she did like the box of dressing-up shoes, clearly her

51

mother's daughter in that respect, and the bright pink scooter got her approval.

Cal was back to being distantly polite with Angel and she with him. She wanted to pretend the kiss had never happened. It was just because it was the first time they had been alone together and Christmas was always an emotional workout, she tried to tell herself. It didn't mean anything.

Michelle and Frank were busy preparing Christmas lunch. Honey was desperate to go out on her new scooter, and Cal suggested that he and Angel took her down to the seafront. After last night Angel wasn't sure it was such a good idea to be alone with Cal, but when Honey found out she might not go with them, she was so upset that Angel had to change her mind.

Both she and Cal were quiet as he drove them down to the seafront in his sleek black BMW. They walked along the promenade towards the brightly coloured children's playground by the old pier, Honey whizzing ahead on her scooter, seemingly oblivious to the biting wind coming off the sea. Cal kept all his comments strictly on the level of small talk. Wasn't it funny seeing all the children on their new bikes/skateboards/rollerblades? Did she think Honey needed to wear a helmet? Would Honey be warm enough in her coat? And Angel returned with small talk of her own.

But every now and then she couldn't resist glancing at Cal. He was wearing a black cashmere military-style coat with the collar turned up, and looked so handsome. She couldn't deny the old pull of desire she felt for him. But this had to stop. Just as Angel thought she had got away without talking about their kiss, he turned and looked at her and said softly, 'That was quite some kiss last night. I haven't been able to stop thinking about it.'

Angel was completely floored. She looked out at the

iron-grey sea and pulled her chestnut aviator UGG hat further down over her face, both to keep herself warm against the bitter wind blowing off to the sea and as if to fend off the question.

'It was a mistake,' she said quickly. 'Please don't talk about it.' She thought about how devastated Ethan would be if he knew, and felt ashamed. All her reassurances to him that there was nothing more between her and Cal suddenly seemed hollow. She had thought she was immune to Cal now, had spent the last months building up her defences against him, but just seeing him again was destroying them, piece by piece, leaving her feeling raw and vulnerable.

Cal shook his head. 'Nothing that felt that good could be a mistake. But if that's how you want to play it.'

'It's not how I want to *play* it! It's not some game. I made a mistake. We all make mistakes.' She paused, colour rushing into her face as she realised what she was saying.

'Perhaps it's time you finally forgave me for mine?' Cal said, an undeniable edge of hope in his voice.

Angel couldn't believe that they were having this conversation. 'I'm with Ethan, I told you.' She made her voice as hard and cold as she could, to try and hide the turmoil she felt, and Cal seemed to realise he wouldn't be able to get through to her and withdrew once again, making it impossible for Angel to read what he was thinking. He was always so good at that.

Back at her parents' house it was the full-on family Christmas experience – champagne, crackers, dinner – where everyone ate too much, except Angel who was too preoccupied with thoughts of Cal. Then the obligatory TV-fest until Gemma and Tony came round in the evening and they played Trivial Pursuit and ate more food. This was exactly how Angel had spent the last five Christmases with Cal when they were together, and today was such a strange experience because everything was at once the same yet completely different. At one moment during the game, Cal received a phone call and went out of the room to take it which immediately put Angel on high alert – who was he speaking to? Was it a woman? Why had he left the room? And even as these thoughts collided in her head she felt furious with herself for being so easily drawn back.

Chapter 4

After Christmas Day, Cal had Honey for a few days and
Angel used the time to catch up with Jez in London.
Even though she knew she wouldn't be apart from her
daughter for long, she still felt Honey's absence like a
physical ache and had to keep busy so as not to dwell on
missing her.

'So how was it with Cal?' Jez asked as they met up in
the bar of the Mayfair Hotel for cocktails, typically
asking the very question that had been preoccupying
Angel herself.

They were sitting on one of the luxurious purple
velvet sofas by the fire, with glasses of pink champagne.
Angel contemplated telling him about the kiss and then
thought better of it, not wanting it to take on an even
greater importance than it already had in her mind.
Indeed, she could not stop thinking about it – and it still
aroused such contradictory feelings of desire, quickly
followed by guilt.

'It was okay at times,' she said slowly. 'And then at
others it felt really strange being with him. He was very
offhand with me.' She shook back her long blonde hair
as if shrugging off the memory, and took a sip of
champagne. 'I don't know, maybe it's just too soon for
us to meet up like that . . . everything is still too raw.'

Jez arched an eyebrow. 'He still loves you, it is so

obvious! He's doing his distant act as a defence, but it *is* just an act.'

For as long as she had known him – which was coming up for eight years – Jez had been one of her closest friends and confidantes. He put on an act of being shallow, and camper than a row of tents, but underneath he had a heart of gold, and was both caring and perceptive – a bit too perceptive sometimes. 'And don't be cross with me, but I think you're still in love with him on some level.'

Angel sighed, 'I don't know, Jez. When I found out that he had seen Alessia for three months – that it hadn't just been a one night stand, not that a one night stand wasn't bad enough – it shook everything up. I never thought Cal would do that to me – ever.'

'I know, Angel, but he bitterly regrets it, and it wasn't as if things between you were going well back then.' It was true, of course. After Honey was born, Angel had completely shut herself off from Cal, had been impossible to live with, snapping at him one moment, withdrawing the next; nor did she feel able to tell anyone as she felt such a failure as a mother. Post-natal depression had been one of the worst experiences of her life.

'Sorry, I didn't mean to bring it all back,' Jez added, seeing sadness invade Angel's face.

'Shall we talk about something else?'

But even though they then chatted and gossiped about which celebrity was doing what to whom, the mood of sadness stayed. It was as if Angel had been so caught up in the whirlwind of her infatuation with Ethan and her determination to leave Cal and start a new life for herself, that she hadn't given herself any time to grieve for her broken marriage.

After cocktails she treated Jez and Rufus, who had finally finished work at the gym, to dinner at Nobu in

Mayfair. It had always been one of Angel's favourite restaurants and she knew Jez and Rufus loved it too, but hadn't been able to go for a while because of their money worries.

Rufus was the perfect partner for Jez, being calm, quiet, thoughtful and totally loyal. Before Rufus, Jez had flitted from affair to affair, pretending to be happy but inside always craving a stable relationship. It was lovely to see them together, they suited each other perfectly.

Angel was just in the middle of telling Rufus that he must come out to LA in the New Year when she caught sight of someone she had hoped she would never have to see again. Ever. She was the former soap-star actress Simone Fraser, the woman Cal had left to be with Angel. Simone had never forgiven her – though Angel never knew whether that was because she had lost her position as an A-list WAG or whether it was truly because of her feelings for Cal. After Cal, Simone had gone out with a succession of footballers, slipping further and further down the leagues. The last Angel had heard, Simone was dating someone from Torquay.

'Don't look now,' she muttered to Jez, trying to be discreet, 'but I can see Simone Fraser over there.'

'Where?' Jez demanded, instantly turning round and craning his neck to get a better look at the fallen WAG. Simone had always been stunning-looking, with a heart-shaped face, huge brown eyes and a slender figure, but she had become obsessed with ageing, had gone down the Botox route by the look of her immobile forehead and had had work done on her lips, which were pumped up and now looked out of proportion with her delicate features. She also rarely smiled and had a permanent sulky pout, which only accentuated the inflated lips.

'Oh my sweet Jesus! What *has* she done to her

mouth!' Jez exclaimed. 'It looks like two bloated chipolatas coated in lip gloss. *So* not a good look!'

'Shush!' Angel warned him, worried that Simone would overhear them. She really wasn't up to a confrontation. Over the years Angel had learnt to her cost that any meeting with Simone would end up with her coming out with a stream of bitchy comments. But unfortunately for Angel, Simone had clocked her. Instead of simply giving her the evil eye, she rose from her seat and started walking unsteadily towards their table. A walk made precarious by her skin-tight black leather pencil skirt and staggeringly high silver-studded black Louboutins, as well as by the fact that she seemed to be pissed. Somehow she made it to their table without falling over and stood next to Angel.

'Long time no see, Angel,' she said, slurring her words slightly. 'Having fun with your basketball player?' She fumbled to push up her red satin bra strap which had slipped down one arm.

'It's baseball,' Angel said through gritted teeth.

'Whatever.' Simone swayed and grabbed the table for support, nearly knocking over Angel's wine glass. 'Oops!' she said, and plonked herself down on the free chair next to Rufus. 'Don't mind if I sit down for a minute, do you?' It was a bit late now, she was sitting there. She flicked back her long brunette hair, which seemed to be modelled on Cheryl Cole's lovely locks, nearly catching Rufus in the eye. 'So, you left Cal. I never saw that one coming! I thought you'd be together forever . . . like swans or is it geese?' She giggled, while Angel looked at her in appalled fascination – the woman was totally caned. She had never seen Simone like this before. Simone picked up Rufus's glass of wine and took a large swig from it.

''Course, I phoned Cal offering a shoulder to cry on, but the bastard never even returned my call.'

Another swig. 'And I really wasn't trying to get back with him; I just wanted to be friends. It would be nice to have a friend like Cal.' It was like watching an emotional car crash. Even Jez, who was never usually lost for words, was speechless.

'Don't you want to go back to your friend?' Angel asked, desperate to get rid of Simone.

'Oh, he probably won't even notice. He's too busy checking his CrackBerry or letching after the twenty-something waitress. And, if you must know, I can't bear being with him another minute . . . he makes my flesh crawl.'

To Angel's horror, tears began snaking their way down Simone's cheeks, leaving streaks of black mascara. While Angel and Jez sat there frozen, Rufus put his arm round her and said gently, 'D'you want me to call you a taxi?'

Simone shook her head and tried to brush away the tears. 'I can't leave yet, I have to spend the night with him . . . it's part of the package.'

Oh my God! Was Simone a hooker now?

She looked at Jez. 'I just wondered if you had anything on you? I'd pay you back next time. I need a little pick me up, something to get me through . . . I can't get hold of my usual source.'

A coke-snorting hooker?

'Sweetie, I don't do drugs, I've always had a strictly just-say-no policy . . . well, except to poppers, but I don't think you need those right now. I think you should go home and have a nice cup of tea then go straight to bed. We'll get you a taxi, and explain to your gentleman friend that you're not feeling too good.'

'Would you really do that?' Simone gazed at him, her eyes still brimming with tears.

'No problem,' Jez replied, and stood up, holding out

his arm for her to take. She struggled to get up and then looked once more at Angel. 'You're mad to think you'll ever find another man like Cal. And it won't be long before he finds someone else. I mean, come on, this is Cal we're talking about . . . he could have *anyone*. I saw him the other month with about three model types hanging round him.'

Bloody hell! Now Angel could feel tears pricking her own eyes. She tried to tell herself that they were tears of sympathy at seeing the wreck Simone had made of her life as she watched her totter towards the door, clinging on to Jez and Rufus for grim death, but knew that her words about Cal had struck home.

Angel expected that Jez would return and make some bitchy quip about Simone being on the WAG scrap heap, but he was unusually subdued when he sat back down. 'I never really liked her, but it was just awful seeing her in that state. She really cried when we got her in the taxi . . . said that men were never nice to her like we had been,' he said quietly. 'Makes you realise what's important, doesn't it?' He reached across the table and took Rufus' hand. 'If I hadn't met Rufus when I did, I could see myself going down that route.'

'What! Being an escort and taking drugs?' Angel asked, trying to inject a bit of humour into the situation. But Jez was having none of it. He shook his head. 'Drink more likely, and a succession of one night stands . . . anything to fill the emptiness. It was Rufus who saw the real me, saw beyond the camp act that I put on.'

He smiled at Jez, then looked at Angel. 'So are you okay about what Simone said to you? I don't think she meant it to upset you.'

'It made a change from her usual slating of me,' Angel tried to say lightly because Simone's words had really shaken her. Yet again, she couldn't seem to escape from thoughts of Cal.

She ended up calling him when she got back to her hotel suite, on the pretext of finding out if Honey was okay, but really to hear his voice. 'Did you have a good time with Jez and Rufus?' Cal asked. He sounded sleepy, as if he was lying in bed. Angel had a sudden unexpected longing to be lying next to him.

'It was eventful,' she replied, going on to tell him about seeing Simone.

'Christ, she sounds a mess!' Cal exclaimed. 'I had no idea. Perhaps I'll send her a text, see if she wants to meet up sometime.'

Angel knew Cal well enough to realise that he didn't have feelings for Simone any more. After they had split up she had turned into something of a bunny-boiling stalker, and he very nearly had to take out an injunction against her. Angel should have been able to stay dispassionate at the prospect of them meeting up, but rational thought seemed to have gone out of the window and she was gripped by the most intense feeling of jealousy at the thought of Cal seeing Simone. Who was to say that his old girlfriend wouldn't charm him again? She'd managed it before in the past. She might have been a wreck tonight but it probably wouldn't take much to get her looking good again . . . The jealous thoughts swirled round Angel's head like a sickening fair-ground ride even as she wondered why the hell she was getting so wound up.

The following day she tried to ignore the emotional battle being waged inside her and focus on business and work as she went to see her agent, Carrie Rose, in her office in the heart of Soho. She'd been with Carrie since she'd started out as a glamour model and on the whole they got on well, even if at times Carrie's love of making money over everything else did grate. But Angel appreciated her agent's business acumen.

Carrie was working out on the Power Plate she'd recently had installed in her office. Pam, the PA, told Angel before she went in to see her that Carrie was obsessed with using it and literally hopped on it after every single snack or drink she consumed. She was paranoid about keeping slim.

'I'll be with you in a minute,' she called as Angel walked in.

She sat down on the mint-green leather sofa and tried not to look at Carrie's tiny bum vibrating away on the Power Plate. Despite being in her mid-fifties Carrie dressed like someone in their twenties, today in black skinny jeans and a tight white tee-shirt with the word *Juicy* printed across her perky silicone boobs. She had recently had her long blonde hair cut into a bob and looked better for it.

She finally stepped off the Plate, slipped on her heels and walked over to Angel to give her the obligatory two air kisses.

'You look gorgeous, darling. LA must be agreeing with you . . . and that divine baseball player. You sure know how to pick the good ones, don't you? First Cal, then Baseball Boy . . . and the fact that he's such a star in the US is doing your profile no end of good. You must talk to Susie, I want her to work on your profile with you.' She click clacked over to the door and called out, 'Susie, babe, come see Angel.'

She turned back to Angel who looked at her inquiringly, surprised that Carrie wanted to involve Susie, who was her junior agent.

'I'm taking more of a back seat in the agency,' Carrie explained, 'since I married Dave. I've discovered that there's more to life than working all the time.' She looked adoringly at the large photograph of a boyishly good-looking man on her desk.

Dave was the twenty-five-year-old builder Carrie had met six months before when he came to convert her loft. It had been love at first sight apparently, and by all accounts he was a lovely man who worshipped Carrie. She, in turn, could not stop telling everyone how wonderful he was – on Facebook, on Twitter, in texts. Angel was only surprised Carrie hadn't put Dave's name on her tee-shirt!

'I know everyone thinks it won't last and that he's the boy toy to my Cougar, but I know he's the man I've been waiting for all my life. You just know don't you?' Carrie said seriously. Her words reminded Angel of her feelings for Cal and Ethan. Damn! She really didn't need an emotional heart to heart right now.

Fortunately, at that moment Susie walked in and more air kisses followed, with comments from Susie about how great it was that Angel was with Ethan. Angel felt like saying that it hadn't been a career move, she was in love with the guy! Susie, who was in her mid-thirties, and pretty with long auburn hair and big brown eyes then turned serious. 'I've been looking at the press stories about you and Ethan and I really think you need to go to more premieres. And you absolutely have got to go to the Oscar parties in March. Profile, profile, profile Angel! There are thousands of beautiful women in LA!'

Angel sighed, 'I don't want to go out every single night, I want to be there for Honey.'

Susie pursed her caramel glossed lips together, clearly disapproving, but managed to say, 'Okay but a few events wouldn't go amiss. I've had Benny Sullivan on the phone asking if we can liaise and get some publicity for you guys. I'm not averse to the idea of working with him, he's got amazing contacts.'

Angel grimaced. 'He's so arrogant and full of himself. He even suggested I got my boobs redone.' She looked across at Carrie, who just shrugged and said, 'Don't if you don't want to, they still look good to me!' She really had mellowed! Angel thought.

But Susie raised her eyebrows, 'Well you have had a child, darling, maybe it is time for a freshen up.' She said it as if it was equivalent of a trip to the hairdressers for a cut and blow dry. 'And Benny could be useful to us. We could be talking big money here.'

Susie sounded like Carrie back in the day. Angel glanced at Carrie again, expecting her to be nodding her approval, but she was busy looking at her emails. Angel returned her gaze to Susie. 'He's already hinted that I should have an American agent.'

Carrie's ears pricked up at this. 'Don't be silly, darling. Susie will go out to LA and look after you, won't you, Susie? I might be married now, Angel, but it doesn't mean I've lost interest in your career. I'm as committed as I ever was.'

Susie looked very eager at this. 'Absolutely. I think one of us needs to be there, and I really want to pick up some clients out there. In the meantime keep me posted on anything Benny comes up with.' Susie was certainly coming across as a force to be reckoned with.

They finished the meeting by going through all Angel's work commitments – she had several shoots coming up for her own lingerie range and for various magazines, plus in the spring she would be returning to the UK to launch her second fragrance. She also had plans to launch her own range of children's clothes. Angel had always had a good head for business.

Usually Angel would have felt energised by the prospect of new work projects but she still couldn't shake off the memory of Simone's comments about Cal. Angel had once believed that she and Cal would be together forever; that he was the only man for her. She worked herself up into such a state, remembering this, that she almost had butterflies about seeing him when she went to pick up Honey from his Brighton apartment. But Cal was offhand with her when he opened the door. There was no smile, just a matter-of-fact, 'Hi, Honey's in the living room. Come in.' Angel's excitement faded; she couldn't bear it when he was like this.

Honey was sitting on a rug in the living room, playing happily with her toy cat. Angel rushed over to give her a hug and kiss.

'I think I've packed up all her things,' Cal said as he handed over Honey's rucksack, giving off the vibe of wanting to get rid of Angel as soon as possible. He was dressed in a sharply cut black Prada suit and looked as if he was about to go out.

'Thanks,' Angel replied. 'No worries if not, Honey's got plenty of other things. In fact, I think she might have more clothes than me!'

She waited for Cal to make a joking comment back – he'd always teased her about how much stuff she had when they were together – but he simply said, 'Please call me when you get back to LA. I'd like to know that you've landed safely.'

'So are you going out somewhere tonight?' Angel asked, wanting to know if he had a date.

'Yep, I'm meeting some friends in London. I never like to be on my own when Honey goes. I'm sure you understand that.'

Angel wondered if the friends were female, thinking back to Simone's words. Cal avoided eye contact and remained standing. Angel gathered up Honey and her rucksack and said goodbye. There was no sign that he was thinking about her. She felt stupid giving Cal so much headspace when it was obvious he was getting on perfectly fine without her, and found herself questioning why she was even wasting her time thinking about him.

Chapter 5

'So did you miss this, Angel?' Ethan asked as they lay
in bed together after making love. She had been back in
LA a week and Ethan had been very attentive, wanting
to make love twice a day. Frankly it was getting
knackering! But Angel guessed it was all down to his
insecurity about her seeing Cal again; his wanting to
prove that she belonged to him and not her ex-
husband.

'Of course,' she said lightly, stroking his shoulder,
when the truth was she had been so caught up with
wondering about Cal that she hadn't thought about
Ethan much while she was away. And Ethan's insecurity
had only intensified when pictures of Cal, Honey and
Angel, being reunited at the airport, made it into the
celeb mags.

'Your ex is very good at playing happy families,
isn't he?' Ethan had commented, looking totally pissed
off.

'He loves Honey, I can't deny that.'

'Yeah, let's hope she isn't too disillusioned when she
finds out what her daddy's really like.'

Angel hadn't wanted a full-scale row and so had let
the comment go, but she knew Ethan was still brooding
about it. She herself was finding it hard to block out her
feelings for Cal, but had returned to LA determined to

try . . . and especially to stop thinking about that kiss. However intoxicating it had felt, Cal belonged to her past; Ethan was her here and now.

'There's nothing I need to know about, is there?' Ethan asked unexpectedly, taking her right back to the night of the kiss. Maybe she should confess. That way it would be out in the open and she could deal with it better. Then she considered how hurt he would be.

'No, there's nothing you need to know about,' she told him.

Ethan sighed, 'It's just that sometimes I feel as if you're holding something back.'

She shook her head. 'No, there's nothing, I swear.' Even as she came out with the lie she felt awful. She held him tighter, as if Ethan's physical presence could somehow shield her from thinking about Cal.

But Ethan was moving away and getting out of bed, putting on his white bathrobe. 'Benny's due here soon, he wants to talk to us about a TV project.'

'What's that?' Angel asked, inside recoiling from the prospect of seeing Benny. She hadn't forgiven him for his comments about her needing another agent and new implants. The man was a complete asshole, in her opinion.

Ethan looked evasive. 'It's kinda best if Benny tells you himself.' He paused then added, 'It would be great if you could keep an open mind to what he says. I'm going through a real shit time at the moment with my finances. Without boring you with details, it turns out my accountant hadn't been paying my taxes for the last five years – he was taking the money and now he's disappeared and I've got a massive backlog of taxes to pay. He did it to a whole string of people including Benny. And of course Ella Richards is still out for a big pay off.'

'Christ, Ethan! Why didn't you tell me before? Why

68

the hell did you buy me that necklace? I had no idea things were so tough for you.'

'I didn't realise things were quite as bad as they were.' He looked reluctant to say any more on the subject. 'I'll see you downstairs.'

Seeing Benny Sullivan was so not a good start to the day. The minute Angel wandered into the living room, she received the usual double kiss from him, leaving her with an overwhelming desire to wipe her face to remove the damp marks left by his fleshy lips.

'Beautiful as ever, Angel. I saw the shots from your Victoria's Secret campaign – you look seriously hot! A real angel.'

He beamed at his own comment. Angel simply nodded, wanting to keep communication with him to an absolute minimum. But now Benny was opening up a large black portfolio of news cuttings, which Angel saw were all about her. 'While you've been away I've been doing some research on you. Boy, do the tabloids love you! You get so much coverage, Angel, you really should be using it to your advantage . . . and Ethan's.'

And your point is? she wanted to say.

'I think you and Ethan combined make an irresistible package, as I've said before. So many people are interested in you guys. I've been talking to some big-hitting TV executives and we've come up with a killer idea. Everyone is really excited. We could all do so well out of it.' Benny was practically bouncing around on the sofa in his enthusiasm. He was such a wanker, Angel thought dismissively.

'E! want to do a four-part reality show with you and Ethan!' Benny declared as if it was the most momentous news ever. 'They're thinking of calling it *A Player and an Angel* . . . What do you think? We could start filming right now. That's the joy of reality TV – no sets to build, no actors to hire, just you and Ethan, access all areas. And they're offering great money.'

Angel was totally unimpressed. She wasn't interested in doing a reality show. She'd been through so much in the last year that now all she wanted was peace and as much privacy as possible. 'It's not for me, Benny,' she said quietly.

It had clearly never even crossed his mind that Angel would say no, and he turned an unusual shade of aubergine as her words sank in.

'*That's* your answer!' Benny exploded, slamming the portfolio down on the table, so the cuttings scattered on to the floor and Angel was surrounded by images of herself. 'Come on, Angel! This is a perfect launch pad for you into the States. You're starting to get a profile, but you could be so much bigger.'

Angel shook her head. 'I want to concentrate on modelling, and Carrie and I have plans for more lingerie and perfume. That's enough for me. I want my private life.'

'And what about Ethan? He told you about his situation, didn't he? He's been totally screwed, and this deal could really help put him straight. Along with the fee for the show, there are so many new possibilities for advertising and sponsorship. This is a big fucking deal, Angel!'

She just hated being blackmailed. It wasn't her fault that Ethan's accountant had ripped him off or that he had got Ella Richards pregnant.

'Like I said, Benny, I'm not interested.'

He shot a furious look at Ethan. 'You gotta tell her – there's no way E! will want the series without her. We need this fucking deal!' He was speaking to Ethan as if he was a child. Angel couldn't believe that Ethan didn't tell him to fuck off. Instead he turned to Angel and said quietly, 'Is there any way you would consider doing

70

this? It would really get me out of some serious financial shit, and it would be good for your profile.'

'Can we talk about this somewhere else?' she asked. 'Just you and me?' She didn't think she could bear to be in the same room as Benny for another second. And without waiting for a reply she went outside, ignoring the cuttings on the floor. Let Benny clear them up.

Before she'd lived in LA Angel had had the idea the skies there were always effortlessly blue, but she was learning that they could be grey, the sun didn't always shine, and it did sometimes rain, in spite of what the songs said. She was confronted with grey skies as she went outside and headed as far away from Benny as possible.

Ethan came and found her by the pool where she sat in one of the chairs, staring out at the ocean beyond the vivid pink bougainvillea and palm trees as if it could provide the answers. He sat down next to her, seeming tense and on edge.

'I'm sorry to put this on you, Angel, but I've really fucked up.' He ran his hands over his short blond hair. 'I've already had to sell my New York apartment and my villa in Martha's Vineyard. The TV show could really help get me straight. We can do it how we want, I'll make sure of that. And Benny's right. It could make you into a huge star out here.'

Angel didn't want Ethan to put this kind of pressure on her; didn't think it was at all fair. 'I can see that you've got real problems, and I'm sorry. I want to help, but I don't think I can do this. I've had so much shit with the press over the years, I don't know if I want a camera crew following me around. Why can't it just be about you?'

A heartfelt sigh from Ethan. 'Like Benny said, without you the channel won't be interested. I don't want to go on about it, babe, but will you at least promise that

71

you'll think about it? The fee is likely to be around a million and a half dollars, for each of us. I don't want to pressure you into doing something you don't want to . . . but it would really help me out.'

'What about if I gave you some money towards your taxes?' But even as she said it, she knew Ethan would not want this.

'No fucking way,' was his blunt reply, 'I'm not taking your money. That's why I thought you'd go for the TV idea, because there's something in it for both of us.'

'But there's someone else to consider.'

Ethan looked at her blankly. 'You mean Honey?'

'Yes, and there's . . .' She winced as she was about to come out with Cal's name and knew what an impact this would have. Ethan's expression hardened. 'What the fuck's it got to do with your ex?'

'He won't want Honey to be filmed. He's a really private person.'

Ethan shook his head in disbelief. 'And what am I? An asshole who wants the world to know everything about me? Of course I don't. I've just said, we will do the series how we want.' He looked angry. 'You think Cal's so perfect, don't you? Even after he screwed around, you still think he's perfect. I can't win, can I?'

And before Angel could say anything he abruptly got up. 'I've got stuff to do, I'll see you later.'

Angel watched him stride back into the house. She felt helpless in the face of his anger, and by the way her past life kept spilling into her present . . .

Over the next few days Ethan said nothing more about the TV series, but he seemed unusually subdued and, when he wasn't training, was in tense meetings with his accountants and Benny. Angel longed for the carefree days when they'd first got together. It seemed as if one obstacle after another had been put in their way recently, testing their relationship. Benny wasn't going to give up, though, and early one evening Angel received a phone call from Susie who was almost beside herself with excitement.

'Darling! Why didn't you tell me about the TV series? It is the most *amazing* opportunity for you to make it . . . not just in the States but to become a global name!'

How the hell did Susie know about the proposal? Angel soon found out as she gushed, 'Benny Sullivan called and told me himself. He is perfectly okay with us each cutting our own deal. It is *so* exciting. This is the best piece of news we've had about your career in a long time. You must be thrilled?'

'There's just one thing, Susie,' Angel said when she could finally get a word in, 'I don't want to do it.'

Susie made a weird choking noise then managed to splutter, 'But, darling, it is the perfect career move for you. I surely don't have to remind you that in three years' time you'll be *thirty*, which, face it, even with all the cosmetic surgery you can have done these days is still ancient for a glamour model.' Susie said 'thirty' as if it were 'seventy'. 'And we need to explore other career options – the acting route didn't exactly pan out, did it?'

A year ago Angel had had a small part in a film, playing a gangster's moll. It wasn't her finest moment. The camera might have loved her but she didn't have the acting gene and delivered all her lines in a robotic monotone, which was probably why most of the scene was cut.

'Thanks for reminding me, Susie,' she said dryly.

'Of course, there's the reality TV show route as well – *Dancing with the Stars*, *I'm A Celebrity*, blah blah blah. But I think your own series would be much more exciting. Please tell me you're going to think about it?'

Angel gave a non-committal 'Maybe' and made an excuse about needing to check on Honey. She hated feeling under pressure, with everyone telling her to do what they thought she should. It only made her more determined not to give in. Ethan would just have to figure out another way of sorting out his finances. It was clear-cut as far as Angel was concerned, and she wasn't going to cave in.

But she hated feeling so distant from Ethan, who seemed to want to avoid her, choosing to stay up late shut away in his games room when she went up to bed at midnight. Angel read for a while, hoping that he would come up and they could talk, but by 1 a.m. she gave up and switched off the light. Around 5 she woke up and reached out her arm but the bed beside her was empty. This was not what she wanted; she had to talk to him.

She grabbed her robe and padded downstairs, expecting to find him still in his games room, but it was empty. That seemed odd. She didn't think she'd heard his car leave. She quickly checked the rooms downstairs, but there was no sign of him. She eventually found him on the balcony outside his study, slumped on the wicker sofa and mindlessly swigging from a bottle of Maker's Mark. She had never known Ethan to drink on his own before.

'Are you okay?' she asked sitting down beside him.

He turned to her. His eyes were bloodshot and he looked as if he was struggling to focus. 'Not yet,' he replied grimly, 'but I will be when I finish this.' He took another long swig from the bottle.

'Hey, how much have you had?' Angel asked. 'You're going to feel wasted tomorrow.'

'So much the better. I have to tell my grandmother that I may need to sell her house.' He stopped talking for a moment, choked with emotion. 'She's so sick,

Angel. It's *really* not something I want to do, but I've got no choice.' Another long swig.

Angel stared at him, appalled by the news. 'Can't you raise more money on this one? Or, please, let me give you some money.' She couldn't stand by and see his grandmother lose her house.

'I would never take money from you, Angel, you know that. And I'll probably have to sell this place anyhow.'

Angel sat back and looked up at the midnight-blue sky, pin-pricked with glittering stars, and felt very lost. She just didn't know what else to suggest. She moved her foot and it knocked against something. Reaching down, she retrieved what looked like a bottle of pills. She read the label; they seemed to be some kind of strong painkillers. 'What are these for?' she asked, with a sickening premonition.

Ethan took the bottle from her and said bitterly, 'I was going to mix them with the bourbon. Spare myself and everyone else the inevitable shame and humiliation of seeing me made bankrupt. Except, of course, I couldn't do it. Couldn't even do that right.'

Angel couldn't bear to see him so broken, and hated hearing him talk in this despairing way. She remembered a time in her own life when she had felt so low that she had considered ending it. She'd had no idea Ethan felt so bad and so guilty. She should have known.

She reached out and touched his arm. 'I had no idea you felt like this. Why didn't you tell me?'

He hung his head. 'Thought you would despise me for being weak. I'm sure Cal would never have gotten into such a situation, would he? All I wanted to do was give you and Honey a new life out here, a great life, and I've fucked it all up. First I find out about a daughter I never knew I had, then the money problems . . . I've ruined everything, and I know I'm going to lose you.' His voice caught and he put his hand over his eyes.

'You haven't lost me, Ethan, but you will if you carry on like this. It's not your fault that your accountant ripped you off.' Angel gently prised the bottle out of his hand. She suddenly realised how insecure she must have made him feel by being so distant with him. She had been so caught up in her own thoughts, in what everything meant to *her*, that she hadn't stopped to consider what he must be going through. 'Come on, let's go to bed,' she said gently, 'I'm sure things will seem better after you've had some sleep.'

He pretty much passed out as soon as she got him into bed. Angel held him tightly, wanting him to know that she was there for him, that everything would be okay.

But in the morning, as she and Ethan went into the kitchen for breakfast, they were met by Jose, wearing a sombre expression in place of his usual beaming smile. 'Mr Turner, I am very sorry to bring this matter up, but can you tell me when I and the rest of the staff can expect to be paid? Our salaries do not seem to have gone through this month.'

'Shit! I'm sorry, Jose. I'll go and phone Benny right now. Put him on to it.'

'If you could, Mr Turner, I would be very grateful. I'm behind with my mortgage and health insurance payments, and I think I told you my daughter is a diabetic . . .'

Angel felt awful hearing this. Honey was sitting at the table, tucking into her bowl of Cheerios and singing 'The Wheels on the Bus' contentedly to herself. The contrast between her secure, privileged life and Jose's made Angel feel incredibly humble. She waited until he was out of the room before saying to Ethan, 'Let me pay the staff right away.'

Ethan vehemently shook his head. 'No way. This is my problem, I've got to deal with it.'

'Please, think of it as a loan. I can't bear to think of Jose being anxious, it's not fair on him – you heard what he said about his daughter. You can't leave him in that situation.'

Ethan slammed his fist down on the black marble kitchen counter and kicked one of the sleek white units below it, in sheer frustration. 'I can't believe it's come to this!' He seemed a million miles from the man she had met a year ago, who had charmed her with his good looks and easygoing character. He looked grey and unhealthy under his tan, and his blue eyes were still bloodshot from the previous night.

'Okay,' he said quietly, 'if you could sort out the staff salaries this month, I'll pay you back next month, I swear. The last thing I wanted was to drag you into all this.'

Angel spent the next hour with Jose, going through who needed to be paid. As she worked through the list of names she realised that she had to help Ethan get out of this situation, not by loaning him the money, which she didn't think he would accept anyway, but by finally agreeing to do the reality show with him. One series of it should be enough to pay off some of his debts and secure Loretta's house and this one. She just couldn't stand by and let him suffer like this – even if she wasn't keen on filming the show. So long as she knew it would help Ethan, it would be worth it. And surely it wouldn't be too intrusive. Right now Ethan needed her and she wanted to prove that she was committed, that she would stand by him.

Chapter 6

'Angel, if you could just sit on Ethan's knee . . . I want a nice intimate set up for the next questions.' That was Mimi, director of the reality show, now called *When Ethan met Angel*, in full flow. Angel had naively thought that filming the show would involve a couple of days' work a week at the most, and that she would hardly know the cameras were there while she got on with her life. Wrong and wrong.

E! wanted to start airing the series in two months, which meant it was an intensive and full on schedule to record the material for the first two episodes. Mimi, thirty-something, ambitious, with a body to die for but a rather plain face under her long blonde hair – someone that Angel's brother would cruelly have described as 'Body off *Baywatch*, face off *Crimewatch*' – and Todd, the camera man, twenty-something, ambitious, and in love with Mimi, became permanent fixtures at the house. Sometimes it felt as if they had moved in as often they were there filming from the moment Angel and Ethan got up to the moment they went to bed – and if they'd had things their way, would have been in the bedroom as well.

Ethan had the attitude that it was access all areas, and it was left to Angel to lay down the boundaries – i.e. that they couldn't film in Honey's bedroom or play room or in Angel's dressing room. She truly thought she would go mad if she didn't have some kind of space away from the cameras.

And along with Mimi and Todd, Benny was there most of the time as well: checking that they were getting the recordings done, adding his own – usually unwelcome – thoughts about what he thought should be filmed.

'Oh, and Angel . . . could you just unfasten one of your buttons?' Typically that was from Benny. He was always trying to get her to flash as much flesh as possible, something that she stubbornly resisted. Just because she made her living as a glamour model it didn't mean she wanted to show off her cleavage 24/7, especially not with Benny in the room, practically with his tongue on the floor. Ugh! He made her skin crawl!

'I'm fine as I am, thanks, Benny. And I'm going to sit next to Ethan, if that's okay,' Angel said firmly.

A slight pursing of the lips from Mimi showed that she wasn't entirely happy, but she had learnt in the last few weeks that Angel was not some bimbo blonde to be ordered around, she had views of her own – something that Mimi had not really factored in.

'Just make sure you're real close.' The reality show was supposed to be a 'dynamic' mix of Angel and Ethan out and about doing their own thing, plus more intimate footage of the couple talking about their relationship, and Mimi was always trying to push it. Ethan complied and instantly moved closer to Angel, draping his arm round her. He was just a bit too keen to go along with what everyone wanted for her liking. Sometimes she wished that Ethan would say no and stand up for her.

'So, you guys have been together nearly eight months now . . . still the honeymoon period?' Mimi began firing off the questions while Todd zoomed in with the camera. 'Lots of action in the bedroom?'

Ethan treated the camera to his trademark sexy, lazy smile. 'Yeah, I'll say. In the bedroom, in the games room, in the hot tub . . . you name it!' He laughed, though Angel wasn't so happy about him discussing their sex life. 'But it's not just about the sex, though of course that's great. She's perfect in every way – my lover, my soul-mate. Every day is just so special when I wake up with her next to me. She's beautiful on the outside, as everyone can see, and a beautiful person. What else can I say? I love this woman.'

He was laying it on thick for the cameras and Mimi was nodding approvingly, especially when Ethan turned to Angel and kissed her full on the lips. She was practically squirming with embarrassment at his comments and imagining how her friends would react to that description of their relationship, never mind her parents! She would have to warn them not to watch that bit.

'How about you, Angel?' Mimi asked when Ethan had finally released her from the embrace.

'Everything's great,' Angel said in a slightly clipped tone. She felt far too self-conscious, and not able to turn on an act for the camera.

'In the bedroom?' Mimi persisted,

'Great,' she replied, and realising she wasn't going to get away with keeping things so brief, added, 'Ethan's a very special guy.'

'In the bedroom?' Mimi asked again.

'In every way,' Angel replied, still sounding uptight. God, she wished they would stop asking questions – she didn't want to go into such detail about her relationship with Ethan and, perhaps naively, hadn't expected they would want to talk about it incessantly.

'And what about plans for the future? Have you thought about getting married?'

Not this again! Angel winced inside; she had hoped the whole marriage question would be forgotten in the midst of all Ethan's other problems, but apparently not.

He didn't even hesitate before he replied, 'I'd love to marry, Angel. I'd do it tomorrow if I could.'

'There's just one small problem,' she said quietly, 'I'm still married.'

'Oh, yeah, to the English soccer player, Cal Bailey,' Mimi replied. Then added to Todd, 'We could do a cutaway here to him.'

'And how do you feel about that, Ethan? Must be tough when the woman you love is still married to some other guy?' she asked, aiming as always for the jugular.

Ethan shrugged. 'What do you think? But Angel's her own person, and I respect her decision to have a two-year separation followed by divorce, or whatever they do in England.' He didn't sound like he was too happy about it, though.

'Actually it's just a year and a half now,' Angel said quietly.

But Ethan had temporarily lost his charming, everything's great persona. He just shrugged and said, 'Whatever.'

Later that night, when the crew and Benny had finally gone, he confronted Angel about it as she tried to soak away the stresses of the day in a hot bath. 'I just don't get why you don't divorce him,' Ethan said, sitting on the edge of the huge porcelain bath and instantly making her feel claustrophobic. After a day of filming, she needed some space. 'Doesn't it feel weird, knowing that he is still legally your husband?'

Angel shook her head. 'Not really. To be honest, I don't think about it.' A lie. 'And I just want things to end quietly; you've no idea how vicious the English tabloids can be. I don't want the affair plastered all over them again, not because of me but because of Honey. When she's older, I don't want her to think that her parents' marriage ended in bitterness and hatred.' That was true.

'But what if he won't give you a divorce at the end of the two years? I've read cases where that happens, and it drags on and on.'

Angel shook her head. 'Cal would never do that to me. He promised me a divorce after two years, and he would never go back on his word.' As soon as she said it, she thought what a foolish thing that was to say as Cal had gone back on his vows to be faithful. But fortunately Ethan didn't pick her up on it.

'So it's not because you still love him?' he replied, gazing intently at her. 'Benny thinks you must still love him.'

What? Ethan had been discussing her with that wanker? Angel struggled to contain her emotions. 'No, I don't. I'm with you, Ethan. I love you.'

'Promise?' he demanded.

'I promise,' she replied, longing for this conversation to be over. 'Come here,' she added, and when Ethan came closer she raised herself out of the bath and kissed him. 'Now why don't you go into the bedroom and get ready for me, and I'll show you how much?' she said huskily, running her hands lingeringly over his body and caressing him through his jeans. That was one sure-fire way of ending the unwelcome conversation. Ethan didn't mention Cal after the make-up sex, but Angel felt as if he was just biding his time before he brought it up again. It wouldn't be long before Cal Bailey was once more a source of conflict between the two of them.

*

'*My saviour Cal, I'll never forget what he did for me*'. Angel stared at the headline on the *News of the World* website that dominated her laptop screen. Since moving to LA she regularly read the British tabloids online; it was one of her evening rituals after putting Honey to bed. She would sit at her dressing table and go through all the stories. She liked to keep up with the celeb gossip, and it would often make her smile. But not this story.

Simone had 'intimately' and 'exclusively' revealed how Cal Bailey had 'saved her' from her life as a high-class escort and drug addict. Angel feverishly scrolled through the article. She'd had no idea that Cal had become so involved in Simone's life again. Certainly he hadn't mentioned it in any of his daily phone calls to speak to Honey, but judging from this article he had paid for Simone to go into rehab and had been seeing her regularly since she came out.

It was like an echo from her own past when Angel herself had got caught up with drug addiction, and it had been Cal who had got her straight. And look what had happened then . . . She had got together with him. Maybe that was going to happen with Cal and Simone? Angel was so jealous she felt physically sick. Cal had saved the poor fragile woman and got her life back on track, all ready to get back with him. And why hadn't he told Angel about it? It must be because there was something more to their relationship than simply friendship.

There was a large picture of Simone post-rehab looking beautiful and fragile, along with several other pictures of her and Cal when they were an item. These were ones that Angel had seen before, but the sight of Cal with his arm around Simone sent a fresh surge of jealousy rushing through her, drowning all rational thought. She reached for the phone. Only talking to a really good friend would help right now. She tried Gemma, but the call went straight to answerphone, and then she called Jez. It was nine o'clock Sunday morning UK time, the only day Jez ever got a lie in, but Angel was so wound up she didn't stop to consider that.

'Is Cal seeing Simone?' she demanded as soon as Jez picked up with a sleepy 'Hi'.

'Angel? What are you talking about?'

'It's the front-page story in the *News of the World*,' she replied, frustrated that he was being so slow on the uptake, and went on to fill him in on the details, stumbling over her words in her hurry to tell him.

'He's just been a friend to her, as far as I know.'

'Yeah, right!'

Jez ignored the bitter sarcasm and said, 'And please don't throw a hissy fit, but Rufus and me have met up with her a few times as well. We've had dinner, and Rufus is trying to get her back on track with her fitness. I was going to tell you next time we spoke. I knew you'd find it strange.'

'Strange' was the bloody understatement of the year! Angel was outraged. Simone was a woman who had gone out of her way to be as nasty and back-stabbing to Angel as it was possible to be. And now her best friends and Cal were getting up close and personal with her!

'Well, thanks a lot!' she exclaimed hotly. 'Some best friend you are. Don't you remember how vile she used to be towards me?' She felt bitterly hurt at the betrayal.

'I know that, Angel, and I'll never forget it either, but you saw the state of the woman. We just feel sorry for her, that's all, and underneath that hard image she likes to put out she's actually vulnerable and quite sweet. I imagine sympathy is all that Cal feels as well. Simone's a wreck. I know you two have a history but . . .' He paused. 'We all love you best – even Cal.'

Some of the anger was ebbing away, but the jealousy

Angel felt about Cal's new connection with Simone was still hanging on in there tenaciously. 'I'm sorry, Jez, I probably did over-react. It's just, being so far away from you all, I guess I felt left out and shocked by the story. I wish someone had told me.'

'To be honest, I didn't know it was coming out, but I'm not surprised. Simone is completely broke. I imagine the money was too big a temptation.' He paused. 'And I expect you wondered if there was any more to the story than Cal being nice to her?' Jez voiced the fear that was most concerning Angel. 'Like, has it gone beyond friendship?'

Angel dug her nails into the palms of her hands with anxiety; trying to hold it together in case Jez went on to say that Cal was having a relationship with Simone. 'As far as I know,' he said carefully, 'and Cal doesn't really open up to me – he is just seeing Simone because he feels sorry for her, nothing more. But why don't you ask him yourself?'

'Why should I care?' Angel tried to say breezily, though she felt as if she was speaking through a mouthful of cotton wool. 'I'm with Ethan.'

'I think we both know the answer to that one,' Jez said quietly. 'Don't we?'

'Oh, God, Jez . . . I cannot believe that I'm even talking about this! It's been nearly a year since we broke up, and he still has the power to turn my life upside down!'

'I refer you to my previous question,' Jez replied. 'But, look, try and chill about the Simone thing. You're making it into something that it's not. I promise, it's not important. And tell me how the filming is going? I cannot wait to see the series. I bet you're an absolute star in it and the Americans will love you.'

Angel thought back to how pissed off Mimi was with her for not opening up about Ethan, and how pissed off

Ethan was about the marriage thing, even after their consolation shag. 'Ummm . . . I'm not sure about that.'

But Jez was off on one about how she would soon become a household name, like Kim Kardashian, and wouldn't listen to a word when she objected that she was being too quiet for the director's liking. Or that she had her regrets about ever agreeing to take part in it in the first place. Jez was strictly from the school of thought that believed all publicity was good publicity.

Angel ended the call by promising to be more chilled about Simone, though she wasn't sure how long that promise would last. Almost instantly her phone rang and her heart beat that little bit faster when she saw Cal's name flash up. 'Hi, I just wanted to talk to you about a story that's out in the papers today,' he said, getting straight to the point.

'If it's the one in the *News of the World*, I've seen it,' Angel replied, definitely not feeling chilled.

'I've just been a friend to Simone, Angel, it's nothing more than that. She was in such a mess when I saw her, I felt I had to do something. We were close once, and I know that deep down she isn't a bad person. She just got lost.' Cal sounded resigned.

'It's okay,' Angel said defensively. 'You don't have to justify anything to me, you're free to do what you want; we both are.'

He sighed. 'I know, I just didn't want you to think that I was having a relationship with her. I know in the past she has sold stories that have hurt you. That's all.'

That might be all as far as he was concerned, but Angel had a whole list of questions she wanted to ask Cal. Like, how often did he see Simone? Did he really just see her as a friend? And did he think she still had feelings for him? But now he was asking after Honey.

Angel filled him in on their daughter's latest exploits and was then suddenly aware that Ethan had walked into the room and was looking over her shoulder at the story on the computer screen. He remained standing behind her, making Angel feel awkward.

'Quite the saint, your ex,' he said snidely when she'd finished her call. 'I bet he's fucking her, though. There's got to be a trade off for paying for someone to go into rehab. And she looks hot and up for it! He's only human. You surely don't think he's been living like a monk since you broke up, do you?'

Angel spun round on him, furious to hear Ethan give voice to the one thing she was most afraid of. 'He's not fucking her, actually. Is that what *you* would do then? Yeah, I just bet you would . . . with your track record with women. Fuck them and then leave them with a baby to bring up without you! But you're not in a position to pay for anything right now, are you?' She lashed out with all the things she knew would really hurt him. 'Have you even bothered to make contact with your daughter?'

'I'm working on it. Like I said – it's complicated,' he shouted back. 'And why are you always defending Cal? Do you never stop to think about what it's like for me, knowing that man is still your husband? Always wondering if the reason why you won't divorce him is because you still love him? Why can't you ever see anyone else's point of view? It's always just about *you*!' He slammed his hand down on the dressing table. 'Jesus, Angel, you make it so damned hard for me sometimes!'

Angel had had enough. First the news about Simone, then Ethan having a go at her. 'Just leave me alone!' she shouted back. 'I only fucking agreed to do the reality show because of you, and you're doing my head in with your jealousy!'

She stormed out of the room, almost shaking with fury, wishing that she was back home in England where she could have gone out with Gemma and Jez and let rip about Ethan. The couple avoided each other for the rest of the evening which was easy to do in Ethan's vast house. Angel watched *The Proposal* on DVD, though she was in no mood for a rom com right now. Ethan was no doubt holed up in his beloved games room or working out in his state-of-the-art gym. Well, fuck him, she thought, in no mood for making up. As far as she was concerned, he was the one in the wrong.

That night Ethan slept in one of the many guest rooms, and left for training before Angel and Honey got up the following morning.

'You know, you guys should really make up. Ethan's not in a good place right now, Angel. Surely you can see that?' Benny nagged her while Molly, the make-up artist, got her ready for the lingerie shoot. Angel and Ethan still hadn't spoken since the argument two days ago, but Angel was damned if she would make the first move. Ethan had been bang out of order as far as she was concerned, saying those things about Cal, and what's more she really didn't need Benny giving her grief. He was at the shoot because it was being filmed for the reality show, but the last thing Angel wanted to do was to pose seductively with him ogling her.

She kept looking straight ahead of her while Molly applied bronzer to her cheeks. 'Not that it's any of your business, Benny, but Ethan really needs to apologise to *me*.' Angel was trying to keep her cool but Benny was seriously winding her up.

He chewed hard on his gum, working his plump cheeks as if psyching himself up for his next attempt. 'He worships you, Angel, you know that. And of course he feels insecure about your ex-husband . . . not that he *is* your ex-husband yet . . . what guy wouldn't? You've just got to cut Ethan some slack. I think it would make a big difference to his confidence if you speeded things up with the divorce. He feels he's in limbo . . . like you're keeping him hanging on, but deep down not committing to the relationship.'

What was Benny now – a fucking shrink?

'Ethan is a great guy, Angel, don't you realise how lucky you are to have him? He could have his pick of anyone – Oscar-winning actresses, models, that top tennis player – and he chose you, a glamour model from England. Count yourself one very lucky girl!'

Benny was not going to give up. Angel just hated him talking to her like this. It felt as if the man was trying to take over her life, and for the first time she got the distinct impression that Benny really didn't like her. It was the way he had said 'glamour model', as if it was the lowest of the low professions. He paused before going in for the kill.

'And, you know, if you guys got married it would be a ratings winner for the show. No question. A wedding would guarantee a second series, maybe even a third. It would be an amazing coup. E! would love you big time.'

Now Angel did turn and look at Benny, incensed by his remark. Did he think she would get married just to score good ratings! What kind of planet was the man living on? Well, actually, she knew exactly the planet he was living on – Planet Only Money Matters, and screw everything and everyone else.

'If I ever got married again, believe me, it would not be in front of the cameras,' she said in a low voice, trying to keep a lid on her emotions. She was itching to inflict physical violence on Benny, except that would involve physical contact.

He shrugged. 'My advice? Don't rule anything out. I'll see you out there.' And he sauntered out of the dressing room.

'What a fucking fuckwit! Slimeball . . . mother-fucker!'

89

Angel exploded, nearly causing Molly to jab her in the eye with the mascara wand.

'I guess you don't like him much,' she said perkily, blowing a perfect pink bubble with her gum. She was a sweet enough girl, who had worked as Angel's make-up artist for a number of shoots, but Angel missed having Gemma who had always done her make-up in the UK and who got Angel completely. Molly only seemed to do perky and 'have a nice day' bollocks, and that all seemed so fake to Angel.

'I guess not,' Angel replied dryly. She flicked back her long hair, which had been straightened and now hung perfectly down her back, and considered Molly's handiwork in the mirror. Smokey eyes, check; glossed lips, check; perfectly contoured cheekbones, check. She would do.

Angel wandered into the studio where Ashton Walker, the photographer, was getting everything ready for the shoot. The studio had been dressed to look like an intimate boudoir, and occupying central position was an elegant double bed with a delicate wrought-iron bedstead. It was covered in a rich purple silk throw, with pale pink and violet silk cushions scattered over it, making it the perfect backdrop for Angel's shoot. Usually Ashton was the most laid-back, easygoing photographer she knew and Angel loved working with him, but today he seemed on edge. Angel soon found out why. Mimi and Benny kept getting in his face, acting as if they were running the shoot, rather than being guests there.

'Hey, Angel,' he said, walking over and giving her a hug in place of a kiss, not wanting to spoil her make up. 'Shall we get started? First up, can I have you kneeling up on the bed and smiling at the camera, head to one side, hand on your hip?'

'Wouldn't it be better if she was lying down?' Benny

put in. 'Kinda sexier that way, I'd have thought. Or how about she's kneeling on all fours?'

'That's not the look we're going for here,' Ashton replied, and took up a camera and began clicking away, clearly wanting to avoid any further conversation.

Angel slipped off her white robe to reveal the lingerie: a cream silk and lace bra with a matching thong. It took a while for her to get into her posing groove – she was just too aware of Benny ogling her, along with Todd zooming in on her with the film camera. She needed to get into her zone and tried to block out everyone and everything except for Ashton and the stills camera. Fifteen minutes later he was happy with his shots and Angel was off to the dressing room to change into the next set of lingerie. Indeed, she was just about to whip everything off when she turned round and discovered, to her annoyance, that Todd had followed her in with his camera running, closely followed by Benny. Did they seriously think she was going to strip off in front of them? Was Benny about to come out with some bollocks about it being good for ratings? Well, if they thought they were going to get a shot of her Brazilian, they had another think coming!

She put on a fake smile and held her hand up to the lens. 'Sorry, guys,' she said in a mock-sweet voice. 'You don't get to see this bit.'

Extremely reluctantly, Benny and Todd left the dressing room and Angel slammed the door shut behind them, turning the key for good measure – she wouldn't put it past Benny to try his luck again.

Some three hours and ten changes of lingerie later, Angel was finished with the shoot. She had arranged to meet Alisha, one of her newfound LA friends, for cocktails at Chateau Marmont. Alisha was a stunning

African American woman, with looks to rival Halle Berry and a knockout figure even after having three sons. She also had the dirtiest laugh Angel had ever heard. She was married to Logan, one of Ethan's team mates in the Dodgers and his closest friend.

Alisha was already sitting at a table when Angel arrived, looking as effortlessly beautiful as ever in a gorgeous bronze silk wrap dress, sipping a glass of champagne. 'Angel, so good to see you!' she declared, standing up and kissing her lightly on the cheek while enveloping her in a cloud of exotic floral perfume that, knowing Alisha, was bespoke.

Her high standards of grooming put Angel to shame. Alisha was forever having her nails manicured, feet pedicured, regular facials and waxing. It seemed like a full-time job to Angel. She had to be groomed for her glamour work but it wasn't something she loved doing, more something she knew she had to do.

'So how are things with you guys?' Alisha asked once Angel had ordered a Cosmopolitan.

She shrugged. 'Okay.' She was tempted not to go into more detail, knowing it would put her on a downer, but then she found herself opening up about what had been going on. Alisha had known Ethan a long time; she would probably have some insights into his character.

Alisha smiled. 'I guessed something was up. Logan said Ethan has been real moody at training these past days, but when I asked him if he knew what was wrong, he had no idea! Men are so bad at dealing with emotional stuff. I can only hope that I'm raising my boys with more emotional intelligence than Logan has.'

'I just think Ethan needs not to get so wound up about Cal. I mean, he has to face it. Cal is always going to be in my life because of Honey. There is nothing I can do about that.' Angel spoke in a rush then realised she was sounding pretty wound up herself. She took a sip of her cocktail and tried to calm down.

Alisha smiled at her. 'I'm not going to take sides in this, but it is tough for Ethan. He's really in love with you . . . I've never known him be like this with any other woman. You're the one, as far as he's concerned. So of course he's going to find it difficult to accept that you haven't divorced Cal yet. Hell, a lot of women would have done it straight away, after what Cal did to you. Ethan just feels insecure, especially when it came out about him having a daughter. I know he was terrified he would lose you over that.'

Angel knew that Alisha was right, but it didn't necessarily make her feel any better. She hated there to be conflict in her life – she'd had enough of that during the last few months before she left Cal. She just wanted things to be happy and light, wanted it to be back to how it was when she first met Ethan.

'He's not going to lose me,' she replied. 'Even though he really pisses me off with his jealousy.' She looked around the intimate bar, the lights casting a soft, flattering glow on all the hip, beautiful people sipping their cocktails, and suddenly had a pang of longing for Ethan. Bar Marmont was where they had first met and it had always been their special place after that. It seemed wrong to be sitting here and not to have made up with him.

'So how do you feel about Ethan? Whenever I see you guys together, you always seem so perfect for each other.'

God, lately Angel seemed to be surrounded by people telling her what they thought she should do!

'I do love him, *really* love him, but as for the whole marriage thing, Alisha . . . I just don't know if I ever want to get married again.'

'So what about Cal? Is Ethan wrong to be worried

93

about him?' Alisha paused. 'Are you still in love with him?'

Damn, that wasn't a question Angel wanted to answer! Alisha was being a bit *too* emotionally intelligent for Angel's liking. 'I guess I'll always have feelings for him but it's over, and Ethan just has to accept that. So,' she paused, wanting to change the subject, 'how do I get him to cheer the fuck up?'

Alisha gave her trademark dirty laugh which attracted stares from the other drinkers, no doubt stunned that such an elegant woman could produce such a sound. 'Girlfriend, you've just got to fuck his brains out! Works every time with Logan. Hell, sometimes the sex is even better when you're angry with them. And then it's over, the air is cleared, your man's happy, and hopefully you'll have a smile on your face too. Men are simple.'

Several cocktails later Angel was feeling more mellow herself; maybe it was time to clear the air; she could head back home and act on Alisha's advice. She didn't want further conflict between her and Ethan. She made her way to the bathroom, determined that when she got back to her table she'd suggest to Alisha that they should get a cab home. She quickly got out her phone and texted Ethan, asking if he was at home. She was just reapplying her berry lip gloss when he replied, *Sorry, babe, am out and sorry about everything, love you x.* The 'sorry' was sweet but Angel was disappointed that he wasn't home; she had planned to take him straight to bed. Ah, well, she thought, flicking back her hair and heading back to the bar, the make-up sex would just have to wait. But when she got back to the table, to her great surprise Ethan and Logan were there, laughing and talking with Alisha.

'Hey,' she said, kissing Logan in greeting and then sitting down next to Ethan.

94

He smiled but looked unsure of how she was going to react. 'You don't mind us crashing your night, do you? I really wanted to say sorry, and I wanted to do it in person.'

'He made me come with him in case you gave him a hard time. He's such a baby,' Logan put in, smiling broadly. He was a strikingly handsome African American, well over six foot, with the cheekiest smile.

Alisha swiped a punch at her husband's arm. 'Just let the man say his piece.'

Ethan looked at Angel. 'Well, that was basically it. I'm sorry, I was completely in the wrong. Can we just forget about it?' He ran a hand through his blond hair, looking awkward. 'God, I can't believe I'm doing this in front of an audience!'

Angel took pity on him. There weren't many men she could imagine who would be prepared to apologise in front of their friends. She reached out for his hand. 'I'm sorry as well. And, yes, let's forget it.'

At this Logan clapped his hands together. 'Does that mean we can eat now? I didn't like to say anything with all that emotional stuff going down but, man, I am hungry.' That comment earned him another swipe from Alisha but Ethan and Angel just laughed, and Angel added, 'Let's eat.'

While Logan helped Alisha on with her jacket, Ethan put his arms round Angel and lightly kissed her neck, murmuring, 'I've missed you. Don't let's fight any more.'

It ended up being one of the best nights out Angel had had in LA. The four of them had dinner at the Chateau and Angel felt as if she had some real friends in Alisha and Logan. As for Ethan, well, she really admired him for being the first to say sorry. She had a stubborn streak herself which meant she was usually the last person to admit that she was in the wrong, and

Cal had been stubborn too, which had made for some fierce rows where neither of them would back down.

Ethan wasn't like that, and she liked the change. When they went back home, the make-up sex was just as good as she'd known it would be . . .

Chapter 7

Filming for the reality show dominated Angel's and Ethan's lives for the next month. Mimi came up with the concept of teaching Angel all about American life – for a part of the show she hilariously called *My Fair American*. So they set it up for Angel to learn how to play baseball (though it was still rounders to her); take cheerleading lessons – which just seemed to Angel an excuse for Benny to perve after her in her outfit of a short white pleated skirt and tight vest; be a waitress in a fifties-style diner and do the whole what-can-I-get-you-and-have-a-nice-day shit.

Practically every night the couple were filmed going out to some event or other – film premieres at Grauman's Chinese Theatre, a celebrity launching their fashion line or perfume, an opening of the latest new hip bar or club. It was getting exhausting. Angel had to guard the time she had with her daughter – Mimi was constantly wanting to film her with the toddler. Cal had expressly said that they could only film a few inserts, but that didn't stop Mimi from trying.

To make life even more full on, Susie had just moved over to LA for six months, saying that she wanted to be near her famous client, and so Angel had to deal with her instructions to get out there and be seen. Weirdly, Benny and Susie hit it off. Angel had been convinced that Susie would be terrified that he would try and poach her. Instead she had simpered and flirted with him as he flirted back, and Ethan was pretty certain that they had become lovers – Angel *so* did not want to know about that! And, on top of all this, Cal was flying over to spend the next week with Honey, something that was obsessing Ethan, in spite of his promise not to fight with Angel about it any more.

'So will you take Honey to his hotel?' Ethan asked as they hung out in the games room watching *Goodfellas*, one of his favourite movies, on a huge plasma-screen TV. The games room was his special den, large enough to accommodate a full-size pool table, several arcade games, including a motorbike racing game with a real motorbike that looked like a small toy in the vastness of the room, and an entire wall given over to a huge photograph of the Dodgers in action. You almost felt as if you were in the game yourself.

'Well, I suppose I'll drop her off and collect her, but that will be all. Cal and I don't exactly have a lot to say to each other,' Angel replied, her heart sinking that they were talking about this *again*.

'Couldn't Lucy take her over and pick up? Isn't that her job as a nanny?' There he went again, making difficulties where there weren't any. Ethan picked away at the hard skin round his thumb, a sure sign that he was feeling stressed. Angel sighed, reached for the remote and paused the film.

'If I'm going to be away from Honey for a few days, then I'd rather I was the one who dropped her off. I thought we weren't going to do this thing again?' And even though she felt Ethan was putting unfair pressure on her, she snuggled up closer to him and kissed him. 'Come on. There are advantages to Cal having Honey for a few days . . . like we've got the whole house to ourselves.'

Ethan put his arm round her. 'Yeah.' But he didn't sound convinced.

'So you don't want a lot of stuff like this going on?' Angel slid to her knees and unbuttoned his jeans, flashing him her best sultry, temptress look.

'I guess I can live with it,' he replied, anticipating what was coming next.

Until he found a house to rent, Cal was staying in a suite at the luxurious Shutters on the Beach hotel on Santa Monica beach. Angel and Honey pulled up outside the hotel, with its pretty white wooden balconies and yellow-and-white-striped awnings, in her midnight blue BMW. Instantly they received the five-star treatment, with a valet opening the driver's door and helping her get Honey and her bags out of the car. This would be the first time Angel had seen Cal in nearly a month. Would there be any thawing in his attitude? she wondered, or would he still be Ice Man?

She held Honey's hand and the two of them walked into the elegant lobby, which had a stylish but intimate feel, with old-fashioned lamps giving off a warm glow, and comfortable arm chairs and sofas arranged for private conversations. She was just about to ask the receptionist to phone up to Cal's room but he was waiting in the lobby for them, sitting in one of the arm chairs having coffee. Angel was determined to be cool but her body had other ideas. Her heart treacherously raced that little bit faster. Why, oh why, did he still have that effect on her!

As soon as he saw them he leapt up and came rushing over, obviously thrilled to see Honey as he swept her up in his arms and kissed her.

'Hi,' Angel said when Cal finally looked at her, and suddenly felt self-conscious.

'Hi,' he replied. He was wearing a plain white tee-shirt and jeans, and looked gorgeous – so much for her resolve not to notice such things.

'Well, I'd better go then,' Angel said, kissing her daughter where she was still snuggled in Cal's arms. 'I'll call you later to speak to Honey.'

But the child didn't want her mummy to leave and burst into noisy tears, stretching out her arms, appealing to Angel.

'Look, why don't you stay with us for a while?' Cal said quickly. 'Honey needs to get used to me again. If that's okay with you?'

Angel was due back at the house to do some filming for the show, but reckoned they could wait just this once. She texted Mimi to say she couldn't start for a couple of hours then turned her phone off, knowing that otherwise Mimi or Benny or both would bombard her with calls.

'So how about we go swimming?' Cal asked his daughter, who instantly cheered up then said, 'Mummy swim too?'

Angel didn't have her bikini with her. 'No, Honey, but I'll watch.' That wasn't good enough for Honey who looked as if she was threatening an epic tantrum. 'It's the terrible twos, I think,' Angel told Cal.

'Why don't you buy a bikini from the boutique and charge it to my room?'

'I can buy it myself, I don't need to charge it,' Angel replied. She never liked feeling beholden to anyone.

Cal rolled his eyes. 'Still like this about money? It's only a bikini! Go on, charge it. Break the habit of a lifetime.'

While Cal took Honey up to his suite to get her ready for swimming, Angel bought herself a white bikini with gold ties in what was probably the quickest purchase ever. She didn't charge it to Cal's room and didn't care if he thought she was being predictable, it just didn't seem like the right thing to do. Honey was already in her Hello Kitty costume with matching armbands and bouncing energetically on the double bed when Angel walked in. Cal had changed into a pair of black Calvin Klein trunks. Angel nearly did a double take, he looked so sexy. Although he wasn't playing football any more, she couldn't help registering that his body was as fit as ever, in both senses of the word.

'The bathroom's through there if you want to get changed,' Cal said casually, putting his clothes back on over his trunks. Angel hurriedly went in and changed into the bikini, fumbling to do up the gold ties, feeling she could hardly ask Cal to assist her. What the hell had happened to being cool? Yet again, she was behaving like an inexperienced teenager around him and it was ridiculous! She took a critical look at herself in the mirror and instantly all kinds of inappropriate thoughts began colliding in her mind. Was the bikini sexy? Would Cal still find her attractive? And why the fuck was she thinking such things! She quickly slipped her skirt and tee-shirt back on.

Outside the pool was empty and there were just a couple of other guests relaxing on the loungers on the deck, looking out over the beach and ocean. Honey instantly demanded that both her parents get in the water with her so Angel stripped down to her bikini and lowered herself into the warm water. In spite of her best intentions, her gaze kept being drawn to Cal – in particular to the pair of angel wings he had tattooed on his right shoulder. He'd had the tattoo just after news of his affair had come out, as if he wanted to prove to Angel that in spite of what he'd done he belonged to her. A sudden image of lying in bed with him, tracing her fingers over the tattoo, flashed into her mind. Cal had always been the most sensuous, erotic lover. Just because she had left him, didn't mean she didn't still remember that.

At one point her eyes locked with his. 'It's good spending time together, isn't it?' he said. And he was right. But it was also bittersweet. Cal had always been a very hands on dad, and they'd had great family times. Angel missed that in her life with Ethan – he was good with Honey, but he was never going to fill the gap left by Cal. Fortunately Honey then demanded her parents chase her round the pool, stopping Angel from brooding on the past.

After a good thirty minutes Honey finally agreed to come out of the water. Angel was about to say her goodbyes, she was late for filming as it was but Cal asked if she wanted to stay for lunch. Angel hesitated. She really should get back, but she was having such a good time with Cal and Honey. Cal seemed more relaxed around her than he'd been for a while, he wasn't doing his distant thing, and frankly Angel just wanted to enjoy that and not have to put on an act for the cameras.

'Stay,' Cal repeated, and she found herself saying yes.

They sat in the beach-side café. All of them had a healthy appetite after the swimming. Cal and Honey shared a rotissière chicken with French fries while Angel had Caesar salad with shrimp. Angel had always thought that her daughter was thankfully too young to realise that her parents had split up but Honey seemed especially happy today, as if she couldn't quite believe her luck in having both her parents at her beck and call. Maybe Angel was reading too much into it, she didn't know, all she knew was that she was in no hurry to leave and break up the happy scene.

'I can see why you love it out here,' Cal said, looking out over the expanse of white sand, the brilliant blue ocean just beyond with several white yachts cutting jaunty trails through the water. 'I mean, I love Brighton and couldn't really imagine living anywhere else, but the sea's never this blue, is it?'

'And there's no sand, and the sun doesn't always shine. And the chips aren't this good.' She sneaked a French fry from Cal's plate. 'I do get homesick, though,' she added quietly.

'I'm sure everyone misses you.'

And what about you? Angel burned to ask. Talking about Brighton made her wonder what was going on in Cal's life back home. She knew little about it other than that he saw Tony and Gemma regularly, and worked hard. Was he seeing anyone yet? It would hardly be surprising if he was. Cal Bailey was a very eligible man. He must have women throwing themselves at him . . . women like Simone Fraser. Angel just had to ask, 'So how's Simone getting on?'

'She's okay. She moved down to Brighton about a month ago and is helping her sister run a fashion boutique in the Lanes.'

Instantly Angel felt a stab of jealousy. Now Simone was in Cal's home city, she was bound to see him. 'I hope she's learnt how to be nice to people then or I can't imagine they'll get many customers,' she said bitchily. 'So, do you see much of her then?'

Cal shrugged. 'Every now and then. And I suppose she calls me a quite a lot,' he admitted. 'She hasn't got that many friends. She was never really that good at making them, if you remember.'

That's because she's a complete cow! Angel thought, and then felt another stab of jealousy. Didn't Simone have another ex-boyfriend she could ring up? Did it have to be Cal? Angel hated herself for caring so much but she couldn't help it. She avoided looking at Cal and took a long sip of her mineral water, hoping he hadn't noticed how unsettled she'd become.

'And I think she realises what a bitch she was to you,' he went on. 'She's always asking after you.'

'Probably hoping that she'll hear some bad news,' Angel muttered sulkily.

A sigh from Cal: 'I don't think so, but let's not talk about her. I know it winds you up. So, this afternoon I was going to take Honey to the beach and maybe go to the pier. D'you want to come with us? I'm sure she would love it if you did.' He paused. 'And I would like it as well.'

Angel hesitated. She really should be getting back, and she knew that Ethan would be angry about her spending time with Cal, but she couldn't say no. She wanted to spend more time with Cal and Honey. All her good intentions of playing it cool had deserted her.

And so she spent the rest of the afternoon with them going on the white clapboard Santa Monica pier with its long boardwalk – too long for Honey, who demanded a piggy back from Cal. Angel had always been a thrill-seeker and loved fairs and theme parks, so she went on the Ferris wheel and roller-coaster and screamed her head off in delighted terror, while Cal and Honey waved to her from below. They all went on the dodgems – Cal and Honey going in one car, Angel in another – and raced each other, much to Honey's amusement.

'This definitely beats Brighton Pier,' Cal told her as they sat down having coffee.

'How can you say that?' Angel said in mock outrage. 'I had my first snog on Brighton Pier, in the ghost train with Tommy Jackson.'

'Was it a good one?' Cal asked, smiling, though Angel was pretty sure he knew the answer.

'It was atrocious; he bit my tongue and then gave me a massive love bite on my neck. You can just imagine what my dad said about that, can't you? Proper read me

104

the Riot Act and threatened to ground me for a month, until Mum reminded me what *he* was like as a teenager.'

'Yeah, I can imagine it. I remember when . . .' Cal paused, then shook his head and frowned. 'No, probably best not to go there.' Angel looked at him, wondering what he was going to say, and suddenly the moment seemed charged with emotion. So many memories, so many regrets. Cal gazed back at her and she felt as if he could read her thoughts.

'One of those!' Honey exclaimed, shattering the moment as she pointed to a little boy carrying an enormous stick of pink candy floss, almost bigger than his head.

'No way, Honey!' Cal told his daughter. 'Or you will have the sugar rush to end all sugar rushes.'

Honey's bottom lip trembled, and Cal, fearing toddler meltdown, quickly added, 'Let's go on to the beach and make sand castles. I bet I can build a bigger one than Mummy. Come on!' And he picked up his daughter and began walking briskly back along the boardwalk.

Santa Monica beach stretched out into the distance, miles of glorious white sand, fringed with palm trees. It was the perfect setting and one of Angel's favourite places. She often came here with Honey; she would bring her bike, put Honey in the child seat and cycle along the ocean-front path, looking at the swimmers and surfers, watching the rollerbladers weave their way along the path. Now she sat cross-legged on a rug and watched Cal and Honey hard at work, digging in the sand. The pair of them looked so happy together. The sun was warm on Angel's skin and a slight breeze from the sea lifted her hair. She suddenly wished this moment could last forever, wanted to shut out all the complications in her life.

'Shall I take a picture?' she asked Cal.

'Yeah, thanks,' he replied, brushing the sand off his hands before retrieving his phone from his jacket and handing it to Angel. But instead of pressing the button to activate the camera she somehow accessed Cal's pictures and found herself staring at the image of a beautiful dark-haired woman with stunning blue eyes. She was wearing a revealing evening dress and a seductive smile.

'Who's this?' Angel demanded, holding the phone up so Cal could see the image.

He frowned. 'Just a friend of mine.'

Angel immediately had a burning desire to look through the other pictures on Cal's phone, to see if there were any more pictures of this 'friend' or any others. She suddenly felt such a fool for allowing herself to be caught up in the moment.

'What's her name?' She couldn't stop herself from asking the question.

Cal shrugged. 'Madeleine.'

'And what does Madeleine do?'

'She's a model. I met her at some charity event.'

And why have you got her picture? Angel was dying to ask, but didn't.

She quickly took the photograph and handed back the camera. She was about to make a move when Cal asked a teenage girl who was passing by with her friends to take a picture of all three of them together. He put his arm round Angel, with Honey sitting between them. It could have been a scene from their past.

'Thanks,' Cal said to the girl as she returned the phone.

'You're welcome.' She beamed back at him, showing off perfect teeth. 'You guys looked so cute together. What an awesome family!'

Cal showed Angel the picture – she herself might not use the word 'cute' to describe it, but they certainly looked good together. Angel felt she was wandering on to dangerous territory; knew she could not let Cal have this much power over her emotions again.

'I have go now,' she said abruptly. It was 5 p.m. She should have been back over four hours ago. She stood up, brushing sand from her skirt. There was a pause when she almost wondered if Cal was going to ask her to stay longer. And if she hadn't seen that picture, she knew that she would have been tempted. But instead he said, 'We'll walk back to the hotel with you.'

She hated saying goodbye to Honey but tried not to show it, realising that it must be only a fraction of the pain Cal experienced when he said goodbye to his daughter knowing that he wouldn't see her for weeks. 'I'll send you the picture,' Cal told her as they stood in the lobby.

Angel thought she didn't need a picture to remind her of what she had lost, but she simply nodded.

'I had a great time,' Cal said. 'Maybe we could do it again this week.'

'Maybe,' Angel replied, but all she could think about was that she had to keep him at a distance again. Seeing the picture of Madeleine had proved that.

'My car's here, I have to go.' And blowing Honey a kiss, she swiftly walked out of the hotel, pausing at the doorway to turn and wave goodbye to her daughter.

'Where the fuck have you been?' Ethan shouted at her the moment Angel stepped into the hallway. He was tense with anger, his eyes narrowed. 'You should have been here hours ago. And why didn't you have your phone switched on?'

Angel had never seen him this furious before.

'Sorry. I did text Mimi to say I would be late. Honey

didn't want me to go so I ended up spending a few hours at the hotel, that's all. I didn't think it was such a big deal.'

Angel made to go upstairs, she didn't want to argue, but Ethan grabbed her arm. 'And why is your hair all messed up? You look like you spent the afternoon in bed. Is that where you were . . . fucking him?'

Angel shook her arm away. 'Don't be stupid! I was on the beach; it was windy. End of.'

'No, it's not! You've messed everyone around today. It was so selfish of you, Angel. We're behind in filming now, but all you could think about was him, wasn't it?'

'Fuck off! I was thinking about my daughter. It was nice spending time together as a family. I miss that, if you must know.' She didn't care if that comment hurt him. She was so angry at the way Ethan was having a go. But he wasn't going to let up.

'I wonder if you ever think about me at all? What am I . . . a convenient fuck buddy you use to get over your husband? Or do you want to get back with him? Is that it? You think he's so fucking perfect, but he's not. He cheated on you, Angel, and let me tell you – that kind of guy doesn't change! He would do it again and again. I would never cheat on you. *Never.*'

'Oh, just leave it, can't you?' she exclaimed, and ran up the stairs before Ethan could say anything else. She didn't need this. The day had been emotional enough without Ethan piling on the pressure with a fucking forklift truck. She stomped into the shower. She hadn't been in the wrong, had she? Ethan was over-reacting as usual about Cal, wasn't he? But as she let the hot water cascade over her, she began to reflect on the day and realised that Ethan had a point; she had been selfish. She should have come back sooner, or at least phoned. Cal had asked her to stay and she'd done what she'd always done: dropped everything for him.

She'd been so caught up with thinking about how Cal made her feel that she had relegated Ethan to second place when he deserved more. She tried to imagine how she would have felt if he had gone off with his ex-wife and switched off his phone – would she have felt that was a reasonable thing to do? She knew she would not. Ethan had every right to be angry and jealous. And yet again, why was she jeopardising what she had with him when, for all she knew, Cal was seeing Madeleine, and possibly even Simone? God, she was so stupid! She dried off quickly, and dashed into her dressing room. She slipped on a black silk tee-shirt dress, leaving her underwear off. She had some more making up to do.

'Sometimes I feel you fuck me when you don't want to think,' Ethan said afterwards, 'You're very good at using sex as a distraction.' They were lying stretched out on the vast double bed, hot, sweaty and very satisfied, after what had turned out to be a marathon sex session.

'No way,' Angel protested, languidly pushing back the hair from her face. 'I wanted to have sex with you because I wanted to have sex, there wasn't any hidden agenda. I don't have anything I need to be distracted from.'

Ethan turned and looked at her. 'I'm not sure if I believe you . . . but I'm not sure it even matters if the sex is as smokin' as that!' And he kissed her on the lips, sealing the deal.

Angel lay back. She didn't want to analyse his comment about her using sex as a distraction. Everything would be okay, she and Ethan were back on track, she could handle Cal. But later, when Ethan was in the shower, she checked her phone and there was a message from Cal along with the picture of the three of them. *Thanks for a great day, Angel, hope we can do it again. Cx.* It was the warmest message he had sent her in a long time and instead of feeling that she had a handle on the Cal situation, she went to sleep feeling as conflicted over it as she ever had been.

It didn't help when, the following day, Cal texted her at breakfast to say that Honey was desperate for her favourite toy elephant which Angel had forgotten to pack, and could he drop round and get it? Of course, this would be the one day when Ethan didn't have training until the afternoon. One of her worst night-mares was about to be realised, with the two men coming face to face again. In fact, Ethan insisted on answering the door to Cal, in what Angel was pretty sure was some kind of macho, this is my house, my woman act.

'Hey,' Ethan said, without any of his usual charm.

'Hi,' was Cal's response. No warmth there either.

'I've got the elephant,' Angel put in, coming forward and giving Honey a hug. She could sense the two men sizing each other up. This was beyond awkward! The last time they had met had been when Angel had left Cal for Ethan.

'Okay, thanks,' Cal replied. 'She's been really upset without it. Well, we'll leave you to your day. We're going to the beach.'

Honey stretched out her hand. 'Mummy come?'

'You go with Daddy, Mummy's going to work. Love you, Honey.'

Instantly the child's face crumpled and she burst into tears. Cal picked her up and Angel rushed over to her daughter and kissed her, aware that she was just inches away from Cal. And aware of Ethan watching her every move.

'I'm just going to go,' Cal said. 'I'll text you later. 'Bye.' And Angel had to stand by and watch as Ethan

110

opened the door and Cal carried a still crying Honey out to the car.

Ethan shut the door after them. 'Why will he text you?' He sounded pissed off.

Angel sighed, 'Just to let me know how Honey is. That's all. Thanks for letting him come by and pick up the toy.'

'Of course I would let him, what d'you think I am? Some jealous prick? You chose me.'

Ahhh! Angel wanted to scream with frustration. She'd thought she had put things right with Ethan and now it was all unravelling. Men were so infuriating! Though she didn't imagine she'd be that cool if one of Ethan's exes turned up. She shook back her hair and walked over to him. 'Yes, I chose you,' she murmured, putting her arms round him.

Once Ethan had left the house later that day, Angel texted Cal and said she was busy for the rest of the week and wouldn't be able to take time off from filming for any more outings with him and Honey. He must have realised that her mind was made up as he didn't try and persuade her, just texted back that he understood. She also couldn't resist Googling Madeleine and Cal, and instantly got a hit. Madeleine Fournier was a French supermodel, hugely wealthy and successful. She and Cal had met at Elton John's White Tie and Tiara Ball, and had subsequently been photographed having dinner, though both of them denied there was anything going on between them. But Angel found herself wondering, as she gazed at the beautiful brunette with her dark blue eyes, gorgeously chiselled cheekbones and bee-stung lips . . . and was then furious with herself for even caring.

That evening Angel and Ethan paid a visit to Loretta, Ethan's grandmother, at her house in neighbouring

Malibu. He was really close to her. When he fell out with his parents as a wild teenager, it was Loretta who'd taken him in and put him straight. Now their roles were reversed and Ethan looked after Loretta while she recovered from breast cancer, except she wasn't recovering and her prognosis was not good. She was fiercely independent, though. Despite the help Ethan had paid for, it was Loretta herself who opened the door to them.

Angel was shocked to see how much she had aged in the past weeks. Even in her late-seventies Loretta had always been a stylish and attractive woman, but the illness had left its mark on her and she suddenly looked every bit her age. Her skin was deathly pale, with deep lines etched in it, and she was slightly stooped, without her usual poise and ramrod-straight posture. When Angel hugged her Loretta felt frail and terribly thin.

'Now come on in,' she declared, showing her old spirit, 'I want to hear all your news. I've been bored to death this last week. The radiotherapy has left me feeling utterly wretched and I haven't been able to get out. I'm beginning to have some sympathy for Jack Nicholson's character in *The Shining*, when he goes mad after being snowed up in that hotel.'

'Just promise me you won't come after me with an axe, Grandma?' Ethan smiled at Loretta, linking his arm through hers and escorting her back to her cosy living room which looked out on to a beautifully tended garden.

'I know I probably shouldn't, but I really feel like a glass of champagne. Will you do the honours, Ethan? I think there should be a bottle of Dom Perignon in the fridge.' As Loretta settled herself in the high backed arm chair and Ethan went off to the kitchen, Angel sat down on the opposite sofa, careful not to disturb

Charlie, Loretta's haughty white Persian cat, who was stretched out on one of the cushions.

Loretta had once been an actress – and a great beauty – and the room was full of photographs of her in various roles, along with many, many photographs of Ethan, from baby to adult. Loretta was a doting grandmother. Angel spotted a picture she hadn't noticed before of a teenage Ethan with long blond hair falling across his eyes, scowling at the camera, and holding a skateboard. At sixteen he hadn't quite perfected the trademark sexy smile that had won him so many female admirers plus sponsorship and advertising deals. Loretta noticed what she was looking at. 'Hadn't quite grown into his looks then, had he?'

Angel smiled and shook her head. 'But I bet he still broke some hearts.'

'A fair few, I don't doubt. Ethan tells me your husband is over here at the moment?'

'Yes, just for a week.' Angel wondered what was coming next. Loretta could be very perceptive and straight-talking at times.

'And have you had any thoughts about the divorce?' Yes, here it was. Was there no escape from this question?

'I'd still like to do the two years' separation with consent,' Angel replied, as calmly as she could. 'I know that Ethan finds that tough, but it's just something I want to do. I don't want to upset him, but it's how I feel.' She knew that she sounded as if she was justifying herself. Sometimes she even wondered whether she was right.

Loretta smiled at her and rearranged the white pashmina round her shoulders. As she did so her gorgeous diamond and sapphire engagement ring caught the light and sparkled. 'Of course you must do what you think is right, Angel, and please forgive an old woman for asking annoying questions. I just want Ethan to be happy. It's taken him a long time to find love. And, selfishly, I would like to see him get married and be settled.' She paused, good actress that she was, before delivering her killer line. 'I'm not sure if I have two years. I'm not sure if I even have six months.' She said it without an ounce of self-pity. It was Angel who had tears in her eyes.

Loretta looked at her with piercing blue eyes, the same irresistible shade as Ethan's. 'I'm really not trying to guilt trip you into marrying my grandson. I'm just . . . how does the expression go? . . . telling it like it is.'

At that moment Ethan returned with a tray carrying three flutes of champagne and conversation switched to how the Dodgers were doing that season – Loretta being an ardent fan. Angel tuned out of the conversation. She had been so convinced that she was right not wanting to divorce Cal, but now she was starting to have serious doubts. Was not divorcing him the reason why she felt in limbo? Was it stopping her from moving on with Ethan? Maybe she had got this all wrong.

After an early supper, Ethan and Angel drove back to the house. Loretta had suddenly felt exhausted and had to go to bed. It was sad seeing her so diminished; before her illness she had been the life and soul of any social event, witty, charming and full of energy. Angel was silent, gazing out of the window, looking at the shadowy black expanse of the ocean.

'I'm sorry if I've been putting pressure on you about Cal,' Ethan suddenly said. 'I've been thinking about it and realise I've been coming on too strong. I understand about the divorce, and I understand why you wanted to spend the day with him and Honey. Sorry if I've made you feel trapped. It's the last thing I would ever want to do.'

Sometimes Angel felt she had a lot still to learn about

Ethan. It must have taken a great deal of courage for him to say that. She reached out and lightly touched his arm. 'Thanks, and I'm sorry if I made you feel insecure about Cal. You've no reason to be, I promise. You're the man I want to be with, Ethan.' An image of Cal flashed into her mind, but she pushed it away.

'So, will you come with me tomorrow to see Megan? The lawyers have finally set it up; I think we're meeting at her grandmother's house. Ella won't be there.' He certainly was full of surprises – Angel had had no idea he had been planning to see his daughter.

'Wow, Ethan, I'm so glad you're going to see her! What changed your mind?'

Ethan gave a rueful smile, 'You and Loretta. She was shocked that I hadn't met Megan. As soon as I've got to know her a little bit, Loretta wants to meet her as well. First great-grandchild and all.' The smile went from his face. 'I know she hasn't got long, but at least she's seen me with you. That means a lot to her, I'm sure. She despaired of me ever settling down even though she told me I would know when I found the right girl for me.' He briefly turned towards Angel. 'She was right, of course. She's always right.'

Angel suddenly felt a fierce surge of love for him. This man loved her, wanted her, was willing to change for her. Maybe it was time finally to put her past behind her.

Chapter 8

'Honey, be gentle with Megan, remember she's littler than you!' Angel called out to her daughter as she watched the two girls splashing about in the pool. It had been two weeks since Ethan had met his daughter and since then he was a changed man. He was absolutely smitten with the little blonde-haired girl, wanted to spend as much time with her as he could. The transformation was wonderful to see. It was as if he'd been in denial about even having a daughter, but as soon as he had seen her for himself she had instantly wormed her way through all those defences and denials. Not that it was going to be easy – Ella was continuing to hold out for the big money, and far from her being the struggling single mother portrayed by the tabloids, it turned out that her mum was mainly bringing up Megan while Ella got on with trying to make it as an actress and rarely saw the little girl.

Ethan came up behind Angel and slid his arms round her waist. 'Isn't it great how they play together? I love how Honey looks out for her as if she really is her big sister.'

Angel leant back against him. 'It's so sweet. And I'm so glad you're seeing Megan.'

She was genuinely happy for Ethan; she didn't have a moment's jealousy about it or feel insecure. Instead,

Ethan facing up to his responsibilities meant a great deal to her, showed his strength of character.

'So am I. Now I've met her, I can't believe I left it so long. I just have to make the most of the time now. I don't want to miss out on any more of her life.' He kissed Angel's neck then said, 'And thank you for being so understanding and supportive, and for pushing me to do the right thing. I know a lot of women would have found it hard to deal with the situation.'

'You had to accept Honey,' Angel replied, 'so it's only right that I accept Megan.'

'Well, well, well, what an adorable sight!' Benny was marching towards them. He tended to come and go in the house as he pleased, which drove Angel to distraction. 'You know, it would make a fabulous scene for the show, seeing your daughter and Angel's getting along so well. The audiences will love it . . . it's beyond cute.'

Angel was just about to jump in and say no way, but Ethan got there first. 'I'm not having Megan filmed for the show, Benny. Besides, I haven't got Ella's consent.'

Benny pursed his fleshy lips and fiddled with the enormous diamond ring on his left hand, which could probably be seen from Mars. 'What about an interview with *OK* and photographs of the girls then? We need to think of some good publicity angles in the run up to the first episode airing. You're not the only people with reality shows. We have to make yours stand out, give it the wow factor.'

'Maybe,' Ethan replied. 'But I'll need to discuss it with Angel.'

Wow, she thought, that was a first! She liked the change.

Benny didn't. He was used to being the person Ethan discussed everything with, but he tried not to show his displeasure. 'Okay, well, can we sit down and go through what's coming up? We've got a helluva two weeks, guys.'

Angel and Ethan waited until Lucy was ready to take over looking after the girls before going inside with Benny to go through their schedule; they had a number of press and TV interviews, including a prime-time interview with E! and several other channels. The trailers were already going out for the show and creating quite a buzz, not least because Ethan and Angel were so stunning-looking and because of the obvious chemistry between them. And, of course, the press were still obsessed with Ethan having a daughter, even more so since he had issued a statement saying that he was going to see Megan. Stories about their meeting had dominated the American tabloids, who had entered a bidding war to get the first pictures of father and daughter together, but so far Ethan still hadn't decided if he wanted the child to be photographed. On the whole the press had been positive, saying it was good that he was facing up to his responsibilities.

Closer to home, Angel had had to deal with more sceptical comments from Gemma, who with typical bluntness said she would wait and see how Ethan got on with the girl before giving him any award for Father of the Year. Ouch, that hurt, but Angel tried not to let it get to her. She had already had Cal on the phone being snide about Ethan, which had led to a frosty exchange when Angel reminded him that he hadn't been taking his own responsibilities as a father very seriously when he'd shagged Alessia. Maybe a low blow, but sometimes Cal brought out the worst in her.

It took a good hour to go through their publicity schedule, and Angel was itching to get back outside to the girls and the pool, but just as she stood up at the end of the meeting Benny said, 'Oh, Angel, I have something to show you which might be of interest.' He typed away at his laptop.

No doubt he was going to try and persuade her to do something she didn't want to. Angel sat back, folded her arms and looked questioningly at Ethan, who shrugged and said, 'What's this, Benny?'

'Just some photographs I thought Angel might appreciate having a heads up on. They're going to be in the British press next week. It pays to have contacts like me.' Benny looked extremely pleased with himself and Angel suddenly had a feeling that she wasn't going to like the photographs one little bit. Benny spun his laptop round so she could see the screen.

'Oh my God!' she exclaimed before she could stop herself, as she confronted an image of Simone and Cal, arm in arm, leaving his apartment in Brighton. They were both smiling and looked like the perfect couple. Angel was aware of both Benny and Ethan waiting for a further reaction, so she tried to keep a lid on her emotions.

'They look pretty into each other, don't they?' Benny put in. He seemed to thrive on her discomfort.

Ethan reached out and rubbed Angel's back. 'You okay?' he said sympathetically.

'Of course! Why wouldn't I be? I'm just pissed off that he lied to me. I hate that.'

'Your nearly-ex is quite the man,' Benny put in, clicking on his mouse and bringing up another picture – this time of Cal and Simone sitting in the back seat of a limo. Simone was leaning into him and he was gazing at her; it seemed an incredibly intimate moment. For Angel that image was bad enough in itself, but it also threw up many troubling memories of Cal's infidelity, which she had first found out about when someone sent her a photograph of Cal and the beautiful Italian woman Alessia embracing. Irrational as it was, it felt to

Angel as if Cal was betraying her all over again. She couldn't bear to sit there with Benny gloating over the pictures any longer and abruptly stood up. 'If that's all, Benny, I've got things to do.'

She managed to walk out of the room with her head held high but, as soon as she was out of sight, she bolted upstairs and locked herself in her dressing room. On top of feeling hurt and churned up she also felt bitterly humiliated – hated the fact that Cal had lied to her. He had *promised* there was nothing more than friendship between him and Simone. She felt so stupid for believing him. To Angel it felt like Cal knew that she still had feelings for him, and enjoyed knowing that he still had a hold over her. She couldn't face telling any of her friends; Jez and Gemma most likely already knew and were wondering how to break it to her.

A soft knock at the door roused her from her thoughts. 'It's me, babe, can I come in?' Wearily Angel got up from the sofa and unlocked the door. Ethan stood there looking concerned. He reached out and lightly touched her cheek. 'Hey, I had no idea Benny was going to show you those pictures. I'm sorry, babe. I've told him it was really inconsiderate.'

Angel managed a half smile. 'It's okay. It's better to know, isn't it?' They both sat on the sofa, Ethan with his arms around her. 'You don't have to put on a brave face for me, I'll understand if you're hurt. It must bring back memories of . . .' He broke off, clearly sensitive to mentioning the affair.

'Cal shagging Alessia,' Angel put in for him. 'D'you know what? Fuck him. I hate the fact that he always makes me feel guilty for leaving him when *he* was the one who was unfaithful, and I hate the fact that he lied to me about Simone. Can we go out somewhere? I just want to forget that I was ever married to him.'

*

When Cal phoned later that evening to speak to Honey, Angel made sure that Lucy took the call. She had instructions to say Angel was out. From now on, Angel decided, she was going to have as little contact with him as possible. She had softened towards him and he had hurt her; an all-too-familiar pattern that she wanted to break, once and for always.

Neither Jez nor Gemma believed her when she mentioned that she thought Cal was seeing Simone, saying that they were sure the pictures were either old or just showed them as friends, and Angel was jumping to the wrong conclusion, which made her feel even more isolated as if even her friends weren't being honest with her. She was so glad she was living in LA. The thought of bumping into a loved up Cal and Simone in Brighton was just too painful.

Fortunately she had plenty to distract her, and Benny was right: it was indeed a helluva two weeks in the run up to the first show – a whirlwind of press calls and interviews. Angel's face almost ached from smiling so much for the cameras, but she couldn't complain because the publicity for the show was going brilliantly well and they had secured a great deal of press attention. It seemed as if the show would be a 'must see'. Ethan was lovely to her during this time. He made her feel safe and loved, and it was hard to imagine him ever lying to her like Cal had done.

And then it was time for the big TV interview with Sam Ferrara on E! in front of a live studio audience. Angel was extremely nervous as Susie put the finishing touches to her make up in the dressing room. She had never liked doing TV, never mind live TV, always got anxious that she would come out with the wrong thing and sound like an idiot.

'Just be yourself, babe,' Ethan told her from the adjacent chair where his hair was being carefully gelled into place by his make-up artist. 'And they'll love you.'

'I know that I can come across as being wooden sometimes. What if he asks me a really awkward question?' Angel fretted. She had already changed into three different outfits in her anxiety about the interview, in the end settling for black skinny jeans, a pair of gold peep-toe Jimmy Choos, white vest and white boyfriend blazer plus the diamond necklace Ethan had bought her from Tiffany's. She could almost hear Gemma in her head saying, If in doubt go classic, but now she wasn't sure if she looked spectacular enough. Maybe she should have gone for the leather trousers . . . but they were way too hot under the lights!

Ethan reached out for her hand. 'Seriously, you'll be great.'

Still, Angel reflected as she and Ethan made their way onto the set during an ad break, ready to meet the host Sam Ferrara, at least he wasn't known for doing difficult interviews. The chat-show host, in his early-fifties, radiating good health and dentistry, instantly leapt up and shook Ethan's hand. He slapped him on the back and kissed Angel. 'Thanks for coming on, guys. Just make yourself comfortable, we'll be with you shortly.'

Angel sat down on the beige leather sofa and had to press her legs together to stop them from shaking with stage fright. She didn't dare look out at the audience, knowing that if she saw all those anonymous faces staring back at her, she really would freak out. A sound engineer quickly attached a microphone to her jacket, and Ethan, sensing her nerves, reached for her hand and squeezed it reassuringly.

'Don't let go,' she whispered.

'Just chill, you're going to be fine.' And he turned

and kissed her which had the audience cheering even before the show had started.

Then, all too soon for Angel, the ad break finished and Sam was beaming away at the cameras and introducing the couple. Angel clutched even more tightly to Ethan's hand, while he seemed supremely confident. Sam kicked off with plenty of compliments to Ethan about having such a beautiful girlfriend. He had also seen the show and loved it – thank God for that, Angel thought, she really wasn't up to an interview with someone ripping the piss out of her. All Angel was required to do at this point was smile and come out with the odd comment, she left all the talking to Ethan, but then Sam asked about Megan and Angel knew she would have to say something more.

'So, Ethan, it's been quite a year for you – you're with Angel and you've just discovered you have a daughter.' He leant forward expectantly, knowing that this was where the interview would get juicy.

'Yeah, it was a bit of shock finding out about Megan, but I think we're dealing with it.' Ethan no longer sounded so confident; he half turned to Angel as if seeking her approval.

'We're more than dealing with it, Sam,' she replied, knowing from the media training she'd had that it was important to use the interviewer's name wherever possible as it made you sound friendly and as if you were in control, even if you felt nervous as hell, as she did now. 'Megan's a fantastic little girl and I think Ethan's going to be a great dad.'

Cue cheers from the audience. 'So you didn't mind?' Sam asked, with his concerned, you-can-tell-me-everything look.

'Sam, we've all got pasts. Maybe I was shocked when I first found out, but now . . . not at all. I just want us to be happy together. After all, Ethan has to get used the fact that I have a daughter from a previous relationship.' Phew! She'd managed a decent couple of lines without mishap; maybe this was going to be okay.

Ethan smiled his appreciation at her.

'Well, that sounds great, Angel, good for you. I know a lot of people might not be quite so understanding under the circumstances. So what about the future for you guys? Can I ask if marriage might be on the cards?' Sam looked eagerly at the couple, no doubt desperate for a heads up on every other media outlet.

Ethan put his arm round Angel. 'No plans yet, we're just happy the way things are. And you know the expression, Sam. If it ain't broke, why fix it?'

He didn't do the gushing number he'd done for the reality show, which Angel had found so off-putting and corny. She looked at him with new respect; she really did love this man. Suddenly she had an overwhelming desire to show him how much. She had put him through a great deal in their short relationship – first having an intense affair with him, then rejecting him and going back to Cal, then back to Ethan, then refusing to get divorced. And during all that, his love for her had been constant.

She felt an opportunity opening up before her, something she had to seize with both hands in case she lost it. She had been so wrapped up with thinking about the past, she'd forgotten to appreciate what she had with Ethan.

She looked back at Sam. 'Actually, I do have something to say.' Ethan stared at her, clearly wondering what she was going to come out with, as did Sam. Angel gave a nervous laugh. Her stomach felt full of butterflies.

'I've never done this before, and I can't quite believe that I'm going to do it now, but Ethan . . . will you marry me?'

The audience let out a collective gasp of astonishment – no one had seen this coming! Sam looked as if he might explode with happiness that he'd had the announcement made on his show.

Ethan looked completely stunned. He turned to Angel. 'Is this what you really want?' It was hard for him to make himself heard over the audience, who were now applauding, whooping and whistling loudly. Sam held up his hand to silence the crowd, as right in front of their eyes a very private drama was unfolding.

Angel felt as if every eye was on her, but for once she didn't mind the attention – she wanted everyone to know what was in her heart. She felt completely calm and in control, knowing that she was doing the right thing.

'It is. I haven't been fair on you. I've been in a kind of limbo, not able to let go of my old life, but now I know that I want to and I really want to marry you, Ethan.' She paused, then bit her lower lip with anxiety as realisation dawned that she would never live down the humiliation if he said no.

'So what's your answer?' she asked nervously.

'What do you think?' Ethan exclaimed. 'Yes!' And then he pulled her to him and kissed her passionately, which drove the audience into a frenzy and caused Sam to exclaim, 'Get a room already!'

As soon as the couple came off the set Benny and Susie were there to greet them with a bottle of champagne, along with Mimi, Todd and the ever-present camera.

'Way to go!' Benny exclaimed. 'That is the best fucking news ever! Though maybe a heads up would have been good, Angel, so I could have got a press announcement ready.' He hugged Ethan and then Angel. She was feeling so happy that for once she didn't even mind having physical contact with him.

'I'm thrilled for you, Angel!' Susie seconded him, and air kissed Angel and Ethan. They all drank champagne in the dressing room while Mimi attempted to interview Angel and Ethan for the show, but the couple were too delirious, too high on love, to answer her questions seriously. They couldn't keep their hands off each other and Ethan alternated hugging and kissing Angel with saying, 'She's going to marry me!'

And his phone kept ringing with people wanting to congratulate him, though the first thing Angel had done was to switch hers off – tonight she wanted to focus on Ethan, didn't want to hear anyone's opinion on whether she had done the right thing or not.

'So this means you better get that divorce, Angel,' Benny put in. 'Last time I checked, bigamy was still illegal in the State of California. And I'd hate to see a pretty little thing like you behind bars. Mind you, that could *really* boost the ratings.' He paused, seeing the shocked expression on her face. 'Just kidding, Angel. You don't think I'm that desperate, do you?'

It was so typical of him to come out with something like that! Angel thought bitterly. She wanted tonight to be all about her and Ethan; absolutely did not want to think about Cal.

'Man, you can kill a moment.' Ethan turned to Benny. 'Angel knows that she's got to get a divorce but tonight is just about us. Where d'you want to go, babe? We can go anywhere you like?' He had his arms round her waist and had pulled her to him. Angel thought for a moment then said, 'I'd like us to go and tell Loretta in person, though I guess she'll have seen the show and knows already.'

Ethan smiled at her. 'That would make me so happy.'

Benny, Susie, Mimi and Todd were all set to follow them, thinking of the emotional drama they could whip up for the series with Ethan telling his dying, beloved grandmother the good news. 'Sorry, guys,' he said, realising what they expected. 'This one is just for me and Angel.'

'What if you give her the good news first without the cameras and then we film you? It would make great viewing,' Benny said. Angel waited for Ethan to give in to Benny like he had so many times before. Instead he shook his head and replied, 'You've got the great scene with Angel proposing to me live on air. Now let us have our privacy.'

'Ethan, you're not thinking straight. This could be a killer moment . . . you telling your sick grandma the news she never thought she would live to hear. Surely you want the world to know that!' Benny had taken hold of Ethan's arm for extra emphasis. He was persistent, Angel gave him that.

But Ethan stood his ground. 'I don't need reminding how ill Loretta is. I'm not doing it, Benny, and that's final. I'll speak to you tomorrow. Goodnight.'

For a few seconds Benny kept his hand on Ethan's arm and looked shocked, as if he couldn't quite believe Ethan was saying no to him. Then he snapped out of it and removed his hand. 'Sure, Ethan, we'll talk tomorrow. You guys go head and celebrate. Congratulations again. And give my love to Loretta.'

Ethan and Angel said their goodbyes, but as Angel turned to pick up her bag she caught the look Benny was directing her way. His usual lecherous leer had been replaced by one of pure venom. He saw her looking and quickly switched to a fake smile. What was that all about? she wondered as she and Ethan walked out of the building. Then she forgot all about it as they stepped out of the studio and into a volley of flashes from the waiting paps. Instantly Angel put her head up

127

high and smiled. She had made her choice and she was proud of it.

It was wonderful seeing Loretta's reaction to the news. She was thrilled and couldn't stop smiling, briefly back to looking the way she did before she was ravaged by cancer. She insisted on them drinking yet more champagne and they stayed for a couple of hours, chatting to her. As they came to leave, she slipped off her beautiful sapphire and diamond engagement ring and handed it to Ethan, saying, 'I want you to give this to Angel.'

'No way, Loretta!' Ethan exclaimed. 'I couldn't possibly take it from you.'

He held it out in the palm of his hand, but she gently closed his fingers around it. 'Nothing would make me happier than knowing you had given that ring to Angel. Besides, I've lost so much weight the ring keeps falling off and I'm afraid I'll lose it.' Ethan still looked unsure, so Loretta added, 'Please, Ethan.'

And so he took Angel's hand and gently slipped the ring on to her finger, where the jewels sparkled brilliantly. It even fitted. Angel held up her hand to show Loretta who smiled her appreciation. 'You don't mind that it's not a new ring?' she asked. 'It was my mother's, and before that my grandmother's, and is a bit of a family tradition.'

'I'm honoured,' Angel replied truthfully. She felt buoyed up with happiness.

It was only when she and Ethan were driving home that she switched on her phone and saw she had several missed calls from Cal. She realised she had better face up to some explaining. Ethan saw her frown. 'I take it Cal has phoned you?' She nodded.

'So what are you going to tell him?'

'The truth. That I need a divorce because I love you and want to marry you.'

'He's not going to take it well,' Ethan replied. 'You'd better be prepared for that.'

But when, back at the house and filled with apprehension, Angel phoned him, Cal was completely cool and offhand. She had no idea what he was thinking, other than the slight edge to his voice, they could have been discussing the weather.

'Congratulations,' he said as soon as he answered her call. 'Of course, it might have been nice to know you were planning to do that, but I'm guessing it was a spur-of-the-moment decision.' He wasn't giving anything away. But she could hardly blame him, could she?

'I'm sorry I didn't tell you, I hadn't planned it but it wasn't just a spur-of-the-moment thing. I know I really want to marry Ethan.'

'You don't have to convince me, Angel. Fine, why don't you arrange for your solicitor to contact mine and we'll get this over and done with quickly, if it's what you really want. And your mum and dad and friends might appreciate a call as well. I've just had your dad on the phone . . . and Gemma. They both sounded pretty shocked.'

Angel hated the way he was trying to make her feel guilty and was instantly on the defensive,

'Yes, it's what I really want. I don't know why you're sounding so offhand,' she replied. 'You're seeing Simone, so what difference does it make if we get divorced and I marry Ethan?'

'What the fuck are you on about?' Cal sounded extremely pissed off. 'I've told you, Simone is just a friend . . . that's all there is to it.'

'Oh, please, spare me the denials, it's so fake! I've seen the pictures, Cal!'

'Seriously, Angel, I don't know what you're on about.'

She couldn't believe that he didn't 'fess up. 'Well, whatever, Cal. I know what I saw.'

'I *really* don't know what you're talking about.' He sounded exasperated. 'But I've got to go. Give Honey a kiss from me.'

Angel thought fleetingly of the day she had spent with them in Santa Monica. She was turning her back on any chance of a reconciliation with Cal if she went ahead with marrying Ethan – not that he had even suggested there should be one. Indeed, she had no idea what he thought about her any more apart from that one kiss. Maybe that was all it was, a kiss that meant nothing. And she realised something else. Actually it didn't matter if Cal was or wasn't seeing Simone, in a way that was irrelevant, the fact was she couldn't trust him any more. There was no going back.

Chapter 9

Angel spent a difficult few days fielding concerned calls from her family and friends. No one she knew seemed that thrilled by the news. Both her parents thought she was rushing into things and her dad even came out with the old chestnut of 'Marry in haste, repent at leisure', which went down very badly with Angel, who felt he was being really unfair. He was so blinkered where Cal was concerned. Had always thought he was perfect; and when he wasn't, it seemed to Angel that Frank was very good at burying bad news. As for her friends, while Jez was cautious in giving his congratulations, Gemma didn't make any attempt to hide how shocked she was.

'But it's so soon after you breaking up with Cal. Are you sure this is what you want?' she demanded.

She didn't seem to be listening when Angel replied that, yes, this was exactly what she wanted.

'Has Ethan been putting pressure on you to do this?' Gemma carried on. 'It just seems so sudden, especially after you've only just found out about his daughter. How do you know there aren't any other secrets he's been keeping from you?'

Angel hated hearing her friend talking to her like this; hated everyone judging her, expecting her to do what they thought she should do. It was like a red rag to a bull. 'Why did I even think that you would be happy for me?' she shot back. 'Fucking hell, Gemma, you're my best friend and all you can do is criticise me! All *everyone* ever does is criticise me! Sometimes I think you all believe it's my fault that Cal was unfaithful.'

'Of course I don't think that,' Gemma said quickly. 'What Cal did was wrong and I can understand why you feel you could never trust him again, but is marrying Ethan the way to get over Cal? Because that's what it looks like from here.'

'I'm not marrying Ethan to get over Cal!' Angel exclaimed. 'I'm marrying him because I love him! And anyway, I don't have to justify myself to you or to anyone.' Then it was Angel's turn to put the phone down on someone. She felt as if her friends and family were doing all they could to take the shine off her big news.

Ethan came and found her, curled up on the sofa in her dressing room, looking at her engagement ring. This room had become her sanctuary from the outside world and from her past, it seemed.

'Tell me you're not having second thoughts,' he said, sitting down next to her.

She shook her head and leant against him, breathing in his fresh clean smell, cut with his musky aftershave. 'No way.'

'Folks giving you a hard time?'

She sighed, 'You don't mind if we have a small wedding, do you? I don't want people coming if they're going to be negative.'

'Angel, I don't mind what kind of wedding we have, I just want to marry you.'

At this he kissed her and Angel kissed him back, and it wasn't long before they were pulling off each other's clothes, culminating in a brief, intense fuck, putting Angel's worries right out of her head. And nothing that

132

felt this good could be wrong, she thought, lying back in Ethan's arms.

While Angel received such a lukewarm reception to her big news from the UK, the reaction from the States couldn't have been more of a contrast. All Ethan's friends were delighted for him, the media couldn't get enough of the golden couple and it made a refreshing change to have the attention on a positive event in her life. Angel tried to block out the negative comments and enjoy the congratulations.

Benny insisted on throwing the couple a huge star-studded engagement party. It was the first time Angel had ever been to his house and she'd had no idea it was so grand. It was in the heart of Beverly Hills, a huge Italian-style villa, complete with two impressive marble pillars at the front entrance, bronze statues of naked Greek youths dotted around the garden, and inside it was all marble floors, huge glittering chandeliers, and everywhere you looked photographs of Ethan: Ethan playing baseball, Ethan at various celebrity parties and premieres, Ethan posing for his after-shave and car commercials, Ethan relaxing on the beach. Angel realised that there didn't seem to be any other pictures of anyone else. That seemed weird. Although Ethan was Benny's most successful client, he did look after other players.

She was about to say as much to Ethan when Susie caught sight of her. 'Angel!' she screeched. 'Why haven't you returned my calls? We've got so much we need to talk about!'

Angel had indeed been ignoring Susie's messages, knowing that her agent would go off on one. She could do with some head space at the moment. In contrast, she had received a lovely bouquet of flowers from Carrie and Dave congratulating her, with no mention of work. Angel rather wished that Carrie was out here with her instead of Susie who had clearly decided that she was a kick-ass agent who wouldn't take no for an answer. Susie was certainly dressed to impress in a clinging gold dress which resembled fish scales and seemed to be staying on her 32Ds by sheer will power alone, or more likely a roll of tit tape, along with staggeringly high gold sandals. 'This is just the best news ever for your career! I couldn't have wished for anything better. You could have told me before though, I didn't like to say anything in front of Benny and Ethan but I am your agent. I mean I know I'm junior to Carrie, but she has left me in charge.' There was a slight petulant edge to Susie's voice here. Angel looked over her shoulder, hoping that Ethan was nearby and could rescue her.

'Susie, I know we've got a lot to talk about, but this is a party and I've got people I need to say hello to,' she replied, knowing that her agent was always nagging her to talk more to other people or rather 'network'.

'Yes!' Susie exclaimed, instantly perking up, 'Go mingle! There are people here you absolutely *must* invite to your wedding, and I guess it would be nice if you met them first. You're thinking of a fall wedding, I take it – we need at least six months to plan it, though to be honest a year would have been better. The best venues are most likely all booked up . . . But I'm sure we can pull a few strings.'

Now was not the time to inform her that Angel planned on having the smallest wedding possible – maybe even getting married on the beach with just two witnesses, Honey and Megan as flower girls and strictly no photographers. She could just imagine how well *that* would go down with her agent.

Angel was just about to move over to where Ethan was chatting to Alisha and Logan when Susie took her arm again and whispered, 'I might even be planning my own wedding soon.'

Angel looked at her, trying not to show how surprised she was.

Susie nodded, 'Yes, it's true, I'm sure Benny is close to popping the question.'

Angel had had no idea that the Benny/Susie love fest was so far advanced.

'We're a perfect match in so many ways, we both love our jobs, our independence, we make each other laugh and –'

Angel winced, praying that Susie wasn't going to share what Benny was like in bed.

'And we've got the most fantastic sexual chemistry.'

Oh no, please, let her stop now! 'But isn't Benny a little old for you?' It wasn't the most polite of questions but Angel couldn't bear to hear about the couple's sex life.

But Susie didn't seem to take offence, 'I've always loved older men and so Benny's just perfect for me and he's got so many contacts!'

At that Susie caught sight of Benny, and headed over to him, leaving Angel free to find Ethan, relieved to have escaped hearing any more revelations.

As she walked across the room, other guests caught her eye and smiled at her, raising their glasses in congratulation. Benny had certainly pulled out all the stops. There were beautiful arrangements of flowers everywhere, a jazz band was playing in the corner of the palatial room, waiters whisked by with trays of vintage champagne and delicious canapés. Angel smiled to herself, noticing that the champagne was going down far more quickly than the canapés – everyone here was simply too image-conscious to be caught scoffing any food. She recognised Ethan's team mates, various movie stars, rap stars, socialites, a couple of gossip columnists – she gave the latter a wide berth. Bitter experience had taught her never to trust journalists.

Ethan looked so handsome as he chatted to his friends – usually he was to be found in baggy tee-shirts and jeans, but tonight he had scrubbed up well in an exquisitely cut dark grey Dior suit. Angel had gone all out for glamour as well, wearing a white floor-length Grecian-style dress with diamante straps that emphasised her gorgeous curves.

'Hey! Congratulations!' Alisha and Logan exclaimed, taking it in turns to kiss her.

'I never thought I'd live to see the day that Ethan Turner got married!' Logan joked. 'And I can't think of anyone I'd rather see him married to than you.' It was lovely basking in their warm wishes after the cautious way her old friends had received the news. If only they knew Ethan like Angel did, they would understand that she was most definitely doing the right thing. A succession of other guests then came up to wish them well, and the next half-hour was a blur of introductions. Angel didn't find it easy mixing with people she didn't know, but Ethan was so easygoing he made her feel relaxed. Every time she felt unsure of herself, he would catch her eye and smile. At one point one of the gossip columnists came over, eager for some juicy titbits about the engaged couple, and Angel made her excuses and wandered off to find a bathroom, having no desire to talk to them.

She made her way up the vast wood-panelled staircase and on the landing above paused to look down over the guests, who had spilled out from one of the spacious living rooms and into the hall. This was a really great party, she thought to herself happily, then had a sudden pang that none of her family and friends were here to celebrate with her. Neither was Loretta, who was simply too frail for a big event like this.

She tried to shake off the feeling of sadness and opened a door off the long landing which she thought was the bathroom. Instead she found herself in Benny's office, which like the rest of the house was furnished in an over-the-top extravagant style: gold taffeta curtains, a zebra-print sofa with red heart-shaped velvet cushions scattered over it, the ceiling painted sky blue with white fluffy clouds and cherubs darting round the edges. But what really stopped Angel in her tracks was the huge black-and-white photograph of Ethan which took up an entire wall. While it wasn't a surprise to find yet another photograph of him, this one was a shock as in this photograph Ethan was lying on his side, naked save for a Dodgers' cap covering his manhood and flashing one of his trademark sexy smiles. It seemed a very full on choice for a study. For a moment she stood transfixed in front of the photograph.

'Admiring the view?' It was Benny.

She spun round. 'I'm sorry, I came in here by mistake.' She made to walk out of the room, but Benny stood blocking the door.

'Great party, isn't it?' he commented.

'Yeah, thanks, Benny. It was really nice of you to put it together for us.'

Benny narrowed his cold grey eyes and said with an edge to his voice, 'I did it for Ethan.'

'Well, he really appreciates it . . . we both do,' Angel replied, wondering why he was giving off this vibe.

'I hope you realise how lucky you are to be marrying him. He is such a big star, and you – you could be one of any number of girls. What's so special about you, Angel?'

He seemed drunk and Angel really didn't want to get into an argument with him, so she didn't reply. But Benny carried on, 'Played it well, though, didn't you? I have to give you that. Very clever. Kept him hanging on with your coy, "Oh, Ethan, I do love you but I don't want to go through the trauma of a divorce",' here Benny put on a simpering expression, 'till Ethan didn't know what the hell was going on between you. And all along you *knew* you were going to marry him. Of course you were! You hit pay dirt; you weren't going to turn down the chance to marry Ethan Turner. You're a fucking glamour model, for Chrissake! He's a multi-millionaire, a sporting hero!'

Benny had never sounded so hostile towards her before and Angel was shocked, both by his tone and by his words. She inched forward, hoping that he would get the message and move away from the door, but he remained standing where he was.

'Benny, I don't know what your problem is, but I do love Ethan and I was never playing any games with him.' She took another step. 'Now I'd really like to get back to the party.'

At this Benny finally moved aside, but as she walked past him he reached out a huge hand and grabbed her arm, gripping it so tightly it drew a gasp of pain from Angel.

'Just don't even think about fucking Ethan about. He loves you for whatever dumbass reason, but if you ever hurt him, I will personally fucking ruin you.' Benny shoved his face in hers, so close she could see the pores on his nose, smell the brandy on his breath.

'Let go of me!' Angel exclaimed, frantically trying to shake off his hand. His blatant aggression and hostility were frightening.

He abruptly released her. 'Enjoy the rest of the party, Angel,' he said, perfectly normally, as if nothing had happened.

Angel took a few minutes to compose herself in the bathroom; there was an angry red mark on her arm where Benny had gripped her. He had sounded as if he hated her. Maybe he was just being really protective of Ethan . . . but, no, it was more than that. She leaned against the wall – even this bathroom had pictures of Ethan all over it. In fact, the whole house was like a shrine to him. She had always thought that Benny was straight, but maybe his feelings for Ethan went beyond those of an agent for a client; maybe he was in love with him? Maybe she'd completely misread him. But then, why would he start up a relationship with Susie? Angel couldn't imagine.

She returned to the party but felt pretty shaken up for the rest of the evening, staying close to Ethan. Every now and then she would catch Benny watching her.

'Great party,' Ethan said sleepily as they curled up together in bed. 'Everyone loved you.'

Not everyone, Angel thought, thinking of Benny and wondering how to bring up her encounter with him. She hesitated, then blurted out, 'Ethan, do you think Benny likes me?'

'He adores you! Thinks you're the best thing that's ever happened to me. Why do you ask?'

'Just something he said at the party, along the lines of did I realise how lucky I was to be marrying you, and that if I messed you around, he would personally ruin me. He even grabbed my arm.' She rubbed it. It still hurt, and even as she spoke an image of Benny's cold grey eyes flashed into her head.

'What the fuck!' Ethan sat up in bed. He looked shocked. 'D'you want me to call him now?'

Angel shook her head. She didn't want the incident with Benny to ruin what had otherwise been a good night. She sighed, 'I think he was drunk, most likely he had no idea what he was saying.'

Ethan frowned. 'It's no excuse but I guess he must

have been drunk. He can get aggressive when he has too much, I've seen it myself, which is why he rarely drinks. He's bound to wake up in the morning and feel terrible and phone you up to apologise. And if he doesn't, I'll have something say to him. Let's forget about him.' He lay back down, murmuring, 'Love you.'

But Angel had something else she wanted to ask. 'I wondered if Benny might be . . .' she hesitated, not knowing if she should come out with her theory about Benny; she really didn't want to upset Ethan.

'Might be what, babe?'

'Gay.'

Now Ethan roared with laughter. 'Benny's one of the straightest men I know! He's had more women than me! Not that it would matter if he was gay, but seriously, Angel, there's no way. I've known him for ten years and there's never been a hint of that.'

Angel didn't like to say that people could be in the closet for years and maybe never come out. Ethan might be cool with people being gay, but she was willing to bet other people in his sport wouldn't be. 'What about that picture of you that he has in his study? You know, the one where you're practically naked.'

Ethan frowned, considering her comment, 'I guess that's a bit out there. I'd never really thought about it before. Still, I bet your agent has got pictures of you in her office and that doesn't make her a lesbian, does it?'

Okay, maybe Ethan was right, maybe she was reading too much into the picture, but could she simply put Benny's threatening tone down to drink? Angel didn't think so, but then again she didn't want to make a big deal of it; she wanted to be happy about marrying Ethan, not have to think about anything else, and so Angel did what she always did with unwelcome thoughts. She pushed them to the back of her mind.

*

The first episode of their reality show aired a few days later and went down a storm with the viewers – the channel was thrilled, Benny and Susie were thrilled, even Angel didn't think she came across too badly when she watched it back. And when she saw Benny he apologised profusely for anything he might have said to upset her, claiming that he had drunk too much and couldn't even remember what he'd said. Apparently he'd spent the last few days apologising to several other people he had offended.

It was a plausible explanation, given how freely the champagne had been flowing, but Angel couldn't help wondering if it really had been the drink. She vowed to avoid him even more than she did usually.

To celebrate the success of the show and to give them both a break, Ethan whisked her off to the Caribbean island of St Lucia, leaving Honey with Lucy for a weekend. It was luxury to the max. They had their own beachside villa, where they did nothing but make love, eat, sunbathe and have spa treatments. As they lay out on their balcony, sharing a hammock and counting the shooting stars, Angel thought it had been a very long time since she had felt this happy and content. She felt at peace. She had finally got closure on the past. Her new life was with Ethan. A fresh start without the shadow of Cal's betrayal hanging over her, tainting everything.

Chapter 10

'God, I'll miss you,' Ethan said, pulling Angel to him and kissing her, much to the delight of the paps who were crowding round them, clicking away with their cameras to get the best shot. Angel was just about to go through the departure gate at LAX to board a flight back to the UK. She was spending a week there for work, and to celebrate Gemma's birthday. Ethan had an important game so couldn't come with her.

'I'll miss you too,' Angel murmured, then headed for the security check, holding on to Honey's hand, pausing only to turn round and blow Ethan a kiss. She hated leaving him, even for such a short time. Since her marriage proposal she felt as if she'd fallen more deeply in love with him, he was wrapped round her heart and she felt intoxicated with love for him. Finding out about Cal and Simone had been a big wake up call, telling her to move on with her life because Cal certainly wasn't waiting for her. The photographs Benny had showed her had turned up in the British press but there had been no more since then. Simone was quoted as saying that she and Cal were just friends but Angel didn't believe her. And Cal never gave interviews. She had continued to avoid speaking to him on the phone.

Landing at Gatwick, Angel faced the usual scrum of paps. She had already prepared by putting on her largest pair of black Chanel sunglasses and had arranged for Ray to meet her along with her mum and dad. Since the news of her marriage to Ethan had broken the paps had become even more desperate to photograph her, particularly as she had yet to do an interview – Benny and Susie were in the process of setting up an exclusive deal with one of the mags.

'I thought Dad would come and pick us up,' Angel commented, holding on tightly to Honey as Ray cleared a path through the photographers.

'He's not feeling too good at the moment, so I told him to stay at home.'

It was unlike Frank to be ill; Angel had never known her dad to even have a day off work.

'What's wrong?'

'I think it's just a virus and he feels under the weather.' Michelle paused. 'He's also a bit upset about you, love, not that he would ever say.'

Angel was just about to ask why, but then realised she had deviated from her plan not to show any expression at all before the greedy paps otherwise the next thing she knew they'd be writing some load of bollocks about how she had landed in a foul mood because she'd argued with her American lover, or something like that. 'Let's talk in the car,' she said quietly.

But it turned out to be a conversation she really didn't want to have. Michelle explained that Frank was really upset about Angel marrying Ethan, convinced that she was making a terrible mistake, that it was far too soon and that she should be with Cal. Angel didn't want to say too much in front of Honey but she was really angry. It felt to her as if Frank was ruining her big moment, and what's more was being really unfair on her.

'Well, Dad's completely wrong on that score. I am doing the right thing marrying Ethan. I'm really happy and I'd have thought that my parents would be happy for me as well, especially after what I went through with Cal.'

'I am happy for you,' Michelle said quietly. 'And I understand. It's just your dad, you know what he can be like sometimes. He probably needs to see Ethan again and then he'll realise that he is right for you. He just doesn't know him well enough yet.'

Great. So instead of having a chilled out time with her family and friends, she was going to have to deal with her dad giving her grief. Angel sat back in the car seat and folded her arms, looking moodily out of the window as the car sped along the A23 into Brighton. She could always rely on her dad to make her feel like an awkward teenager again. She wondered when that feeling would ever stop.

But a day into her visit her dad had resisted saying anything about her engagement or Cal, so either Michelle had said something to him or he was waiting for the right moment – and Angel definitely wasn't going to bring up the subject if she could help it. She was getting enough ear ache from Gemma, who continued to make it clear that she thought Angel was rushing into the marriage. After a quiet day with her mum and dad, Angel had gone to the beauty salon run by Gemma's mum, Jeanie, to get her nails done ready for her shoot the following day. But she was definitely getting more than a manicure as Gemma talked at her over the nail bar. She had noted Angel's sapphire engagement ring, briefly commenting that it was very beautiful before launching into a tirade.

'Why don't you wait a year? Why the big rush?' she demanded, carefully applying bubble-gum pink varnish to Angel's nails.

'Because I really love him!' Angel exclaimed. 'And it's what I really want!' She moved her hand in her

144

agitation, causing Gemma to scowl as a blob of varnish went on to Angel's finger. Angel couldn't help feeling hurt by her friend's attitude. She turned her head and appealed to Jeanie who was sitting at reception.

Jeanie was one of her mum's closest friends and Angel had known her all her life. She was down-to-earth, warm and funny, and could always be relied on to defuse any difficult situations.

'Jeanie, will you tell your daughter to stop giving me such a hard time!'

Jeanie looked over and smiled. At fifty-something she was still a very attractive woman, who was as into fashion as her daughter, though had to put up with mutton-as-lamb jibes from Gemma on a regular basis. She also changed her hair style as often as Danni Minogue – currently Jeanie had a long black bob with an asymmetric fringe, and had gone for the casual look in a black velour track suit with diamante love hearts on the sleeves, an Ed Hardy tee-shirt and black furry UGG boots.

'You know what Gemma's like. I can't tell her anything! All I will say is that you need to follow your heart, Angel, and no one can tell you what you should or shouldn't do, babe.'

'See?' Angel turned back to Gemma who had finished varnishing her nails and was just admiring her own handiwork. 'You should listen to your mum for a change. She's right about this.'

'First time for everything,' Gemma muttered. Once she had made up her mind it was practically impossible to get her to change it, Angel knew that from experience.

'So have you seen much of Cal?' she asked as casually as she could.

Gemma shrugged. 'Not that much lately, he's been

really busy. He might be coming to my birthday. You don't mind, do you?'

Angel did mind and wished that Gemma hadn't asked him. Recently she felt she had been very successful in compartmentalising her feelings for him and didn't want the complication of seeing him. ''Course not,' she replied. 'So is he bringing anyone?' She was fishing now to find out about Simone.

'Don't think so. I told you, I don't think he's seeing anyone.'

'Not Simone?'

That comment earned her an eye roll from Gemma. 'Why are you so obsessed with her and Cal? I'm sure there's nothing going on between them.'

Gemma's defence of Cal angered Angel. It seemed to her that everyone was quick to jump to his defence. Saint fucking Cal!

'And you'd know, would you?'

'If he was seeing Simone, he'd have told Tony and Tony would have told me.' Gemma shrugged. Angel could well believe that her brother would find it hard to keep anything from Gemma, who no doubt had ways of making him talk. But quite possibly Cal hadn't told anyone that he was seeing Simone. He could be intensely private about his life sometimes.

'And have you seen her?'

'She comes in here for beauty treatments, but to be honest I get one of the other girls to work with her. I feel sorry for her, but I'll never forget how bitchy she was to you.' Gemma smiled, 'And she's fucking high-maintenance still, always moans about everything. Only last week she was in complaining that the spray tan hadn't made her brown enough and that Elaine had left a white patch on her bum. Kicked up a right fuss. Mum had to do a respray for free. The worst thing, is she asked to be my friend on Facebook. I tried ignoring

146

the request but then gave in and accepted, so now I get all her wanky comments about what she's been up to.'

'You can hide them on your wall,' Angel told her, secretly thinking that would be one way to check up if she was seeing Cal, as Simone wouldn't be able to resist blabbing about it. Cal wasn't on Facebook, though his football charity was.

'Good idea. There's only so much of the high-maintenance queen that I can take.' And with that her friend was back to being the Gemma Angel knew. Maybe it was just that she hadn't seen her for a while.

After Angel's nails were dry, Gemma took her lunch break and the two girls wandered through the Lanes, enjoying the April sunshine, and then had lunch in Angel's favourite Italian restaurant – a tiny family-run place she'd been going to for years. As soon as she walked in, the head waiter, Alonzo, made a huge fuss of her. He arranged for her and Gemma to sit at her favourite table in the window so they could people-watch, and brought them both a complimentary glass of champagne. Angel didn't even have to place her order, she always had the same thing and Alonzo knew it: a tricolore salad and garlic bread, followed by Tortelloni Aurora.

Angel felt herself relax. It was lovely spending time with Gemma, especially now her friend had stopped giving her a hard time about Cal and Ethan.

'I can't believe you eat all those carbs!' Gemma exclaimed, delicately picking out all the potatoes from her Salade Niçoise. 'I thought you'd be all healthy.'

Angel shook her head. 'I've been dreaming of eating here. I can get whatever I want in LA but nothing tastes as good as this. And Ethan's always teasing me because I can't live without Marmite and PG Tips.'

'No one could ever call you high maintenance,' Gemma joked. They both laughed and then stopped as they each noticed Cal walking past the restaurant with Simone. They weren't holding hands but Angel got the same sickening jolt of jealousy she had when she'd seen the photograph of the couple. Sometimes Brighton could feel like the smallest place in the world.

Simone was gazing adoringly at Cal. She looked a million times better than she had when Angel had seen her at Nobu. Gone were the overly inflated lips; her make up looked natural, emphasising Simone's beautiful brown eyes, and she was wearing skinny jeans, heels and a tight-fitting black leather jacket. She looked good, very good. Angel suddenly regretted stuffing her face with pasta. She hoped that Simone and Cal would walk by without seeing them but Cal noticed her, waved, and then walked into the restaurant, followed by Simone.

An awkward few minutes followed. Angel never knew how she should greet Cal these days. Did you kiss your soon-to-be-ex-husband or just smile politely? Cal decided for her, by bending down and kissing Gemma and then Angel. He was back to being cool, polite and distant. His gaze momentarily fell on Angel's glittering engagement ring but he didn't mention it.

'I'm just on my way to see Honey at your mum's.' They had already agreed that Honey would stay at her grandparents' for one night before spending the rest of the week with Cal.

'Hi, Angel. Hi, Gemma,' Simone put in, flashing a smile that showed off perfectly veneered teeth. 'I've seen the pictures of Honey . . . she's so beautiful, Angel. You're so lucky.' She seemed sincere. Angel looked at her thoughtfully. She'd never had Simone down as the maternal kind, and it was very unusual for her to say *anything* remotely complimentary to Angel who half wondered if she was taking the piss. But apparently not as Simone continued, 'And you look so well, it must be that LA sunshine.' Angel waited for the sting in the tail, the old Simone wouldn't have been able to resist putting in a dig about Ethan, but none came.

'And you look good, Simone, it must be the sea air,' Angel replied, feeling that she had to return the compliment, even if she didn't feel like it, not one little bit. She hated being fake and putting on an act.

'Better than when you last saw me, I bet, not that I can really remember.' She lost the smile as she added, 'Jez tells me that I was completely shit-faced, which is *so* embarrassing, but that's all behind me now.' Not as embarrassing as everyone knowing you were a high-class escort to fund your drug habit, Angel thought. Simone carried on, 'But we've all done things we regret, haven't we, Angel?'

Ah, so there was the sting in the tail. Angel simply shrugged, refusing to get drawn into a discussion about her own battle with addiction many years earlier. Simone's comment just proved she hadn't really changed, she still knew where to stick the knife. She then turned to Cal and the smile returned as she looked at him adoringly. 'Anyway, it's all down to Cal that I'm getting my life back on track. I really don't know where I would have been without him.'

Sucking some old businessman's cock for money, were the words that Angel did not say, sorely tempted as she was. *If* Simone was a changed woman, then she would *try* and be nice back.

Cal shifted awkwardly, he hated being the centre of attention. 'We'll leave you to get on with your lunch,' he said. 'Speak to you later, Angel. See you, Gemma.'

Simone treated the girls to another dazzling smile and then followed him out. Angel watched her tiny bum wiggle out of the restaurant then exclaimed, 'Is she for real? She used to be such an old cow to me!'

'Apparently so. She's in AA and doing the Steps,

which means she has to make amends for her behaviour. I expect she'll be contacting you to say sorry for all the things she said to you.'

'That will be a *very* long list, and I don't think I can forgive or forget,' Angel said darkly. 'I still think she's a witch underneath her fucking goody-two-shoes act, whatever Cal and Jez think.'

Gemma sighed, 'Just don't let her get to you, babe, I'm sure she'd love that. She can't have changed that much.'

The following day Angel had a shoot to promote her new lingerie range – the designs for the autumn collection were all grown-up glamour in scarlet, purple and midnight blue, decorated with love hearts and lace. She had always loved her work and got a real buzz from knowing that a campaign had gone well. She would have liked Gemma to do her make-up but as it was her birthday felt she couldn't really ask, and so she'd booked Danni, a cheery Australian make-up artist she'd known for years. Jez was doing her hair and it was great to be back with him. He was the same bitchy, fun-loving mate, except for one thing: he refused to say anything negative about Simone. As soon as Angel mentioned seeing her the day before she expected some witty dig back. None came. Instead he told her, 'It's good you've seen her, I know she wants to apologise to you. I hope you didn't make it hard for her.'

Angel stared at him in stunned amazement. What had happened to all her friends? Had Simone brainwashed them somehow?

'No, I didn't make it hard for her!' she shot back. 'But, frankly, would you blame me if I had?'

'I know you find this difficult to believe but she is a changed woman,' Jez replied. 'People can change . . . look at me. Before I met Rufus I never imagined that I would settle down, but I have, and I'm much happier for it.' He lifted Angel's long hair. 'Up or down, sweetie?'

Angel looked at him in the mirror and frowned. 'I want it curled, but don't change the subject. It is weird for me finding out that you're all pally-pally with Simone, can't you see that?'

'I guess, but I can't help feeling sorry for her. And I wouldn't say she's a great friend – you're my A-list friend, Simone is more like a G-slash-F-list friend. She gets my sympathy vote basically. I think she's quite lonely, I don't exactly believe she's got many really good friends. And it's hardly like we see much of her, just every now and then she phones up for a chat. And I do her hair.' He muttered the last part as if hoping it would go under the radar, but Angel treated him to a glacial glare. Jez simply shrugged,

'Credit crunch, sweetie, I can't afford to turn down business.' Angel couldn't really come back on that one, but she still wondered why Simone couldn't find some friends of her own instead of taking hers. However, she made a big effort not to mention Simone any more. It was bad karma.

'So tell me how the wedding plans are going,' Jez asked, also changing the subject as he expertly teased her hair into curls.

'I'm not really doing anything until the divorce comes through, but I was thinking about maybe having a small wedding, on the beach.'

'How very Pammy of you. Didn't she get married to Tommy Lee in her bikini in Cancun? I wonder what I could wear? I suppose I could get a gorgeous pair of designer trunks, or maybe I should go for a white linen shirt, white trousers combo . . . barefoot with a great pedicure,' Jez mused. Angel didn't have the heart to tell him that she was thinking of not having any guests at all. He might do her an injury with the tongs.

He finished curling her hair. 'There you go . . . perfection.'

The shoot was over and done with quickly. Angel was such a professional that she instantly got what the photographer wanted and it was all very smooth and slick. Then she and Jez grabbed a taxi back to the Mayfair Hotel where she was staying to get ready for Gemma's birthday meal, which was at the Michelin-starred, über-glamorous Hakkasan, followed by clubbing at Movida.

'I think I might need a disco nap,' Jez declared, lying down on the double bed in Angel's suite. 'I'm not as young as I was, I just don't think I can work in the day any more and party at night.'

'You old man!' Angel exclaimed, throwing a cushion at him. 'I expect you to have more stamina!'

'Like your sexy baseball player?' Jez rolled over on to his stomach and propped his head up between his hands. 'Go on then, tell me everything. I might perk up if you give me some salacious details. Like, is he is big as I think he must be?'

Angel threw another cushion at him. 'I would never kiss and tell! I'm a lady.'

'Yeah, right!' Jez exclaimed, rolling off the bed and raiding the mini-bar for champagne. Locating a bottle, he held it up.

'Go on then,' Angel replied, thinking it would be good to get in the party mood.

'So is he?' Jez persisted, handing her a flute full to the brim with champagne.

'Massive,' Angel said cheekily, then took a big sip of champagne, loving the sensation of the bubbles exploding in her mouth.

'What? Bigger than Cal?'

Angel snorted with laughter. 'Behave! I haven't measured them! But please, let's not talk about Cal. I don't want to go on a downer, I want to be happy, happy, happy!' She took another sip of champagne. She'd drunk nearly half a glass.

'And so you shall be!' Jez declared, topping it up.

They ended up drinking a bottle of champagne between them, leaving Angel feeling quite tipsy; she wasn't used to drinking that much any more and had always been a bit of a lightweight with alcohol. Thankfully Jez did her make-up and her hair still looked good from the shoot. Wanting to make the effort for her fashionista friend, Angel wore a white Preen dress, which showed off her beautiful figure and golden-brown skin, with a pair of black Jimmy Choo suede ankle boots. Then it was another taxi ride to the restaurant. Angel walked in smiling as the *maître d'* showed her to the table. This was going to be a lovely night.

Gemma and Tony were already there, along with Rufus and Cal. She experienced the familiar rush of nerves and anticipation at seeing him, but as she took her place next to him, was determined not to let his presence unsettle her. This was her friend's birthday, and anyway the champagne had blurred some of her anxiety about being around him.

'You don't mind me being here, do you?' he asked her quietly as Gemma got down to the serious business of unwrapping presents.

'I'm fine about it, Cal,' Angel replied. 'And anyway, it's not up to me who Gemma invites.'

'Thank you, Angel!' Gemma squealed as she unwrapped the Tiffany charm bracelet. 'That is just what I wanted.' She blew her friend a kiss across the table.

'I know,' Angel shot back. 'You dropped enough

hints!' Then Gemma quickly got on with opening the next gift.

'So you're definitely going ahead with it?' Cal again, clearly not able to bring himself to mention the marriage word though he was looking at her engagement ring.

Angel shook back her hair. 'Yeah, nothing's changed, Cal.' He stared back at her, his brown eyes serious, then glanced away as he said, 'If that's what you want.'

How many more times was he going to ask her this! 'It *is* what I want, Cal.'

Angel took a sip of champagne. 'So you're still seeing Simone then?' If Cal could interrogate her about her marriage then she could play the same game.

'As friends,' he replied. 'I've told you, that's all we are. Why won't you understand that?' He seemed frustrated to be repeating himself.

'That's what happens when someone lies to you, it makes it almost impossible to trust them again.' Oops! So much for keeping it light.

And then, thankfully, he stopped talking to her and instead they all became caught up in teasing Gemma about being so obsessed with fashion, and so demanding. Everyone had to buy her exactly what she had asked for: Cal a bright red ToyWatch, Jez and Rufus a dress from Kate Moss's Topshop collection, and Tony a fuchsia Mulberry clutch bag. She simply couldn't bear surprises – even designer ones.

Then Cal filled them in on how his two football academies were going – one was in Lewisham, one in Brighton, and they aimed to coach disadvantaged kids. This had long been a passion of his and Angel admired him for his dedication in seeing the project through. As he talked she reflected on what a good and decent man he was, in spite of letting her down so badly. He wanted to give something back to the community. In fact, the whole evening was going much better than Angel could have anticipated. And then she caught sight of Simone. Oh my God! she thought as Simone waved at them and walked, or rather sashayed, towards their table. Surely Gemma hadn't invited her? Even if she was Cal's girlfriend.

But both Gemma and Cal looked as surprised as Angel by Simone's appearance.

'Happy Birthday!' she exclaimed. She looked gorgeous in a violet Hervé Léger bandage dress – she must be doing okay financially, that dress cost over a thousand pounds. Angel knew as she had exactly the same one. 'I'm meeting some friends here by coincidence and I brought this for you.' She handed over a small parcel.

'You didn't have to get me anything!' Gemma exclaimed, uncomfortable with the idea of Simone giving her a present.

'No, I wanted to. You and everyone else . . .' she paused here to look round the table, drawing on her acting skills, opening her eyes that little bit wider and looking vulnerable '. . . have been so good to me, I really don't know what I would have done without your support.' She left just the right amount of time to make her point, gazing longest at Cal, then said, 'Anyway, I'll leave you to your meal. It was lovely seeing you all.' And turned to go.

'Wait a minute, Simone,' Gemma called after her. 'Why don't you have a drink with us while you wait for your friends to arrive?'

'Are you sure?' she asked. 'That would be nice actually. I don't like sitting at tables on my own in restaurants, I always feel like a right no mates!'

Angel tried to compose her features into a friendly expression as Simone sat down next to Rufus and opposite Cal. Gemma then opened the parcel to reveal a small Tiffany box, inside which was a horseshoe charm made of diamonds and platinum. How the hell had Simone known to get that? Angel stared at her friend as Simone said, 'I heard you mention to your mum that you'd asked Angel to get you a bracelet, and thought I'd get you a charm for your collection. In fact, I hope you don't mind, but it's second-hand – it's one of mine. I hope it brings you more luck than it did me.'

Oh, bring out the violins! Angel thought bitterly while Gemma exclaimed, 'Thank you so much!' It took all Angel's will power to smile instead of grimace. It felt to her as if Simone was trying to buy Gemma's friendship, which was ironic seeing as when she was going out with Cal she wouldn't give either Angel or Gemma the time of day and had totally looked down on them.

Rufus poured Simone a glass of champagne and she chatted to him about her plans to run the marathon, apparently she intended to run it for Scope, the charity supported by Rufus as his sister had cerebral palsy. Coincidence? Or yet another example of Simone trying to get in Rufus' and Jez's good books?

'Have you ever run a marathon?' Simone asked Angel.

She shook her head. 'I don't really have time for training at the moment. I've got so many work projects on, along with the reality show and Honey as well.'

'You're *so* lucky to have a daughter,' Simone replied wistfully. 'I always thought that I would have a baby by the time I was thirty. It was what I wanted most of all.'

'Really?' Angel couldn't stop herself from sounding sceptical; she had always thought that the only thing Simone dreamt of was securing the attentions and wallet of a successful football player.

Cal shot her a warning look as if to say, Play nice,

which made Angel want to scream with frustration. Why was everyone else so blind to what Simone was up to? She finished her glass of champagne and Rufus poured her another. 'So who are you meeting?' Angel asked her. She had the strongest suspicion that Simone wasn't meeting anyone; that most likely she had overheard Gemma talking about her birthday plans at the salon. 'Two girlfriends,' Simone replied. She looked at her elegant white gold and diamond Chanel watch, which Angel knew had been a gift from Cal when they were together. 'I can't believe they're so late.'

I can't believe they're coming, Angel thought, watching as Simone pulled out her phone from a red Swarovski heart-shaped clutch bag. Another coincidence. Angel had one just like that as well.

'What!' she exclaimed as she read a text message. 'They've blown me out! Nina is not well and Tori has gone on a surprise trip to Paris with her boyfriend!' She reached for her jacket. 'I'd better go then. Honestly, I can't believe those girls . . . they're so flakey.'

Cal raised his eyebrows at Gemma, who got the hint. 'Stay and have dinner with us, Simone.'

'Oh, I don't want to crash your birthday party!' she exclaimed.

'You wouldn't be. It would be nice if you joined us,' Gemma managed to say.

Well, that just about took the fucking biscuit! Angel thought. Her friends might be falling for the poor-little-me act, but they obviously had short memories. Simone was the most calculating woman Angel had ever met.

'You don't mind, do you, Angel?' Simone asked, obviously detecting that Angel was less than thrilled by her presence.

'Not at all,' Angel replied as politely as she could; then had to take a very large sip of champagne to compensate.

'That's a beautiful ring. Can I see it more closely?'
Simone commented,

Angel reluctantly lifted her hand so that she could inspect the engagement ring.

'Did Ethan have it made for you?'

'It was his grandmother's.'

'How lovely that it's vintage! So much history there. And when do you think you'll get married?'

Angel could almost feel Cal tensing next to her, and talking about her marriage in front of her not-even-ex-husband was hardly what she wanted to do. Trust Simone to bring it up.

'Oh, we've not thought that far ahead.' Angel tried to say breezily, then shot a look over at Gemma as if to say, Rescue me. Luckily Gemma was so tuned in to her friend she obliged by asking Simone if she had any acting work coming up.

Angel felt so awkward and uncomfortable in Simone's presence that she ended up drinking far too much. She had hoped that Simone would leave after dinner but somehow she managed to get herself invited to the club. Such a bloody cling on! Angel felt the early happiness of the evening ebb away, and bitterly resented Simone for spoiling this precious night with her friends. By the time they came to leave the restaurant she was feeling decidedly unsteady on her legs.

'Don't you think you should go back to your hotel?' Cal asked her as they were about to pile into the car to take them to Movida.

'No way!' Angel shot back. 'I haven't been out clubbing in London for ages, and I can't wait! Bring it on!' She waved her arms in the air, stumbling slightly as she did so. Cal had to put his arm round her to steady her. Angel smiled at him gratefully, but he shook his head as if to say, What are you like?

'Careful, Angel, you don't want the paps to get a shot of you looking caned.' Simone said it sweetly enough but Angel was sure she was taking the piss. There had been many times in the past when Simone had revelled in the unfortunate encounters Angel had with the paps, going out of her way to comment on them. Angel chose to ignore her. Once in the club she insisted on Gemma and Jez hitting the dance floor with her. Cal and Rufus rarely danced and headed for the VIP area with Simone. A couple of vodka and Cokes ensured that Angel's inhibitions about people looking at her went out of the window as she strutted her stuff. This was so much better than sitting with the poisonous Simone. She loved the way the beat of the music got inside her head. After twenty minutes Gemma and Jez pleaded exhaustion and went back to sit with the group but Angel carried on. She was so in her own little bubble that she hadn't noticed that she had attracted the attention of a number of men, including Daryl Webster, an R&B singer with a truly terrible reputation as a womaniser.

Angel had met him a couple of times with Cal. He was an extremely good-looking black guy with gorgeous brown eyes and the most suggestive smile. He had always seemed like a laugh and Angel had enjoyed his company. He caught her eye across the dance floor. He might be a tart but he was a good dancer. Angel found herself watching his moves with some admiration as he danced closer to her.

'Long time no see, Angel,' he shouted in her ear. 'Fancy a drink?'

She looked towards her party; all of them were deep in conversation. It maybe wouldn't hurt to have one drink with Daryl, then she'd carry on dancing.

He led her towards the bar. 'What can I get you?'

'Diet Coke.'

'Nothing stronger?'

Angel shook her head. 'I know my limits.'

'Diet Coke coming up.'

Daryl was an outrageous flirt. Within seconds of handing over her drink he had told her that she looked even more beautiful than when he last saw her, and that he followed what she was up to in the press.

'You've always intrigued me, Angel,' he told her, giving her his melting chocolate-eyed, brooding look, which no doubt knocked the knickers off most other women but wasn't getting him anywhere with Angel. 'I think you're a bit like me, a free spirit who can't be tamed, but maybe that's because you haven't met the right man yet.' He had made his voice go extra low and husky, she thought.

His speech didn't get quite the reaction Daryl would have hoped for as Angel burst out laughing. She was absolutely nothing like Daryl, who if the celeb mags were to be believed had shagged practically everyone who was anyone, including some mother/daughter combinations. She held up her hand so he could see her engagement ring and he reciprocated with a pained expression, and put his hand over his heart, flashing a bling-bling skull-and-crossbones ring. He really wasn't her type but she was enjoying watching him try it on with her and, because she was immune to his attempts to charm her, found it very entertaining.

'So who are you seeing?' she asked him, certain that he would be seeing someone.

'I'm single at the moment, just need some time to sort my head out.' He paused. Cue smouldering gaze. 'But if you were to be free, I reckon my head would be sorted out in no time.'

Angel laughed, and pointed at her ring again. He was so blatant! 'So, who dumped you?'

He frowned. 'Why do you say that?'

'Well, it's just not like you to be single, and I'm guessing you were dumped and haven't had chance to line up the next girl. So how long have you been single?'

Now the wounded frown was replaced with a smile. 'Fuck, you've got me! I was dumped this morning. And, Angel, I have to tell you that *never* usually happens to me. I think it might have had something to do with her catching me out flirting with her best friend. But, like I said, I just need the love of the right woman to keep me faithful.'

They both laughed at this, and then, because he realised he'd been rumbled, Daryl stopped trying it on and they actually had a conversation about his work and about how her life was in LA. In fact, they were getting on so well that Angel lost track of the time. It was only when she saw Cal walking towards her that she realised she must have been talking to Daryl for ages. He gave Daryl the briefest of greetings before saying, 'We're all heading off now. D'you want a lift back to the hotel or are you staying?'

He sounded like her dad! And looked really stern and judgemental. Half of Angel wanted to stay on at the club just to make the point that she could do what the fuck she liked and it had fuck all to do with him, but she figured that she had better go back, otherwise she would be totally wasted in the morning.

'I'll come, I just need to go to the bathroom.'

She waited until Cal had walked away and then turned to Daryl. 'See you then. Nice talking to you.'

'Can I get your number? I'm due in LA in a month or so and it would be good to see you.'

'And Ethan,' Angel prompted.

'Yeah, and Ethan, but you most of all,' Daryl said cheekily as Angel reached for her mobile and they both exchanged numbers. She was still smiling to herself as she went to the bathroom; to her the encounter with Daryl had been a friendly bit of banter, you couldn't even call it flirtation.

'Had fun with Daryl Webster? You seemed to be getting on very well together.'

Simone had joined her in the bathroom, standing next to her as Angel checked her make-up in the mirror. No way was she going to be photographed looking a mess by the waiting paps outside.

'He's a laugh,' Angel replied, rubbing away the smudged mascara under her eyes.

'Very good-looking,' Simone continued.

'Very.'

'So are you going to see him again?'

Angel really didn't like the way Simone was interrogating her. What business was it of hers?

'Maybe,' she said casually. 'He might be over in LA so we could hook up . . . with Ethan, of course.'

'Of course,' Simone said sweetly.

But her interrogation was continued by Angel's friends on the journey back to her hotel. Jez was dying to know all the details of what Daryl was like; Gemma was green with jealousy that Angel had spoken to one of her music crushes; even Tony was impressed. Only Cal was silent, looking out of the window and radiating disapproval. He barely said good night to Angel when she was dropped off at the Mayfair.

As Angel made her way up to her suite some of the euphoria of the evening started to wear off as she registered how sad it had felt, spending time with Cal. It's just the alcohol, she tried to tell herself, thinking that she'd feel okay once she had spoken to Ethan. It was after 3 a.m. and 7 in the evening in LA. Ethan would be chilling out in his games room.

'Hey, what are you doing still up?' he exclaimed playfully.

Angel tried to shrug off the sadness as she said, 'Wishing you were here with me! I'm drunk and feeling very, very naughty. And I wanted to tell you that I love, love, love you!'

Ethan laughed, 'Well, save it for when you get back. Now go get yourself a large glass of water and take some painkillers, otherwise you're going to feel like hell in the morning. You know you can't take your drink.'

'Cheek!' Angel exclaimed. 'Can too! And I feel just fine!' She omitted to mention to Ethan that she now had the spinny-head feeling and the room was revolving before her eyes.

'Call me in the morning your time. You can tell me then.' Angel took his advice and then practically passed out in bed.

In the morning she felt every bit as rough as Ethan had predicted. She was just trying to will herself to get up when there was a knock at the door of her suite and one of the maids presented her with an extravagant bouquet of velvety red roses. She was just about to text Ethan to thank him when she read the card and discovered they were from Daryl, saying how much he had enjoyed meeting her and that he was looking forward to seeing her again. Maybe what she had taken for playful banter, he had taken for flirtation? Angel sincerely hoped not, she didn't want any other complications in her life. She ordered breakfast in bed and thought no more about it before heading off to Jez's Islington salon where he was going to redo her highlights. Just as well. She wasn't up to doing any work and Cal had Honey, so Angel could just relax.

She and Jez were having a great time gossiping when Angel's mobile rang. She frowned when Benny's number flashed up and almost considered not taking the call, then pressed the Accept key. Benny didn't bother with any niceties like saying hello before he launched in with, 'What the fuck were you doing with Daryl Webster last night? I told you if you ever messed with Ethan, I would personally take it on myself to fuck up your life. You've only been engaged five fucking minutes!'.

'Er, hello, Benny. It's none of your business what I was doing . . . not that I was doing anything.'

'Yes, it's my fucking business! Anything that effects Ethan is my fucking business! So did you fuck him? Give him a blow job? What? It would be better if I knew everything. Ethan's saying that he doesn't believe you would do anything like that. But I know better. I know what girls like you can be capable of.' He was back to sounding vengeful and full of hatred as he had at his party, but rather than feeling shaken by his outburst, Angel was quietly furious. No way was Benny going to get away with speaking to her like this.

She held the phone away from her ear as Benny carried on ranting and Jez gave her a WTF look.

Then she moved the handset closer as she said coldly, 'Benny, nothing happened. And if you *ever* speak to me like this again, I will do everything I can to persuade Ethan to get another agent.'

And before he could fire off any more abuse, she ended the call.

'I can't believe that!' she exclaimed to Jez, then filled him in on what Benny had said, though he had heard much of it as Benny had been shouting. 'And how the hell did he know anyway?'

'I guess someone could have tipped off the press that you were talking to Daryl – you're both so well known it was bound to happen.'

'I'd better call Ethan, I don't want him freaking out that something has gone on. Bloody hell Jez, why is my life always so complicated!' He gave a sympathetic shrug.

Fortunately Ethan was completely cool, saying that he trusted her and knew nothing would have happened. That Benny had over-reacted and he would talk to him about it. He didn't know how his agent had found out about her encounter with Daryl, but suspected it was from one of Benny's many press contacts.

But as Angel spoke to Ethan, she found herself wondering if that was the case; found herself wondering if perhaps Simone had something to do with tipping off the press. Angel knew the other woman was short of money, and whatever front she was putting on she had no great love for Angel. Simone would have been perfectly placed to make that call. She had certainly gone out of her way to question Angel about Daryl. Trouble was, Angel had no proof, and if she mentioned it to Jez or Gemma they would no doubt think she was laying the blame at Simone's door because she didn't like her.

She had barely come off the phone when Susie called her, and wasted no time getting to the point. 'So what's all this about you and Daryl Webster, flirting all night and then going back to his hotel? Not that I blame you . . . he is sex on legs! I'd do him any day of the week! So what was he like?'

Angel rolled her eyes at Jez. Some relaxing day this was proving to be! 'There is nothing going on between me and Daryl, it's all crap, Susie, so if any journalists contact you, can you simply say that, yes, I did talk to him. But he was one of many people I spoke to last night and we're just friends. I'm happily engaged to Ethan, remember?' How dare Susie think she would be so quick to jump into bed with another man!

'Just friends?' Susie said suggestively, then laughed.

165

'Not that old line! I always think it's code for "shagging each other's brains out"!'

'Susie!' Angel exclaimed sharply.

'Sorry, Angel, I didn't mean to suggest anything. But just think this story is still good for you profile.'

It was so not! Angel thought crossly and said abruptly, 'Got to go Susie, I'll see you when I'm back in LA.'

And she switched her phone off for good measure. She didn't need any more calls about Daryl Webster. She was starting to regret her little chat with him, she had forgotten how the press here always picked up on every single thing she did, picked it, twisted it and then printed a lie.

Chapter 11

'Has Daryl got a new Angel?' screamed the headline in the *Sun* the following morning. Susie didn't seem to have done a good job of defusing the story, Angel thought bitterly as she scanned the article. A 'friend' had told the paper that the pair had seemed smitten with each other, that Angel had confessed she was seriously having doubts about her marriage to Ethan, and that they had spent most of the night together in the club, hardly able to keep their hands off each other . . . not that old bloody tabloid cliché! The couple were said to have left the club separately, only to meet up at the Mayfair Hotel where guests were said to have commented on the loud noises coming from their suite. As if!

Angel angrily threw the paper across her mum's kitchen table, disgusted by the blatant lies. 'I haven't read that yet!' Frank said accusingly, from his position at the head of the table where he was ploughing his way through a plate of bacon and egg which Michelle only allowed him to have once a week now, drawing the line at fried bread.

'It's all crap!' Angel exclaimed. 'I can't believe they can get away with printing it. And I bet I know who "the friend" is,' she added darkly.

'Who's that then?' Michelle asked, sitting down with her bowl of muesli.

'Simone bloody bitch-face Fraser.'

Michelle winced. 'She was never very nice to you was she?' A typical understatement from her mum.

'And I never knew what Cal saw in her,' Frank put in.

Blimey! Her dad was actually criticising Cal. Angel couldn't resist pointing it out. 'Not like you to say anything bad about him.'

'Why do you say that?' Frank asked.

Angel pushed her yoghurt and blueberries around in the bowl; she was trying to be healthy after overdoing the drink. 'Well, it's just sometimes I feel that you think Cal is perfect, whatever he does.'

Frank shook his head; he hated being criticised. 'I've never thought that. I just think you shouldn't be rushing into marriage with this Ethan.' Okay, finally her dad had come out with what had been bothering him.

'He's not *this* Ethan!' Angel exclaimed hotly. 'And I'm *not* rushing into it. I love him and it's the right thing to do.'

'You could wait a bit longer, though, couldn't you? I don't see the need for the urgency. It seems spiteful somehow.'

'Spiteful to who? Oh, to Cal? He's the one who couldn't keep his dick in his pants when we were married!'

Frank frowned at the expression; he had always been a bit staid in his ways, a little bit sexist. He thought it was fine for men to swear like troopers but that ladies shouldn't. Both he and Angel were getting very wound up – Frank's breakfast lay untouched as did hers. It was left to Michelle, as so many times in the past, to try and smooth things over between father and daughter.

'Come on, you two! Angel's going back tomorrow, don't part on a quarrel.'

'I'm not,' Frank said gruffly, pushing his chair away from the table and getting up, 'I just think she needs to think a little longer about what she's doing. She's got a daughter now; she needs to be more responsible. All this rushing headlong into marriage with a man none of us knows anything about . . . it's not good.'

'It's your fault if you don't know anything about him – I've asked you over enough times!' Angel shouted back. But Frank ignored her.

'Aren't you going to have your breakfast?' Michelle asked as he headed out of the kitchen.

'I've lost my appetite,' Frank called back. 'I'll see you later.'

Angel's bad mood only continued when she met up with Gemma and found herself pursued by the paps round Brighton. 'Simone's got a lot to answer for,' she said crossly as they went into Pret for coffee and to escape the cameras.

'Why do you think it was Simone who tipped off the press?'

Angel glared at her friend who was wearing the Tiffany charm bracelet. She noticed the diamond horse shoe amongst the charms.

'It's precisely the kind of thing she'd do. Or do you think she's turned into a bloody saint?'

'But there were lots of other people in the club, it could have been anyone, and it did look like you and Daryl were getting on well.'

'I was just having a laugh!' Angel exclaimed.

'And you could have come and sat with us, rather than wandering off with the first hot singer who comes your way.'

'I'm sorry, Gem. I was just dancing. And I didn't want to sit with Simone, it was bad enough having dinner with her.'

Surely Gemma wasn't pissed off with her about that?

Simone really was doing a good job of turning Angel's friends against her if so. But luckily Gemma sighed and said, 'Yeah, and now she's given me this charm, I feel like I have to be nice to her all the time!'

'Sell it on Ebay and give the money to charity,' Angel urged her.

Gemma stroked the horse shoe protectively. 'But I've always wanted one!'

'So you are happy to sell your soul for a Tiffany charm?' Angel took the piss out of her friend. They both laughed, but Gemma couldn't resist adding, 'Just because you could buy yourself any number of Tiffany charms and not even notice a dent in your bank account!'

'Okay, point taken. I can't stand the woman. And I don't trust her. I can't help feeling that she's trying to buy your friendship. And what was all that about her suddenly wanting to run the marathon? She never used to be into running.'

'She's lonely, isn't it obvious? I think all her old WAG friends dropped her when they found out about the drugs and everything. Honestly, Angel, don't get so wound up by her.'

Angel gave a wry smile. It was pretty hard not being wound up by someone like Simone, but equally she didn't want it to be the only subject she talked about with her friends. There was a lull in conversation as both women sipped their lattes then Gemma commented, 'Cal didn't seem himself last night.'

'What do you mean? He seemed okay – well, he was being judgemental and uptight because of me talking to Daryl, though I don't know why that was any of his business.' Even as Angel said it, she thought how she would have felt seeing Cal in close conversation with a good-looking woman.

Gemma shrugged. 'He finds it hard being around

170

you. And you marrying Ethan has really thrown him. I think he always hoped you would come back to him, but now he realises that's not going to happen.'

'He's said this to Tony?' Angel asked, unsettled by the comment.

Gemma shook her head, 'Nope, I can tell. I have known Cal for seventeen years. I saw the way he looked at you. But you're marrying Ethan, so I guess he has to get used to it.'

Was her friend trying to make her feel guilty? Tell her that she was doing the wrong thing by marrying Ethan? Angel wasn't having any of it. She shook her hair back defiantly. 'Yeah, I'm marrying Ethan.'

It was Angel's last day in Brighton before she and Honey flew back that night. She and her dad maintained a polite front with each other as Angel returned home to pack. No way was she going to be the first to apologise when he had been so totally in the wrong, and Frank was just as stubborn. Then Cal came round with Honey and Angel got the cold treatment from him as well. So much for Gemma thinking he was pining for her!

'I saw the story, Angel,' he said, not even bothering to say hello but standing in the tiny hallway, looking moody, hands shoved into the pockets of his black leather jacket, a frown on his face.

'Yeah, well, it was all a load of bollocks!' she exclaimed.

'You did talk to him for a long time, and he has got a reputation.'

'Talking being the word!' Angel shot back. 'Nothing happened, Cal. He didn't come back to my hotel room – as you well know. You dropped me off! Do you really not know me better than that!' She just hated him having a go at her, as if it was anything to do with him

171

any more. He didn't have any say in her life. He had forfeited that right a long time ago.

Cal shrugged. 'Like I said, he's got a reputation. So will you see him again?' He sounded so judgemental, it made Angel want to provoke him.

'I might if he comes over to LA. He's a laugh.'

'And d'you think that's a good idea?'

Angel wanted to stamp her foot with frustration! 'I'll see him with Ethan, of course. And maybe he could be in our reality show and that would prove to people we're just friends.'

'I don't think Daryl has women as friends, just shag conquests.' That was so like Cal, he had to get the last word in. Now it was Angel's turn to shrug. She busied herself with getting Honey's things together. She couldn't wait to get back to LA after all this shit, even more so when she got a text from Daryl saying he was sorry about the story and hoped she would still be up for meeting him again. She sent back the blandest reply she could, saying everything was cool and that he was welcome to come round to house for dinner with herself and Ethan.

'So did you miss me?' Ethan demanded when he met Angel and Honey at the airport. 'Not too busy hanging out in night clubs and flirting with singers. You *dirty* girl!' His tone was teasing, thank God, Angel couldn't deal with anyone else being on her case.

'Don't you start!' she exclaimed, wrapping her arms round his neck and not caring that they were being photographed by the waiting paps. 'Take me home and you'll find out how much.'

It was so good to see Ethan again, and he genuinely wasn't wound up about Daryl. He was so easygoing, so uncomplicated. Indeed, he thought the whole thing was hilarious. As soon as Angel had settled Honey in

172

bed and walked into the living room, 'Hot Love', one of Daryl's biggest hits, began blasting out of the speakers. Angel looked at Ethan, who was laughing at her confused expression.

'He sings a bit like a girl, I really don't get his appeal,' Ethan commented. 'He is good-looking, though, I'll give him that. So, you promise you weren't tempted?'

'I really wasn't,' Angel replied. 'Now come here.' She hooked a finger into the waistband of Ethan's jeans and pulled him towards the sofa. 'He's way too girly-looking for me. I need a real man, like you.' She undid the buttons on his shirt, loving the feeling of his bare skin against her hands. It felt so good to touch him again. In the background Daryl sang his heart out. Angel suddenly stopped. 'Babe, can't you turn that off?'

Ethan reached for the stereo remote and silenced the track. 'That's better,' she murmured. 'Now I can really show you how much I've missed you.'

Afterwards they lay in each other's arms on the sofa. 'So I've told Benny that no way can he ever speak to you again like that,' Ethan was saying. 'He swore he wouldn't. He was being over-protective again and realises he was jumping to all the wrong conclusions. He's just not used to me being in a relationship. Before you, the women came and went pretty quickly.' Ethan gave a wry smile. 'And Benny did have to get me out of some sticky situations, shall we say?'

Angel sighed. While she was glad Ethan had said something to Benny, she couldn't see his agent and manager changing his attitude towards her any time soon.

'But I'm also putting out feelers for other agents,' Ethan said, surprising her. 'I've been with Benny a long time, it might be good to have a change. And if he doesn't listen to what I've said about you, I really will fire him.' She had never expected Ethan to come out with *that*.

'I've told him as well, so you should see a big improvement in Benny's attitude towards you. And I've told him he has to apologise to you.' Angel couldn't believe for a second that Benny was going to like that.

However, the next time Benny saw Angel he was back to being Mr Nice Guy, polite, quiet, with none of the leering or poisonous glances and certainly no inappropriate comments.

'I'm sorry I jumped to conclusions about you and Daryl,' he told her when he dropped by to go through the couple's filming schedule. 'It was wrong of me and I apologise. I hope you will accept my apology and that we can move on.' He spoke with apparent sincerity, as he had after his outburst at the party, but Angel doubted he meant it; he was simply saying it out of fear of loosing his best client. And she would never forget the way he had spoken to her.

But in the weeks that followed Benny continued to be polite to Angel. Gone were the snide comments about how lucky she was, a mere glamour model, to be with Ethan. Even if he was just putting on an act it was a definite improvement. It was good not to worry about that side of her life as she had plenty of other things to worry about. Her dad was continuing to be disapproving of her and Ethan, and that had filtered through to her brother Tony who was also giving her a hard time about divorcing Cal. It made for some tense phone calls. As for Cal, he was doing his distant thing. When he phoned to speak to Honey, he kept conversation with Angel to the minimum, with no hint of what he might be feeling. And when he flew over to LA to spend two weeks with their daughter in a rented house just along the coast from Angel, there were no invitations to her to spend the day with them. Sometimes she felt as if she had dreamt about the day with him in Santa Monica all those months ago.

The divorce came through and there was a flurry of interest in the press, but neither Angel nor Cal commented. Even though Angel knew that she was doing the right thing, she still felt horribly sad when she received the decree nisi, ending the marriage. She had never imagined her marriage would end like this. There were several days when she felt incredibly blue and wanted to see Cal, to tell him that she was sorry. But she didn't. Her marriage to him was over and now she had her future with Ethan to think of. Loretta's health was continuing to decline and Angel knew that she must get on with planning the wedding, knowing how important it was that his grandmother should see Ethan married. Realistically, for Loretta to be present Ethan and Angel would have to be married within three months. Angel was still sticking to the idea of having a small wedding, if it was up to her there would be no other guests apart from Loretta, but Ethan talked her round.

'If you don't ask your parents and your brother, things are going to get really tough between you,' he said one evening as they sat outside in the garden. Candles were flickering around them and Jose had thoughtfully lit a fire.

Angel sighed, 'I know. It's just I couldn't bear it if my dad didn't look totally happy for me, and it is *my* day.'

'*Our* day,' Ethan corrected her, smiling.

'Nah,' Angel teased him. 'People only ever care about the bride on her wedding day. What she looks like . . . what's she's wearing. You're just my support act.'

'Tell you what,' Ethan said, reaching out for her foot and massaging it – he gave a very good foot massage – 'why don't we ask your parents over? I'd like to get to know them better.'

It was a really thoughtful gesture, and maybe Frank's attitude would soften once he had spent some more time with Ethan and had seen what a genuinely nice guy he was.

Or not. Angel found out two weeks later when she met her parents off their flight at LAX airport along with Ethan and Honey. From the moment Frank arrived he began complaining – the flight had been so long, he hadn't slept (this in spite of Angel paying for first class tickets for them), he had a headache, it must be because of the heat (it was a lovely 23). Why was there so much traffic on the freeway? (There wasn't by LA standards.) He barely spoke to Ethan, addressing all his comments to Angel.

She made him a cup of tea and packed him off to bed, hoping that his mood would have improved after a good night's sleep. Michelle stayed up a little longer, talking to them both. She tried to make up for Frank's offhand manner by complimenting Ethan on the house, commenting on practically everything, from his pictures to his furniture to the light fittings, in the end driving Angel almost as mad as her dad had. Even easygoing Ethan looked strained.

'I'm sorry about Frank,' she said apologetically, on her way up to bed. 'He's not a great traveller, I'm sure he'll be in a better mood in the morning.'

Angel waited until her mum was well out of earshot before saying to Ethan, 'D'you want a drink? I'm going to have a very large glass of wine.'

Ethan had training the following day and rarely drank, but he nodded fervently and said, 'Can you get me a beer? In fact, get me two, I think I need them.'

Everyone's hopes that Frank's mood would have improved by the morning were dashed when he appeared at breakfast in an even fouler temper. He hadn't slept well, he'd woken at 4 a.m. and been unable to get back to sleep. No, he didn't want to have breakfast by the pool, he wanted it in the kitchen, and did Angel have an English paper?'

'You can go online, Dad, if you need a fix of news. That's what I do.' Angel told him, trying to stay calm but feeling increasingly infuriated by her dad's attitude.

Frank tutted, 'All this money and I can't get to read the paper!'

'Come on, Frank, don't be so ungrateful,' Michelle put in. 'You tell Maria what you want for breakfast. I'm going to sit outside with Angel and Honey. I've got to make the most of this lovely sunshine before I go back to the rain.'

'Nothing wrong with a bit of rain,' Frank replied moodily. 'It's good for the garden. And too much sun gives you skin cancer anyway.'

Even the usually placid Michelle was gritting her teeth as she walked away from her husband, 'Honestly, that man would argue black was white!' she exclaimed to Angel. 'I don't know what's got into him!'

Angel sat down by the pool and served Michelle up a bowl of fruit salad. 'I can see why you love it so much out here, love, it's beautiful,' her mum told her, looking out across the ocean. 'Just ignore your dad, I'm sure he'll snap out of it once he sees how happy you and Ethan are together. He is lovely, by the way. Not just lovely-looking but he seems so kind – and I can see that he really loves you.' It was the nicest thing she had ever said about Ethan, and Angel smiled. 'I am really happy,

I just wish Dad could see that. And I'm sorry about the divorce, but it wasn't my fault.'

'No, it wasn't. I know that, love.'

'Anyway, let's not talk about it. There's nothing more to be said on the subject of me and Cal. It's over and Dad just needs to realise that.'

But in spite of Angel, Ethan and Michelle's best efforts, Frank remained cantankerous for most of the visit. Ethan had arranged for them all to go and watch a Dodgers game and for them to have the best seats in the stadium, but Frank yawned and tutted his way through the game. Angel just hoped Ethan didn't catch sight of his grim expression.

'Is this really a sport?' Frank asked in a loud voice at a particularly crucial moment in the game, earning him several disapproving looks from the spectators around him. Annoying as her dad was, Angel didn't want to see him lynched and so shushed him and whispered, 'We're outnumbered here, Dad, so maybe you could keep your opinions to yourself.'

Frank duly heeded her warning but was morose during the meal out afterwards to celebrate the Dodgers' win. Ethan took them to Koi, a Japanese restaurant where the food was divine. Frank's only comment was that it was 'too rich and fancy' for him, and he would have rather had a steak. Back home he went to bed complaining of indigestion, followed by a long-suffering Michelle, while Angel and Ethan retreated to the games room.

'I think your dad might have broken my spirit,' Ethan exclaimed, sprawling on the sofa. 'I'm usually so optimistic but he's draining me, babe. It's a miracle you turned out so well adjusted.'

Angel flopped down next to him. 'I know, but he's not always like this. Maybe it will help when we see Loretta tomorrow. If she can't charm him, no one can.'

Frank was still complaining about indigestion in the morning and for a time it seemed as if he would miss out on seeing Loretta, but then Angel cornered him in the kitchen where Maria had just served him up a plate of eggs, waffles and bacon. 'So you're not feeling so bad then, Dad?' she exclaimed while Frank looked suitably guilty. Angel whisked the plate away from him. 'I really think you'd be better off with a bowl of yoghurt, or even a glass of hot water and lemon. Unless you do feel better, in which case you can have the breakfast and then we'll go and see Loretta.'

Frank looked longingly after the plate. Angel ramped up the guilt. 'You know, Loretta has really been like a mother to Ethan, and it would mean a great deal to him, and to me, if you met her. I've told you how unwell she is. She's hasn't got much time.' Just talking about it brought a lump to Angel's throat. 'So, you will come won't you?'

Even Frank couldn't maintain his grumpy-old-man act in the face of such a comment. 'Of course I'll come,' he conceded.

'And be nice?'

'Aren't I always?'

Angel rolled her eyes but rewarded him with the cooked breakfast.

Loretta was her wonderful charming self later that afternoon as she greeted them in her living room. She was too weak to get up and was lying on one of the sofas. Although she was dressed in a beautiful lilac silk dress and had obviously taken extra care with her appearance, she looked worse than ever, so frail. Angel bit her lip in concern and looked at Ethan, who seemed to hide how upset he was by fussing over Loretta, asking her if she had everything she needed.

He received short shrift from her. 'Ethan, stop fussing over me! I admit that today is one of my off days, but it's still lovely to see you all. Now you can do something useful – pour Frank and Michelle a cup of tea.' She managed to smile at Angel's parents. 'I even got in PG Tips, on Ethan's orders. And perhaps we can have a glass of champagne to celebrate Ethan and Angel's engagement?'

Angel looked warily at her dad to see how he'd take the comment, but he was smiling. Usually in social situations Frank left Michelle to do all the talking, while he contented himself with monosyllabic replies and most likely thought about football, so Angel was surprised to hear her dad really making an effort. He pointed out the photograph of Loretta on the white baby grand piano, which had been taken when she was in her thirties and starring in a romantic comedy which had been very popular at the time.

'I remember you in that film. You were so beautiful. I never imagined I would get to meet you one day.'

'Alas, no longer looking as I did,' Loretta replied, looking wistfully at the picture of her younger self. 'More ancient withered crone than love interest.'

'Not at all,' Frank replied. 'You're still a beautiful woman, and I see that Ethan has you to thank for those eyes of his.'

Wow! It was very unlike her dad to be charming. Angel could hardly believe what she was hearing. 'Now shall I open that champagne?' Frank went on, standing up and reaching for the bottle from the silver ice bucket. 'We should have a toast.'

Finally Ethan was getting to see her dad in a good light. Angel was hugely relieved. Maybe she would be able to plan for a bigger wedding and involve all her family? They stayed for a couple of hours, Frank insisting on looking through some of Loretta's photo albums, prompting her to reminisce about her film roles. He gently flirted with her, treating her as if she was still the great beauty that she once had been.

'And now have you got any pictures of this young man?' Frank asked, pointing at Ethan. 'I feel I'm getting to know him and he's a real credit to you, Loretta.'

'He's a credit to himself,' she replied, 'I don't know what I would have done this past year without him.' She paused. 'And I know you've had your reservations about him and Angel.' Frank went to interrupt her, but Loretta shook her head. 'I know you have, Frank, but I hope you will see what I do – two people who are very much in love and who need the support of their families behind them. I know it would just about break Angel's heart if you weren't fully in favour of her marriage. She adores you, Frank.'

Not for nothing had Loretta been a leading actress. Frank, who rarely showed any emotion, practically had tears in his eyes at her speech. He looked over at Angel, and said gruffly, as if trying to disguise his emotions, 'I admit I haven't always been pleased that you're marrying Ethan.' An understatement if ever there was one. 'But spending time with you both this week has changed my mind. I can see that Ethan is a good man, and that he really loves you. And if it's what you want, then you have my blessing.'

At this Loretta clapped her hands and declared, 'More champagne for everyone! I feel like I've just played a scene in a soap opera . . . exhausting, but exhilarating too!'

Angel, who often had the feeling that her life resembled a soap opera, could only smile and hug Ethan. That night, back at the beach house, they sat outside having a BBQ, Frank and Ethan bonding over bottles of Bud, and even though Angel felt great sadness for Loretta, in all other ways she felt incredibly happy. She was moving on with her life, no longer stuck in the painful past.

Chapter 12

Angel and Ethan set their wedding date for 15 June, only two months away. They had decided on a private ceremony at the church Loretta went to, with just family and a few close friends, and to have the reception at Ethan's house. Neither of them wanted a grand formal affair. Besides, if they had it at the house, they could make sure it was secure from the paps. And Angel wanted to make this wedding as different as possible from her wedding to Cal, which had been a grand and lavish affair.

But just as they got underway with their wedding plans there was a sudden explosion of negative stories about Angel in the press. '*Secret Shame of Ethan's Angel . . . She's no Angel . . . Threesomes and Drug Addiction: Does Ethan know what he's getting into?*' blazed the headlines on the tabloids and in the celeb mags. Benny and Susie called a crisis meeting at the house to discuss what to do about it.

'Why now?' Angel asked, picking up the *National Enquirer* which had raked up the story of her having a threesome with her ex, Mickey, and a hooker . . . not that Angel had known she was a hooker, and she'd only had the threesome to please Mickey at a time in her life when she was incredibly vulnerable. 'These stories have already been out years ago, they're old news.' She had

183

been through it all before, had lived the humiliation and shame, had her regrets, but knew that brooding over past mistakes would not help.

Benny shrugged. 'You're marrying Ethan, one of the most eligible bachelors in the States. Go figure.'

'Well, what can we do about it?' Ethan asked. 'You know the press. You know how they work. Can't we put some positive stories out there?'

'We could do a photo shoot and in-depth interview with a publication like *OK!*. I'm sure they'd jump at it, especially if we got pics of the kids as well.' That from Susie, even though she knew that Angel did not want Honey to be photographed.

'And we need a publication on your side,' Benny carried on. 'I'm sure if we could sell exclusive rights to photographs from your wedding, that would help. Then whoever buys the rights will be more inclined to put out favourable stories about you now. You scratch my back, I'll scratch yours kind of thing.' Susie looked at him lovingly, as if approving his remarks. Love certainly was blind, Angel thought bitterly.

'Our wedding photos aren't for sale,' Ethan said forcefully.

'Oh, come on!' Benny exclaimed, dropping the Mr-Nice-Guy act he'd been cultivating for the last month. 'This is what we've been working towards! You could each make a million dollars if we set this up.'

'Aren't you forgetting your cut?' Ethan said dryly.

'I'm not thinking about me! I'm just thinking about you. It's what I always do. I always have your best interests at heart. You're not going to be a star baseballer player for ever. You need a back-up plan.' Benny reached into his pocket, pulled out a cream silk handkerchief and mopped at his brow which was gleaming with sweat.

184

'He really does,' Susie added, rubbing Benny's arm affectionately. 'Just as I have your best interests at heart.' She looked over at Angel.

Spare us the bullshit! Angel thought.

Benny looked over at Ethan, ignoring Susie's adoring look. 'Will you at least think about the wedding?' He snapped open his Louis Vuitton monogrammed briefcase and pulled out a selection of magazines, all of which had covered a celebrity wedding. 'Take a look at these, and you'll see it can be done stylishly. And it can be as understated as you want. You set the agenda.' He slid the magazines across the glass table towards Ethan, who looked at them with disdain and didn't attempt to pick them up. 'Or we can sell the pictures through an agency, if you think that will suit you better.'

Ethan didn't reply.

'Okay then, Susie and I will leave you two to have a think. We'll put together a positive press campaign for Angel. It's going to be a tough call, though. That's quite some past you have there, missy – orgies and cocaine. Anything else we should know about? S&M parties? The press always love a bit of bondage. And I'm sure you look real pretty in leather. Still, at least you got it all out of your system.'

There was a flash of the old lecherous Benny there, seeming to want to goad her into saying something. Angel just shrugged. Bullies like him thrived on the oxygen of someone's reaction and she wouldn't give him the satisfaction. But Ethan wasn't going to sit by and allow Benny to speak to Angel like that.

'And your past is perfect, is it, Benny? I suppose you'd love the press to hear about every detail of your private life? Don't ever speak to Angel like that again or you will no longer be representing me.' Benny looked as if Ethan had just punched him in the guts.

Susie was quick to jump to Benny's defence, 'Oh Benny was just joking Ethan, he didn't mean anything.'

Benny turned to her, treating her to a venomous glare from those cold grey eyes, 'I don't fucking need you to speak for me.' Then he looked over at Ethan, 'I'm just watching your back, it's what I've always done. I apologise if I spoke out of line.' A muscle was twitching in his jaw with the effort of being polite.

'Yeah well, Angel and I have got things to do,' Ethan glared at Benny, arms folded, effectively dismissing the couple. Benny got up and strode out of the room closely followed by Susie, who paused to say quietly, 'He really didn't mean those things seriously, Angel. Benny adores you.'

Yeah right! Angel thought as Susie dashed after Benny, her heels clicking against the marble floor.

'That was some start to the day!' Angel exclaimed after she'd heard the front door slam. She expected Ethan to come back with a light-hearted reply but he seemed wound up and paced across the living room.

'Babe, are you okay?' Angel asked. 'Don't let Benny get to you.'

Ethan spun around. 'Christ, Angel, how can you sound so cool! Benny seemed as if he was really getting off on taunting you. No way am I tolerating that! I warned him not to speak to you out of turn and he does it again, blatantly, in front of me. He thinks he's indispensable to me, but d'you know what? He isn't.' He paced some more before adding, 'And I've got a bad feeling about all those stories in the press. It wouldn't surprise me if Benny wasn't the one behind them. That would be his style . . . manipulating everyone, especially us, so that we panic and sign the wedding pictures deal to stop the bad press.'

Angel gazed at Ethan in surprise; he certainly seemed to have woken up to Benny's true nature.

'I'm going to phone my lawyer. Get him to send the letter putting Benny on notice. I'm sick of him causing tension in our lives.'

Ethan stopped pacing; he seemed to have made his decision.

'Hang on a minute,' Angel said, shocked. 'Maybe you're getting this all wrong. Benny isn't my favourite person and he doesn't like me, but he is a good agent. Why don't you at least find out for sure if he's playing straight with you and if you can trust him?' She couldn't believe that she was defending Benny, but she didn't want Ethan to do something he might later regret.

He came and sat down next to her. 'How do we do that?'

Angel thought for a moment. 'Tell him something that only you and I know, and see what happens. If he leaks it, after you make him promise not to say anything, then we'll know.'

'What kind of thing?'

'Oh, I've got a good idea,' Angel replied, smiling. She was really going to enjoy catching Benny out.

They waited a couple of days and then Ethan invited Benny over, telling him he had some important news for him. Benny was back to working his charming act. 'Hey, gorgeous, you look beautiful,' he told Angel as she sat on the edge of the pool, dipping her legs in the water to keep cool. She gave a fake little smile in acknowledgement. Benny retreated under the large parasol. 'So what's the big news, guys?' Benny asked, looking inquisitively at Ethan. He was tapping his foot almost impatiently. Angel guessed that he must hate not being in the position of power.

'Hold on a minute,' Ethan replied, 'I need Angel by my side to tell you. Come on, babe.' She got up and came and sat next to him. Both of them were wearing sunglasses and she could see Benny's overly fake-tanned face reflected in Ethan's Aviator Raybans.

'First off, Benny, this is for your ears only,' he said seriously. 'Neither of us has said anything, not even to our families, and at the moment we don't want anyone else to know. Especially not the press.' Angel thought she might giggle; Ethan was playing his part perfectly.

Benny held his hand up. 'I understand. Whatever you guys tell me will go no further, you have my word.'

Yeah, right, Angel thought. For all that was worth.

'Okay, here goes then.' Ethan actually looked behind him as if to make sure no one else could hear. Damn, he was good! Maybe he could consider an acting career when he stopped playing baseball. 'It's great news actually . . . the best.' He paused to smile at Angel and reach for her hand – and, of course, to prolong Benny's agony. She pretended to cough to mask the giggles that were threatening to escape.

'Okay, here goes – Angel's pregnant, we're having a baby!' Ethan exclaimed. 'Isn't that awesome?'

Benny beamed at the pair of them, flashing his perfect dentistry. 'Congratulations, you guys! Wow! That is awesome!' And he shot up from his seat to hug first Ethan and then Angel. 'So when's the baby due?'

Damn! Angel hadn't thought to work out a due date. 'Ummm . . . just around Christmas.' she blustered.

'A Christmas baby? That's beautiful.'

'Yeah. I've had to put my foot down about naming him Jesus, if it's a boy,' Ethan put in, and Angel really had to fight to stop the laughter.

'So I hope you'd be up for the role of godfather?' Ethan was certainly milking this for all it was worth.

Benny actually put his hand on his heart. 'Me? I would be honoured.' Angel could have sworn there were tears in his eyes.

188

'So, I hope he's taking good care of you, Angel,' Benny asked, doing his concerned act now.

'Oh, he is,' she replied, and Ethan reached out and protectively rubbed her stomach. Now maybe that was going too far. Angel put her hand over his to stop him. 'Wouldn't it be great if we had a boy? I mean, I know all that matters is that the baby is healthy, but can you imagine . . . a boy?' Ethan enthused. 'I could teach him all I know about the game.'

Benny's cold grey eyes were now glinting with greed. He must have been thinking about the press opportunities the pregnancy and birth afforded.

'We're not having a mini-me!' Angel teased back.

'It's a wonderful thing,' Benny mused.

'But like we said, we don't want anyone else to know. When Angel's reached the end of the first trimester, then we'll release it to the press. She doesn't want Susie to know either, Benny. It's a question of trust. So if you could keep it to yourself, we'd appreciate it.'

Benny looked thrilled to have been told the news before Susie. 'You can count on me. So does this affect the wedding plans at all?'

Ethan shook his head. 'Going ahead as before.'

'And have you thought any more about the photographs?' Benny was not going to give up on this.

'We're still thinking about it, Benny.'

'Sure, I understand – you guys have got a lot going on.' He checked the time on his diamond-encrusted watch. 'I've got another meeting to go to, so I'll catch up with you later.' He stood up and gave Ethan a congratulatory slap on the back and treated Angel to another kiss. 'I am thrilled for you both, but hush-hush.' He put his finger over his lips for emphasis then headed back into the house. Angel snuggled up to Ethan and didn't say a word until she heard the roar of Benny's Porsche starting up in the drive.

'What do you reckon?' she asked. 'Think he fell for it?'

'With my superior acting skills? You betcha.'

'Babe, you were good, I give you that, but I don't think Brad Pitt has anything to worry about just yet.'

'He might be able to take me on the screen, but I bet I'm better than him in the sack.'

'Yeah, you've had all that practice!' Angel teased back. 'You should be!'

'Want a reminder?' Ethan slid his hand between her legs.

'I don't know if I should, with the baby and all,' Angel said coyly.

Ethan's caresses grew more insistent. Angel melted.

'Oh, all right then, I'll race you inside,' she murmured.

'I love sex in the afternoon!' Ethan declared some time later. He was lying back in bed with his hands behind his head. He turned to look at Angel. 'I love sex any time with you.'

Angel smiled and rested her head on his broad chest. She felt sleepy now and Honey wasn't due back from nursery for at least another hour, but she was jolted out of her doze by Ethan's next comment. 'I'd really like to have a baby with you. I mean, I know we were kidding around with Benny, but as we were saying it, I suddenly thought how I would love it to be real.'

Angel lifted her head and gazed into his blue eyes. 'You really mean that?'

Ethan nodded. 'Since Megan I've felt it, but I don't want to put any pressure on you. I know it's early days and there's no rush, but wouldn't it be great to have a baby? I'd kinda feel it sealed our life together.'

Angel knew that she did want another baby, had known it for a while, but she couldn't help feeling wary, considering the crippling post-natal depression she'd suffered after the birth of Honey. But if she had another baby, at least she and Ethan would know the warning signs. He was smiling at her and she thought about how much she loved him.

'Okay, maybe we needn't be so careful. Let's just see what happens.'

And as she said it, she felt a rush of excitement at the thought of having a baby with him. That would surely free her from her past; she would have a new family.

Ethan wrapped his arms around her. 'That would make me *so* happy.'

'And what do we do about Benny?' she asked.

'We wait and see what he does. Knowing Benny, he went straight home and started working out a strategy for who to leak the news to first.'

'Maybe he won't leak it at all,' Angel replied, feeling all mellow and loved up. She felt as if she was in a golden glow and didn't want to let the bad thoughts in.

'Maybe he won't,' Ethan replied, but didn't sound convinced.

But there were no news stories in the week that followed, almost lulling the pair of them into a false sense of security. They were in their own bubble of happiness. Other brides-to-be might have been stressing out about the dress and the catering, but Angel was genuinely chilled. Gemma had recommended a new designer who might be able to design Angel's dress, but Angel didn't really mind what she wore. She'd had the big white dress once already, she wanted something different this time. Or at least she thought she did. And as for the catering – she wasn't going to get hung up on hors d'oeuvres and seating plans. Instead they were going to have a BBQ buffet and people could sit wherever the hell they liked.

'What do you mean, you don't mind what you wear?' Gemma sounded outraged on the phone during one of their chats when Angel admitted that she hadn't given her wedding dress much thought. 'You can't just wear any old thing!'

'Gem, I know you can't imagine this, but I really don't care – it's about me and Ethan, not about some expensive dress that I'll never wear again.'

Angel could just imagine Gemma rolling her eyes on the other end of the phone. 'How about I fly over and help you? I've got some holiday and Tony can't take time off at the moment.'

'I'd love it if you came over, but I don't want us to spend all our time looking at clothes – one day only and the rest chilling. Deal?'

'Deal.'

But it was a deal that Gemma had clearly no intention of keeping as she arrived a week later with a suitcase full of magazines and ideas for Angel's dress, which she insisted on getting out the very night of her arrival. Ethan took one look at the table laden down with magazines and headed for his games room.

'But you should be involved in this,' Gemma called after him, 'You need to co-ordinate with Angel.'

Angel had a sudden flash back to Gemma's own wedding and how she had agonised over every single detail, right down to the colour of Tony's socks. Fortunately Tony was head over heels in love with her and had submitted to her every demand.

'I'm going to wear a black tux for the wedding and then I'll probably change into a tee-shirt and jeans for the reception. Angel can wear what the hell she wants, she'll look gorgeous whatever.'

Gemma wrinkled her nose. 'A black tux is so pre-dictable – what about a cream suit? Or maybe white . . .

say with a blue shirt? And have you thought about shoes?'

'See you later, girls,' Ethan replied, and practically jogged out of the room so as not to receive any more of Gemma's pearls of fashion wisdom.

Angel laughed at her friend's appalled expression. 'I told you, Gem, we're just not bothered.'

'But you could have anything you want! Any designer . . . any style.'

'I want simple,' Angel insisted.

'What are you? Bloody Amish all of a sudden? A wedding needs sparkle and bling!'

Gemma flicked through the magazines, every now and then holding up a picture of a stunning dress, none of which fitted into the simple category, unless ten-foot lace trains and whopping great tiaras counted as simple. Angel alternated watching Honey draw – or rather scribble with her crayons – with shaking her head at every page Gemma showed her. Finally, just as Gemma was about to admit defeat, she held up a picture of a beautiful white dress, a strapless creation with a fitted bodice and a full white skirt made up of layers and layers of tulle, studded with crystals Suddenly Angel felt her resolve to keep it simple waver.

'Wow, that is gorgeous!'

Gemma's eyes lit up. 'It is! And it would be so *you*.' She studied the caption. 'Even better, it's by an up-and-coming Japanese designer and it looks like he's based here. I'm going to call him.'

And with that she reached for her phone, found his number, called him up and arranged for Angel to go to his workshop the following day.

Angel looked at her friend in awe. Gemma was like a tornado when she wanted her way: nothing could stop her.

*

Gemma looked as if she might explode with happiness the following day when they went to the airy open-plan workshop. There was rail upon rail of beautiful clothes: sumptuous rich purples, delicate pinks and creams and whites, fabrics of slippery silk, pearly satin, all studded with crystals and pearls.

Kaz, the twenty-something Japanese designer, pulled out dress after dress for Angel to look at, but she had her heart set on the ballerina-style dress. Finally he held it up.

Gemma gave it the critical once over and conceded, 'Yes, it's definitely you.'

'Try it on,' Kaz told her, pointing out a screen in the corner. Angel slipped off her denim mini skirt and vest and slid into the dress. It was slightly too big, but as soon as she looked in the mirror she knew it was the one. It accentuated her curves, her beautiful neck and slim shoulders, and she loved the way the full skirt made her feel like a princess.

But as she looked at her own reflection she couldn't help thinking back to her wedding day with Cal, remembering the look on his face when he saw her in her stunning white dress for the first time. The memory bought unexpected tears to her eyes, which she hastily brushed away as Gemma called out, 'Let's have a look.' She was just upset because anyone would be, thinking of a failed marriage. It didn't mean anything more than that. Angel emerged from behind the screen, standing before Gemma.

'Well, what do you think?'

Her friend smiled with approval and said, 'It's beautiful. You should wear it with your hair up, and maybe a simple necklace. Nothing else. Too many accessories would ruin it. And I would say wear it with ballet pumps rather than heels. Or maybe start with heels for the ceremony and slip into pumps later.'

194

Gemma had definitely missed out on her calling to be a stylist.

Angel twirled round in front of the mirror, watching the full skirt flare out. The dress was beautiful, but suddenly she didn't feel any sense of excitement or anticipation about the wedding.

'Ethan is going to be blown away when he sees you in that,' Gemma told her.

'It is perfect,' Kaz backed her up, 'I just need to take it in here.' He pulled in the fabric round Angel's waist.

'The dress is perfect but maybe I shouldn't be going for something as grand as this.' She turned to Kaz to explain, 'This will be my second marriage.'

'Is that any less of a reason to celebrate?' he replied.

'Kaz is right,' Gemma agreed. 'Your marriage to Ethan deserves a dress like this. You've got nothing to feel guilty about.'

'You mean that?' Angel asked. It was the most positive thing Gemma had ever said about her relationship with Ethan.

'I do. I can see how much he loves you, and you seem really happy together. I didn't get that before, but I do now.' Gemma never said anything unless she really meant it.

Angel was hugely relieved to know her friend was finally on her side. She had missed the closeness she'd had with Gemma. But her next comment floored Angel. 'Cal's seeing someone else now. That French model – Madeleine Fournier. He seems happy too. So everything seems to have worked out for both of you.'

Why then did Angel suddenly feel as if she had lost something? I am happy to be marrying Ethan, she told herself, as if it was a mantra. It doesn't matter if Cal is seeing someone else. He's free to do exactly what he wants. But later that night, when Gemma was in bed and Ethan was out seeing some friends, Angel found herself irresistibly drawn to her laptop to Google Cal and Madeleine – and there they were on several of the tabloid websites, photographed leaving Scott's restaurant in Mayfair together, holding hands. They made the most stunning couple. It shouldn't have affected her but it did, even more so when she read the accompanying article about how 'smitten' Cal was said to be with the French beauty. How theirs was a relationship which had built up over the last few months and was now serious, and how they were supposed to have been seen house hunting in Chelsea. Angel felt sick with jealousy.

Chapter 13

However, she barely had time to obsess over Cal as the following day news of Angel's 'pregnancy' appeared in the press. Benny had excelled himself. The story was splashed across several publications but it wasn't a straightforward leak: he had put a vicious spin on it. *'Ethan's Angel is pregnant, but is he the father?'* screamed the headlines, and the articles went on to talk about rumours that Angel didn't know who the father of her baby was; that she had confided to 'a friend' that it might be Daryl Webster, the singer.

'Son of a bitch!' Ethan shouted when he read the story. He was genuinely rattled. Outside the house the paps were already camped out in force, itching to get their picture. Angel got the familiar feeling of claustrophobia their presence aroused in her. She hated knowing that they were just over the fence and that she and Ethan would be pursued wherever they went, considered fair game for photographers who didn't give a shit about people's feelings. Indeed, Angel often wondered if the paps even saw them as people at all. To them she and Ethan were just commodities, whose image could be sold to the highest bidder.

Giving Benny the false story had seemed like a bit of a joke to Ethan and Angel and they had enjoyed the power over him, but, boy, had he turned the tables. To Angel it seemed that Benny had used the story as a way of getting back at her for the grovelling apologies he'd been forced to make. It showed the full depth of his hatred for her. The man was poison.

'That's it!' Ethan declared. 'That motherfucker is out of my life once and for all.'

'You're sure?' Angel asked. They were sitting by the pool with breakfast laid out, but neither of them felt like eating. Gemma had left for the airport several hours earlier, which was a pity as Angel could have done with her friend's company right now.

'Never been more certain,' Ethan said grimly. 'I've given him enough second chances. Benny was out to get you from the start . . . I should have seen it. He's a jealous, twisted little guy. I suppose I didn't want to think badly of someone who's been such a major part of my life for the last ten years. But that's it, the end of an era. I'm going to phone Abe right now and get him to courier Benny the letter terminating his contract.' He reached for his phone, all set to call his lawyer.

'Don't you want to speak to Benny first? Give him the chance to explain himself?'

'Give him the chance to try and wriggle out of it? No, I'm through with Benny Sullivan.'

It was a mad day with Ethan on the phone first to his lawyer and then meeting with Julia, the woman he had temporarily appointed to do his PR, so that they could put out a statement contradicting the news story and announcing Benny's dismissal. Angel remembered how much Ethan had depended on Benny when she had first known him; how he'd always valued Benny's opinion. It seemed awful that things were ending like this, but Ethan was rising to the challenge and she saw a steely determination in him that she hadn't seen before.

Angel had some calls of her own to make, and had to spend several hours phoning her mum and dad and friends to let them know that, contrary to the news stories, she wasn't pregnant. She even got a cheeky text from Daryl saying he wished that he had been in the position of potentially being the father of her child. She showed it to Ethan who replied that maybe he didn't want Daryl round to the house for dinner after all, if he was going to come out with lines like that.

Benny would have received the letter of termination by early-afternoon. Every time Ethan's phone rang after that Angel kept expecting it to be Benny or that every time the doorbell rang he would be there, trying to talk his way out of what had happened. But there was no word from him. Instead, in the early evening, Susie turned up. She looked as if she'd been crying.

She wasted no time in getting to the point. 'Take him back, Ethan, you'll not get a better manager than Benny, not ever. That man would do anything for you, I swear.' Ethan surveyed Susie coolly from where he sat back on the sofa, arms folded across his chest. He was entirely unmoved by her protestations.

'He broke my trust. There can be no going back.'

'Oh, come on, Ethan – you know the pregnancy story is only going to raise your profile further. It'll make the bidding war for the wedding pictures even more ferocious.'

'I told him I didn't want anyone else to know, and look at the spin he put on it! I'm not having my wife-to-be talked about in the press like that. Benny knew exactly what he was doing when he leaked the story.'

'But he only had your best interests at heart. Believe me, Ethan, the man worships you.' She tried even harder to lay it on. 'You're like a son to him.' She turned to Angel then. 'You must talk him out of this.' There was an edge of desperation to her voice – she was no longer the kick-ass, in-control agent.

'Don't involve Angel, this is between me and Benny, no one else.' However hard Susie was trying, it wasn't working with Ethan. 'In fact, if you could excuse us, Angel and I have several other meetings.'

Effectively dismissed, Susie stood up. 'It's not too late,' she appealed one last time.

Angel and Ethan were silent as she walked from the room, shown out by Jose. Then Ethan spoke. 'You know, maybe you need to speak to Carrie and get her to take over again, if Susie carries on her relationship with Benny. She doesn't exactly seem to be thinking straight at the moment.'

'I'll see how it goes,' Angel replied, wondering how much longer Benny and Susie would last. 'D'you still want to go the cocktail party tonight?'

Tyler, one of Ethan's team mates, was holding a party at Bar Marmont to celebrate his birthday. Angel was sure that Ethan wouldn't want to go; and she had no desire to face the press.

'Of course we're going to go!' Ethan exclaimed, surprising her. 'Otherwise it looks as if we've got something to be ashamed of.'

This was not the answer she had hoped for. 'What if Benny's there?'

'There's no reason why he should be, Tyler's not one of his clients. And, if he is, I'll deal with it.'

Reluctantly Angel went upstairs to get ready; she could have done with a cosy night in to recover from the day. But when they arrived at the swish bar, thankfully without being papped, she felt her spirits lift. No one was looking at her as if she was a whore, they seemed genuinely pleased to see her, and it was clear that no one believed the outrageous stories in the press. She and Ethan spent a pleasant couple of hours drinking Bellinis and chatting to Alisha and Logan.

'Told you it would be okay to come out,' Ethan told her as they got ready to leave.

But he had spoken too soon. Both of them froze as they saw Benny Sullivan weaving his way through the guests, heading straight for them. Angel's heart sank. She really had hoped that she'd seen the last of him. Ethan reached for her hand as Benny arrived in front of them.

'We're just leaving, Benny,' Ethan told him.

Benny glared at him. 'Ten years I've worked for you . . . ten fucking years! I took you on when no one else was interested, helped make you all those millions, and *this* is how you pay me back?' His face was sweaty and he was breathing heavily, as if struggling to contain his emotions.

'You broke my trust, Benny, and I'd had enough of the way you treated Angel. Our business relationship is over, there's nothing more to be said.'

Again Ethan made to go but Benny blocked his way. He jabbed his finger at Angel. 'You chose *her* over me? Some worthless piece of trash? She'll be screwing some other sucker before you know it. The bitch has got form.'

Angel felt Ethan tense next to her and instinctively felt that he was about to punch Benny. She held tightly to his hand. 'Let's just go, Ethan, please.'

'Take back what you said.' He spat out the words.

Benny shook his head. 'The truth hurts doesn't it?'

God knows how Angel would have held Ethan back but thankfully Logan turned up then and moved between the two men. 'Ethan, I really think you and Angel should go. Benny can stay here with me and we can have a little chat about how he is not going to bother you two again or things could get very uncomfortable for him.'

Ethan remained where he was for a few seconds but then seemed to take on board Logan's advice. 'Don't ever come near me and Angel again,' he hissed as he walked past Benny.

Angel felt really shaken up by the encounter. It was so disturbing knowing how much the man hated her. But she tried to keep it from Ethan, not wanting to give him any further reason to want to settle the score with Benny. She just hoped that it would all blow over.

In the meantime she had Cal to deal with. He was over in LA for one of his visits to see Honey. They had done a good job of avoiding each other so far but Angel was due to pick up her daughter the following day. She would have to see Cal then, and no doubt he would have seen the news story and have a view on it. And she still couldn't shake off that feeling of jealousy about him and Madeleine. But she was determined to breeze in, collect Honey and make a quick exit.

Cal's house was just along the coast from hers, an ultramodern place, painted white, with a roof garden, and surrounded by palm trees. He and Honey were swimming in the pool, the housekeeper informed Angel when she opened the door to her. It was strange walking through Cal's house, seeing all the furniture he had chosen for himself and the many photographs of Honey on the walls. Angel looked out for pictures of Madeleine but there were none. Instead, just as she was about to go out to the pool, she noticed the photograph of Honey, Cal and herself taken on Santa Monica beach all those months ago. He's probably just put it up for Honey, she told herself, but couldn't help finding it surprising that Cal would have a picture of her on his wall. Did it perhaps mean that he still had feelings for her, in spite of seeing Madeleine? What did he think when he looked at it?

She stepped outside on to the decking and into the glorious sunshine, a smile on her face ready to greet her daughter . . . and did a double take. Because reclining on a white sun lounger by the pool was a stunning-looking blonde, clad in a tiny red bikini that showcased a knock out figure. Angel didn't think this was Madeleine so who the hell was she? She didn't exactly look like nanny material.

'Mummy!' Honey called out in delight.

Angel averted her eyes from the blonde bombshell and walked over to the pool where she sat down at the edge, waiting for her daughter to swim to her.

'Hey, I didn't realise what the time was,' Cal said. 'I'll just get Honey out of the pool.' He picked up his daughter and climbed out, treating Angel to a view of his gorgeous body as the water ran off his olive skin.

'Hiya, Angel,' called out the blonde. That voice sounded horribly familiar. Angel spun round as the blonde strutted towards her, and then froze as she realised it was none other than Simone bitch-face Fraser!

'Didn't you recognise me?' Simone gave an annoying tinkly laugh. 'I've decided to test out the old saying that blondes have more fun.'

What the fuck was she doing here? Was Cal seeing her as well as Madeleine? Angel bristled at the thought of one of her least favourite people spending time with her daughter, and at Cal's continuing inability to tell her the truth about his relationship with Simone. She was too gobsmacked to reply

'Simone has several auditions over here and I said she could stay at the house,' Cal explained her presence.

Yeah, right! Like there aren't enough hotels in LA, Angel thought.

'It was so sweet of Cal, but you know how generous he is.' Simone flashed him an adoring glance and stretched her arms over her head as if drawing attention to her lithe body, especially her boobs which were threatening to burst out of the tiny red bikini top. 'I love it out here, Angel, I'm really hoping I get a part then I can stay. I've got a new agent who thinks that there will be lots of possibilities out here for me. And you'll have to tell me all the cool places to go. I really want to throw myself into my new LA life.'

This woman was incredible! Did she really think Angel was going to end up as her new best friend? Well, she could spin on that! And the blonde hair didn't suit her, she'd looked so much better as a brunette. Angel busied herself wrapping Honey up in a white fluffy towel, which saved her from having to make a reply other than a cursory, 'Oh, right.'

But that wasn't going to deter Simone who carried on, 'Press giving you a hard time, I see. Still, on the plus side, at least you're well enough known out here that they write about you. And it's not like you haven't had to deal with bad press before, is it?' That comment earned her a frown from Cal and she was temporarily silenced, not wanting to say anything out of turn in front of him.

'Are you okay?' Cal asked Angel. 'I could always delay my flight if you needed me to have Honey while all this is going on.' He was drying himself with a towel; she tried not to look at the angel-wing tattoo.

'Thanks, but I'm fine. It will all blow over soon.' She wanted to say, Don't you have a supermodel you need to get back for? But didn't. 'It always does,' she sighed.

'Actually I was thinking about Honey, I don't really want her to be caught up in the press shit.'

Oh, typical of Cal to try and gain the moral high ground!

'She won't be, Cal,' Angel said defensively, and it was on the tip of her tongue to say that nothing could be as bad as the press attention when they'd found out about his affair. 'Can I get Honey's things? I really should be going.' She had quite enough to deal with already without having Cal doing his judgemental number on her.

'See you around then, Angel,' Simone called out as Angel headed for the door. Not if I can help it, she was sorely tempted to reply, and couldn't resist calling back, 'Be careful in the sun, Simone. It's hotter than you think and so ageing for the skin. I'd wear a hat, if I were you, there are a lot of very *young* actresses looking for work in LA.'

It was a low blow and Cal flashed her a warning glance, but Angel couldn't care less about his disapproval.

Inside the house Cal quickly got Honey dressed and handed Angel her rucksack.

'So there was no truth in the story?' he said quietly. 'I mean, I know the part about Daryl was rubbish, but the other?' He paused, seeming not to want to say the words.

'No, I'm not pregnant.' And Angel had to stop herself from adding 'yet', wanting to show Cal that she had moved on with her life.

'I see,' he replied coolly, his barriers well and truly back in place.

'So does Madeleine mind about Simone staying with you?' Damn, she'd stumbled over saying 'Madeleine', and why the fuck was she mentioning her at all?

'Of course she doesn't, why would she?'

'And how's it going with her? She's very beautiful.'

'It's going well. Why are you so interested?' He reached out and lightly touched her hand with the engagement ring on it, as if to say, You've made your choice. Angel suddenly felt hot and short of breath. Cal was right, why was she so interested? But her next question was no better at defusing the tension.

'So Simone is just here as your friend?'

Cal clenched his jaw, clearly infuriated with her for asking the same question again. 'As I've told you, nothing's changed on that score. She is just a friend. Will always be just a friend. I don't have any other feelings for her and never will have. She's too fucked up and needy.'

It was unfortunate for Simone that she chose that moment to sashay through the French doors into the living room. For a second she faltered as she registered Cal's words and looked utterly crushed. And Angel thought again that while Cal's feelings for her might simply be those of a friend, Simone's were in an entirely different league.

Cal helped her get Honey into the car. Angel was all set to drive off when he stopped her. 'Did you know that you've got some graffiti on there?' He gestured at the door of the front passenger seat. Angel, who loved her car, was livid and shot out of the driver's seat to take a look. Someone had scratched the word 'Bitch' into the door. It looked horribly stark against the pristine midnight blue paint, like some kind of warning. For a few seconds she stared at the crudely scratched letters, feeling chilled. There was something so personal and hateful about the word.

'It was probably some kids fooling around,' Cal tried to reassure her.

'Some kids who knew I was a woman?' In spite of the warm sun Angel suddenly felt cold. She folded her arms defensively and looked anxiously over at the tall wooden security gates. Surely no one would have climbed over them?

'Everything okay?' Simone appeared at the front door, in a sheer white kaftan. Now *there* was someone who really did think Angel was a bitch, however hard she pretended not to. But surely it couldn't have been her, unless she could shape-shift into a bat and fly round the house! Not that Angel would put anything past her. And, of course, there was Benny . . .

Cal filled Simone in. 'That's terrible, Angel! D'you think you've got a stalker!' She sounded almost excited by the prospect.

Way to go, Simone! Why not make me feel really uptight? Angel thought.

'It's just kids,' Cal replied. 'It probably happened when you were out shopping, Angel. Don't make a big deal of it, Simone, can't you see that Angel is upset?'

'Sorry,' she replied, twirling a lock of blonde hair round her finger, 'I was just concerned for her.' Simone sounded neither sorry nor concerned, something that didn't pass Cal by as he gave her a scornful look. Better brush up on the old acting skills if you want to keep in with Cal, thought Angel.

Ethan took a very different view of the graffiti and insisted on calling the police, in spite of Angel's protests. 'Babe, we're in the public eye and there are some nutters out there. It's better to be safe than sorry.' The young officer who was sent out to take a statement some time later that afternoon saw the incident from Angel's point of view. There was no other evidence that pointed to a stalker, but when he asked Ethan and Angel if there was anyone who might have a grudge against them, Ethan came out with the first name that had sprung to Angel's mind.

'Benny Sullivan, I just fired him. And we had a pretty unpleasant encounter with him last night.'

The officer dutifully wrote the name down in his notebook and then advised them to review their security, but it was clear that he thought Ethan was over-reacting and that it was only because he was such a huge star that the police were bothering to follow up on the incident.

'Let's go out and grab a bite to eat with Honey, we'll take her to that diner she likes,' Ethan said once the officer had left. 'I kinda feel I want to show whoever trashed your car that we don't give a shit. In fact, while we're out, I'm going to buy you a new car.'

Angel couldn't help smiling at Ethan's over-the-top offer. 'Seriously, babe, you don't have to get me a new car! We can just get mine resprayed.'

'I'm going to. You can choose whatever model you want.' Ethan wrapped his arms around her. 'Think of it as an early wedding present.'

It was easy to forget about what had happened in the late-afternoon sunshine, surrounded by people out to enjoy the evening. They were pursued by the paps as they drove off and later as they got out of the car, but once they were in the diner they were free from the unwanted attention. Angel didn't have much of an appetite so sipped a strawberry shake and watched Ethan and Honey tuck into burgers and fries, helping Honey out by snitching the odd fry from her plate when she wasn't looking.

'And now on to the showroom,' Ethan declared when they'd finished. His money troubles were far behind him now and he had the Porsche salesman practically falling over himself in his eagerness to serve Mr Turner.

'So, babe, which one do you want?' Ethan asked as Angel surveyed the gleaming motors. She did adore a car. 'I think I like that one.' She pointed out a cream Porsche Cayenne. 'I love the colour!'

'Excellent choice,' Mr Porsche Salesman agreed, and went on to reel off the specifications of the luxury motor, which Ethan pretended to be interested in when Angel knew for a fact that he was just putting on an act. While he loved fast cars, he knew nothing about them.

Some $50,000 later – Ethan would pay the rest in monthly instalments – they were on their way back home. As he punched in the security code on the keypad by the gate, Angel looked around her, wondering if the cars parked alongside the road belonged to paps or to the stalker. Ethan caught her looking.

'I'm going to call in the security guys now, get them to go over the place and make sure there are no weak points. I don't want you to worry about anything.'

Angel couldn't help thinking then that Ethan should have got rid of Benny a long time ago – he was so in control of everything now, and she liked this new decisive side of him. While he made the security arrangements, Angel gave Honey her bath and then put her to bed.

'Daddy say night-night?' Honey piped up just as Angel bent down to kiss her.

'Oh, baby, you'll see daddy very soon,' Angel exclaimed, fearing that the older Honey got, the more she was going to want to see Cal. She sat with her daughter a while longer until she fell asleep, then wandered into her dressing room intending to phone Gemma. She felt like she needed a chat with her friend after the day's events, hoping that Gemma would make her laugh.

She was busy fumbling for her mobile in her bag when a flash of red caught her eye at the far side of the room. 'Oh my God!' Angel exclaimed as she took in the

209

word 'Bitch' written in red lipstick on her dressing-table mirror. She froze for a second then raced back to her daughter's bedroom, terrified that whoever had written it was still in the house. 'Ethan!' she shouted in the hallway. No answer. She shouted again, looking fearfully around her.

Ethan raced up the stairs. 'What is it?'

'Someone's been in here.' She pointed at the mirror in the dressing room and had the unsettling thought that the word looked as if it had been written in blood.

'Shit!' Ethan immediately dialled up the police on his mobile, who promised to send a unit right away.

Angel remained in the doorway of Honey's bedroom as if guarding her daughter. 'What if they're still here?' she whispered, feeling totally creeped out.

'I'm sure they're not,' he reassured her. 'I'll check round with Jose.'

Angel grabbed his arm. 'Please don't leave us! I'm really scared.' It was one thing to find out your car had been vandalised, quite another to discover that there'd been an intruder inside your house. By now Jose and Maria had come upstairs, wondering what the noise had been about, and Maria stayed with Angel while the two men checked out the many rooms.

'Don't worry, Angel,' Maria tried to reassure her. 'I'm sure the police will catch them.'

'But how did they get in?'

Maria shrugged helplessly. 'I don't know, but Jose and I were out food shopping all afternoon. There was no one here then.'

The next couple of hours were taken up with the police getting statements from Ethan, Angel and the staff, and checking through the house. There was no sign that it had been broken into; whoever had got in was either let in or had a key. Ethan had CCTV but when the police checked the tapes they discovered they were blank, the day's output having been erased, most likely by whoever broke in. This showed a level of knowledge of the house which made Angel feel even more uneasy. It didn't seem as if anything had been taken, but when Angel went back into her dressing room with the police to check if everything was there, she opened her walk-in wardrobe and screamed. One of her dresses – a long red Valentino number, one of her favourites – had been slashed all over with a knife. It had been carefully arranged on the floor as if the intruder wanted to make the maximum impact. Angel took one look at the garment which made her think of a woman's body, no doubt the image intended by the intruder, and then bolted into the bathroom to be sick. Even the police seemed to take the break-in more seriously after that and told Ethan they were sending a squad car round to Benny Sullivan's to interview him. Angel couldn't help wondering if there would be some other nasty message left for her to find too.

She couldn't stop shaking, even after drinking the sweet tea Maria had insisted on making and after putting on one of Ethan's sweaters. She couldn't face touching anything in her dressing room, was going to have to have everything washed and the whole room repainted. It felt contaminated, violated. Whoever had done this hated her, really hated her, and wanted to make her afraid. It showed a sick, calculating mind. Angel thought of Benny's cold grey eyes raking over her, his threats to fuck up her life. The police found the third piece of work by the intruder in Ethan's games room where a picture of him and Angel had been defaced. Angel's eyes had been cut out and the word 'Bitch' written on her dress in red.

'Who would do such a thing?' Ethan shouted, visibly shaken.

It was a question the police were no closer to

answering when they finally left at midnight. Their visit to Benny Sullivan had revealed nothing as he had an alibi after spending the day in meetings with clients, all of whom could vouch for him. And yet it seemed to Angel that he was the only one who could have such a grudge against them. But when she voiced her concerns to Ethan, he said that he couldn't believe that Benny would jeopardise his whole career by doing something like this.

That night Ethan and Angel slept in Honey's room. A team of locksmiths had changed all the locks, but Angel had to be close to her daughter and Ethan didn't try and argue with her. Angel hardly slept. Whenever she closed her eyes she saw the red dress lying on the floor. She had the strongest feeling that was how the intruder would like her to be.

The next day Ethan pulled out of training, to be with her and Honey and to sort out new security arrangements. He had hired bodyguards for them. Part of Angel wanted to say that this was an over-reaction, the other part was relieved, especially when she met the two guards, Carlos and Brandon, both of whom were ex-marines and built like tanks.

'I want them with you whenever you go out until this sick fuck is caught,' Ethan told her. 'You and Honey are going to be safe, I swear.'

Even with the security guards and beefed-up security – they'd increased the number of CCTV cameras and put in another alarm upstairs – Angel still felt jumpy and couldn't bring herself to go into her dressing room. Maria had gone shopping to buy her some basics and had sent everything else to be cleaned, but Angel couldn't imagine ever wanting to chill out in that room again.

'We can move house, if it makes you feel better,'

Ethan told her as they sat by the pool watching Honey splashing happily about in a rubber ring, thankfully oblivious to how anxious her mother felt. She looked at Ethan. He absolutely loved it here, but she knew he was serious.

'Of course we're not going to move!' Angel exclaimed, trying to sound as if she meant it. 'Then I would feel like that mad person has won . . . and no way do I want to give them that satisfaction.'

They were brave words but she couldn't live up to them when she went back inside the house to get drinks for everyone and ended up smashing several glasses when she jumped in fright as Maria came into the kitchen. She really needed to get a grip but couldn't shake off the sickening feeling of apprehension that something else was going to happen. It was hardly how she wanted to feel in the run up to her wedding. The only good thing was that she had barely thought about Cal and Madeleine.

'I'm flying back tomorrow,' Susie told her as they sat out on one of the balconies having tea. Her agent had called by two days after the break-in. She was sorry to hear about the incident but seemed distracted. Angel had expected Susie to urge her to give an interview to the press about what had happened, that was her usual style, but she seemed subdued. Susie looked at Angel and she was surprised to see tears in her brown eyes. She had always thought that Susie was really tough.

'He dumped me,' Susie said simply. Angel prepared herself for the inevitable tirade that was sure to follow, about how all men were bastards and she was a million times better than him and he couldn't get it up anyway. None came. Angel was stunned when Susie said, 'I love him but he doesn't love me. I don't think he cares about me at all.'

'I'm sorry, Susie, I had no idea you felt that way about Benny. Though, to be honest, I think you're well out of it. He was so threatening and abusive to me, and I think he might even have been behind the break in.'

'No way would Benny do something like that, Angel! Whatever he said, he's just bitterly hurt about Ethan firing him.'

Angel gave a non-committal 'Ummm' while Susie pressed on. 'For the first time, I felt as if I'd met my match. We could have been a great partnership – and not just at work.' Susie sounded so bitter and hurt. 'With Benny I felt I could finally be myself because he's vulnerable as well, underneath it all.'

About as vulnerable as a cobra! Please let Susie not expect Angel to have any sympathy for Benny Sullivan.

'I don't expect you to understand, Angel. You and Ethan, you're the beautiful people, you can have anything or anyone you want. Benny and I are just there to serve people like you.' God, she was sounding so melodramatic, Angel felt like Susie needed a reality check.

'Susie, that really isn't how I see you, so please don't think that. You're upset, I understand.'

Susie seemed to gather herself at this. 'Yes, well, I had hopes that Benny and I had a future together. But there you go. Life's shit then you die.' What had happened to her perky, can-do-anything optimism? It seemed to have left the building.

She stood up. 'I'll see you back in the UK, Angel. I'm not sure if LA is a place I'll want to be for a long while to come. I'm sorry I'll miss the wedding.'

They exchanged air kisses and then Susie headed out of the house, escorted by Carlos. But judging by the appreciative look Susie shot at Carlos and his bulging biceps Angel thought it perhaps wouldn't be long before Susie got over her heartbreak. She felt sorry for her. She had seemed genuinely upset, but Angel was also relieved – her being involved with Benny had been just too close for comfort.

Chapter 14

In the week that followed, Angel tried to get on with her life and push away her anxieties that the stalker was watching her every move. She did a shoot to promote a swimwear range, had a fitting for her wedding dress and took Honey to her art and ballet classes. But every time she returned to the house she had sense of foreboding that something else would have happened; the house no longer seemed like the beautiful sanctuary it had once been. And every time she had a free moment, she couldn't resist looking up Cal and Madeleine even though it made her experience a toxic mix of jealousy and sadness when she saw them photographed together, something which she didn't want to reveal to any of her friends. No, she would get over it and everything would be fine.

She was jolted out of this when Cal sent her a text asking her if she was okay and could she phone him. As soon as his name came up on her phone Angel felt a flutter of anticipation in her stomach. She thought about leaving it a while before phoning him, but couldn't resist calling him straight back. But Cal only wanted to know about the new security arrangements for the house, asking how secure it was for Honey and then ending the call by saying he was late for dinner, leaving Angel yet again wondering about him and Madeleine.

At the weekend Logan and Alisha were throwing a party to celebrate their tenth wedding anniversary, and Ethan and Angel were forced to socialise. It was the first time they'd been out together since the intruder.

'You're not still worried are you, babe?' Ethan asked as he noticed Angel constantly checking in the wing mirror to see who was behind as he drove them to the party. He had done so much to protect her that she was reluctant to admit her fears, to tell him about the nightmares she kept having. And if she admitted to them, it felt as if she'd be giving them credence – much better to pretend that everything was okay. 'I'm fine,' she lied. 'I was just seeing which bastard photographer was behind us.'

The party was in full swing when they arrived. Angel recognised Ethan's team mates from the Dodgers and many of Alisha's friends and family as she wove her way through the guests to get to their hosts who were greeting everyone in the huge cream marquee. They were surrounded by their three boys, who immediately made a bee line for Honey and promised to take her swimming. The anniversary couple looked blissfully happy as they chatted to their guests. Behind them was a five-tier cake decorated with white chocolate cherubs, which was almost as tall as their eleven-year-old son. The whole atmosphere was one of celebration. For the first time since the break-in Angel felt herself relax. She was amongst friends here, she, Ethan and Honey were safe.

'Hey, you guys!' Ethan exclaimed. 'Alisha, you look even younger than you did when you married Logan, and I'll never know how he managed to attract such a beauty as you.' She smiled while Logan playfully punched Ethan on the arm.

'Careful! That's his playing arm,' Angel put in, adding cheekily, 'and I couldn't marry him if he wasn't a successful baseball player.'

'And to think I would marry you if you had nothing!' Ethan teased back, pulling her close to him.

'I am looking forward to your wedding,' Logan told them. 'I've thought of *so* many things I can say in my speech.' He grinned cheekily, no doubt relishing the thought of putting together some embarrassing stories about Ethan who had recently asked him to be his best man. Ethan checked that none of the kids could see and defiantly flashed Logan a middle finger.

'It's okay, Angel,' Alisha put in, 'I'm going through the speech before he gets to deliver it. There won't be anything that will embarrass Loretta or your folks, I guarantee.'

Angel smiled at her. 'It doesn't matter to me about Ethan's past . . . we've both got pasts. It's what happens now that matters.' She didn't care that she sounded corny; it was what she kept telling herself.

Ethan stayed chatting to Alisha and Logan while Angel made her way to the pool. She trusted Alisha's sons to look after Honey and knew there would be several nannies supervising as well, but wanted to check for herself that her daughter was okay. She spent the next half an hour hanging out round the pool, chatting to the other mums. Honey was in seventh heaven, having three boys playing with her, and Angel thought how much she would love her daughter to have a brother or sister. Sure, Honey had Megan, but her contact with the little girl was always going to be on a part-time basis.

Finally Honey had had enough of the water and wanted something to eat. The two of them made their way back to the marquee. Angel felt happier than she had all week, surrounded by people who liked her and whom she liked, and the events of the past seven days seemed to belong to a bad dream. She found Ethan deep in conversation with a young Dodgers player called Matthew, who had recently joined the team and been taken under Ethan's wing. Matthew was just twenty-two, and looked more like a teenager with his round boyish face. He was also incredibly shy with women. As soon as he saw Angel he blushed.

'Matthew's got some news,' Ethan told Angel. 'Can you guess what it is?'

She looked at him blankly. 'No idea.'

'He's got a girlfriend.' At this Matthew's cheeks became even redder.

'And I've just met her so I know she's not a figment of his imagination,' Ethan teased. 'And the weird coincidence is that you know her.' Another blank stare from Angel. Who the hell could he be talking about? She was distracted by Honey pulling at her hand and wanting to go for a drink. When she looked up again she was confronted by Matthew's new girlfriend who had just joined them. Angel's mouth fell open in total astonishment. It was none other than Simone bitch-face Fraser.

Simone had snaked her arm possessively round Matthew and was smiling at Angel.

'Hiya, Angel, bet you didn't expect to see me here.' She leant forward to do the air-kiss thing.

'Wow, you two could be sisters!' Matthew exclaimed, causing Angel's hackles to rise. What the fuck was Simone doing? How had she met Matthew?

'I guess you're wondering how I met Matthew?' she asked disconcertingly, flicking back her long blonde hair. Angel didn't know whether it was her imagination but Simone's hair colour now looked pretty much exactly the same shade as hers.

'I still can't believe Matthew is going out with someone as good-looking as you,' Ethan put in. He flashed Simone his gorgeous smile, obviously thinking that Angel would want him to be nice to one of her friends. She had never told him about Simone, figuring there was no need, but now was wishing she had as Simone gave him a coy smile back which just about made Angel want to throw up.

'Oh, isn't he lovely, Angel!' she exclaimed. 'Every bit as lovely as you described.'

Angel feared her teeth were in danger of cracking, she was gritting them so hard, but she managed to get out, 'So where did you meet Matthew? I had no idea you were interested in baseball.'

Cue annoying tinkly laugh from Simone, followed by, 'I'm probably as interested in it as you are! I met Matthew at SkyBar; I'd gone there with some friends after an audition.'

Were these real or imaginary friends? Angel was tempted to ask as Simone continued, 'And it was the classic eyes meeting across a crowded room. A bit like you and Ethan in Bar Marmont. Ethan just told me.' She paused to caress Matthew's beefy forearm. 'So now Skybar will be our special place, just like Bar Marmont is yours. And I am having to really brush up on my knowledge of baseball, but Matthew's been taking me through it. It's a fantastic sport, isn't it? So exciting!'

Well, Simone had been through most of the English footballers, it was probably time for her to start on a new sport. And with God knows how many baseball teams in the USA, there was plenty of fodder for her here, Angel thought bitchily.

'You guys will have to come round for dinner soon,' Ethan put in. 'It'll be great for Angel to have one of her English friends so close by, I know how homesick she gets. And, of course, there's a certain event in

June to which you'll both be invited, I'm sure.'

The wedding? No fucking way was Simone bitch-face Fraser coming to her wedding!

Another annoying tinkly laugh. 'Oh, I would love that.' Simone beamed at Ethan.

'So where are you staying out here, Simone?' he asked.

Angel wondered how Simone was going to wriggle out of that one. It would surely do her no favours in Ethan's eyes if she revealed that she was staying with Angel's ex-husband. 'I was in a rented house just along the coast from you but . . .' Here she broke off to smile at Matthew. God, all this smiling must be making her face ache! 'But Matthew suggested I move in with him. I mean, I know it probably seems quick to you, but when you meet someone you just know is right for you, why wait?'

Angel could hardly believe what she was hearing! 'So how long ago did you and Matthew meet?' She tried to keep her tone neutral but hadn't quite succeeded; there was an edge to her voice.

'Two weeks, three days, seven hours and thirty-five minutes,' Matthew said proudly. 'Okay, I was just kidding about the thirty-five minutes. I'm not counting the minutes, honest.'

While Angel tried not to give him a look which said how deluded she thought he was, Ethan slapped him heartily on the back. 'Yep, don't mention the hours and definitely not the minutes, it does make you sound kinda weird. But the days stuff? Chicks love that kinda thing.' He paused to smile at Angel. 'It does remind me of when we first met. If I'd had my way, Angel would have moved in straight away. I knew she was the one.' If this had been said in front of any other couple Angel would have found the comment adorable, but Simone was a fucking mentalist!

And right now she wanted Ethan to zip it. Oh, to be telepathetic and able to tell him so silently! But Angel's super powers were definitely not working today.

'Except, of course, Angel was married, wasn't she?' Simone said it sweetly enough but Angel was sure she'd intended it to hurt. Even Matthew, who was clearly not blessed with the quickest brain in the world, said quietly, 'Honey, that's probably something they don't want to be reminded of.'

'Of course. I'm sorry,' Simone replied, and batted her eyelashes.

Angel was just wondering how to get away from the couple when Ethan noticed a former coach and took Angel and Honey off to meet him. The two men then talked baseball for what seemed like ages, but frankly Angel would have happily sat through a discussion on the state of the International Monetary Fund if it meant she was free from Simone.

However, that wasn't the last she was to see of Simone that afternoon. When she nipped to one of the many bathrooms in the house, leaving Honey with Ethan, she came face to face with Simone as she click-clacked her way down the stairs in her nude Louboutins, which made her long bronzed legs seem even longer.

'Such a gorgeous house,' she remarked conversationally as Angel drew level with her, as if her presence at this party was the most natural thing in the world.

'What are you playing at?' Angel said quietly.

'What d'you mean?' Simone was all innocence and butter-wouldn't-melt-in-her-mouth.

'What are you doing with Matthew?'

A wide-eyed look from Simone. 'I'm head over heels in love with him, isn't it obvious? Just like you are with Ethan.'

Pull the other one, Angel was tempted to say, 'And

what about Cal?' At the mention of his name a shadow passed across Simone's face and she dropped the Little-Miss-Perfect act as she hissed, 'Don't ever fucking mention his name to me! He's with that French woman and I'm with Matthew.'

And before Angel could say anything else another guest came down the stairs, forcing the women to move.

'Looking forward to that wedding invitation,' Simone called out when she reached the bottom of the stairs.

'Don't hold your breath,' Angel muttered quietly.

Thankfully she was spared any further run-ins with Simone. She, Ethan and Honey left soon after that. As they drove home, Angel wondered how to bring up the topic of Simone and tip Ethan off to what she was really like; he obviously didn't recognise her as the woman with Cal in the tabloid picture that Benny had taunted her with all those weeks ago. The danger was that she herself would sound like a number one bitch, raining on Simone's parade, if she revealed how the other woman had gone out with Cal, been a bit of a bunny boiler, got into drugs and become an escort before getting back on track. Maybe she really was a reformed character and was indeed head over heels with Matthew . . . but Angel somehow doubted it. The old Simone would certainly have been in love with his bank balance, though. Angel decided she needed to speak to Jez and Gemma before she tackled Ethan.

'So did you know your friend was over here?' Ethan asked, forcing her to change her mind and talk about Simone now.

'I did, but I had no idea she was seeing Matthew. To be honest, Ethan, we were never that close.'

'Well, Matthew's fallen for her big time, though I guess it's probably because he's never had so much sex in his life – well, at least not with another person!'

'She's had plenty of practice,' Angel muttered, looking out of the window.

'Excuse me?'

'Nothing, babe.'

As soon as Angel had put Honey to bed and Ethan was safely installed in his games room, playing on his Xbox, she shot into her bedroom to make her calls. Jez and Gemma had both been gobsmacked when she had told them about Simone coming over to LA and staying with Cal, and she reckoned this latest piece of news would stun them as much as it had her.

Jez's reaction did not disappoint. 'What the fuck? I think you've just blown my tiny mind! What the hell is she playing at?'

'So you don't think it's a coincidence, either that she's hooked up with Matthew?'

'It seems unlikely, doesn't it? Of all the men in LA, she goes for a Dodgers player? I'm not buying that eyes locking crap. In fact, I'm not having a great feeling about this, cupcake. I'm seeing *Single White Female* – you the Bridget Fonda character, beautiful and successful, and Simone the Jennifer Jason Leigh character, the saddo who moves in and tries to copy Fonda's life.'

'Oh my God! I've seen that film – is that where the Leigh character throws the Labrador puppy over the balcony and pretends he jumped? I hated it when the puppy died!'

'Never mind the dog!' Jez was now getting carried away with the scenario. 'Don't you remember the scene where the Leigh character creeps into the Fonda character's bedroom and pretends to be her, I think she's wearing a blonde wig or something, and the boyfriend is there and she gives him a blow job? And then there's the moment when he realises it's not his girlfriend giving him the old oral, but . . . typical man . . . just lies back and lets her get on with it thinking, Any blow job in a storm. He gets his comeuppance, though, when the Leigh character stabs him in the head with a stiletto. Brutal. Mind you, he had shot his load first so maybe it wasn't such a bad way to go.'

Angel was feeling too disturbed to laugh. 'Simone's got blonde hair now,' she replied in a small voice.

'She never has! She's so much better as a brunette.' Jez, ever the professional hairdresser, was appalled when women chose the wrong hair colour. 'Blonde is totally the wrong colour for her skin tone.'

'Jez! I don't fucking care whether it looks *better*, the fact is her hair now looks like *mine*. Has she turned into a Single White Female? Is she stalking me? Do you think she could have broken into the house?'

Angel was feeling vaguely hysterical; part of her wanted to laugh, it seemed such a mad idea, but then again, Simone turning up in LA and dating one of Ethan's team mates seemed off-the-scale crazy.

Finally Jez seemed to get a grip. 'Of course she didn't break into the house! She's a bit of mad, jealous bitch, but not a criminal mastermind!'

'Maybe she had help to do it. Paid someone.'

'She hasn't got the money to do something like that. That's exactly why she's with Matthew Money Bags. Maybe we've got this all wrong, maybe it is all just an incredible coincidence.' Jez conceded.

'Last time I saw her in London, she was wearing a dress that I'd been photographed wearing and she had the same clutch bag.' Angel had suddenly remembered Simone's outfit at Gemma's birthday party.

'It must be a coincidence,' Jez said again. 'She can't be that much of a weirdo.'

And coincidence was exactly how Gemma saw it, too, when Angel spoke to her. She thought the whole Single White Female stalking scenario madly far-fetched. 'You should have phoned me before Jez, you know how over-active his imagination is. Single White Female, my arse!'

'But what about the blonde hair?'

'What about it? Women change the colour of their hair all the time, and you don't own the colour blonde. Seriously, Angel, don't get hung up on this. You should be concentrating on the wedding. You probably feel jumpy because of the intruder, but don't make Simone a big thing in your life. She'd probably love that. If anything, you should feel sorry for her. She's obviously still in love with Cal but he's not interested, especially now he's with Madeleine.'

'Bloody hell, Gem, you're sounding very serene and chilled.' Angel had expected more from her friend.

'Actually I have been getting into yoga and meditation. I want to feel relaxed about trying for a baby.'

'Oh, yeah, how's it going?' Angel had been keeping her fingers crossed for her friend.

'Good, apart from your brother being back home late because of work every night for the last week, which was supposed to be our prime time for conceiving.' Gemma yawned. 'So I'm knackered, but feeling okay.'

'You really don't think Simone is out to get me then?' Angel asked. 'Sorry to go on about myself.'

'Why break the habit of a lifetime?' Gemma teased back, then added, 'I think she's wildly jealous of you, but that's as far as it goes. And you hardly have to see her, do you?'

'I'll have to see her at Dodgers games and Ethan's asked her for dinner . . . he's even asked her to the wedding! And I don't know what to tell him. I don't want to seem like a total bitch, trashing her, in case this is all a coincidence. And I don't want to drag all that old history between us into my life with him.'

'Don't say anything then. Be cool with her and Ethan will get the message that she's not a good friend, just an acquaintance. Jez and I were only friends with Simone because we felt sorry for her. Since she's been over in LA, she's only texted us once. Seems like we're not useful to her any more, and that's no great loss. Forget about her. Now tell me about what really matters – have you had the final dress fitting?'

Angel filled Gemma in on where they were at with the wedding plans – Ethan had gone to see Kaz for a suit which would complement Angel's dress; and they had decided to give the wedding a fairy-tale theme with two marquees in the garden, one for the kids decorated like a Disney castle, along with entertainers dressed up as Minnie Mouse *et al.*, the other as a circus tent with performers ranging from jugglers to trapeze artists. There were going to be chocolate fountains, candy-floss machines and ice sculptures. Angel had thought about going more sophisticated, then realised how much Honey would love the fairy-tale day and decided to go all out for it. As for Ethan, he was happy to go along with whatever she wanted.

After the phone call Angel tried to take Gemma's advice on board, but Simone had got under her skin and it was impossible not to think about her and wonder what she was up to. Every time Ethan went off to training, Angel wondered if Simone was going to be there watching. She really hoped that Ethan would have forgotten about asking Simone and Matthew round, so it was a nasty surprise a week later when he announced that he had invited the couple for dinner the following evening, together with Alisha and Logan. He announced this as if it should be great news for Angel.

'Oh, babe, do we have to? Can't we go out and meet them?' The thought of seeing Simone was bad enough, never mind having her in the house!

'If we go out we'll have to do all the security shit, have the paps after us. I'd much rather chill round the pool while Maria cooks up her seafood paella. And I've got Megan and don't want to leave her with a nanny on one of my few days with her.'

There was no way Angel could argue with that; still, the announcement didn't exactly put her in the best of moods. But at least she would have Alisha and Logan as allies for the night. They were such good company that hopefully Angel would be able to focus on them and block out Simone. And she was busy – she had two full days' shooting her calendar, would only be back in time for dinner, leaving her less time to brood on Simone. Ever since Angel had become a successful glamour model she had shot a calendar every year, and as she was out here she had decided to give the pictures the full LA treatment. So far she'd been photographed in a gold bikini lying in the sand on Santa Monica beach, eating candy floss on the pier in a tiny pink bikini, and walking down the legendary Sunset Boulevard in a pair of hot pants and a crop top. The next two days were to be used take some studio shots, including Angel draped over a pink Cadillac wearing a white bikini, and dressed as a sexy waitress on roller-blades.

The two-day shoot was as full on as Angel had anticipated; the first night she didn't get back until 9 p.m. While she was sorely tempted to make a late entrance for dinner the next night, she knew that wouldn't be fair on Ethan and they ended up finishing at 7. To ensure she wasn't late, Carlos drove Angel back while she was still in the silver sequined hot pants and bikini top she'd worn for the final series of pictures. She just threw a tee-shirt on, and still had the silver false lashes. With any luck she'd have time to change when she got back. But the traffic was bumper to bumper. Angel phoned Ethan to let him know she was running late and received the most unwelcome news that Alisha and Logan's youngest son was running a fever and they didn't want to leave him. It was just going to be Simone and Matthew.

'Shouldn't we rearrange?' Angel asked, her spirits plummeting at the prospect of an evening with Simone and no Alisha.

But no hope there – Maria had made the dinner already, Simone and Matthew were on their way. Angel was just going to have to deal with it. Fifteen minutes later she opened the front door, intending to sneak in and go straight upstairs. She wanted to be in a killer outfit if she had to deal with Simone, but Ethan heard her and called her into the living room where he was pouring out cocktails. Angel winced and headed in, steeling herself for the encounter.

Simone was wearing a cobalt blue Matthew Williamson silk mini dress, which showed off her lovely figure. Angel only knew it was Matthew Williamson because Gemma had sent her a link to Net-A-Porter illustrating that exact same dress, saying it was totally her. Well, it was totally Simone now. She'd teamed it with a massive diamond necklace. She looked even slimmer than usual and her skin had a gorgeous sun-kissed glow. She might be a total bitch but she certainly looked stunning. She was in a pair of gold Louboutins which meant she towered over Angel, who had kicked off her heels in the car and was barefoot.

'Hey, Angel, how'd it go?' Ethan asked, coming over and giving her a hug.

'Really good.'

'I'm loving those hot pants!' he exclaimed, playfully slapping her on the bum.

'Angel does look great in hot pants,' Simone agreed, coming over and bestowing the inevitable air kiss on Angel. She waited for Simone to come out with a quip about her being white trash or chavtastic, but none came.

Simone had obviously been working on Matthew's 'look' – usually he was to be found in baggy sweatshirts and cut-off jeans; tonight he was in a navy linen suit which looked every bit as designer as Simone's dress. But actually, Angel reflected, Matthew looked better casual. He was so muscular that he looked as if at any minute he was going to burst out of the suit, like the Incredible Hulk. If it had been any other couple Angel would have been perfectly happy to have dinner in the hot pants, but the thought of Simone looking over her body, checking her for any imperfections, had her excusing herself and whizzing upstairs to change.

First she checked on Honey and Megan who were both fast asleep – Megan in her cot next to Honey's bed. Then she walked into her dressing room. It had been completely re-painted and refurbished since the break in, even down to replacing the thick white carpet and the sofa where Angel used to chill out and the desk from where she'd email her friends and family. Gone too was her pretty glass dressing table with the Venetian mirror where 'Bitch' had been scrawled, and in its place was an ultra-modern sleek white dressing table with a huge mirror with lights on the side, in the style of a theatre dressing room. But even with the changes, Angel always thought about the intruder when she went in there. She thought about them now as she went to click open the wardrobe, remembering how chilling it had been to see the ruined red dress laid out for her like some kind of sick message.

She hesitated as her hand touched the cool, polished wood of the door, almost tempted not to open it but to go back down in her silk pyjamas – well, they were Chanel, Gemma would be proud – but she forced herself to go ahead. The lights flicked on in the walk-in wardrobe as she opened the door, revealing the white carpet thankfully bare. Angel picked out a long white maxi dress with the bodice embellished in silver beads.

'This is such a lovely house, Angel,' Simone said as she unexpectedly walked into the room, almost causing Angel to cry out in fright.

Simone registered her expression. 'Oh, I'm sorry I didn't mean to startle you. Matthew told me about the break-in . . . I should have realised that you'd be jumpy.'

No one apart from a very tight circle of friends and family was supposed to know about the break-in and Angel was furious with Ethan for telling Matthew. 'It's really not something I like to talk about, Simone,' she replied, wishing the other woman would clear out of her room. She'd already had to redecorate once. At this rate she'd be doing it again to banish Simone's bad karma.

'Sorry, Angel. I don't want us to get off on the wrong foot, especially since we're going to be seeing so much more of each other.'

Don't count on it, Angel thought grimly while Simone considered her own reflection in the mirror.

'So how do you feel about Cal and Madeleine? I told you he wouldn't be single for long.' Simone turned round to look at her, obviously keen to gauge her reaction.

Angel tried to keep her face as expressionless as possible as she replied, 'Cal's free to do what he wants. I'm marrying Ethan.' There she went again with her mantra.

Simone flicked back her hair. 'Cal's pretty serious about her apparently. But then, it's not surprising – she is beautiful and really intelligent. She speaks four languages, started a charity for Rwandan orphans and is a UNICEF ambassador.'

'Does she split the atom in her spare time? Who are

you . . . her fucking PR?' Angel resorted to sarcasm to hide how shaken up she was by this revelation.

Simone shrugged. 'I'm just someone who is over Cal.' She looked at Angel with a knowing expression and didn't need to add that she thought Angel wasn't. Then she sashayed out of the room, leaving a waft of Agent Provocateur Maitresse in her wake, which Angel had always liked before but definitely wasn't keen on any more.

Angel sat down at her dressing table and tried to pull herself together, telling herself it didn't matter that Cal was with Madeleine. In fact, it was good because he was happy. 'And I'm happy,' she said out loud to her reflection. Then she grimaced, quickly brushed out her hair and peeled off the silver lashes, changed into the white dress and headed back downstairs. She intended to have several glasses of champagne to counteract Simone's presence. With any luck, as she'd hardly eaten all day, they would go straight to her head.

By now everyone was sitting round the dining table outside on the decking and Maria was serving up her legendary seafood paella. 'We couldn't wait any longer!' Ethan exclaimed when he saw Angel. 'Matthew and me have been doing real men's work. We need food!'

Any other time Angel would have bantered something back but now she felt slightly offended that Ethan was dismissing her work, even though rationally she knew he wasn't. It was just having Simone there, sitting at *her* table, delicately nibbling the paella and behaving as if there was every reason in the world for her to be there when the truth was it was fucked up.

But somehow Angel pulled herself together, kissed Ethan on the neck as she sat down, and murmured, 'And you'll need your energy for later,' a kind of signal to Simone that, while she would be shagging Shrek later on, Angel would be having sexy Ethan. If Simone picked up the vibe she didn't show it but in turn held up her hand to caress Matthew's arm. A gesture which was no doubt calculated to show off the frankly enormous blingtastic heart-shaped diamond on her engagement finger. A diamond so enormous that Angel was amazed neither she nor Ethan had seen it before.

'Wow!' Ethan exclaimed. 'Have you guys got something you want to tell us?'

'Fast worker' didn't even begin to describe Simone.

Matthew looked rather awkward and turned to Simone. 'Honey, I thought we agreed not tell anyone yet until we'd broken the news to our folks?'

She looked at him and bit her lip, looking adorably guilty. 'I know, and I'm so sorry, Matthew, but I couldn't bear to take my ring off! It seemed so wrong. It belongs there now, where you put it.' She looked at Ethan and Angel. 'And I know we can trust our friends not to say anything.'

Angel almost looked over her shoulder as if in search of Simone's real friends. Instead she nodded while Ethan exclaimed, 'Way to go! That is awesome news. But please tell me, Matthew, that you're not getting hitched before I am?'

'We could have a double wedding!' Simone said, a comment which thankfully found favour with neither Ethan nor Matthew.

'So . . . congratulations!' Ethan was the perfect recipient of the news, insisting they raise their glasses immediately in a toast to the happy couple, wanting to hear all about the proposal. Apparently Matthew had taken Simone out for the most wonderful dinner at Ago, the Italian trattoria backed by Hollywood heavyweights such as Robert De Niro and Ridley Scott. Back home he'd led her upstairs where she saw that he'd filled the entire bedroom with flowers and scattered white rose petals all over the bed. Then he got down on one knee to propose. Simone apparently didn't know if he was serious at first, but then he'd snapped open the ring box and shown her the diamond and she knew it was for real! They just had to break the news to Matthew's parents, who were quite a religious couple. Simone's parents would be no trouble, they were bound to be thrilled, and then they would set the date for as soon as possible.

'Well, that is incredible news,' Angel finally commented once Simone had finished gushing. She wondered if Cal's relationship with Madeleine had spurred on Simone to get her claws into Matthew. She remembered now how Simone had overheard Cal saying he would never get involved with her – which must have hurt.

'I know what you're thinking, it's too soon, but we love each other.' Simone said. Then threw open her arms and shouted up to the sky, 'I love this man!' As she did so, Angel caught sight of a new tattoo on her wrist: Matthew's name surrounded by love hearts with a baseball bat and ball underneath it. Simone *definitely* didn't hang about. Matthew and Ethan laughed at her over-the-top-gesture. Ethan then suggested another toast and Angel thought that maybe Simone was overdoing the declarations.

There was absolutely no way that she was in love with Matthew, who was a sweet enough guy but had the conversational abilities of a thirteen year old, and that was probably being disrespectful to teenagers. If not ugly – and several of Simone's former footballing lovers had been dog ugly – he was definitely plain, not hot or sexy, or clever, or charming, or funny . . . or any of the things that Cal and Ethan were. Simone had done her time with the footballing fraternity as a WAG and never received a proposal; no wonder she was going for it with Matthew. It was hardly as if her acting career was going to take off.

Angel just didn't know whether to feel sorry for Matthew or not. Maybe Simone would continue to be sweetness and light to him when they were married. But didn't he have a right to know what he was getting into with her? Angel couldn't help thinking that he was being taken for a ride, and that he should at least know the full facts about his fiancée before he took it.

'So maybe Angel could be your maid-of-honour, honey?' he said eagerly to Simone. 'I know that I'd like Ethan to be my best man.'

Cue back-slapping between the two men and exclamations of, 'Oh, man!'

It was possibly the most inappropriate comment Matthew could have come up with, not that he knew any of the history between the two women. Angel just looked at Simone, wondering how she was going to get out of this one.

'Actually, Matthew, I was going to ask Gemma. Remember, I've talked about her? She was so kind to me when I was going through that difficult time just after I left rehab.' Simone turned and shot a challenging look at Angel as if to say, See, he does know about my past. 'And it would be kind of weird as Angel was married to Cal Bailey who I went out with absolutely years ago. Not that there's any bad feeling between me and Angel, as you can see.' Another comment designed to show Angel that Simone hadn't kept things from Matthew, which had Angel reaching again for her glass of champagne.

But does he know you were an escort? she thought. Or that you stalked Cal and he nearly took an injunction out against you? Or that, whatever act you're putting on now, you're still in love with Cal Bailey?

*

'My God, your friend's a fast worker!' Ethan exclaimed after they'd finally shown the couple out. It was after one and to Angel it had felt as if they were never going to leave. Simone was milking her new role as Matthew's fiancée for all she was worth.

'She certainly is,' Angel said dryly, wondering how to break the news to Ethan that his friend's fiancée was a super-bitch. The couple were in the kitchen; Angel had just poured herself a glass of water. She'd drunk far too much champagne and knew she was going to feel rough in the morning, but it had been the only way to get through a night with Simone. 'Did you tell Matthew about the break in?' she asked, remembering Simone's earlier comment.

Ethan frowned. 'No way. I only told Logan and my coach.'

'Simone knew about it.'

A shrug from Ethan. 'Maybe Matthew overheard me talking to Logan in the dressing room. Don't worry about it, babe, she's a friend.'

Ethan was leaning against the breakfast bar. Angel walked over to him and slid her arm under his. 'To be honest, Ethan, I'm really not at all close to Simone. I don't want her to come to our wedding.'

Ethan sighed, 'Babe, I've asked them now. I can't go back on it. Besides, it's only for the reception; you won't have to see much of her.'

'It's just . . . there are things you don't know about her.' And Angel was about to bite the bullet and fill Ethan in on Simone's true nature when her mobile rang. She frowned as she picked up her phone and saw her mum's name flash up. It wasn't like Michelle to phone her so late. 'Mum? Is everything okay?' she asked.

But her mum was crying so much she could hardly get the words out. 'Angel, it's your dad . . . He's had a heart attack . . . he's in hospital.'

A shocking feeling of dread rushed through Angel. 'He's going to be all right, isn't he?'

A sob from her mum as she replied, 'They don't know yet. Oh, Angel, please come home.'

Chapter 15

The rest of that night and the following day was a blur of panic, fear and apprehension as Ethan took control and sorted everything out for her, from booking her tickets to packing. Angel herself was a wreck. She was in no state to look after Honey, and they both felt it was best if the little girl stayed behind with Lucy. Ethan couldn't come back with Angel as he had a really important game coming up and couldn't miss it. On the flight she was unable to think of anything but her dad. The thought of him dying was unbearable. At times theirs had been a difficult relationship, Frank could be very over-protective and often Angel had resented this, taken it to mean that he didn't love her, when the opposite was true.

Angel had expected that her brother Tony would meet her at the airport, but it was Cal. Her intense anxiety about her dad swept away any trace of awkwardness at being with her ex-husband. As soon as he saw her, Cal enfolded her in a hug. 'It'll be okay,' he told her. But he didn't sound certain, and he looked exhausted. 'I'll take you straight there. Tony didn't want to leave him, which is why I'm here.'

Angel looked at Cal, her eyes welling up with more tears, 'Oh my God, is it that bad?' she exclaimed, remembering how her brother had said that he would never be able to forgive himself if he wasn't there when his mum and dad passed away, after missing the final moments of their late granddad whom they'd both adored.

Cal held her gaze. 'I'm not going to lie to you. He's in Intensive Care at the moment.'

His own eyes filled with tears then. Frank had been a father figure to Cal after his own dad had walked out when he was just three years old, leaving him to be brought up, or rather neglected, by his alcoholic mother. Angel knew that Cal believed it was only Frank's intervention in his life that had helped him to make something of himself.

Angel was exhausted after the long flight but nothing was going to stop her from seeing her dad. But even knowing that he was in Intensive Care did not prepare her for seeing him lying there in the hospital bed, attached to a drip and heart monitors, a ventilator breathing for him. This helpless man did not look like her dad who was always so full of life, such a huge presence in any room. She was so caught up in looking at him that she hardly registered her mum sitting next to the bed, along with Tony.

'Angel!' her mum exclaimed, standing up. 'Thank God you're here!' She clung on to her daughter, sobbing into her shoulder. Angel found herself comforting her, stroking her hair, and saying 'It's all right, Mum,' as Michelle wept.

'Managed to drag yourself away from your fiancé then?' Tony said bitterly. His face was a mask of pent-up pain.

Angel was stung by his words. 'I came as soon as I knew!'

'Dad's not been well for a while, and worrying about you marrying that man hasn't helped. You've always been the one who's brought stress on this family.'

It was so typical of Tony to lash out at her as a way of handling his own pain, but that didn't make it any less hurtful. Angel was about to defend herself when Cal spoke. 'Don't be like this, Tony. Frank having a heart attack has got nothing to do with Angel; she's as upset as you are.'

At this Tony's shoulders sagged. He reached out for Angel's hand. 'Yeah, you're right, I'm sorry. Come on, sit down and talk to him, I'm sure he'd like to hear your voice.'

Angel sat by the side of Frank's bed and gently put her hand over his, careful not to disturb the drip. 'Hi Dad,' she said quietly. 'This is quite a state you've got yourself in. I told you to cut back on the beer and the fry ups and the fags, and you promised you would. When you get better, I'm going to give you a real ear bashing. In fact, even better, I'm going to get you a personal trainer . . . a really tough one, to get you back into shape!'

Angel did her very best to keep her voice upbeat in spite of the tears that kept blurring her eyes. Frank gave no indication that he had heard her. His eyes remained shut and the only sound was the regular 'whooshing' of the ventilator and the beep-beep-beep of the monitor. 'Anyway, I love you, Dad, and just want you to get better. We all do.'

She turned and looked at her mum then. Michelle was pale and drawn and looked absolutely exhausted; Angel doubted that she would have been home since Frank was brought in. 'Mum, why don't you go home and get some rest? I'll stay here with Dad. And you, Tony, you both look shattered.'

Michelle shook her head and said determinedly, 'I'm not leaving him.'

'Me neither,' Tony added.

Angel looked at Cal, who shrugged and said, 'I think

it's best if we all stay.' He sat down at the opposite side of the bed from Angel, and so began one of the most emotional nights of her life. They all took it in turn to talk to Frank, or rather to lead the conversation, allowing each of them to shut their eyes for a break while the others spoke about subjects dear to Frank's heart – his beloved Chelsea, the youth team, when Cal was going to teach Honey to play football – and all the time Frank's eyes remained closed and there was no sign that he could hear them. Every fifteen minutes the nurses came to check on him, walking quietly in, checking his drip and the monitor, writing up comments on his chart, but giving no indication about how he was doing. At some point Angel quietly left the room to go to the bathroom and Cal followed her out.

'Do you think he'll get better?' Angel asked, leaning against the wall which was painted a sickly green. The overhead fluorescent lights hurt her eyes and the antiseptic hospital smell was giving her a pounding headache.

Cal looked back at her. 'I don't know, Angel. Your dad's a fighter, but he had a massive heart attack. He nearly died. Your mum and Tony won't admit it, but it's not good. I'm sorry.'

Angel put her hand up to her face and then Cal took a step towards her and put his arms round her and she reached for him. For a while they just held each other tight. They didn't say anything, they just needed the comfort that only they could give each other. Angel felt so safe, so protected in his arms, she didn't want to move.

Gemma arrived around 5 a.m. It was so good to see her friend. They all needed Gemma's bright smile and natural optimism as they were feeling exhausted and low. Angel tried again to persuade her mum to have a break, but Michelle stood her ground and in the end it was she who persuaded Angel to go home and get some rest. She was now so jetlagged and exhausted she couldn't even see straight. Although she tried to protest, they all insisted and eventually she gave in, telling them she'd grab a couple of hours' sleep then return.

Back home she went upstairs to her old bedroom where she didn't even bother to get undressed but climbed into bed fully clothed. She vaguely thought about phoning Ethan but was too tired. She didn't know how long she had been asleep when she became aware of Cal calling her name. It must be a dream, she often dreamt of Cal. But then the voice grew more persistent: 'Angel, wake up.'

Feeling as if her body was made of concrete, she reluctantly she opened her eyes. Cal was standing by the bed. 'I tried phoning but there was no reply. I thought you'd want to know that Frank's awake . . . he's been asking for you. I'll take you back to the hospital.'

'I've got to see him!' Angel exclaimed, summoning all her energy to get out of bed. She was so wobbly with exhaustion she almost lost her balance, and instantly Cal held her to him.

'It's going to be all right, Angel,' he murmured, and kissed the top of her head.

In that instant, with his arms round her, and his body against hers, and all her defences down, Angel felt a flash of desire for him that made her long to stay in his arms. But somehow she pulled herself out of the embrace and went to the bathroom where she quickly showered. She looked terrible, her eyes puffy and bloodshot, but she didn't care. All that mattered was seeing her dad.

Frank was very weak when they saw him, but he managed to speak and hold Angel's hand. 'You haven't got rid of me yet,' he whispered.

'I'd never want to get rid of you!' she exclaimed, tears streaming down her face. She'd cried more in the last few days than at any other time in her life.

He managed a smile. 'I know that, love. I don't suppose you brought that daughter of yours? I could do with seeing her happy face, instead of being surrounded by you miserable lot.' Talking so much made him cough. Instantly Michelle was at his side.

'That's enough now, Frank, you're to rest. You heard what the doctor said.'

For once in his life he didn't attempt to answer back, but shut his eyes and murmured, 'Yes, love.'

Angel then managed to persuade Michelle and Tony to go home and get some rest while she and Cal stayed with Frank. Her dad slept most of the time. When he woke up he would only be able to talk for a few minutes before once more falling asleep. His body had been through so much, it was going to take time for it to recover, but the doctors seemed more hopeful now. Angel and Cal read the paper and talked quietly, mainly about Honey and Cal's football academies. Conversation flowed easily between them. They didn't mention Ethan or the wedding and seemed to be getting on fine until Cal spoke about the future.

'You know, Frank's life is really going to change now, Angel,' he said quietly. 'He'll have to cut back on work and completely change his lifestyle . . . the fags, the booze, the unhealthy food . . . it's going to have to go. Your mum's going to have her work cut out for her. You know how stubborn your dad is.' He paused. 'She'll really need you. Frank as well.'

Why the hell was he trying to guilt trip her now? 'And I'll be there for both of them!' Angel exclaimed, trying to keep her voice down.

'How will you do that if you're in LA?'

'I'll come back here more often, and they can come

out and see me. If Dad's going to work less, he'll have no excuse not to.'

It really didn't seem to her like the place to be talking this way. It seemed as if Cal too realised he'd spoken out of turn as he looked at Frank and then hung his head. 'Sorry. I'm not having a go. This has shaken me up. Made me realise what's important.'

He looked at Angel, and as she gazed back at him it suddenly felt as if everything else had fallen away. She experienced such an intense pang of longing and desire for Cal then that she thought it must show in her eyes. The air seemed charged with an emotion which was only broken when Tony and Michelle returned after their rest.

That day set the pattern for the week that followed. Angel took it in turns with the rest of her family and Cal to sit with Frank, so there was someone with him all the time. She spent hours at Frank's bedside, and hours with Cal, and when Cal wasn't there, she found herself missing him, longing for him to be back. Suddenly her life with Ethan and their impending marriage seemed a very long way away, as if it belonged to another person, another life.

And it seemed she wasn't alone in thinking that. One afternoon when Cal and Angel were with Frank, he said, 'This feels just like old times, doesn't it?' Angel looked over at Cal who gave a wry smile.

Frank sighed, 'I never thought you two would get divorced, but there you go. You can never tell how life is going to turn out, I suppose.'

'No, you can't,' Cal said quietly. 'And it's not always the way you wanted it to either.' He gazed at Angel and she held the look.

For a few minutes everyone was silent, lost in thought. Then Cal checked his watch. 'I'm going to have to go, I'm seeing someone for supper.' He looked at Angel. 'Will you be okay? I can cancel if not.'

Angel shook her head, dying to ask if Madeleine was the person he was meeting. 'I'll be fine.' She knew she sounded defensive, and it was hardly as if she had any right to ask him to stay.

After Cal left, Frank dozed off and Angel slipped outside to call Ethan. She was surprisingly relieved when Lucy picked up the phone and told her he was at some dinner for the Dodgers. Angel wasn't up to doing the whole 'I love you, I miss you' routine. I'm just worn out, she told herself as she wandered back into the hospital. Her mum turned up soon after that, and she, Angel and Frank spent a couple of hours playing cards, until Michelle sent Angel home, saying that she looked exhausted.

It was an early-May evening, and still light as Angel walked towards the car park. As she drew close she saw a sleek silver Mercedes pull up. Cal got out of the passenger side and a woman Angel was certain was Madeleine got out of the driver's side and ran round the car to hug him. Angel felt a sickening jolt of jealousy at the sight of the couple. She looked around, wondering if there was any other way to the car park. She really wasn't up to an encounter with the beautiful model. But it was too late, Cal had seen her. He waved and so Angel had to keep on walking.

'Are you going home? I just wanted to see if you were okay,' he asked when she drew close.

'I'm fine,' Angel replied, suddenly aware of what a complete wreck she must look – she had no make-up on, her hair, which needed the roots re-doing, was pulled back in an unflattering ponytail, which was verging on a Croydon face lift, and she had spilt tea on her pink hoody earlier on in the day, which had left a nasty-looking stain. Madeleine, on the other hand, looked absolutely immaculate in a white trouser suit, her shiny brown hair cascading over her shoulders. She was even better-looking in the flesh – this was no model in need of extensive air brushing.

'This is Madeleine. She just dropped me off on her way back to London,' Cal explained

The beautiful Madeleine stepped forward and shook Angel's hand. 'It's nice to meet you,' she said in her perfect, but sexily accented English. 'I do hope your father is getting better.'

'He is, thank you.' Angel turned to Cal. 'I'll see you tomorrow then?'

''Course.'

'Nice to meet you, Madeleine,' Angel said, and walked quickly towards her car, not wanting to spend any longer with them. But back home, even though she was exhausted, she couldn't sleep. Every time she closed her eyes, an image of Cal and Madeleine embracing came into her head, and then, to really torment herself, she allowed herself to imagine the two of them in bed together. Thought of Madeleine tracing her fingers over the angel-wings tattoo as they made love.

At 3 a.m. she gave up trying to sleep and called Ethan. He was his usual lovely self on the phone, wanting to know how her dad was, telling her how much he loved and missed her.

'So Maria asked if we wanted her to make her seafood paella for the reception. And the cake people need a definite answer on which design you want – the one with the white chocolate roses and cherubs or the one with the red roses and butterflies?' he said. Angel felt so detached from her LA life with him that she almost asked whose reception, before realising.

'Sure, yes to the paella, and I don't mind about the cake – you surprise me,' she replied, thinking that the catering was the very least of her concerns right now. 'I'm going to stay here another week,' she told Ethan. She wasn't ready to leave her dad. Ethan was completely understanding. He said if she needed to stay any longer, he would arrange for Lucy to fly back with Honey as Angel was missing her daughter so much.

How lucky am I to have such a considerate man, Angel told herself after the call. A man who loves me . . . a man I love. But the thought kept sneaking back in that, while she did love Ethan, it wasn't enough. That love didn't stop her from thinking about Cal. And at 4 a.m., when she sat up in bed with the light on and looked over at the wall of photographs of her and Cal, she finally admitted the thing she had been running away from ever since she'd found out about Cal's infidelity. She was still in love with him.

The following morning Michelle took one look at the exhausted Angel over breakfast and insisted that she take herself off to Jeanie's beauty salon and get a facial and her hair done.

'No way!' Angel protested. 'I've got to go and see Dad!'

'Your dad is seeing the consultant this morning and I'm going to be there, so you can take the morning off. And tonight Cal said something about taking you, Gemma and Tony out for dinner as it's Tony's birthday. He was supposed to be having a big do at The Grey's but he cancelled it because of Dad.'

'I expect Madeleine is coming too,' Angel said gloomily.

Michelle shook her head. 'No, I think she's at some fashion show in New York. Apparently she can speak four languages. She must be a very clever girl.'

God! Like she needed her mum to big-up Madeleine. 'Well, I'm sure she and Cal will be very happy together,'

247

Angel said sulkily. 'Though he might need to brush up on his languages. He can only ask for a beer in French and Spanish.'

'Why are you so bothered all of a sudden? You're getting married to Ethan in less than a month.'

'I'm not bothered,' Angel said hotly.

Michelle gave a smile that said she knew better. 'I'll call Jeanie and ask if she can fit you in.'

An hour later Angel was lying back in one of the therapy rooms while Jeanie gave her a blissful aromatherapy facial. 'You skin is great, Angel, just dehydrated. Probably from flying and sitting in the hospital,' Jeanie told her.

'I'm not going to end up with spots, am I?' Angel asked, thinking about the evening ahead. She'd bet beautiful Madeleine never got any spots.

Jeanie shook her head. 'So how's it been seeing Cal? It must be strange, spending so much time with him.' Angel knew Jeanie so well that she didn't mind the personal questions; in fact, she was glad of the chance to talk to someone about how she felt.

'That's the funny thing . . . it doesn't feel strange at all. It feels strange when I remember –' Angel hesitated, aware that she was about to say something really important '– that we're not together any more, and that I'm going to marry Ethan, and that Cal's with Madeleine.'

'He's only with her because you're getting married! He kept thinking you would forgive him eventually and go back to him, but then you got engaged.'

Jeanie was silent after this for a few minutes while she massaged Angel's shoulders and neck, a move no doubt designed to relieve her tension, but Angel was feeling more and more wound up as she turned over the words in her mind.

'There, all done,' Jeanie told her. 'Take your time

getting up and then I'll do your hair downstairs.'

She went to leave the room, but instead of lying still, Angel sat up. 'Jeanie, I think I still love him. Is it too late?'

Jeanie didn't need to ask who she meant. 'No, it's not. You just need to tell him.'

Jeanie was right! She had to tell Cal. Maybe he would say that he had moved on and was happy with Madeleine, hardly the outcome she hoped for, but at least Angel would know. She spent the rest of the day in a fever of anticipation. Every time the door to Frank's room opened she jumped, thinking it would be Cal. But he had meetings in London and wasn't due back until the evening. At 6 she went round to Gemma and Tony's. Tony was on his way back from London and so it was just the two girls.

They sat in Gemma's bedroom, having a glass of wine, and it felt just like old times when she and Gemma would get ready for a night out together. Angel hadn't told her friend what she had told Jeanie – somehow she wanted to wait and see what Cal's reaction would be. Plus she didn't think she would be able to sit through dinner with Gemma watching her every move.

'You look fantastic,' her friend told her. 'It must be that facial.'

Angel smiled. She didn't think the facial had anything to do with it. 'Will you do my make-up, Gem? I've looked such a wreck all week, I'd like to look good tonight. What time are we meeting Cal and Tony?'

'Half-seven . . . and that's the third time you've asked me.' Gemma looked at her curiously; she was always very good at reading her friend.

'And what shall I wear?' Angel asked, holding up a black asymmetric mini dress and a fuchsia tunic dress she'd bought from French Connection that afternoon, trusting that the clothes question would throw her friend off the scent.

Gemma gave the outfits a critical once over. 'I'd go for the black dress, and you can borrow my black peep toe Louboutins, so long as you promise not to damage them. If you do, I'll be forced to kill you.'

'Or I could buy you some more? That way you won't be in prison wearing a scuzzy prison outfit.'

Gemma shuddered. 'Yes, it would be a sea of man-made fabrics . . . I couldn't cope.'

The two women looked at one other and laughed then, and Angel was almost tempted to tell Gemma what she planned to do. Almost. Instead she kept her secret.

She felt like a teenage girl going on a date as she and Gemma spent the next hour getting ready, and then grabbed a taxi to Hotel du Vin even though it was only a ten-minute walk away. Neither of them wanted to walk in heels, and there was a brisk sea wind which would have played havoc with their hair. Tony and Cal were already there when they walked in, sitting in an intimate corner area of the bar. Gemma sat next to Tony on one of the squashy brown leather sofas, while Angel sat next to Cal on the opposite one. The news from the consultant was very positive, and as a result they all felt they could enjoy themselves. Cal ordered champagne to celebrate Tony's birthday.

While Tony and Gemma chatted about their day, Cal turned to Angel. 'You look better,' he told her.

'Better than I did yesterday,' she replied, remembering the encounter with Madeleine.

'You always look beautiful, but tonight . . . I don't know. You're glowing.'

Angel's stomach flipped over at the compliment, but typically she downplayed it. 'Must be the facial I had at Jeanie's.'

Cal smiled, instantly making his handsome face even more handsome, and how Angel wanted to bask in that smile. 'I missed you today,' he said softly, so that only she could hear. 'It felt strange, not seeing you after seeing you all week.'

'Yeah,' Angel replied, just as softly, 'I know what you mean.' For a few seconds they gazed at each other, then a couple walking past called out Cal's name.

'Hey, Sapphire . . . Jay! How are you?' Cal stood up and shook hands with an extremely good-looking mixed-race man in his twenties and then kissed an equally good-looking woman, with long jet black hair, who looked to be about seven months pregnant. Angel recognised Sapphire as she owned a hen party business and beauty salon in Brighton, though loyalty to Jeanie and Gemma meant Angel had never been there. 'Why don't you join us for a drink?' Cal suggested.

'I was at school with Cal,' Sapphire told Angel as she lowered herself on to the sofa. 'God, Jay, you're going to have to pull me off this or I'll never get up!'

'I've heard him talk about you.' And Angel had seen Sapphire photographed with Cal in the past, and always wondered if there had been something between them.

'Yeah, he's gorgeous, isn't he? But I never fancied him,' Sapphire continued as if reading her mind.

'Why not!' Cal demanded, pretending to be offended.

'I don't know. But you never fancied me either, did you?'

'You had a lucky escape, mate,' Jay put in. 'She's well high-maintenance.' But the look he exchanged with Sapphire was one of total contentment and Angel suddenly envied them. They seemed so happy.

Sapphire and Jay stayed for ten minutes or so, before the *maître d'* called them to their table. As Sapphire prepared to leave, she said quietly, so that only Angel could hear, 'It's so good to see you two back together. I know Cal went through hell when you moved to LA.' There was an awkward moment when Angel wondered if she should say that she was marrying someone else and Cal had a French supermodel for a lover, but Sapphire blew the party a kiss and headed for the restaurant.

Cal watched them leave then said, 'I'm so glad to see those two finally got it together. They're one of those couples that are meant to be.'

He turned and looked at Angel then, his expression serious. 'I know what you mean,' she replied. Cal seemed as if he was about to say something else when they too were called to their table.

Angel could hardly eat a thing, she was too aware of Cal sitting opposite her. She really did feel exactly as if she was on a date, which was surely crazy seeing as Cal was her ex-husband. After failing to eat her first course of sea bass and receiving a raised eyebrow from the waiter, Angel went to the bathroom. There she saw Sapphire checking her make-up.

'Hiya again,' Sapphire said cheerfully. 'This is the third time in the last hour that I've had to pee.' She rubbed her baby bump affectionately and said, 'Get off my bladder!'

Angel smiled. 'I'd like to say it gets better, but it doesn't really until you have the baby.' She paused. 'By the way, I meant to say earlier . . . Cal and I aren't back together. I'm supposed to be getting married in three weeks.'

Sapphire looked awkward. 'I'm so sorry, I just assumed when I saw you here tonight that you were. But that's great, that you and Cal can still be friends. Not many divorced couples can do that. It took me and my ex several years and it's still kind of weird between us.'

Angel shook her head. 'The trouble is, I don't want to be Cal's friend.'

Sapphire smiled. 'So I *was* right the first time? I don't know you, Angel, but I know Cal and he's a good man. He made a mistake and he's really sorry. He's not one of those footballers who cheat all the time and then lie. And if I were you, I would go get him. I know he loves you.'

Angel returned to the table with Sapphire's words beating out a rhythm in her head, *Go get him*, drowning out the *I'm marrying Ethan* mantra. And so when Tony and Gemma headed back home as Tony had an early start the following day, and Cal suggested they stay for a brandy, she readily agreed.

'You seem different tonight,' Cal said as they sat in the bar area.

'How do you mean?' Angel asked, pushing back her hair, aware of Cal's gaze on her body and liking it. She wanted him to want her again, wanted to see the desire in his eyes.

'I don't know how to describe it, but usually when we're together you're defensive. It's like you've built this high wall round yourself and I can't get through. But tonight you seem . . . open.'

Angel took a sip of brandy. She suddenly felt on high alert, all her senses tuned to Cal.

'It's how I feel.'

They took another sip of their drinks then he said softly, 'What are we doing, being apart?'

'I don't know.'

He put his glass on the table and moved closer. Close enough to kiss her. He was looking into her eyes and she was the one who kissed him first. The feel of his lips on hers, the taste of him, felt so right, felt so good. They were meant to be together. He kissed her back . . . an

253

intoxicating, passionate kiss that made them both forget where they were. Cal was the first to pull back.

'Come back to mine.'

Angel didn't hesitate as she replied, 'Yes.'

As soon as Cal had closed the door to his apartment they fell into each other's arms, kissing with a feverish intensity. And then Cal picked her up and carried her into his bedroom, and they were frantically pulling off each other's clothes. And Cal was kissing her breasts, sliding his hand between her legs and caressing her so she melted at his touch, and she was pulling off his tee-shirt, unfastening his jeans feverishly to free his hard cock, which she longed to feel inside her.

'Oh, God, Angel, I want you,' he groaned as she rubbed herself against him. He pushed her back and kissed her entire body, ending up between her legs, kissing and licking her until she came in delicious, exquisite waves that pulsed through her body. And she was still riding those exquisite waves of pleasure when Cal guided his cock inside her and then they were fucking, a deep, intense fuck, Angel arching her body towards his as he drove into her, and it had never felt so good. All she could think was that she wanted him like never before. She didn't think of Ethan, didn't think of anything except how much she wanted Cal. For that moment nothing existed except their desire for each other.

As they lay in each other's arms afterwards Angel could hardly believe that she and Cal had ever been apart. She kissed his neck, his lips, traced her fingers over his face, kissed his angel-wing tattoo. She had been apart from him for too long; they belonged together. When she was with him everything made sense. And then Cal said the words she'd longed to hear him say again: 'I love you, Angel. I always have, always will.'

'I love you too,' she replied. 'I never stopped. I was just too hurt and too scared to admit it.'

Cal held her closer to him. 'I will never hurt you again, I swear.' He gazed at her, and his eyes were so full of love and hope. 'We're going to be together again.' But even as he said it Angel felt a wave of guilt.

'Oh, God, Cal, what am I going to do about Ethan and the wedding? I don't want to hurt him.'

'You'll have to see him and tell him it's over, there's no other way. But it'll be okay, I promise.'

Angel laid her head on his chest, so she could hear his heart beating. Cal was right, it would be okay. It would be horrible having to tell Ethan, but it would be for the best.

Chapter 16

Until Angel had broken it to Ethan that their relationship was over, she and Cal had decided to keep news of their reunion a secret from friends and family. It didn't seem right telling anyone else until she had told Ethan; he deserved that at least. Madeleine was still away in New York, and Cal planned to end it with her as soon as she returned the following week.

The secrecy gave Angel's relationship with Cal an added intensity. It was as if they were new lovers again, snatching time together whenever they could, hating every second of being apart from each other, and as soon as they were alone they inevitably ended up in bed, making up for all the time they had been apart. Frank had been discharged from hospital and was getting stronger by the day. Angel was to fly back to LA at the end of the week, then she would return with Honey and move into Cal's penthouse until they could return to their old family house just outside Brighton.

They had it all mapped out and Angel could hardly contain her excitement, though every time she thought of telling Ethan she felt sick with guilt and apprehension. He had already asked if there was something wrong during one of their phone calls, saying that she seemed distant. Angel felt such a liar when she claimed it was just because of the situation with her dad. She was very tempted to tell him the truth then and get it over with, but knew she had to tell him face to face. She owed him that.

'Are you hungry?' Cal asked her when Angel let herself into his flat on her last evening in Brighton; she was flying back to LA first thing in the morning. 'I'm making risotto.'

'Yes, I'm hungry,' Angel told him, walking over to him and kissing him. 'But definitely not for food,' she murmured, coming up for air, as she slipped her hands into his jeans.

'I'd forgotten what a bad influence you were,' Cal murmured. 'My risotto will be ruined.'

'So you don't want me to do this?' Angel slid to her knees and unbuttoned his jeans.

'Well, if you put it like that.'

An hour later Angel finally felt satisfied – she had sucked, licked, and kissed Cal until her lips felt numb, and they had made love with a fierce intensity, knowing that they would not see each other for at least a week, which suddenly seemed an unbearably long time. Now they were lying in bed together and Angel was gripped with nerves again about seeing Ethan; she hated knowing that she was going to hurt him so much, but there was no other way.

'It will be okay,' Cal told her, stroking her hair, instinctively knowing what she must be thinking about.

She sighed. 'I really hope so. I wish I could fast-forward time. That it could all be over and Ethan would be happy with someone else, and you, me and Honey would be together.'

'It will happen, stop worrying.'

Reluctantly Angel got up and reached for her clothes. It was time for her to go back to her parents and pack.

She was just pulling on her jeans when the front door opened and a voice that sounded like Madeleine's, called out, 'Cal, are you there?'

'What the fuck!' he exclaimed. 'I didn't think she was due back . . . just give me a minute to talk to her before you come out.' He quickly pulled on his tee-shirt and jeans and headed for the living room, closing the bedroom door behind him.

Angel rolled her eyes and sat back on the bed. Like she needed this right now! Why did she and Cal have to have such complicated lives? She expected he would break the news quickly to Madeleine and then she would leave, but some twenty minutes later Angel was still sitting on the bed and there was no sign of Cal. She tiptoed over to the bedroom door and listened but could hear nothing. Cautiously she opened the door, wanting to find out what was going on. What she heard completely stunned her.

'So obviously my parents would like me to have the baby back home in Lyon but I'm thinking London. The Portland would suit me much better.'

Madeleine was pregnant!

'Well, there's plenty of time to decide,' Angel heard Cal reply. 'You're only ten weeks.'

'And I was thinking about the wedding . . . should it be before or after the baby? I mean, hopefully I won't show for at least five months . . . but then, it takes longer than five months to plan a wedding, doesn't it?'

So they were engaged! Madeleine clearly had no idea that Cal was supposed to be leaving her to be with Angel. 'Supposed' being the word. Angel waited for him to say that there wasn't going to be a wedding but he replied, 'I don't know right now. I'm still taking in the news about you being pregnant.'

Suddenly Angel was seized with the most agonising thought; maybe Cal had no intention of leaving

Madeleine now that she was pregnant. She wanted to go out and confront him, but was held back by the thought of Madeleine. She just couldn't do that to another woman, however much she loved Cal. She heard Madeleine say that she was starving and could they go and eat, and then the two of them were leaving the flat. Angel grabbed her jacket and bag, and stormed into the living room. What the fuck was going on? At that moment, Cal let himself back into the flat.

'I had no idea about the baby,' he told Angel, walking swiftly towards her. He looked serious.

'And you're engaged?' She was once again full of all the insecurities and doubts about Cal that had haunted her since his infidelity. How could she ever trust him again?

'I only got engaged when I found out you were determined to marry Ethan.' He sighed. 'I couldn't deal with it. I'd waited for you for so long.'

'But I thought you said you wanted to be with me?' Angel said passionately.

'And I *do* want to be with you. I love you . . . I've loved you all this time . . . but how can I leave Madeleine now? She's only just found out she's pregnant.'

Cal had an expression of pure anguish on his face, but Angel could feel herself withdrawing from him again, her barriers going up.

'So when are you going to tell her? After she's had the baby?' She could feel herself withdrawing from him once more. She couldn't believe that he hadn't told her about the engagement.

'Christ, I don't know! I'm as shocked as you are. But I can't just dump her. Surely you can see that?'

Angel shook her head. 'No, I don't see it. All I can see is that you didn't tell me the truth about your relationship with her. It's sort of a pattern with you, isn't it?'

Cal groaned, 'No, please, Angel, this has nothing to

do with the past. Just let me sort it out in my own time. I'm going to have to go.' He put his arms round her and hugged her, but Angel couldn't bring herself to hug him back, she was too shocked. 'I love you. Call me as soon as you get back to LA,' he told her as he headed for the door. 'It will be okay, I promise.'

Angel just looked at him; to her the words sounded unbearably hollow. She knew Cal so well; knew how hard he would find it to leave Madeleine now she was carrying his baby. He had been abandoned by his own father when he was just three years old. Had always vowed that he would never do that to a child of his own.

Angel nearly cried when Ethan and Honey came to meet her at the airport. While it was wonderful being reunited with her daughter again, she felt such a confused mix of emotions as Ethan embraced her. She knew she loved him, knew that he wanted to be with her, and if it wasn't for Cal she could be perfectly happy with him. She didn't know what to do any more. Everything had seemed so clear while she was with Cal, before the bombshell news about Madeleine's pregnancy. Angel had checked her phone as soon as she had landed, hoping for a message from Cal letting her know that he had told Madeleine, but there was none. Now everything seemed so uncertain. Ethan was as loving to her as ever, and somehow that made her feel even worse. He and Honey had made a 'Welcome Home, Mummy' banner – well, Honey's contribution was some scribbles in purple but the thought was there – and Angel was very touched when she saw it hanging on the front door.

'We've had a good two weeks, haven't we, Honey-Bunny?' Ethan said to the little girl as they all went into the house. 'I feel we've really got close. Give me five,

Honey!' And Angel watched as her daughter solemnly held up her hand. If she married Ethan then no one would get hurt – not Ethan, not Madeleine. If she got back with Cal, then she would be hurting both of them and taking a huge risk: trusting Cal not to betray her again. That risk had seemed worth taking before she knew about Madeleine. Now it seemed like a step in the dark.

'I missed you so much,' Ethan told her later as they lay in bed. 'I guess you were too worried about your dad to think much about me.'

Angel thought of all the hours she had spent in bed with Cal and felt horribly guilty. She put her hand up to Ethan's face. 'Of course I missed you.' He ducked down to kiss her, but when the kiss turned deeper and it seemed as if Ethan wanted to make love, Angel pulled away. 'I'm sorry. Ethan, I'm exhausted. D'you mind if we don't?'

'Sure, I understand.'

He sounded slightly pissed off, so Angel felt compelled to add, 'I'll be okay tomorrow.' She felt such a fraud. When he went to the bathroom she couldn't resist checking her phone to see if there was a message from Cal. There was none. But perhaps, Angel thought bitterly, that was the message.

She couldn't sleep that night; it was partly because she was jetlagged, but more that she was tormented about what she should do. At 5 a.m. she thought she had decided. She would tell Ethan that she couldn't marry him. That was surely the right thing to do, regardless of whether Cal had left Madeleine or not. She went downstairs to make herself some tea, needing some kind of comfort.

She was just about to go outside and watch the sun rise when the phone rang. Thinking it was most likely a wrong number, she was all set to ignore it, but then she heard the caller leaving a message on the answerphone which had her rushing to pick it up. It was Loretta's nurse. She'd taken a turn for the worse. Could Ethan come right now?

Angel had been so caught up with her dad's illness that she hadn't realised how close Loretta was to the end. These past two weeks, Ethan had spent nearly all his time with her when he wasn't with Honey. He hadn't let Angel know as he didn't want to put that on her, on top of all she was going through with Frank. At Loretta's house, Angel put her arm around him, trying her best to comfort him as he held his grandmother's hand. It was so typical of Ethan, wanting to protect her, and not thinking of himself. Even though he had known this was coming he was still shell-shocked, trying to put on a brave face for his grandmother, who was drifting in and out of consciousness. There was nothing more to be done for Loretta now and the nurse told Ethan it was a matter of hours.

He told Loretta how much he loved her and about the wedding plans, as if she could hear him, while all the time her breathing was getting more and more shallow. It was late-afternoon when she opened her blue eyes for the briefest of moments, seemed to seek out Ethan's, then closed them.

'I think she's gone,' the nurse said gently.

Ethan got up and lightly kissed Loretta's forehead and stroked her hair. Then he turned to Angel, who held him to her as he wept.

'I really wanted her to be there for the wedding,' he said through his tears. 'It would have meant so much to her.'

Angel stroked his head. 'At least she knew we were getting married. She was so happy for you, Ethan, and so proud of you.' How could she tell him now that she didn't want him, and that she was in love with Cal? She just couldn't do that to him.

That night Cal finally texted her: *We have to talk x.* Ethan was asleep beside her and so Angel crept out of the bedroom and shut herself in her dressing room to call Cal back. She didn't waste any time saying hello.

'Have you told Madeleine?'

Cal sighed. 'No, it hasn't been the right time. She's had some bleeding and is worried she might lose the baby. I just can't tell her yet. Please understand, Angel?'

'I don't want you to tell her at all,' Angel said in cold, hard voice, trying desperately to hide the emotion she felt.

'What do you mean? Of course I'm going to tell her!' Cal exclaimed passionately.

'Don't. I'm going to marry Ethan. It's what I want. What happened between us was a mistake; it was wedding nerves or something.'

'Don't say this, Angel! You don't mean it. You love me, I know you do. And I love you. I just need time to break the news to Madeleine. Something else must have happened to make you say this?'

'Nothing's happened. Whatever we had, Cal, it's over. I'm marrying Ethan.' She was back saying the mantra. 'I have to go. Please don't call me again. I really have made up my mind. Goodbye, Cal.'

And before he could reply, she ended the call and switched off her phone. Somehow Angel held it together as she walked quietly through the house until she got outside and curled up on one of the sun loungers, where she lay and sobbed in the darkness.

Somehow Angel got through the next few weeks by focussing all her attention on Ethan. He was devastated by Loretta's death. She had always been there for him, and without her steady influence and unconditional love, he seemed to be floundering. Angel had constantly to reassure him that she loved him. She suggested they should postpone the wedding, but he wouldn't hear of it. 'That's the one thing that's keeping me going,' he told her, making her even more certain that she had to go through with it. Cal continued to leave messages and texts but Angel found the strength to delete them without either listening to them or reading them.

Back in the UK the press got hold of the news of Madeleine's pregnancy, which made her relationship with Cal seem fixed, as what kind of man would walk out on the mother of his child? Not Cal, that was for sure. Of course, Gemma and Jez both saw the story and called Angel to see how she had taken the news. She managed to get through the call from Gemma without giving anything away, but broke down with Jez and finally admitted what had happened.

Very little shocked Jez, but he was stunned when she told him that. 'Oh my God! You slept with Cal?'

'I thought we were going to get back together, but then he found out Madeleine was pregnant and I found out he was engaged to her.'

'Oh my God! You and Cal are *destined* to be together. You're like Richard Burton and Elizabeth Taylor.'

This was not helpful.

'We're not – he's having a baby with someone else. I'm going to marry Ethan.'

'Yeah, so you keep saying. Do you think if you keep saying it, it will come true?'

'I love Ethan,' Angel insisted. 'And he really loves me.'

'But you love Cal as well, don't you?'

Angel didn't need to answer that question. 'I have to

marry Ethan,' she said again. 'Please don't tell anyone about what happened with Cal?'

Jez sighed, 'Of course I won't tell anyone, but you really need to think this through.' He paused. 'I was going to say that it was like a situation from a Jeremy Kyle show, but it didn't seem appropriate.' Trust Jez to try and find the funny side.

'It's not appropriate,' Angel said grimly. 'Even if it is true.'

She'd thought she would feel better after confiding in someone; instead she felt even more conflicted. And she was having to put on the appearance of a happy bride-to-be. Never more so than at Simone and Matthew's engagement party. Angel had hoped that Ethan would cancel. Instead he seemed keen to go, said he wanted to socialise as they had hardly been out these past weeks. It was the very last event Angel wanted to go to.

Ethan caught up with her as she went through the clothes in her dressing room. 'Why don't you wear that white dress? It makes your figure look phenomenal,' he suggested.

'Oh, it's at the cleaner's, I was going to wear my black halterneck.'

Ethan shook his head. 'You can't wear black to someone's engagement party. It seems like really bad taste.'

Well, the bride-to-be will be coming on her broomstick, Angel was tempted to reply, but instead she held up a Roland Mouret turquoise silk mini dress which Gemma had urged her to buy. It was off the shoulder and showed off her legs and back.

'Perfect.' Ethan gave her the thumbs up. 'Though you'd look better naked.' And he took her in his arms and kissed her. He checked his watch. 'How about a quick one?' And even though sex was the last thing on

265

Angel's mind, she followed him into the bedroom. As long as she could keep him happy, then maybe she could be happy too.

'So how long have you known Simone?' Alisha asked Angel as they stood chatting at the engagement party, sipping from glasses of pink champagne.

'Six or seven years, I think, but it's kind of awkward as she was Cal's girlfriend before me and Cal got together.' Just mentioning his name caused Angel's heart to race faster. She lowered her voice and checked that Simone was nowhere nearby before adding, 'To be honest, we're not friends at all – I don't think she's ever forgiven me for marrying Cal, and I think she's still in love with him.' As soon as she said it Angel thought how bitterly ironic it was that she should find herself in the same situation. They were both marrying other men to try and forget the love of their lives. Maybe she should feel more sympathy for Simone.

'Wow, that's some heavy shit! So you don't think she's madly in love with Matthew?'

Alisha and Angel looked across the room, to where Simone was clinging on to Matthew and sending him adoring gazes. She was wearing a stunning red asymmetric mini dress, which Angel was sure was by Valentino and which suddenly made her think of the dress which had been ripped up during the break in – something which had been pushed to the back of her mind with everything else that had been going on. Simone was obviously still working hard at Matthew's re-style as he wearing a sharply tailored white suit and had had his hair cut and highlighted, but he still looked plain. As Angel's dad was fond of saying, 'You can put lipstick on a pig, but it will still be a pig.'

'I think it's unlikely, don't you?'

At that moment Simone's gaze fell upon Angel and

Alisha and she let go of Matthew and sashayed across the room towards them. Angel steeled herself for the inevitable air kisses and congratulations. Fortunately Alisha made up for Angel's slightly lacklustre good wishes by exclaiming how beautiful Simone looked, and how exciting the news was. Angel listened to the two women talking wedding plans for a moment and then excused herself to go to the bathroom; there was only so much of Simone that she could take. As she walked across the marble hallway, her phone rang. Thinking it might be Lucy she took the call without checking the caller's name. It was Cal. She was about to hang up but something stopped her. It was so good to hear his voice.

'Finally you answer! I just wanted to see how you were.' He hesitated. 'And to see if you've changed your mind? I haven't changed mine. I love you, Angel.' It was so bitter-sweet hearing him say the words. Tears prickled Angel's eyes as she managed to reply, 'No, I haven't changed my mind. I'm marrying Ethan in two weeks' time. And I don't suppose you have told Madeleine?'

'If you marry Ethan, there's no reason to upset her,' Cal said flatly. 'Please don't marry him. Whatever reasons you're doing it for are all the wrong ones. I love you, and I know you love me.'

Hearing him say those words was unbearably painful. 'I'm marrying Ethan,' Angel repeated. 'Please understand that, Cal.' She forced herself to end the call. It's going to be all right, she tried to tell herself, brushing away the tears.

'How is Cal?' It was Simone. God, she had such an unpleasant knack of turning up when you least wanted her to. Angel swung round, hoping the emotion didn't show on her face.

'He's fine, he was just calling about Honey.'

'Oh.' Simone looked as if she didn't believe a word of this. She smoothed back her glossy blonde hair. 'So how does he feel about being a father again?'

'I don't know; you'd have to ask him yourself.'

'And is he going to marry Madeleine?' Simone seemed determined to torment her.

Suddenly Angel snapped, 'Why don't you fucking ask him yourself if you're so interested? And while you're at it, you can tell him that you still love him and that you always have loved him and you always will and your wedding is just one fucking big charade! And that you don't love Matthew. You're marrying him for his money and because you can't stand to be alone.'

Simone stared back at her. For a second the raw hurt showed on her face, then her expression hardened as she performed a slow hand clap. 'Well done, Angel, you worked it all out. For your next trick you can admit that everything you just said about me goes for you as well. You're still in love with Cal, you don't fool me.'

Both women had been so caught up in their exchange that they had failed to notice Matthew walk into the hall. 'What's going on?' he asked, a bemused expression on his boyish face. 'I came to tell you we're about to do the toast.' God knows how much he had overheard.

Simone looked stricken. 'It's nothing, darling. Angel and I were just having a tiny disagreement, but it's all cleared up now.' She turned to Angel as if to appeal to her.

Part of Angel wanted to tear down the lies and tell Matthew the truth, but she couldn't be that brutal. Instead she said, 'Yeah, I'm sorry, Matthew, it was nothing.' She forced herself to smile. 'You know what brides-to-be can be like! A pair of Bridezillas! It's just wedding nerves.' God, she made herself want to be sick, trotting out these lies. She really was no better than Simone.

'I do love you, darling, don't ever doubt it,' Simone exclaimed, putting her arms round him. 'Come on, let's do the toast.' Matthew still looked uncertain, but he let her kiss him.

They were about to return to the party when there was a knock at the door. Simone walked over and opened it. Angel was completely stunned when Benny Sullivan walked in. He kissed Simone in greeting and shook Matthew's hand, then gave a sly smile as he noticed Angel.

'I don't imagine you expected to see me again, did you?'

Angel was pretty much speechless.

'Benny's representing Matthew and me,' Simone said smoothly, having quickly recovered her composure. 'We're doing a two-part reality show about our wedding. I'm really surprised you didn't want to film yours.'

This was too much for Angel. 'I'm going to find Ethan,' she replied, and practically ran from the hallway.

Ethan was in the middle of a game of pool with Logan and another couple of team mates when she tracked him down to Matthew's vast games room. While Simone had stamped her style on the rest of the house – with chic furniture, huge black-and-white photographs of her and Matthew, and plenty of pictures of Simone on her own, looking sexy and air brushed – Matthew's games room was clearly his sanctuary. It was designed to look like a bar, with dark green walls and subdued lighting; framed *Playboy* centrefolds hung on the walls, including Pamela Anderson and Carmen Electra.

'Hey, are you okay?' Ethan asked, seeing Angel walk in. He smiled warmly at her, and she felt even worse, because she knew that what Simone had said to her had been true.

'Yeah, I just had a bit of an unpleasant surprise. I saw Benny Sullivan.' Seeing Benny was the very least of her problems, but he was a good distraction to offer Ethan.

'What the fuck's he doing here?'

'Apparently he's now representing Matthew and Simone. They're doing a reality show of their wedding.'

She expected Ethan to be shocked. Instead he simply shrugged and said, 'Whatever. They're welcome to him; it's nothing to do with me. He was okay to you, wasn't he?'

'Yeah, slimey as ever.' She paused. 'I just wondered when we can leave?'

'Not till after the toast, I guess.'

Alisha then wandered into the room. 'Wow, I see Simone hasn't got her hands on this room yet! D'you know, I counted twenty-five pictures of her, including one of her butt naked right above their bed when I sneaked in the bedroom to take a look.'

'Where is their bedroom? I'll have to check that out,' Logan joked. 'Not that Simone is my type, baby, way too skinny. But just for research. How about we get one of you for our bedroom?' he added quickly.

'Yeah, 'cos I would just love the boys seeing that!'

'What about you just do the picture for me to have in my wallet, for my own personal use?'

'And your team mates, when you get drunk and show them? Dream on. Anyway, I came to tell you guys that the happy couple are about to do a toast and cut the cake.'

Angel and Ethan had just walked back into the vast living room when they came face to face with Benny Sullivan.

'Ethan, long time no see!' Benny gave a fake smile, flashing his whiter-than-white teeth. He made to shake Ethan's hand, but Ethan didn't offer his.

'Let's not pretend to be friends, Benny.'

He dropped the pretence of being nice. 'Fuck you, Ethan,' he muttered, then moved away as Matthew clapped his hands together and called out, 'Hey, guys, we're going to do the cake thing now.'

Everyone stopped talking then and faced Matthew, who was red-faced with embarrassment. He certainly wasn't good at public speaking but spluttered out his thanks to everyone for coming.

Simone took over then, saying smoothly, 'I know some of you were probably surprised by our engagement, but all I can say is that when you meet the right person, you just know, don't you?' It was the same speech she'd delivered when she'd come round for dinner and she'd obviously been working on it since as she sounded very sweet and loving. Angel sensed that she was winning over the doubters. 'I guess you all know that I'm slightly older than Matthew, and when I met him I'd almost lost my faith in love. He's restored that. Now all I want to do is spend the rest of my life with this gorgeous man.' Steady on! Angel thought. Gorgeous was surely pushing it? And as for *slightly* older . . . well, that really was a stretch. Simone was easily ten years older. But no one else seemed to share Angel's cynicism. There was a collective 'Ah' from the audience and someone started the clapping.

Benny cut across the applause then to call out, 'Let's have a toast to the happy couple – Matthew and Simone!' Everyone raised their glasses and dutifully repeated 'Matthew and Simone'.

But Benny hadn't finished. 'There's so much love in the room, I can almost feel it. I think we should have a toast to love!'

'Can you pass me a bucket so I can throw up?' Ethan whispered into Angel's ear as everyone once more raised their glasses. 'Let's get out of here.'

Chapter 17

Angel sat up in bed. She'd had the dream again . . . the one about her wedding. She was walking up the aisle, Ethan was standing in front of her with his back to her, and then when she reached him he would turn round and she would see that his face was blank. It was the most disturbing sight.

Beside her he lay sleeping peacefully. She lay back down and curled her body round his, trying to feel reassured by his warmth, but couldn't get back to sleep again. The wedding was now only three days away. Cal had left more messages, but as before Angel had ruthlessly deleted them. There was speculation in the UK press that he and Madeleine were to be married after the baby was born. And everyone will live happily ever after, Angel thought bitterly.

She had done her best to throw herself into the preparations for the wedding. Fortunately Ethan had hired a wedding planner, so that had taken away a lot of the pressure, and Angel just had to sign off the catering, flowers and music, and get Honey and Megan fitted in their flower girl dresses. She felt as if she was going through the motions. Everything she did took her further and further away from Cal. She forced herself not to think about the passionate time they had spent together in Brighton, but too often the memories would flood her mind. She would be making love with Ethan and have her eyes closed, and when she opened them it would be a shock to see that it was him and not Cal. Maybe when she was married she would stop thinking of Cal. She could close the door on that part of her life. Somehow she doubted it.

She finally fell asleep around 6 a.m. and didn't hear Ethan leave for training. When she woke at 9 she had a mad dash to get ready and pick up Gemma, Jez and Rufus from the airport.

'You look more knackered than we do!' Gemma exclaimed when she saw her friend at Arrivals.

'Don't say that!'

'Ignore her, you don't look so bad,' Jez declared, giving Angel a welcome hug. They headed towards the exit. 'Are you all right?' he whispered while Gemma and Rufus walked ahead of them.

'Not really,' Angel admitted. 'I just want this to be over and done with. But it's only pre-wedding nerves, isn't it?'

Jez sighed, 'When I married Rufus it was the happiest day of my life. I'm not trying to tell you what to do, but don't you think that's how you should be thinking of your wedding day? Not as something you need to get over and done with.'

Angel couldn't bring herself to answer. Back at the house the friends chilled out by the pool. Fortunately Gemma was too jetlagged to notice that Angel seemed subdued, and Rufus was too discreet to say anything. In the early evening they all went out for a supper at Spago and met up with Ethan. But even with the company of her friends, Angel still felt flat. Jez seemed to sense this and compensated by being extra-flamboyant.

'Should you two even be together so close to the wedding?' he said at one point, in mock-horror. 'Shouldn't Ethan be staying in a bachelor pad and relishing his last few days of freedom? Some kind of James Bond-type luxe apartment with bikini-ed lovelies, wearing flowers in their hair – I'm thinking purple orchids or some kind of hibiscus – tending to his every whim, but obviously not crossing the line.'

Ethan smiled. 'It's an interesting thought. I was considering spending the night before the wedding away from Angel, but at a hotel. I was thinking more along the lines of me and Logan having a steak, shooting some pool and watching a movie. Logan doesn't look good in a bikini, and his hair is way too short to have flowers in it.' He turned to Angel. 'What do you say? I just thought it might make the wedding night feel even more special if we'd been apart.'

Angel, who could only get through the nights knowing that Ethan was beside her, felt her spirits plummet at the prospect. 'I'll miss you,' she said quietly.

'It'll be for one night,' he said. 'And just think, you can hang out with Gemma, Jez and Rufus. Knock yourself out on Marmite sandwiches and watch a rom com.'

'Perlease!' said Jez, outraged. 'We'll watch something French and sophisticated.'

'Yeah, right.' Ethan had Jez's number now. 'I know for a fact that it will be a rom com, something with Sarah Jessica Parker or Sandra Bullock in it, so don't pretend otherwise.'

'Oh, all right,' Jez muttered, and turned to Angel. 'So can we?'

She felt that a horror film was probably more suited to her mood right now. It would at least take her mind off her own worries. 'Sure, Jez, so long as you promise not to blub.'

'And don't forget, you need to pack for the honeymoon.' Ethan reminded her.

After the reception he was whisking her away for four days, while Angel's mum and dad looked after Honey. He hadn't yet told her where. 'Though you won't need any clothes for what I've got planned,' he said flirtatiously.

Angel forced a smile. Perhaps by the time they went on honeymoon she wouldn't have this sick feeling of dread in the pit of her stomach.

Back at the house the marquees had been put up in the garden along with the fairy lights in the trees. The following day the flowers would arrive, along with the champagne and wine. Plus her mum, dad and Tony had arrived and checked into their hotel.

'Only one more day to go before you're Mrs Turner,' Ethan said as they snuggled up in bed later that night. 'I cannot wait!' He sounded blissfully happy. Not for Ethan the pre-wedding jitters, the niggling worry that he was signing away his freedom.

'Nor can I,' Angel said, knowing that was what was expected. I do love this man, she reminded herself as she lay awake for the next few hours, listening to Ethan's even breathing while he slept. But when she finally fell asleep once again her dreams were full of Cal. She was running after him and never quite able to catch up with him. He remained out of reach.

'Just as well we're going to the spa today, you look like shit!' Gemma exclaimed when she saw Angel at breakfast by the pool.

Angel groaned. She could do without Gemma being quite so plain-speaking for once. 'Do I really look that bad? I just haven't been sleeping lately.'

Gemma took pity on her. 'Well, obviously, you still look gorgeous . . . just shit by your standards. But I'm sure today will sort you out.' She picked up the brochure for One Spa at Shutters on the Beach, which was supposed to be one of the best in LA. 'I can't wait to go here! It looks amazing, and it will be so nice to be pampered for a change.'

Angel managed a smile. Today was her treat for her friends and her mum, and usually she'd have been as up for the pampering as they were, but right now she wasn't bothered if she went or not. It was almost as if she didn't think she deserved it.

Angel had offered to book places for Tony and her dad, too, but the men had declined and instead were going to play golf with Ethan. He had asked Jez and Rufus along, but Jez looked at him as if he had gone stark raving bonkers. As if he would want to hit a little white ball with a stick when he could be having a Beach Buff!

'That's a Swedish Massage and Scrub and Buff with Re-texturising Sea Mineral Scrub followed by Tropical Rain Rinse to you,' he declared, reading from the brochure. 'And then I'm having a facial which is an "anti-gravity complexion treatment, a firming oxygenating anti-wrinkle hydrating treatment", followed by a manicure, and rounding it all off with a pedicure.'

'You're going to look so hot after that that I'll probably fancy you as much as my wife-to-be!' Ethan teased. 'Sure you won't change your mind?'

Jez and Rufus both shook their heads and, after kissing Angel, Ethan set off to pick up Tony and Frank from their hotel and take them to the exclusive golf course where he was a member.

While Jez, Rufus and Gemma tucked into scrambled eggs and smoked salmon, Angel just picked at some fruit salad. She had no appetite.

'You should eat more than that,' Gemma told her,

277

noticing how little Angel had eaten. 'At this rate Kaz is going to need to alter your dress again! You've lost weight since I last saw you.'

Angel grabbed a cup of tea and went upstairs. After her shower she put on a pale pink Juicy Couture tracksuit and the largest pair of sunglasses she owned. Gemma was right, she really did look like shit; she just hoped her friend could work her make-up artist magic on her tomorrow.

Michelle was already at the spa waiting for them. Angel almost cried when she saw her mum. She wished she could tell her what had happened with Cal and ask her if she thought she was doing the right thing marrying Ethan. But she felt that it wouldn't be fair to burden her so soon after Frank's illness, and she knew that only she could make up her mind.

Everyone went off happily to get changed into fluffy white robes ready for their various treatments. Angel spent the next couple of hours having a facial that she hoped would make even her tired complexion look peachy again. The therapist knew she was getting married and was so perky and relentlessly cheerful, asking her questions about the wedding, that Angel had to tell her that she had a headache and would she mind not talking. And then it was lunch at One Pico, the lovely outside restaurant with its stunning views of the beach. 'If only I could have those treatments every single day!' Jez exclaimed over his shellfish and avocado salad. 'No wonder celebs look so bloody good if they get pampered like that on a weekly basis.'

'That was so gorgeous, Angel, thank you so much,' Michelle said, looking radiant and a good ten years younger. 'I wish I could have got your dad to come along, it would have done him the world of good.'

Gemma snorted with laughter. 'I really can't see

Frank agreeing to that! Can you imagine him stretched out on a massage couch. He'd be so embarrassed he'd probably have to make conversation all the way through and completely ruin the experience.'

'Yeah, he'd probably start trying to explain the offside rule to the therapist,' Angel put in. She had ordered the seared tuna Niçoise salad, but yet again found she could barely eat anything and was just pushing the food round on her plate. She hoped Gemma didn't notice.

Talk turned to the wedding and to speculation about where Ethan was going to take Angel for the honeymoon. Her friends and mum were so happy for her, though Jez would give her an occasional sympathetic look when no one else was looking, guessing that she was obsessing over Cal.

'Oh, hiya!' Angel's party swivelled round to see Simone standing by their table, looking slimmer than ever in white skinny jeans and white halterneck, with a diamond necklace spelling out her name. Angel had one just like it. She hadn't seen Simone since the party and it definitely wasn't a case of absence making the heart grow fonder. She remembered their last run in only too clearly.

'Excited about tomorrow?' Simone flashed a smile at Angel that didn't reach her eyes. 'And Gemma, Jez and Rufus! How lovely to see you!' She sauntered round the table to treat the three of them to air kisses. She didn't dare do that with Angel. 'Did you see the story about Cal and Madeleine planning to get married? It's wedding bonanza! Soon we'll all have our own happy ever after, won't we?'

Angel just looked at her. How could she be so insensitive?

'So how's it going with Matthew?' Gemma asked, diplomatically trying to change the subject and avert a cat fight. She had noticed the dangerous glint in Angel's eye, which said she wanted to inflict some serious damage on Simone bitch-face Fraser.

Angel wasn't sure if it was her imagination but a shadow seemed to cross Simone's face. She answered in typical upbeat style, though. 'Fantastic. We've set a date in the fall – you're all invited. It's going to be a really big wedding.'

'So his parents are okay about you getting married?' Angel asked.

'Oh, yes. I mean, I've got to convert to their church, which is an evangelical something or other, but that's fine by me. I'd do anything to marry Matthew.'

Angel just bet she would. Ethan had showed her an article about Matthew which put his yearly earnings at well over $10 million dollars and that didn't even include the recent advertising deal he'd signed to pub-licise some luxury watch. He might not have Ethan's looks or charm, but the general view was that he was shaping up to be one of the greatest players of all time. It seemed Simone had chosen extremely wisely. She trotted off after that to meet him for lunch, leaving a waft of Maitresse behind her.

'Blonde . . . so not her colour,' Jez said, shaking his head.

'It is a bit weird, isn't it?' Gemma commented. 'I didn't get it before when you told me, but she really does look a bit like you.'

She caught sight of the thunderous expression on Angel's face and added hastily, 'I mean, nowhere near as beautiful. Obviously. Please don't hurt me! It's the hair and that outfit and the necklace . . . I swear you've been photographed in something just like it.'

'Tell Ethan not to buy you a golden Labrador or accept a BJ off a woman pretending to be you. A stiletto in the head has got to hurt! Sorry, Michelle,' Jez added.

Michelle was looking at him in bemusement. 'What are you talking about?'

And so Jez had to explain the entire plot of *Single White Female*. Fortunately everyone was so caught up in his summary that no one noticed Angel had hardly eaten anything by the time the waiter removed their first courses.

There were more pampering treatments in the afternoon – pedicures and manicures for the women and Jez while Rufus hung out by the pool.

'How are you feeling?' Jez asked Angel when they found themselves in the relaxation room several hours later. It was the first time the pair of them had been alone together. He was lying on one of the couches sipping herbal tea, but even after the treatments Angel was too wound up to relax and literally couldn't sit still. She was pacing round the room.

She paused for a moment to say, 'I'll feel so much better when I'm married. I keep having these night-mares that something goes wrong with the wedding.' She shuddered as she recalled the image of the faceless man from her dream.

'Nothing is going to go wrong,' Jez tried to reassure her. 'Everything is going to be fine . . . brilliant, in fact.' He checked his watch. This time tomorrow afternoon you will be Mrs Turner. That's if you really want to be?' he added.

'I do . . . I really do,' Angel replied.

'It's okay, you don't have to convince me,' he said gently.

'You heard what Simone said – Cal is going to marry Madeleine. I'm going to marry Ethan. We'll all be very happy.'

When they returned from the Spa, the men all sat chilling by the pool, drinking bottles of Bud, while

281

around them the final preparations were being made for the big day. Tony, Frank and Ethan had all enjoyed their game of golf and were happy and laid-back. It seemed to Angel that everyone was except her. The closer it got to Ethan leaving for his hotel, the more anxious Angel felt. As she said goodbye to him the hallway, she couldn't stop herself from asking, 'Are you sure you want to spend tonight apart?' She wrapped her arms around him as if she could physically stop him.

He kissed her lightly and said, 'It'll be fun. And if you look under your pillow, you'll find a little something.'

'I'd much rather have you,' Angel replied.

'Babe, I can't fit under the pillow,' he teased. 'I'll see you in the morning.' He kissed her again, this time more deeply. 'Love you.'

'Love you too,' Angel replied, reluctantly letting him go. Her mum and dad left soon after that, they had to be careful that Frank got plenty of rest. Tony was really suffering from jetlag and so took himself off to bed. Angel couldn't help thinking he was also trying to avoid her. She knew that Cal wouldn't have told him what happened between them, but guessed that her brother still thought she was wrong to be marrying Ethan.

Jez, Rufus and Gemma were in the living room. They had cracked open a bottle of Sauvignon Blanc and were arguing about what to watch.

'Angel should decide,' Jez said. 'You have to choose between *The Hangover* and *Did You Hear About the Morgans?* I'm torn between lusting after Bradley Cooper and worshipping at the altar of SJP.'

Angel shrugged. 'I'm really not bothered.' She poured herself a large glass of white wine and sat on the sofa next to Gemma. Even though it was a warm night she wrapped herself up in a fake fur throw as suddenly she felt freezing cold.

Gemma was quick to pick up on her mood. 'Pre-wedding nerves?' she asked. 'It's going to be such a good day tomorrow.' She gestured at the marquees already set up on the lawns, visible through the large French windows. 'Everything's ready. Your dress is perfect, your hair looks fab, I'm going to do your make-up. So stop frowning or I'll have to book you a last-minute Botox appointment!'

Angel looked over at Jez and Rufus who both shrugged sympathetically. Suddenly she had an urgent need to know if Gemma thought she was doing the right thing marrying Ethan.

'There's just one problem, Gem – I'm still in love with Cal,' she announced. There was a pause, then Gemma spoke.

'I'm tempted to say, "Tell me something I don't know",' she said dryly, but she looked sympathetic. 'You can't go ahead and marry Ethan feeling like this. Why don't you tell Cal how you feel? I'd swear he still loves you.'

Angel gave a heartfelt sigh 'It's complicated.' And she went on to describe how she and Cal had planned to get back together, and how Madeleine's pregnancy had changed everything.

'He didn't tell me they'd been planning to get married! I just don't think I can ever trust him, and I can't live my life like that. Ethan loves me and he's such a good man . . . and Loretta died and I'm all Ethan's got and I couldn't hurt him by leaving . . .' Angel had been calm as she started to speak but now the tears rained down her cheeks. 'I don't know what to do!'

'Oh, babe, and I can't tell you. None of us can. But look at yourself, crying before you get married. How can that be right?'

Angel didn't answer and Gemma went on, 'Cal gave me something for you. He wanted you to have it the night before the wedding.'

She reached into her bag for a small parcel wrapped in gold tissue paper. Angel unwrapped it to reveal a pink leather jewellery case. She snapped it open. Inside was a silver love heart on a silver chain. She turned over the heart and saw it was engraved with the words: *i carry your heart with me* – the first words of the poem Cal had read out on their wedding day. Angel had never forgotten that poem and Cal must have known that he didn't need to say anything else. It was his way of reminding her that he loved her.

Silently she handed the necklace to Gemma who then passed it to Jez and Rufus. Finally Rufus spoke. He had been quiet all this time. 'Only you know what to do for the best, Angel, but whatever you decide, we're all here for you.'

The four friends stayed up for a while longer. Angel tried to encourage the others to watch a movie, but no one was in the mood now. All the happiness and sparkle they had felt during the day seemed to have drained away. In the end Angel made an excuse about needing an early night and went up to bed, though she doubted she would sleep.

She checked on Honey first. Her daughter had flung her duvet off and Angel gently put it back over her and sat by the side of the bed for a while. Her thoughts seemed as jumbled and confused as ever. She felt more lost than she ever had before in her life. She just didn't know what to do. Eventually she went into her bedroom.

The bed felt horribly empty without Ethan and she longed to feel his reassuring warmth beside her. In the end she got up and went through his wardrobe. She pulled out one of his sweatshirts which smelt of him and wrapped that around her. But it was no good, she couldn't sleep. Then she remembered his comment about the gift under her pillow. She discovered a Tiffany box and inside was the dazzling green tourmaline pendant, surrounded by diamonds, that Ethan had wanted to buy her all those months ago. There was also a note in the case: *'Angel, you have made my life complete. I love you more than I can say. Here's to the rest of our lives together.'*

She held the pendant up and the gemstone caught the light and sparkled. It was beautiful, but it didn't mean anything to Angel. She put it by the side of the bed and reached instead for the silver love heart necklace which Cal had given her, re-reading the inscription. He loved her, she knew that, but was it enough? He hadn't been completely honest with her about Madeleine, and he had cheated in the past. How could she trust him again? And how could she hurt Ethan? She should marry him and accept that she would always love Cal, shouldn't she?

By the time Honey came racing into her room at eight o'clock, full of excitement about putting on her flower girl dress and most of all about the chocolate fountain, Angel had probably only slept for two hours. She felt a physical and emotional wreck. She took Honey's hand and the two of them went down to the kitchen to have breakfast, or rather for Honey to have breakfast. Jez, Rufus and Gemma joined them a few minutes later. They all looked at Angel questioningly as if to say, What have you decided?

'I'm getting married to Ethan,' she told them. Gemma bit her lip and didn't say anything. It was left to Jez to respond, 'If that's what you want, Angel, we're right behind you. Hair and make-up in twenty minutes.'

285

He looked meaningfully at Gemma, who managed to say, 'Yep, I'll grab some breakfast and see you up in the dressing room.'

'Don't worry, we have the technology, we can rebuild her!' Jez declared an hour or so later after Angel had emerged from the shower. But she doubted that as she sat in front of her dressing-table mirror while Jez made a start on blow drying her hair. Across the hall Lucy was getting Honey ready, downstairs she could hear the clatter of the caterers, the door-bell kept ringing as last-minute supplies of food arrived, along with the chocolate fountain and ice sculptures.

'Love the necklace, by the way,' Jez said, noticing Ethan's present which Angel was wearing.

Gemma wandered into the dressing room next with her make up case. It seemed to Angel as if Jez and Gemma had agreed not to talk about what she'd revealed last night as both of them were relentlessly cheerful, constantly telling her how wonderful she looked. Angel would far rather they had said nothing at all.

The only thing that brought a smile to her face was seeing Honey dance into the room wearing her pale pink dress. She looked so cute, and was so enormously proud of her appearance she kept twirling round and round to make the skirt flare out. Finally, after Gemma had worked her magic on her face and Jez had arranged her hair up, it was time for Angel to put on her wedding dress.

She looked in the mirror. Her hair was perfect, her make-up was perfect, the white dress was perfect. The trouble was, it all felt like a charade. A lie.

'You do look beautiful!' Gemma exclaimed, backed up by Jez and then Rufus. They were all trying so hard to be nice.

'Thanks, guys,' Angel managed to say, but inside she felt as if her heart was breaking.

Finally her brother made an appearance as they prepared to get into the cars to take them to the church. 'You make a beautiful bride,' he told her. 'And I'm happy for you, if this is what you really want.' He paused then. 'But if it's not, and you don't want to go through with it, we'd all understand.'

Angel just nodded and got into the car.

The small church had been decorated with exquisite arrangements of white flowers; the air was heady with the fragrance of lilies and roses. Angel could see her friends and family already seated. At the end of the candlelit aisle, dressed in a black tux and looking heart-stoppingly handsome, was Ethan. He was chatting and laughing with Logan, his best man and ring bearer. He turned and caught sight of Angel waiting at the back of church, and smiled and blew her a kiss. He looked as if this was indeed the happiest day of his life. Jez and Rufus took their seats, leaving Gemma and Angel and Frank, who was going to give Angel away.

'You look beautiful, love,' he told his daughter, beaming at her; then got caught up with giving Honey a hug and admiring her dress.

'I'll go and sit down now, shall I?' Gemma asked. She hesitated before whispering, 'Are you sure you want to do this?'

Angel nodded, not trusting herself to speak, and Gemma walked quickly up the aisle.

At a signal from the minister, a young male singer began singing 'Love Me Tender', and Angel and Frank began their slow walk up the aisle while Honey skipped behind them. Angel kept her eyes fixed on Ethan, though she was aware of everyone looking at her. Then she was standing next to him. He was still smiling and looking so happy. She should marry him and make him even happier. He loved her. The minister began the wedding service . . . but suddenly Angel knew with absolute certainty that she couldn't go through with this. It would be living a lie, and it would be unfair on Ethan. It wasn't even that she was thinking about being with Cal, she just knew she would rather be on her own than be with someone she didn't love with her whole heart.

The minister's words seemed to wash over her until he said, "'If there is any here present who knows any reason why these two should not be lawfully married, you are to declare it or forever hold your peace.'"

Angel felt a rushing noise in her head then, thought she might actually faint as she looked at the minister and said quietly, 'I need to speak to Ethan alone.'

From behind her she heard a collective intake of breath from the guests. Ethan looked completely stunned as he said, 'Is this some kind of joke, Angel?'

She shook her head and said, 'Please, I need to talk to you.' She could hardly bring herself to look at him. Instead she focused on the minister who, if he was surprised, didn't react but instead said smoothly, 'We're just going to take a short break, folks, I'm sure we'll be back.' He nodded at the string quartet who began playing again to fill the awkward silence and led the way to a small side room. 'Would you like me to be present?' he asked.

Angel shook her head and he left the couple alone together, closing the door behind him.

'What is this, Angel?' Ethan asked urgently. Gone was his smile as he looked anxiously at her.

She clutched at the layers of tulle in her skirt. 'I'm so sorry, Ethan, I can't marry you.'

He looked stricken. 'What are you talking about? Why not?'

'I love you but there's someone I love more. I can't marry you.'

'You're talking about Cal? But it's over between you two – he's marrying someone else. You love me . . . you just said you did! Come on, Angel, this is because you're thinking of your first marriage, thinking you can't trust me, but you can. I love you. I want to spend the rest of my life with you.' He sounded frantic as he pleaded with her. It was unbearable knowing that she was putting him through so much pain.

'I know I can trust you, it's not that. But I love Cal, and I can't marry you feeling like that. It wouldn't be fair on you; you deserve someone who can give you so much more.'

'But I love you,' Ethan said again, an anguished expression on his face. And Angel knew she had to be brutal by telling him the truth, so that he would know once and for all that it was over. There was no hope.

'You wouldn't if you knew the truth. I slept with Cal when I was back in England last time.'

Ethan looked as if she had just punched him; anguish was replaced by jealousy.

'How many times?'

'I don't know.'

'What, you lost count?'

'Something like that.' She hated saying this but it seemed like the only way.

Ethan raised his hand, and fleetingly looked as if he was going to hit her. Angel didn't flinch, she almost wished he would. Instead he lowered his hand with an expression of disgust. 'You bitch! Why the fuck did you come back and go ahead with the wedding?'

'I know I should have been honest, but I loved you too and I was so confused. Then Loretta died.'

'So what was I . . . your fucking sympathy case? Well,

I don't fucking *need* your sympathy. How could you do this to me, Angel?'

'I'm so sorry, Ethan.'

She had promised herself that she wouldn't cry, but could feel the tears blurring her eyes. She was destroying any hope of a future relationship with him. She was making this man, for whom she cared deeply, hate her.

Ethan stared at her with such hurt and pain in his blue eyes. 'He'll fuck you up, just like he did before. He'll cheat and lie because that's what men like him do. And I won't be there to pick up the pieces. Maybe Benny Sullivan was right about you after all. You are just a cheap whore. Someone who just happens to be beautiful, but whose beauty doesn't go below the surface.' He was walking out of the door when he stopped and turned back. 'How ironic that you left Cal because he cheated on you, and you did just the same to me. You must deserve each other.'

For a second he looked at her then said, 'I'm only glad about one thing. That Loretta wasn't here to see what you just did. I'm going, you can sort out the guests. By tonight I want you out of my house. I never want to see you again, Angel.' He left the room, slamming the door behind him.

Angel watched, feeling numb, as the minister broke the news; saw the shocked expressions of the guests; felt shame as she saw Logan and Alisha hurriedly leave the church to comfort their friend. She hated herself for not calling off the wedding before; she had humiliated and hurt Ethan so badly. All the guests filed out of the church, leaving just Angel's parents along with her friends. She looked at them, wondering what they must think of her.

'You did the right thing,' Michelle said, hugging her

daughter. 'It would have been far worse to marry him and then leave.'

'Oh, Mum, I feel so bad that I hurt him! He didn't deserve that,' Angel sobbed. She just wanted to get away, return to the UK as soon as she could. She didn't even want to go back to the house to pack up her things, but realised that wouldn't be fair on Ethan. He wouldn't want any reminders left of the woman who had humiliated him and broken his heart.

Jez, Gemma, Rufus and Tony rallied round, phoning the additional guests to tell them that the reception was cancelled. Some were already on their way, and while Angel was packing she heard the doorbell ring and could hear Gemma explaining to visitors that the wedding was off. Her mum and dad had to deal with the caterers, while Rachel, the über-efficient wedding planner, promised to sort out everything else and ensure the house was cleared of everything connected to the ceremony as soon as possible. Angel told her she'd take care of the bill. By six o'clock Angel and her friends had packed up her things which Jose would arrange to have shipped back to the UK. Angel found it hard even to look at him when she gave him her instructions. He must despise her for putting Ethan through such hell. But thankfully Jose was a consummate professional, as ever. If he thought Angel was a bitch, he didn't let on.

Ethan didn't come back to the house. She took off the engagement ring and the necklace he had given her, and left them by the side of the bed. She knew he wouldn't want to read any excuses for what she had done, but felt she had to leave him something so wrote, '*I'm sorrier than you will ever know. I wish more than anything that I hadn't hurt you.*' The words seemed so feeble in the face of his pain, but they were all she had.

'So have you called Cal?' Jez asked as they finally got into the car to take them to the hotel.

Angel shook her head. 'I'm not going to. I think I really need to be on my own.'

Chapter 18

Angel stared at the headlines on an array of tabloids: *'Runaway Bride!'* *'Angel Does a Runner!'* She had promised herself she wouldn't look at any newspapers, but as she and her family walked through Gatwick her gaze was irresistibly drawn to the stand of papers just inside W. H. Smith.

'Mummy!' Honey pointed excitedly at the pictures of Angel on all the front pages, making her feel even worse. She picked up her daughter and lowered her head. The paps were surrounding them, pushing and shoving each other, desperate to get their shot of the woman who had dumped Ethan at the altar and broken his heart. Angel felt as if she was doing the walk of shame as the press shouted out questions to her: 'Where's Ethan?' 'Does this mean you're getting back with Cal?'

Now *there* was a question. He had called Angel but she wouldn't talk to him. The recent break-up with Ethan just felt too raw, she needed time. She knew from Tony that Cal was away in Dubai for the next two weeks, hoping to raise money for his football academies. Tony didn't know what was going on with Madeleine. It was such a relief when they reached the car and shut the doors on the cameras and the shouting.

'We'll be home soon, love,' Michelle told Angel,

seeing how upset her daughter was. 'And then you can put all this behind you.'

Angel gave a small smile. She doubted it very much.

Back at the house the press attention didn't let up. Angel's parents lived in a terraced house on a narrow street in Brighton, but that didn't stop the paps from camping outside, blocking the pavements, double parking on the road. Inside Michelle had to draw the living-room curtains to stop them looking in, and the minute anyone opened the front door the cameras went berserk.

Angel spent two days there, feeling like a prisoner. 'I've got to get out of here, Mum,' she said on the morning of the third day, 'it's doing my head in! I can't even take Honey to the park.'

She still felt awful about Ethan, and the situation with the press was making everything feel even worse. Hard as it was, she had continued to ignore Cal's phone calls but she kept the love heart necklace close to her, and every night before she went to sleep she would read the inscription, as if it could tell her what to do.

'It'll die down,' Michelle told her, seeing her daughter pace round the house like a caged animal. But when Angel stomped up to her bedroom and switched on her laptop she saw from the online coverage that the story was only gaining more momentum. Ethan had done an interview with one of the US papers where he said that Angel had been unfaithful to him. The only saving grace was that he hadn't named Cal. She must have hurt him very badly for him to lash out like this; he never usually spoke to the press about personal things.

Angel forced herself to read on, hating herself even more when she read how Ethan described the way he was still getting over the death of his beloved grandmother, how he had thought Angel was the love of his life. She was about turn off her computer, feeling that she couldn't bear to read any more, when a familiar name caught her eye: Simone Fraser, described as a former friend of Angel's: 'Her treatment of Ethan is unbelievably cruel and heartless, but I've always found her to be cold and selfish. The bottom line is that Angel has only ever cared about herself. She told me that she had never really loved Ethan and that she was marrying him for publicity and to raise her profile in the States. I guess she must have had an attack of conscience when it came to the actual wedding. Ethan is well out of it. He's a lovely, lovely man who deserves to be with someone who loves him unconditionally. I am going to do all I can to support him.'

Angel wanted to scream with frustration! How could Simone be such a two-faced bitch! Then she realised the other woman was finally getting her revenge for Cal's leaving her for Angel all those years ago. For the first time Angel understood what the expression 'Revenge is a dish best served cold' actually meant. Simone had waited a long time. Now must have seemed like the perfect opportunity to stick the knife in.

But she couldn't bear to think of Simone cosying up to Ethan, and spreading her poison. He was vulnerable and wouldn't be able to see Simone for what she was. She picked up her phone and selected Ethan's number. Of course his phone went straight to voice mail.

'Ethan, I wanted to say again that I'm sorry for everything. And please don't be taken in by Simone Fraser. I did love you, very much. I know it doesn't feel like that can be true right now, but it is. Simone's always hated me because Cal left her for me. She's still in love with him and is only marrying Matthew for his money

295

and status. She doesn't love him. She practically admitted as much to me. Anyway, I don't suppose you'll even listen to this message, but if you do, please take good care of yourself.'

She switched off her laptop and went back downstairs where Michelle was making fairy cakes with Honey in the kitchen.

'I've just had your estate agent on the phone,' Michelle told her as Angel slumped at the kitchen table and dipped her finger into the mixing bowl. 'And the tenants have moved out. You can go back to your house by the end of tomorrow, once it's been cleaned and they've moved the furniture out of storage.'

'Oh, that would be so good, Mum. That way we can have our lives back again.' Angel's house had walls all around its extensive grounds, and CCTV cameras to deter any incursions by paps.

'Yes, it will be just as well. Your dad nearly decked a photographer this morning when he went out to get some milk – and him ending up in court for assault is the last thing we need. Oh, Gemma called. Wanted to know if you could get out for a drink tonight?'

'I'd love to go out, but I don't want that lot chasing me down the road!'

'Ah, I have a plan,' Michelle said, smiling. 'I'm not going to let those bastards have it all their own way.'

'Mum!' Angel exclaimed, pointing at Honey, who luckily was concentrating hard on stirring the cake mixture.'

'I'm sorry, love, I despise them so much.'

Two hours later Angel was climbing over the fence of her parents' next-door neighbour, Sandra, a feisty single parent with three boys. Then over her other fence and into Simon and Adam's garden – the gay couple who had just moved on to the street and who were lovely and well up for getting one over on the press.

Adam showed her through the house. 'I'll go out first, pretend to be putting out my rubbish and stand so they can't see behind me. Then you can nip out. Your mum said the car is round the corner. She's going to open the door and distract the photographers.'

'It'll be like *Mission: Impossible!*' Simon exclaimed.

Angel smiled; she would have found the situation entertaining as well if hadn't been about her. Fortunately the paps were so taken in by Michelle's door-opening diversion that Angel was able to slip out of the house and run down the street entirely undetected. Serve the fuckers right, she thought grimly, getting into her dad's Peugeot and driving into Brighton.

She was meeting Gemma in a small pub just up from the sea front. It was the kind of place you only knew about if you lived in Brighton and was definitely not a celeb haunt. Angel's mum and dad were good friends with the landlady, so Angel knew she could trust her not to say anything to the press, and none of the other people in the pub paid her any attention when she walked in, especially since she was wearing a baseball cap pulled down over her face. Gemma was already there, tucked away in one of the corners.

'Hey, shall I get you a drink?'

'God, yes,' Angel replied, sitting down at the small table. 'I'll have a double vodka and Coke. I reckon I need it.'

While Gemma nipped to the bar, Angel checked her mobile. There was another voice mail message from Cal, which she didn't feel strong enough to listen to. She felt she had made a mess of everything, and couldn't face hearing him explain again why he hadn't told Madeleine. She pressed Delete and shoved the phone back in her bag.

'So, how are you?' Gemma asked, sitting back down.

Angel took a large sip of her drink before replying, 'I don't know, Gem, I feel all over the place. I hate that I hurt Ethan like that.'

'You had to do it. I mean, maybe not at the actual wedding, but better then than two months down the line. Ethan will see that one day.'

'Yeah, right, I'm sure he'll ask me to his wedding, and to be godmother to his next child.' Angel hid behind sarcasm.

Gemma shrugged. 'And what about Cal? Have you spoken to him?'

Angel shook her head, 'I can't even bring myself to listen to his messages! I don't know what to tell him. I can't bear to know that he's still with Madeleine. I need some space. I just want to be a good mum to Honey, and to get back into my work. Maybe I shouldn't be with anyone for a while.'

'Some space would be good for you, but I think you and Cal are meant to be together.' Gemma smiled. 'I think everything will be okay, Angel.'

Oh, God, Angel could not bear to talk about it any more! 'I don't know, Gem. But, please, can we change the subject? It's doing my head in!'

Thankfully Gemma obliged by updating Angel on the latest gossip from the salon, and where she and Tony were planning to go on holiday – all a welcome change for Angel who was absolutely sick of thinking about herself. Towards the end of the night she remembered what Simone had said about her in the newspaper and filled Gemma in.

'God! I wish I'd never been nice to her!' Gemma exclaimed. 'I really believed the act she put on about being a changed woman. I can't believe I fell for it.'

'Yeah, well, Simone's obviously a better actress than

any of us gave her credit for. I just wish she would keep away from Ethan, the last thing he needs is to have Simone bitch-face Fraser in his life.'

'Simone two-faced-bitch Fraser,' Gemma replied. 'Well, at least now she's shown her true colours, none of us will ever have to pretend to be nice to her again.' She fiddled with her charm bracelet, and looked regretfully at the platinum diamond horse shoe. 'Now I really will have to sell it on eBay!'

'I'll buy you another one, babe, or something else to make up for it.'

The landlady called last orders from behind the bar. 'I guess I'd better get home,' Angel said. 'Dad's going to be pissed off with me when he finds out I've left the car in town. I'm going to have to take a taxi back.'

Angel woke up with a slight hangover the following morning, but on the whole felt in much better spirits. She still felt a searing sense of shame every time she thought about Ethan and telling him the wedding was off, but that was counter-balanced by the knowledge that she had done the right thing, and by her optimism about being back in England surrounded by her friends and family. And today she could move back into her own house. It would be a fresh start.

She spent most of the day sorting out dates for shoots with Susie, who seemed to have recovered from her heartbreak over Benny. She had recently begun a passionate affair with her Cuban decorator, twenty-three-year-old Eduardo. 'He tells me he loves older women,' she announced.

Especially ones with money, Angel thought, but didn't voice it.

'And I'm thinking if a younger man is good enough for Madonna, it's good enough for me. I realise now that young men are so much more open to new experiences. And that's what I want as well.'

Great. Just please don't give me any details, Angel thought.

'So how do you feel about doing an interview about what happened? I know it may all seem raw, but it would be a good way of putting your side across. I saw what Ethan said about you and several of the tabloids here have picked it up. They've made you look a bit of a heartless bitch.'

Usually Susie would have been on the phone to Angel the minute she sensed a story, but hadn't hassled her straight after she'd left Ethan, which Angel had appreciated. Perhaps Susie had changed for the better.

'Yeah, I think I should do it. At least it will get the paps off my back.'

Angel peeked out of her bedroom window, down at the street below which was still heaving with photographers. The call ended with Susie promising to fix up the interview for the next couple of days. Angel was just about to say goodbye when Susie said, 'Have you heard from Cal?'

'No, as far as I know he's with Madeleine.'

'You did the right thing, Angel. He was lovely but Ethan wasn't the one for you, even I could see it, besotted as I was with that jerk Benny. You're a one-man woman. It's always been Cal for you, and I think it always will be. Why don't you call him?'

Blimey. Relationship advice from Susie? Angel must be in a bad situation! 'I think I need space right now, but thanks, Susie.'

It was a glorious evening in June when Michelle and Frank drove Angel and Honey to her house in a small village ten miles outside Brighton. The police had been called earlier to clear the paps from outside the

Brighton house as neighbours had complained that they were blocking the road and pavement. Angel and her parents were able to get into their car without being pursued.

Angel's home was along a narrow private lane lined with trees. She felt a pang of longing for Cal when she finally saw the Edwardian mansion through a gap in the trees. It was strange going back there without him. Inside the house, the managing agents had been busy putting all the pictures back on the walls and getting the furniture out of storage. Her parents stayed a while to have something to eat. Angel didn't want Frank overdoing it, and even though her mum and dad said they would stay longer, she promised them she would be fine. In fact, she was looking forward to having some time on her own, the first in what seemed like a very long time.

She gave Honey her bath and read her a story, then wandered round the house. As it was still light, she went outside and for a while sat on the terrace, sipping a glass of chilled white wine and looking out at the grounds, and the green fields beyond where she could see her two horses. She nearly jumped out of her skin when the entry phone rang.

It must be the press, she thought grimly, marching over to the screen inside to check, intending to give whoever it was a piece of her mind. But she was stunned when she saw it was Cal who was standing by the gate. Angel's stomach felt as if she had just dropped ten floors in an elevator.

'I've come straight from the airport to see you, can I come in?' he said.

She couldn't even answer but pressed the button to open the gate. Then she went and waited in the living room, needing time to collect her thoughts. A few minutes later she was gazing at Cal as he stood in the doorway. Looking back, Angel was never exactly sure what happened next. Whether she had run to Cal or him to her, but without saying anything they rushed into an embrace, kissing each other with urgent, passionate kisses. Angel forgot all about her resolve to be on her own. All her talk of wanting her own space crumbled away as she felt Cal's lips upon hers. 'Oh, God, Angel, I thought I'd lost you,' he murmured.

'No, never.' And then they were pulling at each other's clothes, with a desperate need to possess each other. They fell on to the sofa. Angel gave up trying to unbutton Cal's shirt and ripped it open. She reached down and unbuttoned his jeans, wanting to feel his hardness, wanting to feel him inside her and to know that he belonged to her and that she belonged to him. Cal pulled her lace knickers to one side and thrust inside her. And with every thrust it was as if they were moving away from the past, starting again with this intense fuck.

Afterwards they lay entwined in each other's arms. 'Did you listen to any of my messages or read any of my texts?' he said finally.

'I didn't.' Now Angel raised her head. What Cal said next would decide everything.

He shook his head. 'If you had then you would know that I ended things with Madeleine the day you were supposed to get married. I knew that even if you married Ethan and were lost to me, I couldn't be with her. Not for her sake, and not for the sake of the baby.'

'We've made such a mess, haven't we?' Angel replied.

'We have, but it's behind us now. We can be together, if that's what you want? You're all I want; all I've ever wanted.'

Cal gazed at her and Angel gently laid her hand on

302

his chest, over his heart, and said softly, "'I carry your heart with me.'"

'I'll take that as a yes,' he replied, and kissed her once more.

'Hair up or down?' Jez asked Angel as he and Gemma got her ready for her shoot. They were installed in Angel's bedroom, in front of her large dressing-table mirror, and it felt just like old times between the three of them as they drank coffee, gossiped and listened to music. Jez had been very nearly driving Angel and Gemma mad with his impression of Lady GaGa singing 'Paparazzi'.

'Don't mention the fucking paps to me!' Angel had told him, but Jez was carried away and it was only when she pointed out that the shoot was in twenty minutes and her hair looked shit that he snapped out of it.

'Down, I think, and give it that beachy, sun-kissed look,' Angel replied. She had already done the interview about her break-up with Ethan, saying how sorry she was that she had treated him so badly, and that she wished him well. When the journalist pressed her about Cal, Angel just said that was something she wasn't prepared to talk about. She and Cal had decided they would say nothing about their relationship, though of course the press knew as he had moved back into the house and they had been photographed together when they were out in Brighton.

Madeleine was staying on in New York and so far hadn't said anything about breaking up with Cal. Maybe she was hoping that he would change his mind. Cal assured Angel that he wouldn't, though obviously there were going to have to be some complicated custody arrangements when the baby was born as he wanted to be able to see his child.

As Jez got to work on her hair, Angel flipped through

the *Mirror* and came across a photograph of Ethan, his arm round a stunningly beautiful woman, tall and slim with long honey-coloured hair and dark brown eyes. She looked a little like the gorgeous model Bar Rafaeli, who had dated Leonardo Di Caprio. *'Ethan Gets Over Heartbreak With Model'* was the headline, and Angel went on to read how he had gone on several dates with Kayla White, winner of *America's Next Top Model*. Jez looked over her shoulder. 'You don't mind, do you?' he asked.

'Of course not! I can honestly say that one hundred per cent. He's a lovely guy. I want him to be happy.'

'There's someone here who's not so happy,' Gemma commented. She had been sitting cross-legged on the carpet, drinking a latte and flicking through various celeb mags. She held up *heat* and Angel saw a picture of Simone hurrying through Heathrow airport, huge shades clamped on her face along with a sulky pout, wearing black skinny jeans and a black blazer, a hot pink Hermès Birkin bag dangling from one arm, a large silver cuff on her other wrist, obscuring the tattoo with Matthew's name. The headline above it read: *'The Wedding's Off'*.

'Wow! How come?' Angel couldn't help wanting to know, in spite of loathing Simone. Or maybe it was because of loathing her.

Gemma scanned the article. 'It just says that Matthew realises he's too young to settle down yet and that he wants to concentrate on his baseball career.' She paused. 'He must have discovered what an über-bitch she is. Mind you, she'll be okay financially for a while as that bag she's got over her arm is worth loads. It must have been a present from Matthew before he dumped her.'

'It's gonna hurt getting that tattoo lasered off her

wrist, though, isn't it?' Jez put in. 'Or she'll have to hope that big cuffs stay in fashion.'

'I wish she was staying in the States, I don't ever want to see her again.' Angel said.

'Me neither,' replied Jez, while Gemma made the sign of the cross as if warding off a vampire and said, 'That reminds me, I must unfriend the witch from Facebook.'

Then Stewart, the photographer, arrived and it was time to get on with the shoot. Luckily he was someone Angel had worked with a lot in the past and it was fun taking the pictures in her living room and outside in the grounds. Everything suddenly seemed to be going so well for her, even the sun was shining. Cal had taken Honey out for the day and the plan was that he would drop her off at Angel's parents and then meet Angel and the gang at Havana, a restaurant in Brighton, for cocktails then dinner.

Angel, Jez and Gemma arrived at the restaurant first and quickly got into chill out mode by ordering frozen Margaritas. When Cal walked in, followed by Rufus and Tony, Angel actually had butterflies at seeing him, as if they were new lovers again. He kissed her and sat down next to her. 'Hi, I missed you today,' he whispered, while the others were caught up in ordering more drinks.

'I missed you too,' Angel told him, and kissed him again. Until Gemma called out jokingly, 'Oi! Get a room, you two!'

As they chatted and joked easily over dinner, it was as if Angel and Cal had never been apart. Everything felt right, just as it should be. A table at the far side of the restaurant burst into a chorus of 'Happy Birthday', causing Angel to look over. A group of women were holding up glasses of champagne.

'I don't believe it!' Gemma exclaimed. 'That's Simone's sister over there.'

'You can't see bitch-face, can you?' Angel asked. That would seriously take the shine off her perfect day.

'No,' Gemma replied, but then the brunette with her back to them turned round. It was Simone, back to her natural hair colour. She looked right over at them, and if looks could kill Angel and her entire tableful of friends would have been wiped out.

'Bollocks!'

'Just ignore her,' Cal replied. Angel had told him about Simone's interview. 'She's a bitter and twisted woman. I'm not going to waste any more of my time being friendly to her. She had my sympathy once, but no longer.'

Angel had a horrible feeling that Simone might come over, but clearly she thought better of it as she turned round again. Angel changed places with Rufus so she did not have to see even her back view. Talk then turned to the party Cal wanted to have at the house for all their friends and family, and Angel tried to forget about Simone. The fact was that she had burnt her boats now, neither Cal nor Jez or Gemma would be friends with again, so she would be out of Angel's life. Hopefully she would never have to see Simone again. Or, if she did, then Angel felt perfectly entitled to ignore her.

As Angel and Cal were driven back to the house in a taxi, Cal's BlackBerry beeped with a message. He frowned as he opened it. 'Someone's winding me up,' he commented. He started to hand his phone to Angel. 'Before you look, I've never met this woman before.'

Angel looked at the picture of a topless blonde, who looked like a right slapper – all parted glossed lips and come-hither eyes. The accompanying message read,

Thanx for last nite cant wait to play with u again.

'Who's it from?'

'It's not a number I recognise. It could just be a mistake . . .'

'Or it could be someone hoping that I would see the message and wonder if you had been playing away with Miss Tits Out.'

Cal shook his head. 'That seems a bit paranoid.'

'You know the saying. Just because you're paranoid, doesn't mean they're not out to get you,' Angel said darkly.

'Just forget it,' Cal told her, then lowered his voice. 'So will *you* play with me later?'

Angel swiped a punch at his arm, but whispered back, 'Maybe,' knowing full well that she couldn't wait to get Cal into bed. He turned her on like no other man.

But Cal was wrong in thinking the picture message had been a one off. By the following morning five more pictures of the blonde had been sent to his phone, with the accompanying texts getting more explicit. He ended up having to call his phone company to get them to block the number.

'I bet it was Simone,' Angel said when he told her what he'd done over breakfast. 'She's such a vindictive bitch, I bet she's beside herself now we're back together.'

'Forget about her, she's unimportant.' Cal checked his watch. 'I'm going to collect Honey in twenty minutes, how about we go back upstairs first?'

And by the time they'd finished making love, Angel had forgotten about Simone.

Chapter 19

The Saturday of the party Angel and Cal were holding was turning out to be a glorious summer day; the hottest of the year, the forecasters were saying. The red-and-white-striped marquee was already up on the lawn; the caterers were about to arrive; Cal had gone off to buy last-minute supplies; Honey was with her grandparents. All Angel had to do was get ready. She had just spent the most blissful month with Cal and Honey. She and Cal had taken time out from work. They'd spent two weeks in the South of France, and then more chilled out days in Brighton or staying by the pool in their garden. She had heard nothing from Ethan – not that she'd expected to. According to the press, he was still seeing Kayla. Angel hoped he was happy.

Meanwhile Simone was back on the London clubbing scene and had been photographed looking the worse for wear coming out of Movida and The Embassy, several weeks in a row. Angel was hugely relieved that Simone had moved back to London; clearly she realised she was never going to bag a wealthy footballer in Brighton. Mind you, Simone was going to have her work cut out for her, as she would be competing against women who were way younger than her. Angel only thought about Simone when she was confronted with a picture of her, otherwise her antics seemed to belong to another time.

She pottered happily about the house, making sure everything looked okay, then went back upstairs to change. She was just slipping into a white, thin-strapped sundress when the entry phone rang. 'It's the caterers,' the caller informed her. Angel buzzed them in. They had been to the house several times before and so knew where everything was.

It was so hot that Angel couldn't be bothered with wearing much make-up. Her long hair felt too hot against her bare skin so she arranged it into two loose plaits. She chose a pair of silver flip-flops, put on the love heart necklace and was good to go. She was sure Gemma would have something to say about her looking so casual, and not on-trend enough for a party, but Angel couldn't care less. She wanted to feel relaxed, and did not want to be uncomfortable in some Body Con dress or tottering about in heels.

Pleased with her appearance, she headed downstairs, expecting to have a chat with the caterers. But when she walked into the kitchen there was nobody there. Maybe they were on the terrace, setting up the BBQ? She wandered outside but there was no sign of them and their van wasn't on the drive. That seemed odd. 'Hello,' she called out, as she went back into the house. 'Who's there?'

There was no reply, and Angel wondered where they were. She walked along the hallway and into the living room where she froze. Scrawled on the huge Venetian glass mirror above the fireplace was the word 'Bitch' in blood-red lipstick. Whoever had written that must still be in the house.

Angel was gripped by fear. For a second she didn't know what to do, then adrenaline kicked in and she kicked off her flip-flops and sprinted back along the hallway, desperate to get out of the house. But the front door was double-locked and the key wasn't where it usually was. Someone must have moved it. The feeling of fear intensified as Angel ran towards the kitchen. She'd left the door there open to the terrace. She could get out that way. But that door also had been shut and locked. She let out a gasp of terror. It was no good even trying any of the windows which were all locked and barred. She crept back along the hallway, heading for the phone. But the sound of a key jangling caused her to spin around. She was completely stunned when she saw Simone walking towards her.

'Going somewhere, Angel?'

'What the fuck are you doing here?' But then Angel's voice failed her as she saw that Simone was holding a large kitchen knife. She kept walking towards Angel, forcing her to cower against the wall.

'You always ruin everything for me,' Simone said in an unnervingly calm voice. 'Wasn't it enough that you stole Cal from me? Why did you have to ruin things with Matthew as well?'

'What are you talking about, Simone?' Angel didn't know whether to keep her talking or try and make a run for it.

'He was with Ethan when you left that message and he heard. He refused to believe me when I told him it was just you being a vindictive bitch. Said he'd always had his doubts about me. I mean, what is so fucking special about *you*?' Now the calm voice had turned passionate. Simone pointed the knife directly at Angel. 'Why does every man always want you?' She gave a bitter laugh. 'Why do you always get who you want? Even Matthew said he'd fuck you.'

Angel was aware that she was trembling. She could feel the sweat trickling down her back. Her mouth felt dry. She swallowed, trying to stay calm. 'Was it you who broke into the house before?'

Simone shook her head distractedly. 'Don't be thick. I paid one of the gardeners to do it . . . he was about to be sacked. You see, not everyone loves you, Angel. I hate you for what you've done to me.' She took another step forward. Angel pressed herself against the wall. She could smell the alcohol on Simone's breath. There was a sheen of sweat on her face, and her usually immaculate eye make up was smudged. Angel tried to push away the thought that Simone looked unhinged, like a woman who had nothing left to lose.

'And you sent the pictures to Cal of that blonde, didn't you?'

Simone smirked. 'Maybe I did, maybe I didn't. You can never tell with Cal, can you? I thought he was faithful to me, but he was shagging you. You thought he was faithful to you, but he was shagging that Italian. I wonder who it will be next?'

Simone was ranting now and Angel felt sick with fear but she was sure she'd just heard a car pull up in the drive. It must be Cal! Simone was so focussed on Angel, she seemed not to have noticed.

'He's still got feelings for Madeleine, I mean, why wouldn't he? She's so beautiful and sophisticated, and she *is* having his baby. But I think he still wants me . . .'

'Please, Simone, I'm sorry if I've upset you . . . I didn't mean to. Why don't you put the knife down? You don't want to do anything you'll regret.' Oh, God, Cal! Come now! Angel thought desperately.

Another bitter laugh. 'Believe me, if I hurt you, I wouldn't regret it.'

Simone took another step forward and grabbed at the silver necklace round Angel's neck, ripping it off her. Angel let out a cry of pain and terror as Simone swung at her with the knife. She was sure it was going to strike her and was powerless to do anything about it. But suddenly Angel saw Cal running up behind Simone and taking her completely by surprise. He seized her arm, forcing her to drop the knife. It was Simone's turn to scream out in pain as she tried to free herself from his grip. But he held on to her tightly, pinning her arms behind her back.

'Christ, Angel, are you all right? Did she cut you?' Cal sounded frantic with worry.

Angel thought her legs might give way with shock, but she managed to say, 'I'm okay,' and walked over to him, keeping well out of Simone's reach.

'Of course she's okay!' Simone exclaimed. 'She was the one who was going to use the knife on me! I managed to get it off her just in time. It was self-defence.'

She tried to turn and face Cal to plead her case but he didn't slacken his grip. Instead he looked at Angel. 'Are you sure you're okay? I can see blood on your neck.'

Angel reached up and touched the mark the chain had left. 'She ripped my necklace off.'

Cal clenched his jaw and tightened his hold on Simone, causing her to wince with pain, 'What the fuck have you done?'

'I just dropped in to say hi and she turned on me when I told her that you were planning to leave her and come back to me. I grabbed the knife as she lunged at me.'

Cal looked as if he didn't believe a word. 'I'm with Angel, Simone, and I'm never going to leave her. I love her, I don't love you.'

Something in Simone seemed to give way at that but she burst out, 'No, Cal! I know you love me . . . we're meant to be together. She's been ruining our lives for too long!'

He ignored her pleas and said to Angel, 'You'd better

go and call the police.' As she quickly made her way towards the phone, Simone continued to beg.

'Cal, please, don't be like this. We can work it out, I know we can. And anyway, it's her word against mine.'

'Every room downstairs has security cameras.' Cal turned her round so she could see the tiny white camera in the corner of the hall ceiling. 'You'll be seen on film, threatening Angel with the knife. So smile, you're on CCTV. And don't ever come near my family again!'

It was early evening by the time Angel and Cal finished giving their statements at the police station. Simone had been charged and was being held overnight. The detectives seemed confident that she would be sent to prison, and in the meantime they would get a restraining order preventing her from going anywhere near Angel and her family. The party had been cancelled, but when the couple arrived back at the house, Frank, Michelle and Honey were outside on the terrace, with Gemma and Tony, Rufus and Jez. 'Are you okay, love?' Michelle asked anxiously.

Angel felt tears spring to her eyes. It had been a terrifying ordeal, and she dreaded to think what Simone would have done if Cal hadn't arrived when he did. But she wanted to forget about it now.

'I'm okay, Mum. We can talk when Honey's in bed.' Then Angel was hugging her family and friends.

Jez couldn't resist quipping, 'The whole scenario is just so *Single White Female* meets *Dynasty*! But Angel is so brave, she's my hero now. Well, after Rufus, of course.'

'Jez,' Rufus said in a warning voice, worried that Angel didn't need comments like that.

But she smiled and said, 'Actually I need to laugh about it. And Cal is *my* hero.' She turned and lightly touched his face. 'And I've got something else to say . . .'

She felt as if she would burst if she didn't get the words out. She hadn't realised quite how much she needed to say them until now.

'So have I,' Cal said quietly. 'For a moment back then, I thought I might have lost you, and I've got to say this now.'

They looked at each other and both said at the same time, 'Will you marry me?'

'Yes!' Angel exclaimed at the same time as Cal.

'Oh my God! You *so* are Liz Taylor and Richard Burton, I love it!' Jez exclaimed, clapping his hands in delight. 'Maybe we should get divorced and then re-marry?' he said hopefully to Rufus. 'Just think of the presents. And I would get to wear another great designer suit.'

But Rufus was smiling and shaking his head as he handed out glasses of champagne to everyone. 'Let's have a toast to Angel and Cal. We always knew they belonged together.'

'To Angel and Cal,' everyone declared, raising their glasses.

Cal reached out for her hand. It was time for Angel to forget the past and embrace what she had always known: that Cal was her soul-mate and her lover, and she wanted him to be her husband again.

'To us,' Angel said, clinking her glass against his.